Praise for Carolyne Aarsen
and her novels

"*Twin Blessings* is another delightful romance
by Carolyne Aarsen sure to bring a smile
to your lips."
—*Romantic Times BOOKclub*

"In *Love Is Patient*, Carolyne Aarsen crafts
an exciting romantic suspense that shows
truth always triumphs over deceit."
—*Romantic Times BOOKclub*

"Carolyne Aarsen just keeps getting better,
and *A Hero for Kelsey* is proof of that."
—*Romantic Times BOOKclub*

D1196822

CAROLYNE AARSEN

A Bride at Last

A Mother at Heart

Steeple Hill®

Published by Steeple Hill Books™

STEEPLE HILL BOOKS

Steeple
Hill®

ISBN-13: 978-0-373-65265-5
ISBN-10:   0-373-65265-8

A BRIDE AT LAST & A MOTHER AT HEART

A BRIDE AT LAST
Copyright © 1999 by Carolyne Aarsen

A MOTHER AT HEART
Copyright © 2000 by Carolyne Aarsen

www.SteepleHill.com

Printed in U.S.A.

CONTENTS

Books by Carolyne Aarsen

Love Inspired

*Stealing Home

CAROLYNE AARSEN

and her husband, Richard, live on a small ranch in northern Alberta, where they have raised four children and numerous foster children, and are still raising cattle. Carolyne crafts her stories in her office with a large west-facing window through which she can watch the changing seasons while struggling to make her words obey.

A BRIDE AT LAST

We do not know what we ought to pray for,
but the Spirit himself intercedes for us....
—*Romans* 8:26

This one is for Jesse, Cheyanne, Fern and Amiel,
my dear children, who have had to make do
with a part-time mother when deadlines loom.
Thanks, kids, for your patience and understanding.

Chapter One

Nadine folded the letter she had just read and carefully slipped it into the envelope, as if any quick movement might jar and rearrange the disturbing words. She laid the envelope on her desk and ran her thumb along its sharp edge. As she weighed the information the letter held, her thoughts were intermingled questions and prayers.

She leaned back in her chair and drew her hands over her face. *Is this it, Lord?* she prayed. *Are we finally going to find out the truth?*

Nadine, along with her mother and sisters, had speculated on the mysterious circumstances surrounding her father Jake Laidlaw's death over six years before. It was midwinter and he had been working for Skyline Contractors as a tree faller. The only information his grieving widow and daughters had received was the official incident report the company had released, which stated that Jake had died because of his own carelessness.

But Nadine and her family knew better than anyone Jake's penchant for safety, the care with which he had performed his work. Although they didn't believe the company, they had never found out more.

Until now.

The anonymous letter gave out no specific information, but hinted at knowledge of the events surrounding her father's death.

From the day of the accident Nadine and her mother had been determined to find out the truth. Nadine's sisters, Sabrina and Leslie, had lost interest after a few years.

This letter was the first break Nadine had had in six years. Her only regret was that she wouldn't be able to share a breakthrough with her mother.

Six months ago after a protracted battle with Lou Gehrig's disease, Brenda Laidlaw had died. Her determined nature could not help her conquer her illness any more than it could help her find out what had really happened to her husband.

Nadine picked up the envelope and slipped it into her backpack. Her workday as editor of the *Derwin Times* was over.

She caught her suede bomber jacket off the coatrack against the wall and slipped it over her bulky knit sweater. Fall clothes, she thought, flipping her shoulder-length hair out of the collar and retying it into a ponytail. Last week she'd worn a T-shirt. And then the temperature had suddenly dropped.

She glanced with dismay at the bits of straw still clinging to her corduroy pants and picked the pieces off, dropping them in the overflowing trash can under her desk.

The afternoon had been spent out in farmers' fields taking harvest pictures. She had never been able to stay as neat and tidy as her sisters. Growing up, she was always the one with dirt on her elbows and rips in her jeans.

"Hey, Naddy, you still hanging around here?" Donna, her friend and the office manager of the weekly newspaper, stopped in the doorway, her arms full of computer printouts. Donna blew her copper-colored bangs out of her eyes and leaned tiredly in the doorway.

"Actually I'm heading home." Nadine smiled up at her friend. "What's with the papers? Some light evening reading?"

"Circulation records. Clint wants to bring some of the ex-subscribers back into the fold." Donna plopped the stack of papers on Nadine's desk, then dropped into one of the chairs across from Nadine's desk.

"You look tired yourself," Nadine said, noticing the faint shadows beneath Donna's usually bright green eyes.

"The big boss is a different kind of general manager than Dory ever was," said Donna with a sigh. "I just have to get up to speed, that's all."

"Excuse me, can I come in?" The deep voice coming from the doorway made Nadine and Donna both jump. Donna threw Nadine a look of dismay, and turned to face Clint Fletcher.

"I was just coming with the printouts, Clint."

"That's fine, Donna. I'm in no hurry." Clint stepped into the room, his presence suddenly dominating it. The collar of his crisp gray shirt was cinched by a burgundy tie, his thick brown hair was attractively tousled, his face, as usual, impassive. His hazel eyes were on Nadine. "I received this with my mail and mistakenly opened it. I wasn't aware it was addressed to you personally until I started reading it. I apologize."

Nadine took the envelope. "Thanks, Fletcher. I'm sure you were discreet," she said, unable to keep the flippant tone out of her voice. Clint always managed to keep her on edge, and sarcasm was her favorite defense.

Clint only nodded. "I was also wondering if I could see you in my office first thing tomorrow morning?"

"Another editorial mini-summit?" Nadine laughed nervously, uncomfortable with the somber tone of his voice.

"You might say that," he said, his tone cryptic, his expression still serious. "Just bring those papers to my office whenever it's convenient, Donna."

Ever since Clint had started, the usual routines at the paper had been rearranged, changed and turned end over end. Dory Strepchuk, the previous general manager, favored a looser editorial style and had pretty much let Nadine, as editor, make a lot of her own decisions.

Clint, however, had made it quite clear that he wanted to be involved in the major editorial decisions of not only the *Derwin Times,* but also its sister papers, the *Eastbar Echo* and the *Riverview Leader.*

"I wonder if our esteemed boss knows that I have a name?" Nadine said after he left. "You get called a name," she said to Donna. "Wally has a name. He even called our ex-reporter Bradley Nichols by name. But somehow he studiously manages to avoid calling me anything."

Donna shrugged. "Doesn't help that you always call him Fletcher."

"He's been Fletcher to me for the past nine years. From the first day he went out with my older sister," Nadine groused, "to the last." She hefted her knapsack onto her back, still flustered by Clint's visit and the seriousness in his voice when he had spoken of their meeting tomorrow. "And what's with the clothes?" she huffed. "He never used to dress like that when he lived in Derwin before."

"He's not like you, wearing some of the same clothes he wore in grade twelve."

"My mother made me this sweater," protested Nadine, glancing down at the bulky cream sweater.

"And the pants?"

Nadine simply shrugged. She disliked shopping for clothes. Once in a while her sisters would come home and drag her off to a store. They would laugh together, trying on clothes and having fun coaxing each other to buy new things. Nadine would take her new outfits home, hang them in the closet and pull on her old faithful jeans or cords. Usually, she dressed up only for church.

"It wouldn't destroy your tough editor image to dress up once in a while yourself," continued Donna. "Put on a skirt. Show off your legs."

"Give it a rest, Donna. I'll just stick with pants. Makes it easier for climbing up on tractors and fences, anyhow."

"And fending guys off..." Donna let the sentence trail off as she straightened the stack of papers on the desk.

"Been there, done that," Nadine replied, fishing in her pocket for her car keys.

"Four years ago, I might add. And I don't think your heart was ever in that relationship," Donna admonished her. "A boyfriend wouldn't really cramp your style, you know."

"Don't start," Nadine begged. "You sound just like my grandmother. I thought I had a few days' reprieve from her matchmaking. My sister Sabrina's not been feeling well since she had Megan. With any luck, Grandma will stay there and drive Sabrina crazy for at least a week."

"Is Grandma *that* bad?"

"Not really. I'd just prefer to live alone, I guess."

"I know your grandmother. She won't leave until you have a boyfriend or until you very firmly say, 'Danielle Laidlaw, time for you to go back to Calgary.' And since you won't do either, you're stuck with her." Donna settled in a chair across from Nadine, her legs stretched out in front of her. "So my advice to you is get a boyfriend."

Nadine rolled her eyes. "Sure. I'll just head down to the nearest 'guy' store and pick one up."

"Well, there's lots of eligible guys in Derwin."

"Besides the ones Grandma keeps dragging home?"

Donna winked. "Our dreamy boss, for one."

Nadine skewered Donna with an angry gaze. "Give me a break."

Donna pursed her lips as she looked Nadine over. "I think you would make a good couple."

Nadine ignored the soft sting of Donna's words. She had grown up a dark brunette between two tall, slender blondes. She loved her sisters dearly, but while they loved going out, she preferred to stay home. But that Clint Fletcher, whom she had secretly admired from afar, had gone out with her older sister and flirted with the younger had been harder to deal with. "I'm not his type," she grumbled.

"You never give yourself enough credit." Donna studied her friend, her head tilted to one side.

"I like myself just fine. But I'm not his type. End of story."

"Okay, no Clint. But what are you going to do about Grandma?"

"I should just tell her to move out," Nadine said after a moment.

Donna laughed. "That sweet, tiny woman will just bat those blue eyes, smile at you and hand you a plate of cookies. And then she'll tell you that she's having yet another single, totally unsuitable man over for supper.'' Donna straightened. ''I think the best way to get Grandma to go home is to make up a boyfriend who conveniently doesn't live in Derwin.''

''Like I could pull that off,'' replied Nadine. ''I don't have a good enough memory to lie.''

''The Lord helps those who help themselves.'' Donna grinned at her friend.

''That's not even in the Bible.''

''So I'm an office manager, not a theologian.'' Donna pushed herself to her feet, pulling the stack of papers off Nadine's desk. ''I'd better get going. I promised my family real food for supper tonight. Want to join us?''

''Thanks, but tonight I'm going to enjoy being in an empty apartment, put on some music and eat *two* bowls of cereal for supper.''

Donna pulled a face as they walked out of Nadine's office and down the hall. ''Sounds like a big night.'' Donna stopped outside Clint's office door. ''See you tomorrow, wild thing.''

''That's what they call me,'' Nadine teased back as she tossed her friend a wave.

Nadine stepped outside, into the late-afternoon warmth of September. In spite of the shared laughter with Donna, a feeling of melancholy washed over her.

It was a glorious fall day, and with a sigh she pocketed her keys. She didn't feel like driving home. It would take just twenty minutes to walk and she had to come straight back to the office anyhow. She could leave her car parked at the office overnight and she knew it wouldn't be harmed.

Nadine ambled down the tree-lined sidewalks of her hometown, hands in the pockets of her pants, her jacket hanging open and her knapsack slung over one shoulder. She scuffed her running shoes through the layer of leaves lying on the sidewalk.

It's a beautiful world, Lord, Nadine thought, squinting upward. The sharp blue Alberta sky stretched up and away, contrasting sharply with the bright orange and yellow leaves of the aspen trees lining the street. Derwin was the proverbial small prairie town. It had the requisite grain elevators solidly planted along the railroad track, streets in the older part of town sitting at right angles to it disregarding true north and south. Nadine had been born and raised in Derwin. In typical small-town-girl fashion, she had planned her getaway ever since high school started. Her plans had been to take journalism and photography courses and find a job with a city newspaper or small magazine and work her way up. She'd had two semesters of school and the city and a boyfriend. Then her mother became ill, Dory offered her a job and Nadine gave up all three.

For five years Brenda Laidlaw had fought Lou Gehrig's disease. When the disease was first diagnosed, the doctor had given her only three years, but he hadn't counted on Brenda Laidlaw's temperament or persistence. She vowed she wouldn't rest until she found out what had happened to her husband. But she couldn't win this losing battle. In spite of her prayers, God had other plans for her. And in spite of Nadine's sorrow, her mother's death had also been a relief. The saddest part of the disease was that while Brenda's body failed her, her mind still understood all that happened around her. The death of her mother six months ago, while not unexpected, had plunged Nadine into a deep grief that could still rise up unexpectedly, the feelings still fresh and intense.

Nadine drew in a deep breath of the fall air, a heaviness of heart accompanying thoughts of her mother. Must be the season, she thought. Fall always brought a pensive air.

She shook her head as she turned the corner to her apartment, willing the mood away. At least she could look forward to a quiet evening at home. Whistling softly, she approached her house, then caught sight of a small red car parked in front of the two-story, red-brick walk-up.

Grandma.

Nadine glanced upward as if to question God, shook her head and unlocked one of the double glass front doors. She walked down the hall to her suite and sent out a prayer for patience as she opened the unlocked door and stepped inside. The mouthwatering smell of peanut butter chocolate chip cookies drifted down from the kitchen into the entrance and began an ominous growling in her stomach, reminding Nadine that she had skipped lunch.

With a groan she dropped her knapsack on the table in the side entrance, toed her runners off her feet and stepped around the corner into the kitchen.

A tiny lady, no more than five feet high, soft gray

hair cropped short, was perched on a stool in the small U-shaped kitchen area, singing softly as she rolled cookies, laying them in precise rows on the baking sheet beside her.

Nadine pulled a face and cleared her throat, announcing her entrance.

The sprite whirled around, and the strains of "Nearer My God to Thee" faded away as she beamed at her granddaughter. "Naddy! You're home." Grandma jumped down from the stool, walked over and lifted her head for a kiss.

"Hi, Grandma." *What are you doing back here, Grandma? How long are you staying here, Grandma?*

"Sabrina was doing just fine and didn't really need my help with the baby," Grandma explained, "so I thought I would come back here."

Nadine's heart sank as her silent questions were answered. She felt frustrated with her sister's recuperative ability.

"From the look of the place, I'm not a moment too soon." Grandma shook her head.

Nadine ignored the reprimand in her voice and glanced around the kitchen for any changes her grandmother might have wrought. Sure enough. She had moved the kitchen table into the corner again. She claimed it made the kitchen roomier. But Nadine liked it directly under the chandelier. It shed a better light, with no shadows.

The timer rang out and Grandma went back to her cookies. She pulled open the oven door to take out the next batch. "When I saw all those piled-up cereal bowls in the sink, I knew I shouldn't have left."

"Cold cereal is a well-balanced meal," huffed Nadine, shoving the high-backed wooden chairs back under the table with one knee. "It says so on all the commercials."

Danielle rolled the cookie balls vigorously. "Tonight it's just good, warm food for you. So go wash up. I'll have supper on the table in a few winks."

"You're only staying for a while longer, right?" Nadine asked, remembering past promises blithely broken by her grandma.

Grandma threw an innocent look over her shoulder. "I'll stay as long as you need me."

Nadine held that guileless stare a moment as if to decipher what that meant, but Grandma only winked at her. Nadine straightened the last chair and headed down the hall to the bathroom.

She glanced around the bathroom and wrinkled her nose. This morning she had been rushed and had dropped her clothes and towels on the floor. Now the bathroom taps sparkled and clean peach-colored towels hung on the towel bar, with a gray facecloth the same shade as the walls lying in a perfect triangle across them. The bathtub shone and a clean rug lay in front of both the sink and the tub.

As she tugged a brush through her thick hair she thought about her dear, sweet, interfering grandma.

When Nadine's mother had been in the first stages of Lou Gehrig's disease, Danielle Laidlaw had moved in to help Nadine and her sisters take care of Brenda and the housekeeping. When Brenda was transferred to the hospital, Grandma stayed on. Sabrina and Leslie, Nadine's sisters, got married and moved out. Grandma didn't. Danielle was perfectly capable of living on her own, but preferred to rent her house out and stay to help Nadine.

Grandma "helped" Nadine by cleaning, baking, organizing and inviting "suitable" men over for supper. She thought it was better for Nadine to be involved in church, and regularly volunteered Nadine's services.

Nadine got a break from Grandma only when an anxiously placed call to one of her sympathetic sisters would result in a sham mission for Grandma Laidlaw. From time to time, Grandma would promise Nadine that someday soon she would move back home.

But that day never came, Grandma always insisting that poor Naddy still needed her.

The biggest problem was that poor Naddy was still single.

Not that poor Naddy didn't have a chance. She'd dated Jack for slightly more than a year when they got engaged. Then Nadine's mother got sick and Nadine wanted to move back to Derwin, but Jack didn't. Nadine knew she had to come home. When Jack failed to understand, she knew she had to break up with him.

Nadine pulled a face at herself in the mirror. Maybe if she'd been an alluring blonde, he might have waited, he might even have come to Derwin to be with her.

As always, she was critical of the upward tilt of her own brown eyes, the heaviness of her hair, the fullness of her jaw. It was, as her grandma was wont to say when trying to console her, an interesting face.

Nadine ran the tap and washed her interesting face and hands.

She opened the door to the room that doubled as bedroom and office and breathed a sigh of relief. The old rolltop desk still overflowed with papers, magazines still lay in various piles around it. Grandma hadn't invaded her domain. So far.

After changing, she stepped out of the room and with a furtive glance down the short hall, opened the door to the spare bedroom across from hers. In "Grandma's room" the suitcases were put away and the Bible lay on the bedside table. Framed family pictures marched across the dresser.

It looked as if Grandma never planned to go.

Nadine squared her shoulders and walked determinedly down the hallway. She would step into the kitchen, take a deep breath and say...

"Sugar or honey in your tea?" Grandma set a steaming mug on the table just as Nadine marched into the kitchen. Her determined step faltered as Grandma caught her by the arm and led her toward a chair. "Supper's ready."

Nadine opened her mouth to speak, but Grandma had already turned her back and begun putting the food on the plates. Nadine sighed as Grandma set them down on the ironed tablecloth, then settled into a chair and beamed at her granddaughter. "It's nice to be back again. I missed you, Naddy." She held out her hand. "Do you want to pray, or shall I?"

"You can." Nadine was afraid that she would voice aloud her own questions to God about her grandmother's presence in her home.

Danielle asked for peace and protection and a blessing on the food. When she was finished she began eating with a vigor that never ceased to surprise Nadine. "So, what happened while I was gone?" Danielle asked.

"Not much," Nadine replied, thinking back over the quiet of the past few days.

As they ate, Nadine told her grandmother about the articles she was working on.

"I thought maybe that nice young man David might have called," Danielle said with a lilt on her tone. "I can't remember his last name. We met him at the grocery store."

"David Branscome is unemployed by choice and lives at home. Hardly dating material."

Danielle appeared unfazed. "A good woman can make a huge difference to a man."

"David already has a good woman. His mother." Nadine finished off the food on her plate and laid her utensils on it. "That was delicious, Grandma. Mind if I pass on dessert? I've got some work to do."

"You work all day—surely you don't have to work all night?" Danielle asked.

"It's nothing really important. I just want to get it done before tomorrow," Nadine said vaguely. She rose and picked up her dishes.

Nadine was hesitant to mention the letter she had received. Jake was also Danielle's son, and she was loath to raise any false hope that they might finally solve the mystery surrounding his death.

"I need to look over some information about Skyline," she added carefully.

Danielle turned to Nadine, her expression sorrowful. "Oh, honey, that always makes you so angry. Don't you have anything better to do?"

"They just received some government grants that are questionable," she said, keeping her tone light. Nadine took her dishes to the counter and set them down. "It won't take long."

She left the room before guilt over her evasive answers overwhelmed her. *I could never fib well,* she thought as she walked down the hall.

Chapter Two

Nadine closed the door to her bedroom and leaned against it, thinking of the mysterious letter and all it portended.

She had a letter that promised some answers and possibly hard proof she could bring to Skyline. Once again Nadine wondered at God's will in all of this. Why had the letter come now, after all this time?

With a short sigh, she walked over to her desk and switched on the computer. While it was booting up, she pulled the envelope out of her knapsack and reread the letter.

Dear Ms. Laidlaw,

I've read your pieces about Skyline in the paper. I know you don't have any love for Skyline. Neither do I. You are right. I need to talk to you about your father. In person. I have some information that I think you can use against Skyline. I'll call.

It wasn't signed, and there was no return address. It had been dropped off at the office while Nadine was out and, according to Sharlene, their receptionist, it was lying on her desk when she returned from lunch.

Nadine refolded the letter and pulled out the other one that Clint had given her just before she left the office.

She skimmed it quickly. An official-looking letter announced the opening of a new farm equipment dealership in Derwin. The cover letter was addressed to her personally, and Nadine glanced over it, as well. It asked about advertising rates and the writer wondered if the newspaper would be willing to give him some coverage on opening day. Nadine glanced at the return address, but didn't recognize the name. She would have Donna contact the business and give them the information they needed.

For now she had work to do.

Nadine turned back to her computer and called up Skyline's file, where she kept copies of all the letters she had written to the company's management, as well as various government departments dealing with industrial safety. The correspondence had netted her a few polite responses couched in the vague language of bureaucrats. These replies had been scanned back into the computer and saved on file.

Nadine opened them all up and read each one in chronological order to refresh her memory. Rereading the letters reminded her once again of what she and her family had lost. A loving, hardworking father whose sincere faith in a loving Savior had tempered their mother's harsher view of God. A father who listened with a sympathetic ear, who fixed temperamental bicycles and vehicles for daughters too busy to realize how fortunate they were to have been raised by such a man.

Nadine leaned her elbow on her desk, recalling pictures of Jake Laidlaw striding up the walk in the late evening smelling of diesel and sawdust, swinging up each of his daughters in his strong arms and laughing at their squeals, pulling Brenda away from the stove, spinning her around and enveloping her in a tight, warm hug. Her father whistling as he organized his tools, readying them for the next day's work. Her parents had never made a lot of money, but they had achieved a measure of contentment that often eluded people with much more. Jake was convinced of God's ability to care for them. Unfortunately that conviction created a measure of lassez-faire over his personal dealings with banks and insurance companies, who were less forgiving.

Because her father was considered a contract worker, he'd had no company pension plan and no private life insurance. Neither was the loan against the house insured. The pittance paid out by Worker's Compensation had barely paid expenses. Brenda Laidlaw had worked for barely a year as a cashier in the local grocery store before her illness made her housebound. The house was sold and the family moved into an apartment in the same building where Nadine now lived.

Nadine pulled herself back to the present and looked around the room. When her sisters had got married and moved out, she and Grandma and her mother had moved to this first-floor suite that was more easily accessible for Brenda, then confined to a wheelchair.

Now, with her mother gone, the apartment was too large for a single girl. She had her eye on a smaller, newer apartment complex. But moving away felt as if she was breaking the last tie with her mother.

And you've got Grandma, she reminded herself with a sigh. Moving to a smaller place would probably be the best way to get Grandma to go back to her own place but it seemed an unkind and disrespectful solution. When it came to facing down Danielle, too many memories intervened.

Echoes of her grandmother reading devotions to her mother, singing while she carefully gave Brenda a sponge bath and fed her, lovingly wiping her mother's mouth as Brenda's control decreased.

Grandma's service to her and her mother had been a blessing at the time, but now it seemed to entwine itself around her. Nadine didn't know how to shake free of Grandma's gentle grip of generosity without feeling ungrateful and unloving.

Nadine rolled her shoulders, rubbed her eyes and turned back to the computer screen. Grandma and a new apartment would have to wait.

A gentle knock on the door interrupted her.

"What is it, Grandma?" she asked, frowning in concentration.

"We have company," Danielle announced loudly.

Nadine glanced over her shoulder at her grandmother, who stood in the open doorway smiling at her. "Who is it?" she whispered.

"Don't you want to do your hair?" Danielle whispered back.

"No," Nadine replied irritably. She would have preferred to stay in her room, but it wasn't in her to be so rude to their unnamed visitor.

Nadine followed Danielle down the short hall, through the kitchen into the living room. The pewter table lamps shed a soft light on the room. Nadine couldn't help but feel a measure of pride in the fawn-colored leather couch with matching chair. Burnished pine-and-brass coffee table and end tables complemented the warm tones of the leather. She had made the plaid valances that hung by tabs from the pewter curtain rods and the matching throw pillows herself.

A man stood with his back to her. He turned as they came into the room and Nadine bit back a sigh.

"Nadine, I'm sure you remember Patrick Quinn. Didn't he used to live four houses down from us when we lived on 55th?"

Nadine smiled at Patrick, praying the fake expression she pasted on masked her seething thoughts. She tried to suppress memories of Patrick as a boy—selfish, overbearing and constantly teasing her.

Other than rudely turning around and returning to her office, which would be most un-Christlike and unforgiving, she had little choice but to sit down and try to make some kind of small talk.

The talk turned out to be *very* small, with Grandma and Nadine asking Patrick polite questions about where he worked and lived. Patrick had changed little, Nadine reflected, or possibly he had become even more boring.

After a while Nadine had to do something. Stretching her leg under the coffee table, she gave her grandmother a gentle nudge.

Danielle didn't even flinch.

"Our Nadine is quite the little cook…" Grandma continued, ignoring Nadine's next push, delivered with a little more force.

"I'm neither little nor a good cook," interrupted Nadine. She gave her grandmother a warning look, then glanced back at Patrick. "Grandma would love me to be more domestic, but for me, gourmet cooking means putting brown instead of white sugar on my cereal."

Grandma didn't miss a beat. "She's such a joker, our Nadine."

Thankfully, at ten o'clock Patrick rose and excused himself. He thanked Danielle and Nadine for a lovely visit and, with a playful smile at Nadine, left.

Danielle turned to Nadine. "He's such a nice boy. Don't you think?"

"If you like that type," Nadine said dryly.

"He wanted to see you again. I can tell." Danielle bent over to put the mugs on the tray and then, as the clock struck, straightened. "Goodness, Nadine. You had better get to bed. I'll clean up. You need your sleep.''

And with that, Danielle bustled off to the kitchen.

Nadine shook her head. She had to do something about Danielle, or her meddling grandmother was going to take over her life.

She yawned a jaw-cracking yawn and glanced at her watch. But not tonight.

It was still early morning when Clint Fletcher pulled open the door to his office. He smiled as he looked around the neat room. The sun had just come up, and lit the eastern sky outside his window, illuminating the space with a gentle light.

His office, he thought with a proprietary air. During the years he'd worked in the city for one of the large newspapers, he had been lucky to have his own desk in a large, crowded newsroom. Even then he would often come back from an assignment to find it appropriated by a colleague whose computer was down.

Now, not only did he have his own desk, he had his own phone, his own door and an element of privacy. He set his briefcase down on his desk and walked to the window. His uncle Dory had occupied the office farther down the hall. It was larger, but when Clint had taken over the papers, he'd also moved to this office. He preferred the view. He liked to look up from his desk and see people in the park across the street or walking past the office busy with their town errands.

It had been Nadine's office before he came, and he

was sure there was a certain resentment over that, he thought as he idly watched the play of wind in the trees arching over the street. He still didn't know what he had done to create Nadine's guarded looks, the touchy attitude. Nor did he understand why she still called him Fletcher.

She had always called him that. His first memory of her was of brown eyes watching him warily from a porch swing as he came to their home to pick up her older sister. She had been reading a book, and when he came up the walk she put it down and demanded to know who he was. After that he was simply addressed as "Fletcher." It became a challenge to coax a smile out of her, to get her to speak more than a few words.

He had gone to church with Sabrina as much to see how Nadine would react as to please his girlfriend. She wasn't impressed. Nor was she impressed when he started showing up occasionally at the Bible studies on Wednesday nights. He had more reasons to attend than just to impress Nadine, but he hadn't been ready to admit his seeking to anyone.

Nadine was indifferent and Clint's ego was provoked. He wasn't used to having girls indifferent to him. Consequently he began to show up earlier for dates, seeking out Nadine, talking to her, drawing her out. He found he spent more time talking to Nadine about serious issues while he waited for her sister than he did with Sabrina. He enjoyed their time together and thought Nadine did, too. He knew it was time to break up with Sabrina when he found himself loath to leave Nadine when it was time to leave the house with her sister.

He had gone out with a number of girls when he left Derwin, but none of them challenged him intellectually the way Nadine had. None of them had her appeal. Nor did they ever keep him at arm's length as she did.

Now she was working for him, and it seemed that the intervening years, with all the sadness they had brought to her life, had once again put a prickly shell of defensiveness around her. He had returned to Derwin with the hope of seeing her again, raising their relationship to another level, but each of his overtures had been rebuffed. After his first weeks here, he held back, sensing that Nadine was still dealing with the grief of her mother's death.

Their relationship had become a cordial business one, but in the past few weeks he had begun to see glimpses of the Nadine he'd always loved.

Clint shook his head at his own thoughts. Regardless of his feelings for her, he had a job to do.

He walked back to his desk and, snapping open his briefcase, pulled out the letter he had received yesterday from Skyline Contractors. Correction, he thought. Skyline Contractors' lawyers. He didn't look forward to discussing it with Nadine.

"I made pancakes, Nadine," said Grandma as Nadine came into the kitchen.

"Pass, Grandma. I'm not in the mood for a big breakfast."

"You never are," complained Danielle, looking up from the newspaper.

Nadine tugged open the refrigerator door and pulled out a carton of yogurt, a container of milk and an apple. She juggled the three items, carefully set them on the table, then dropped into a chair. Last week's newspaper was spread out on the table. Grandma was reading the first section, so Nadine grabbed the other.

She opened the pages, skimming over the stories that she knew almost by rote, stopping at her kindergarten feature.

She thought she had done some pretty effective work with the pictures she had taken. She had pasted them in a montage of children's faces, eager, expectant and excited. The mix had energy and exuberance suited to the first day of a new venture. It was the kind of picture she knew parents cut out to put in their child's scrapbook.

"Listen to this item from the 'Court Docket,'" Grandma said, her voice scandalized. "Holly Maitfield fined for allowing her dog to roam the neighborhood unleashed. Again." She clucked anxiously. "They're going to put that poor mutt in the pound one day."

"They'll have to catch him first," murmured Nadine, skimming over the text opposite her feature. Halfway through she sighed in frustration. Another typing error. She had missed that one. Clint would be annoyed. Maybe that's what he wanted to see her about this morning.

"That's an amazing picture," commented Grandma, leaning over to look at the paper.

Nadine couldn't help but glow. In this line of work people commented more often on what the reporter had done wrong, rather than right. Her grandma's compliment warmed her. "Thanks, Grandma. I had a lot of fun with this feature." She smoothed the picture with a proprietary air and turned it so her grandma could see it better. Nadine was about to turn the page when her grandmother stilled her hand.

"Wait a minute, I want to read 'About Town.'" Danielle held her hand on the paper while she read the bits of local gossip gleaned from a variety of sources for this regular feature. Nadine never read it. She couldn't be bothered. But Grandma read it faithfully. If she read it in "About Town," it had to be true.

Nadine finished her breakfast and prepared herself to face down Danielle Laidlaw.

"Grandma, I need to talk to you."

Danielle blinked, put down her fork and crossed her hands on the table in front of her. "This sounds serious."

"It is. I like organizing my own social life, choosing my own friends. I don't think you need to invite suitable young men over for tea."

"I didn't really invite Patrick. He asked himself over. He wanted to see you," Danielle insisted.

Nadine stared across the table at her grandmother, ignoring the remark. "I don't want you inviting anyone over for tea, okay, Grandma?"

Grandma Laidlaw smiled back at her, unperturbed by Nadine's pique. "I'm sorry, Nadine," she continued, her tone contrite. "I'm sorry you feel like I'm interfering in your life. I just want you to be happy, settled. That's all." She got up and took the teapot off the stove. "Do you want a cup of tea yet, honey? It's your favorite kind. I got it in that store on the corner. The one with that good-looking young cashier."

"No, thanks." Nadine frowned, her anger fading. But somehow, she knew her grandma had done it again. Taken the wind out of her sails and then changed tack.

"Well, then, you probably should get going. Make sure you're home on time tonight. We've got company for supper."

Nadine stopped, her frustration trying to find an outlet, trying to find words. "Who?" she sputtered, angry with her own reaction, angry that she couldn't seem to find the right words to make her grandmother understand.

"I know you said no more interfering, but I had invited Dr. McCormack for supper tonight a couple of days ago. I can't change that now. He works in the new clinic I've been visiting," Grandma said quickly.

Nadine's resolve from the previous evening returned with a vengeance. Grandma just didn't get it. If Nadine couldn't come up with her own boyfriend it looked as if she was going to spend the rest of her life across the supper table from potential suitors as her grandmother recounted her accomplishments, going back to kindergarten. Well, two could play that game.

"I won't be home," she said firmly.

Grandma frowned. ''Why not? You're not working, are you?''

She wasn't and she knew she had to do some fast work to avoid a repeat of last night and many other nights. ''Actually…'' What, what? She actually was going to do…what? Her mind flew over the possibilities and then latched on to one in desperation. ''I have a date.'' She smiled in triumph.

''A date? With who?''

Oh, brother. Who? ''Uh…Trace.''

Grandma frowned again. ''I've never heard of this Trace fellow. What kind of a name is that? What is his last name?''

This was getting harder. She didn't even know where she had pulled the name Trace from. It had just popped into her mind. Now he needed a last name, to boot. ''Trace…Bennet,'' she quickly added. Nice name, respectable name, she thought to herself. ''He's a great guy. I met him a couple of months ago at the Agribition in Edmonton when I was doing a story on the farm family of the year.'' She rinsed off her bowl, unable to look her grandmother in the eye, and bit her lip to stop the flow of drivel mixed with absolute fibs.

''You never told me about this.'' Grandma sounded hurt.

Nadine shrugged nonchalantly, ignoring a stab of guilt. She reminded herself of the stories Grandma had spun to Patrick and the fact that Grandma had told her Dr. McCormack was coming over only seconds after Nadine had specifically asked her not to invite prospective boyfriends.

"I'm meeting him in Eastbar," Nadine said, turning with a smile at her grandmother. "I have to do a review on a new movie showing there." Time to quit, Nadine, she thought.

Grandma sat back in her chair, almost pouting. "That's so too bad. I was really hoping for you to meet Dr. McCormack. He's quite good-looking."

"Well." Nadine lifted her shoulders in a shrug. "Sorry, but I can't break a date with Trace." She brushed a quick kiss on her grandmother's cheek. "So long," she added, straightening.

Grandma caught her hand and squeezed it as Nadine straightened. "Do you like this man?"

Nadine almost relented at the sight of her grandmother's worried expression. Grandma really did only mean the best, she thought. But she steeled herself, knowing that Grandma's strongest ammunition was her concern and consideration. "We're just getting to know each other, Grandma. These things take time."

"Well, then, it shouldn't matter if I ask someone else over, should it?"

She just wouldn't give up, thought Nadine incredulously, holding her grandmother's gaze, determined not to back down. "I have a boyfriend now, Grandma. You don't have to worry about me. You never had to." And with that she turned and left before she was forced to make up any more lies.

Trace Bennet, Trace Bennett, she repeated to herself as she walked out the door. I've got to remember that name! She stepped out and hurried down the walk, her guilt hanging over her like a dark cloud.

Chapter Three

Clint stepped out of his office into the airy, spacious foyer. It still held that new smell of paint and carpet glue. He had ordered the renovations as soon as he took over, knocking out one wall and putting a curved, chest-high divider that acted as reception desk. The room was done up in shades of cream and hunter green. The staff referred to it as the restaurant, but most agreed that it made the office look more professional and inviting.

Sharlene was already at her desk, answering the phone and trying to bring a measure of order to the office.

"When Nadine comes, can you tell her I'd like to see her right away?" he instructed the receptionist.

Sharlene nodded, and just as he was about to go back to his office, the door opened with a jangle of chimes and Nadine stepped into the room, rubbing her hands. A flow of cold air accompanied her and as she looked up, she stopped, glancing at Clint, then sharply away.

Clint couldn't stop the nudge of disappointment at her reaction. It was no different than usual, but it still bothered him.

He cleared his throat. "When you've got a few minutes, Nadine, I'd like to see you."

"Okay. I'll be there right away." Without giving him another glance, Nadine walked to Sharlene's desk and leaned on the divider. "Any mail for me?"

"Just these. And a letter with no return address."

Nadine caught the letter, turned it over and shoved it in her ever-present knapsack. "I'll get the others when I come back."

Finally she turned back to Clint, her head back as if challenging him. Clint bit back a sigh. Why did he even bother with this woman? She would never let down her guard with him. She would never come to care for him as he did for her. But as he caught her eyes, he saw pain and weariness behind the light of challenge, and he felt the impulse to hold her, comfort her.

He would just have to be patient. After all, didn't the Bible tell us that love is patient?

"You wanted to see me right away?" she said.

"If you have a moment."

Nadine shrugged. "Better get me now before the phone starts ringing."

Clint ushered her into his office, but before she sat down he offered her a cup of coffee, which she declined.

''You mean I don't even get to show you what a sensitive, caring guy I am?'' he joked in an attempt to alleviate the mood.

She looked up quickly, a smile teasing the corners of her mouth. Clint smiled back as he sat down.

''I know what kind of man you are,'' she said quietly.

That stopped him. Things were looking up. And he needed all the optimism he could muster.

''So what did you want to talk to me about?''

Clint took a breath, trying to find the right words, reminding himself that he was the general manager and protecting the newspaper was his first priority, not furthering his personal relationship with his editor. He rested his arms on his desk. ''I wanted to ask you about an article on Skyline Contractors that I found in the computer archives. It was under your byline, but obviously not ready for press yet. Is it news?''

Nadine's face hardened and Clint sighed. ''I got some information from a former employee about some discrepancies in their accident reports…'' she said slowly.

''Who verified it?''

''A former employee who used to drive Cat for them. Of course, the operative words are 'used to.' He heard a few things he shouldn't have, repeated them to me and now he, too, is a former employee.'' She leaned forward. ''Trust me, Clint. This is a story and it's good.''

''I don't want you to write the story.''

''If you want to pull rank on me, Clint, that's fine.

But before we go any further, I want to talk to the editors of other papers in the organization. They have as much a stake in this fight as we do. You know they'll take my part. I have to run this story.''

"Skyline will kill themselves in the long run. Do you really think they need our help?''

Nadine held his gaze. "Well, it seems to me to be a good cause, so I say why not?''

Clint knew she was right, but he also knew that he had to make sure she wasn't setting out stories just for the sake of antagonizing a company that had their lawyer's number on speed dial. "Why not? Because this time they might take us to court, for one reason.'' He pulled back his frustration. The newspaper business was a tough go and he was thankful for the loyal readership and the comfortable living he was making. He wanted to keep it that way.

Nadine shrugged. "Their lawyers make a lot of noise, but they always back down when we respond.''

"Have you talked to anyone who works for Skyline now?'' he persisted.

"C'mon Clint. The management likes me as much as you do.''

Her comment hit him, hard. "What do you mean by that?''

Nadine shrugged, not deigning to reply, looking anywhere but at him.

He got up from his desk, puzzled that she should think that, and wondering if maybe that wasn't the key, the true reason she kept herself at such a distance from him. "Why would you think I dislike you?''

As he came to stand beside her, she stood as well, looking up at him, her dark eyes wide.

He remembered the smile she had given him just a few moments ago, wondering what she would do if he touched her cheek, if he ran his fingers through her hair as he always wanted to, if he…

"WordCo is on line two for you, Mr. Fletcher." Sharlene's voice on the intercom pierced the heavy atmosphere. Clint blinked, Nadine took a step back.

"Well, I'd better get going. You look pretty busy," she said with a short laugh. She picked up her knapsack, slung it over her shoulder and left.

Clint turned back to the phone, frustrated and angry at the intrusion. He punched the button and answered curtly, "Hello."

"Hey, Clint. Don Pederson here. How are you?"

Clint sighed at Don's fake friendliness. Sounds like a salesman, he thought, even though Don wasn't selling. He was buying, and what he wanted to buy was Clint's small string of newspapers.

"You actually did it?" Donna stabbed her French fry in the ketchup with a grin. "My pure, unadulterated friend actually fibbed to her grandmother?"

Nadine blew her breath out in a sigh and leaned her elbows on the pink tabletop of the Downtown Deli. "I had to. First it's Patrick Quinn last night for tea, then Dr. McCormack tonight for supper."

"Dr. McCormack?" Donna grimaced and shook her head. "He's about fifteen years older than us and, while I think bald men can be very attractive, on him it's not.'' She leaned forward. ''So what name did you give this pretend guy?''

Nadine closed her eyes in concentration. She had to write his name down somewhere or she was going to blow it completely. ''Trace Bennet.''

Donna pulled her mouth down. ''Sounds like a country and western singer. What does he look like?''

''Goodness, Donna. He's fake.''

''Knowing your grandma, she's going to phone me asking about all the gory details. We're going to have to do a biography on this guy.'' Donna laughed. ''We need hair color, eye color...'' She pursed her lips, thinking. ''Job, place of employment.''

''Don't bother.'' Nadine waved a hand over the table in dismissal. ''I just blurted it out this morning because I was angry, and wanted to keep her off my back. There's no getting around it. I'm just going to have to go home and tell her, 'Grandma, move out.'''

''Why don't you let her stay and you move out?''

''Don't tempt me.'' Nadine pursed her lips as she looked out of the café's window, which faced the newspaper office. Some days it seemed as if her life stretched ahead of her like a prairie road. Predictable and the same. Not that she needed high adventure, she added to herself. She was content here in Derwin. She enjoyed her work, enjoyed her life. She just wished she had someone she could share it with. She recalled her morning meeting with Clint. The way he'd looked at her just before the phone call. For a moment it had seemed as if something was building between them.

Nadine shook her head, dismissing the notion. Just wishful thinking. She wasn't his type.

She glanced up at the clock. "Yikes. I've got to get going. I promised Fletcher I'd get pictures of the rodeo."

"And you've got to get ready for a big date," Donna teased.

"Right." Nadine paid the bill, tossed a wave at Donna and left.

Donna watched her go. She knew her friend wouldn't be able to face down dear little Grandma Laidlaw. Nadine might be able to poke holes in Clint Fletcher's composure and fast-talk her way out of awkward interviewing situations, but family situations were another story. There Nadine always avoided rocking the boat.

And now Nadine was making up fake boyfriends in a bid to keep her grandmother off her back. But Donna knew, if Nadine had her way, she wouldn't keep up the sham very long. A very principled person was her friend Nadine.

Well, Donna was going to give things a little push and help Nadine persuade Grandma that Nadine was just fine. She grinned. Donna knew Grandma Laidlaw and knew exactly how to go about it.

The movie was a dud. Nadine struggled through it, scribbled a few comments and as soon as the credits began to roll, fled the theater. Outside, the streetlights had just come on, competing with the setting sun. The evening still held vestiges of the day's warmth, and beyond the town Nadine could hear the faint drone of combines and tractors harvesting the fields.

She knew she should have been home, working over some stories for the next issue, but she had told Grandma she would be out tonight.

If Grandma found out she'd gone alone to the film, she would start her matchmaking all over again. It was frustrating, not to mention slightly humiliating. Before Jack, Nadine had never gone out with many guys, just a few casual dates. But nothing had ever clicked. And after she broke up with Jack she ended up back in Derwin, taking care of her mother.

Nadine loved her job, loved where she lived. The time she had spent going to school in the city had cured her of any desire to work and live there. But the other reality was staying in Derwin, slowly seeing her friends move away or marry the boy they had gone out with since high school.

Nadine hadn't dated much in high school, and had never really minded that much. Until Clint Fletcher. How acutely she'd felt the lack of a boyfriend once Clint began dating her older sister. How awkward and boring she'd felt watching Sabrina make him laugh, when all Nadine could do was debate the most ponderous issues. How it had hurt to watch him leave the house with Sabrina for their dates, even though she would never admit that she had been attracted to Clint from the first moment she'd seen him.

When Clint came back to Derwin, it was as if her life had suddenly turned back. Old emotions melded with new ones and it seemed that each time she and

Clint met it was with wary cynicism on her part and an impassive seriousness on his. Nadine was left to wonder at the irony of life and puzzle out what exactly God planned for hers.

Nadine squinted up at the darkening sky, past the streetlights of Eastbar. The crescent moon hung in the sky above her. A few of the brighter stars showed themselves in the blue-black sky. Beyond these lay more stars, more constellations, other galaxies. She stared upward, aware of what a small part of creation she really was. Just a small speck in the whole cosmos that God had created. She kept busy with the Mission Committee at the church. She went to the Wednesday-evening Bible study when she wasn't on assignment. Each Christmas she joined the choir to sing at the nursing homes and the city jail. She enjoyed her work, but lately, when she came home, she felt as if something was missing. Did she really have a right to expect more?

She knew she didn't, but once in a while a deep yearning overrode her desire to be alone. A yearning to have someone waiting at home besides an older grandmother who didn't really need her.

Her parents had had that, thought Nadine, giving an empty can a tinny kick. She remembered her big, burly father, his warm hugs, smelling of diesel and sawdust. When his work required it, he would stay in the bush for a week. This was in the days when hand harvesting was more common, before mechanical machines took a week to chomp their way through what would have been a full winter's work. Nadine remembered how he used to grab her mother around her waist and swing her off the floor, singing loudly. Her mother would laugh, wrap her arms around his neck and sing along. The waiting was over. The man of the house had returned. All was well.

Now, instead of life amidst her parents and sisters, all she had at home was her dear, meddling grandmother.

Nadine thought back to her conversation with Donna and wondered if she could put Grandma off the scent with her fake boyfriend. She knew beyond a doubt that she didn't have the resources to maintain the fib. This "date" would have to be a one-time thing, she mused, pulling out the keys to her car. She was surprised she'd gotten this far.

Nadine glanced at her watch. Too early to go home. It would have to be coffee at the Derwin Inn.

"I'll just have a coffee, Katya." Nadine smiled up at the waitress, who nodded and tucked her order pad back into her apron.

Nadine sipped the hot brew, wondering how long she dared draw this out. It was only 10:30 p.m. Grandma would still be up.

She looked around the coffee shop of the Derwin Inn, a place known more for its food than its coffee. The Derwin Inn had new owners since the last time she'd been here. Skylights had been installed framed by boxes of ivy, leaves cascading downward, echoed by umbrella plants strategically located to break up the space. The room was painted a soft yellow, and the windows had scarves of ivory and green draped across them. It looked more like a spacious living room than a coffee shop.

Nadine tried to imagine hefty truckers sitting at the delicate, glass-topped tables and smiled at the picture.

"Share the joke?" The deep voice beside her broke into her thoughts. She jumped, her hand hitting her coffee cup.

She grabbed a handful of napkins and, still mopping up, turned to face Clint Fletcher. "You scared me out of my wits," she accused him, her heart pounding.

"Now, that conjures up an interesting image. Nadine without her wits," he said dryly, still towering over her, his one hand in the pocket of his pants, the other resting on the table.

Clint hesitated a moment, then pulled out a chair. "Mind if I join you?"

She tried not to let his height intimidate her, tried not to notice how broad his shoulders looked covered by a suit coat. Tried to ignore the increase in her heartbeat at the sight of him.

She shrugged in answer. He could take that how he liked, but deep down, she felt a faint hope that he would stay, then berated herself for still feeling attracted to him after all these years. Feelings he clearly had never shared. Clint Fletcher was her boss and nothing more.

"What story are you covering that keeps you out so late?" he asked as he sat down.

She fiddled with her cup. "I caught the movie in

Eastbar, which was dreadful, and thought I'd kill some time before I go home.''

''I take it the review won't be favorable.'' Clint folded his hands on the table and leaned forward.

''Not likely.'' Nadine laughed and sat back against her chair. ''I'll probably have Evan Grimshaw accusing me of trying to put him out of business again.''

''Who did you go with?'' asked Clint, a little too casually, as he smoothed down his tie.

''No one you'd know,'' she replied evasively.

Clint nodded and for a moment Nadine was tempted to drop Trace Bennet's name. But she knew Clint with his quick, incisive questions would catch her out, and that would look worse.

''So does your grandmother still live with you?'' he asked conversationally.

Nadine traced her finger through the circles of moisture the mug had left behind on the table. ''Yes, still,'' she replied with a sigh. ''She's a dear old lady, but I do wish she'd go visit my other sisters and bother them for a while.''

A moment of silence hung between them. Clint cleared his throat. ''How are your sisters?'' he asked hesitantly.

Nadine caught the tone in his voice and, looking up at him, caught a melancholy expression on his face. She wondered if he still missed Sabrina. For a moment she felt sorry for the usually self-possessed Clint Fletcher. She knew exactly what it felt like to be the one spurned, the one left behind. ''Sabrina had her first child a few months ago and has just returned to work.

Leslie is expecting as well, but she's quitting her job before the baby is born.''

"She always was a homebody. Just like you." Clint smiled at Nadine, his expression softening. Then, just as suddenly, the moment was gone. He stood and straightened the cuffs of his shirt and once again became her boss. "Well, I'd better be off. I have a busy day tomorrow."

"'Court Docket.'" Nadine grinned at him. "A little bit of a comedown for our esteemed G.M. to have to cover for Wally."

He paused and for a heartbeat looked as if he was going to say something else. Then, lifting a shoulder, he turned and left.

Nadine looked down at her half-full coffee cup. Suddenly she felt very alone. A lonely alone, she thought as she set the cup down and dropped a few quarters on the table for Katya, grimacing at her watch.

Grandma would still be up and she would have to answer some tough questions about her "date."

Chapter Four

"C'mon Nadine," Grandma called down the hall. "We're going to be late for church."

Nadine stifled a wave of impatience with her dear grandma as she straightened a cream-colored sweater over her rust wool skirt and tugged on the elastic holding her hair. It snapped against her hand and her hair slid loose.

"Are you coming?" Grandma called again.

Nadine glanced at the clock and, with a frustrated sigh, grabbed her purse from the bed and slung it over her shoulder. She stopped at the bathroom long enough to quickly brush her hair and grimace at yet another reflection of herself. She felt self-conscious wearing her hair down. A ponytail was far easier, but she could find no elastics in the bathroom, either. Down it would have to stay, she thought.

"Nadine." Grandma's voice was uncharacteristically sharp, and Nadine threw the brush into the drawer. "Coming, coming," she muttered as she ran down the hallway.

Grandma waited in the porch, her mouth pursed in disapproval. "What took you so long?" she grumbled.

Nadine caught her car keys from the little pegboard hanging by the back door. Without deigning to reply to her grandma, she stepped out on the porch, then strode down the sidewalk to her car.

"You are certainly not in a Sunday mood today," Grandma chided as she stepped into the vehicle.

"Sorry, Grandma," Nadine said automatically as she started up the car and backed it onto the street. "But after you cleaned up the other night, I couldn't find my clothes."

"I'm sure you didn't want a mess." Grandma folded her hands over the small purse she had on her lap. Staring primly ahead, she remained quiet for the rest of the trip.

Church was full again. Over the summer, attendance had waxed and waned, with people leaving for holidays, but now the children were back in school, the harvest was in full swing and the congregation was back to full strength.

"You just go on ahead, Nadine. There's someone I want to talk to." Grandma gave Nadine a gentle push into the sanctuary. Nadine frowned at her, wondering what she was scheming now, but when she saw an elderly woman wave toward Danielle, she relaxed.

"Don't wait too long, Grandma. Church is pretty full," she warned.

"Don't worry about me," Grandma chirped as she

walked over to her friend. Nadine shook her head and
let the usher show her to an empty spot.

Nadine dropped into the pew and scanned the bulletin that came with the order of worship. It was filled
with the usual announcements. Church school was
starting again, catechism classes, Ladies' Society and
choir. Nadine made note of the choir practice and began reading a handout from the Mission Committee.

Out of the corner of her eye she saw Grandma stop
beside the pew, glancing backward down the aisle.

Without looking up, Nadine scooted over for
Grandma and her friend, turning the page of the bulletin as she did so.

"Come sit with us," she heard her grandmother
say. Nadine glanced up idly to see who her grandma
was talking to. Her heart sank.

Clint Fletcher stood in the aisle, one hand on the
pew in front of them, the other in the pocket of his
trench coat. Underneath he wore a tailored navy suit,
a white shirt and a patterned tie in shades of deep gold
and russet. Nadine felt her heart lift at the sight of
him.

"Here Nadine. Let Mr. Fletcher sit between us."
As Grandma sat down, she nudged Nadine over. Nadine silently fumed, but could do nothing without creating a scene. So she merely moved aside so Clint
could sit between them.

Nadine picked up the bulletin, trying to ignore both
her grandma and the tall figure seated beside her. It
couldn't be done. Clint's presence exerted a force that
she couldn't ignore. So she thought it would be better

to do as she always did and face him head-on, hoping he wouldn't read anything into Grandma's little machinations.

"So, what brings my esteemed boss to church this morning?" she said, forcing a teasing grin.

He glanced sidelong at her. "Same thing that brought you."

Nadine couldn't resist. "You have a nagging grandma, too?"

Clint smiled and shook his head. "No. A nagging conscience."

Nadine was taken aback at his quiet admission. No quick reply came to mind, so she picked up her reading where she had left off. But she couldn't forget what he had said, and during the service she cast sidelong glances at him. His expression was, as usual, serious. He sang along with the hymns, obviously familiar with them. As he listened to the minister Nadine recognized that firm-jaw look that came over his face when he absorbed some particularly important idea.

Nadine was surprised at his intensity. Clint had accompanied Sabrina to church, but she had never gotten the impression from him that his attendance meant anything. She had challenged him once on it and had received a sarcastic remark. But he didn't look sarcastic right now.

When the offering was passed, he took the plate, dropped in an envelope and handed it to her. He didn't let go, however. Nadine looked up at him, puzzled.

"Your hair looks nice like that," he said quietly.

Nadine raised her eyebrows, almost dropping the

plate. Flustered, she handed it to the person beside her, forgetting to put in her own contribution. She tried to stifle the flush that warmed her throat and crept up her cheeks.

Compliments from Clint Fletcher? That was something she had no defense for.

Nadine felt more and more uncomfortable sitting beside her boss. She would manage to bring her mind back to the sermon, but then he would shift his weight, move his long legs or brush her arm with his elbow and she would have to start all over again. Periodically she caught a spicy hint of aftershave. Mentally apologizing to God, she took a deep breath, pulled out a notepad from her purse and focused her entire attention on the minister. The reporter in her made it easier to remember sermons when she took notes.

When the congregation rose for the last song, she finally risked a sidelong glance at him. He looked down at her from his considerable height, and Nadine looked hurriedly away, feeling even more confused.

What did he want from her? Why was he here?

She was relieved when the organist and pianist began the postlude. It wasn't often that Clint could throw her for a loop, but his presence in church beside her and his unexpected compliment did.

As she made her way down the crowded aisle to the exit, she glanced over her shoulder. Clint had been waylaid by Mr. and Mrs. Enright, the owners of an auction business that advertised frequently in the *Derwin Times*. He was smiling now, his features relaxed. Nadine's step faltered as she saw him grin, then laugh.

He was attractive enough when he was serious. Smiling, he became irresistible.

Nadine shook her head at her own reaction. With a forced shrug, she continued out to her car. Grandma already sat waiting, and Nadine slipped in behind the wheel.

"By the way, Nadine." She smiled, turning guileless blue eyes to her granddaughter. "Mr. Fletcher is coming over for lunch."

"What?" Nadine almost dropped her car keys. "But, Grandma…"

"I know what you said," Grandma interjected, "but he invited himself over. What could I do?" she asked innocently. "I always thought he was too smart for Sabrina. Leslie flirted outrageously with him, but I think he secretly liked you the best," Danielle continued, undaunted by Nadine's expression.

"He kept that secret well," Nadine said dryly, looking away. "I sure never got that impression."

"Maybe because you were always so snippy to him. I'm sure he'd have spent more time with you if you'd softened a little."

"May I remind you it was Sabrina he went out with. Clint never looked twice at me," Nadine remarked, pulling her keys out of her purse.

"He has eyes for you, Nadine. I can tell," Grandma persisted.

Nadine shook her head. "Grandma, I already have a boyfriend."

"Yes, I know. I keep forgetting." Danielle smiled at Nadine. "I'd like to meet him."

Nadine glanced at her grandmother, but made no reply as she pulled out of the parking lot.

"What are you doing in the kitchen?" Grandma caught Nadine by the arm, frowning up at her. "You go talk to Clint."

Nadine neatly laid out the cheese slices, quelling her irritation. "You invited him, you talk to him," she whispered back.

But Grandma would not be swayed. "You pour Clint some coffee," she said loudly, smiling at Nadine. "I'll finish up in here."

Nadine counted to ten, grabbed the pot and marched out of the kitchen. Clint sat on the edge of the couch. He smiled hesitantly up at Nadine as she filled his coffee cup. Nadine straightened, still holding the pot. She couldn't help but smile back. Nor could she help the soft flip of her heart as their eyes met. It was just like the other morning in his office when the atmosphere held a hint of a promise of other things to come.

"Lunch is ready," Grandma announced from the kitchen, and once again the mood was broken. Clint picked up his cup, motioning for Nadine to precede him.

After grace was said by Grandma, it was her game. She chatted amiably with Clint, praising her granddaughter, drawing her into the conversation. Nadine felt uncomfortable and embarrassed by Grandma's obvious matchmaking, and was positive that Clint felt the same.

But he gamely answered Grandma's questions, and if Nadine didn't contribute much to the conversation, he didn't seem to mind. However, it was an awkward affair and Nadine silently promised herself that once Clint was gone, she would have it out with her dear grandma. Once and for all.

Thankfully, after dessert and more polite conversation, Clint said he had to hurry off to another appointment. Grandma didn't hide her disappointment, and Nadine was grateful for his tact. He bid them both farewell, and as soon as Nadine closed the door behind him, she turned to face her grandma.

Danielle yawned delicately and glanced at her watch. "I'm tired, Nadine. I think I'll lie down. Can you clean up? Thanks." With that, Grandma walked away.

Nadine watched Danielle close the door to her bedroom. Then she turned to the kitchen full of leftovers and dirty dishes, left to wonder how she had let Grandma finesse her way out of both the dishes and another confrontation.

And wonder why Clint had accepted the invitation.

Monday was the usual deadline chaos—phones ringing, typesetters requesting changes in articles that didn't fit the layout.

A fire came in over the police scanner and Clint ended up running out to cover it. To make room for the fire, Nadine had to scuttle her plans for her harvest article taking up the top half of the page.

"C'mon, Clint. I can't finish the layout for that page until I get your story," one of the typesetters groused.

Nadine walked past Clint, who sat, head bent over the keyboard of a computer he had taken over. She paused, looking over his shoulder. Clint seldom wrote articles, but since they were still short a reporter, he had offered to cover the story. She remembered all too well how disconcerted she had felt yesterday, first at church, then at her home. She was determined today to get the upper hand once more in their relationship.

"Accident has two *c*'s," she said lightly.

"I'll run the spell-check once I've finished," he muttered.

"If you remember," Nadine said, leaning one hip against the desk, watching him. He looked agitated, a mood she seldom saw overtake the usually self-possessed Clint Fletcher.

"Don't you have some pictures to paste together or cut apart, or something?" he snapped, pausing to loosen his tie, undo his cuffs and roll up his sleeves.

Nadine paused at the sight of his muscular forearms. "Now *this* is a real first," she said, laughing to cover her reaction. "Clint Fletcher loosens his tie!"

Clint frowned at her. "You should be someplace else."

"I have a newspaper to lay out, and I can't until you hand in your copy."

"Well, if you want my copy, you should be any-place else but right here." He continued frowning at her and, as their eyes met, Nadine felt her heart slow.

She blinked, and the moment was lost. She abruptly pushed herself away from his desk.

"Okay. I'll go check on your courthouse notes for the 'Court Docket.'" Nadine left the room, frustrated with her changing emotions.

The day rambled on. Clint got his story done. A few pieces had to be edited, a few photos resized to fit. By late afternoon the bulk of the work was done. Nadine and a typesetter would be at the paper until late evening setting it all out. Tuesday morning the staff of the *Derwin Times* would start all over again on the next edition.

"What are you doing later tonight?" Donna paused by Nadine's office on her way home to her own family. "We're going to rent a couple of movies, and eat greasy hamburgers and popcorn in front of the television. Want to join us?"

Nadine wrinkled her nose, considering. "We'll be done early tonight, but I should go home. I told Grandma I would spend some time with her instead of my imaginary boyfriend."

"And how has she taken to the idea that her granddaughter has a boyfriend?"

Nadine pulled her hands over her face. "She wants to meet Trace."

"Oh-oh."

"Yeah. Big oh-oh. And where am I going to haul up a boyfriend named Trace Bennet?" Nadine shook her head. "I shouldn't have started this business, Donna."

"No. It's definitely a one-way path to ruin and destruction, this fake boyfriend," Donna gibed.

"Don't joke about that, Donna."

"Don't you always tell me to trust? Maybe you should do the same."

"This is completely different. I can't possibly pray that the Lord will miraculously send me a boyfriend to support a lie I told my dear grandmother." She sighed. "I had hoped just the mention of it would be enough."

"Well, go home, sleep on it. Who knows what will happen?" Donna winked at Nadine, leaving her to ponder what to do about a certain Trace Bennet and the consequences of her lie.

Clint leaned back in his chair reading the most recent edition of the *Derwin Times,* taking a moment to appreciate the new leader they were using. It was a struggle to update the fonts, clean out a lot of the deadwood and encourage the reporters to be more creative. Some had resisted change, but others were eager to take a new direction.

He snapped open the paper, skimming the stories, not reading as much as measuring impact. All in all it was a clean, sharp-looking paper that had the potential to win an award this year at the Weekly Newspapers Association convention. It was one of his goals.

Instituting changes had been a struggle, but slowly the editors of all three papers were coming around.

He turned to the editorial section and was immediately confronted with a picture of the one who wasn't.

Nadine Laidlaw.

Clint tilted his head, looking at the grainy picture on the top of her column. Her large eyes stared back at him, her full mouth unsmiling. The picture didn't do her justice. He studied her face wondering as always why Nadine kept him at arm's length. Just won't fall for your irresistible charm, he thought, laughing lightly at his own egotism.

Grandma Laidlaw, however, was always kindness and consideration. And not above a little matchmaking, he thought wryly, remembering her machinations of Sunday. He was pleased to have such a strong ally in his corner, and hoped the time he'd spent with Nadine on Sunday had brought them a few steps closer.

He turned the page to "About Town," giving it a cursory glance. But it was the usual. The name of a town councillor spotted at the golf course during one of the meetings, other well-known people and their goings-on. Local reporter Nadine Laidlaw spotted at the theater in Eastbar with...

"What?" Clint frowned, shaking the paper as if to bring the name into focus. "Who in the world is Trace Bennet?"

He suddenly realized he had spoken aloud, and quickly glanced through the open door to see if Sharlene had noticed. Thankfully, she wasn't at her desk. He looked back at the paper and reread the piece. Was he a boyfriend?

And why was that name so familiar? Maybe Nadine had mentioned it when he'd met her the other day at the Derwin Inn. Thinking back, he remembered she had been evasive about who she'd been with.

He suddenly felt very foolish. She already had a boyfriend, and kept making it clear that she wasn't interested in him. Yet he continued to try.

Sharlene was now at her desk. She looked up and smiled as Nadine walked in. "Hey, Nadine," she heard her call out.

Clint couldn't help the tingle of awareness as he heard Nadine's name. He straightened as she entered the main office area and dropped her knapsack on the reception desk. Clint allowed himself a moment to look at her. She had an athletic build, which appealed to Clint far more than the slenderness of her sisters. Her cheeks were ruddy from the morning air. Her thick, dark hair was pulled back into the ever-present ponytail he remembered so well. As usual, she wore pants.

"Let's see the latest news from the bustling metropolis of Derwin," Nadine said, her grinning face in profile to Clint.

Sharlene slapped a paper into Nadine's outstretched hand, and she laid it out on the counter, eyeing the front page. She glanced Clint's way and, holding up the paper, winked at him. "Nice shot, eh?"

He sauntered over, hands in the pockets of his dress pants holding back his suit coat. "Looks great, Nadine. Good job."

Nadine smiled. "Thanks, my sartorial boss." She turned her gaze back to the paper, flipping the pages just as he had done a few moments ago. Clint could tell by the way her soft brown eyes traveled over the pages that she was looking at them the way he had. Not reading, just checking for overall impression.

He watched her a moment, feeling almost sorry she had pulled her hair back into a ponytail again. Sunday, wearing a dress and with her hair hanging loose on her shoulders, she had looked softer, more approachable. Less the sassy reporter and more womanly.

He let his eyes travel over her face. She had a firm mouth offset by exotic-looking eyes that tilted upward at the corners, accented by narrow eyebrows. Her striking features drew him again and again. He had been attracted to her from the beginning, yet was put off by her prickly manner. But somehow the intervening years had softened her features. Sorrow had granted her an air of vulnerability he was sure she was unaware of.

Nadine seemed to sense his gaze and looked up at him, their eyes meeting. Clint felt once again the spark of awareness he experienced each time their eyes met.

''Cute little piece in 'About Town' on your trip to Eastbar,'' he gibed, needing to know about this boyfriend.

She frowned and turned to the section. As she read the piece he could tell to the second when her eyes hit her name. A flush shot to her hairline. She swallowed and, without looking at him, slapped the paper shut, caught her knapsack with her other hand and marched down the hallway.

Clint raised one eyebrow in surprise, his curiosity further aroused by Nadine's reaction. Not typical of a woman in love, he thought, feeling a little better. Maybe all was not lost.

"You did this. I know you did," Nadine hissed, shaking the paper in front of her friend's face.

Donna rose and shut the door to her office. "Of course I did," she said. "I know your grandma always reads that section. Doesn't she?"

"But…the paper," Nadine sputtered. "To put it in the newspaper…"

"Oh, c'mon. Most people know it's idle gossip. But your grandma puts as much stock in it as anything she hears from the pulpit on Sunday. I knew if she read it, it would bolster your cause." Donna walked over and patted her friend on the head. "Trust me. It's for the best."

She looked up at Donna and then back at the paper. "So what do I do?"

"Nothing, you ninny. Grandma will read it, believe what you told her, and then she'll move out. Which I might remind you," Donna said, her voice stern, "was the point of this whole exercise."

"But she wants to meet this guy. I have to do something."

"Just hope that this little piece in the paper will be enough. Send her on her way and tell her you'll bring him up for Thanksgiving." Donna sat back on her desk, her arms crossed. "Then, just before that, you break up with him. Easy as can be."

"Easy for you to say, that is." Nadine looked once

more at the offending section, shaking her head. "I still can't believe you did this."

"Hey, I could have put in Clint Fletcher's name."

Nadine shot her a murderous look. "You dare."

"Hey. You could do worse," Donna said with a laugh. "Clint's pretty easy on the eyes and whether you like to admit it or not, I think you agree."

The problem was, she did agree. She agreed most wholeheartedly.

Nadine swatted Donna on the head with the paper and left.

Donna crouched down and filled the cubicle under Sharlene's desk with the latest editions of the paper for walk-in customers. The door jangled and as she straightened, a tall, darkly handsome man stepped through the door. He wore denim jeans and a hunter green cable-knit sweater. He had wavy dark brown hair, and his gray eyes scanned the interior of the office almost hesitantly.

"Can I help you?" Donna asked, curious as to who he was.

He shrugged and slanted her a self-deprecating grin. "I'm actually looking for..." He paused a moment. "Nadine Laidlaw."

"She's in her office right now. Can I ask who wants to see her?"

"Trace Bennet."

Donna felt her jaw drop. "Okay," she said stupidly. Then she thought, What am I going to tell Nadine?

She caught sight of Clint in his office staring at them both, and she knew she had to do something.

"I'll show you to her office." She walked around the high, curved desk, caught Trace Bennet by the arm and literally dragged him down the hallway to Nadine's tiny office. "This is a real surprise. I'm sure Nadine isn't expecting you. She's talked about you, but I've never met you and I'm sure she's never met you…" Donna babbled. "I mean, she would like to meet you." Or maybe not, she thought despairingly. What am I going to do? She'll kill me for sure. She stopped at Nadine's office. Thankfully the door was open.

Nadine looked up from her desk, frowned at Donna and then at Mr. Bennet.

"Nadine," Donna said, her voice falsely cheerful, "such an interesting coincidence." She turned to the good-looking man. "This is, um…"

"What is going on?" Nadine asked, getting up from her desk. Trace stared at Nadine. He looked as if someone had punched him in the stomach.

Looks like it's up to me, thought Donna. "Nadine, I'd like to introduce you to Trace Bennet."

"Oh, dear," Nadine whispered, looking as bewildered as Trace did. "What have I done?"

Trace took a breath and then smiled. "I'm a little confused here."

"*You* are?" Nadine replied. "Please, sit down."

"I think I had better check on some coffee." Donna took a few steps backward, bumping into the door before she beat a hasty retreat.

Nadine sighed and looked once more at Trace Bennet. What coincidence had caused her to come up with this man's name? This man who happened to be very good-looking and frighteningly real, now seated in a chair, smiling hesitantly at her?

"I have to apologize, Mr. Bennet..." She let the sentence drift off. Her usual interviewing skills disappeared.

"That's okay." He smiled and leaned forward. "I'm guessing it was a coincidence. I had to come to this office this morning, anyhow. When I noticed my name and yours in the paper, I thought maybe I should talk to you."

Nadine frowned at him, his name echoing from some other source in her mind. "What did you have to come to the office for?"

"I'm starting a new business and needed to talk to you, as the editor, about covering our opening day. I had sent you some information."

Nadine looked at him, and suddenly it all fell into place. There'd been a letter. A new farm implement dealership. "That's where I got the name."

"Pardon me?" Trace frowned.

"The papers you sent me. I must have pulled your name from there. That night, when Grandma..." She shook her head to clear her thoughts.

"When Grandma..." he prompted.

"It doesn't matter," Nadine replied, feeling embarrassed. "It's a long story and you're a complete stranger who, unfortunately, got caught up in a bunch of lies. I'm very, very sorry."

"No. Don't be. Nothing bad came of it." Trace smiled. "I'm really glad I came down to the office today."

Just then the door opened and Donna bustled in carrying a tray bearing two steaming mugs of coffee and a plate of some broken cookies. "Sorry," she apologized. "I had to rescue the bag from Wally." She almost dropped the tray on the desk by Nadine and was about to execute another hasty exit when Nadine reached over and caught her friend by the arm.

"You've already met Donna, but I bet she didn't tell you that she was instrumental in this whole business." Nadine forced a smile at her friend, squeezing her fingers on her arm.

"What?" Donna sputtered. "You're the one who came up with the name." Donna turned to Trace, pressing one hand against her chest. "Honest. I just worked with the raw material provided to me by my friend Nadine. What I did was just embroidery."

Nadine let go, shaking her head at her friend's duplicity. "I didn't think you'd go and put it in the newspaper for everyone to read...."

"No. I put it in the newspaper for your grandma to read." Donna turned to Nadine, an exasperated expression on her face. "That was the point, wasn't it? To let Grandma know that you had a boyfriend so she would move out of your house and leave you alone?"

"Well, somehow it worked out that the whole county got to read that little tidbit, as well...."

"Excuse me, girls," Trace interrupted with a laugh. "It's really not a problem."

"No?" they both said at once, turning in unison to him.

"No. Not at all. I'm new in town." He lifted his hands in a gesture of surrender. "I wanted to meet Nadine anyway."

"That's great," Donna said, turning to Nadine. "Isn't it, Nadine? Here's your boyfriend. You bring him home to Grandma, tell her that you've found the man of your dreams."

"Just a minute, Donna…" sputtered Nadine, seeing an instant need to take control of the situation. "Mr. Bennet is a complete stranger. He's here to do business." She shook her head, feeling overwhelmed. "I think I've had enough of your helpful schemes."

Trace Bennet clasped his hands behind his head, looking perfectly at ease. "Why don't you tell me the history of this little episode? I think it's the least you can do," he added in a teasing tone.

Nadine bit her lip, looking contritely at him. "If I had known…"

"I said it's okay," he said, grinning. "So I gather there's a grandma in this sordid tale."

Donna sat down beside him, more than ready to fill him in, Nadine could see.

"Donna, maybe you had better see if Sharlene needs any help out front?"

Donna frowned, then, taking the broad hint, stood up. With one more smile at Mr. Bennet.

"Anyhow, the story," Nadine began again. "My grandma has been living with me for the past five years, ever since my mother got sick. I've always been very thankful for what she's done, but she was never content to sit back and let other people live their lives. The problem is she won't rest until her only single granddaughter, being me, is married or, at the least, settled down with a boyfriend.''

''Which was supposed to be me,'' Trace said with a grin.

''Which was *supposed* to be a completely fictional character,'' Nadine said with emphasis. ''Your name popped out one day when I found out she was inviting all kinds of single men over for supper.'' Nadine lifted her hands in surrender. ''I'd had enough and told her that I had a date that night and somehow, I guess from skimming over the material, your name came to mind. Donna ran with it and this is the result.''

Trace shook his head, his smile reassuring. ''Believe me, I'm not one bit sorry that our names were linked in the newspaper. But now the next question is where do we go from here?''

''We break up, of course.'' She had to put an end to this for Trace Bennet's sake and her own.

Trace stroked his jaw with one hand, his eyes still on her. ''But why? You need a boyfriend and I could use the help of someone who knows the people of this town. I don't think we should end such a compatible match over such a little misunderstanding.'' He smiled, a dimple winking back at her from beside his mouth.

Nadine felt a softening. Trace had a gentle charm about him, and she was only a weak woman who felt guilty about using this man's name. But the thought of hoodwinking not only her grandma but also the citizens of the town she lived in made her hesitate.

"If we actually went out together, you wouldn't be lying to your grandmother. And dating a beautiful girl like you would hardly be a hardship for me." Trace stood up, his hands in his pockets. "I don't mind, if you don't."

"No," squeaked Nadine. "Not really."

"Good. We can start off with dinner tonight at the Derwin Inn. You can fill me in on the town and its occupants."

Nadine nodded, feeling once again as if someone was taking control of her life. But as she looked up at Trace's handsome face, she didn't mind.

"Great." He reached out a hand, and automatically Nadine caught it. "It's a deal, then. I'll pick you up from your place tonight and we'll celebrate our first official 'date.'" He winked at her. "Where do you live?"

Nadine gave him her address, then he left and she stared at the closed door, feeling bemused, overwhelmed and oddly satisfied. Trace Bennet was a charming, fine-looking man. And the thought of spending an evening with him made her feel wanted.

Okay, Lord, was this it? Was this the answer to my prayer? She smiled. She figured she would find out in time.

Chapter Five

As Nadine poured herself some tea from a miniature silver pot she looked across the table at Trace, studying him as he stirred his coffee.

He glanced up at her and smiled. "And what is Nadine Laidlaw thinking of now?"

"Actually, I'm wondering why you wanted to take me out." She stopped, realizing how that sounded, then added, "I mean, after what we did to you."

"I'm lonely, I'm new in town and I want to get to know you better." He set his cup down, lowering his voice to a more intimate level. "I've been wondering about you for a while."

Nadine frowned. "What do you mean?"

"I've been subscribing to the paper for a while, reading your articles." He covered her hand with his, twining his fingers through hers. "You are a very principled person. You've got strong values...." He hesitated, squeezing her hand. "That comes out in your writing.'' He leaned forward, holding her hand tightly now, as if he was afraid to let go. ''I want to get to know you better. I think that little mistake your friend made wasn't just a mistake. I think this meeting was meant to be.''

Nadine blinked, trying to absorb what he had just said. While his declaration had been pleasant, it created a feeling of discomfort she couldn't put a finger on. Nadine carefully pulled her hand out of his.

He smiled then, easing the intensity of the moment. ''I feel it is only right that we spend this evening getting to know each other better.'' He lifted his coffee cup and took another sip. ''Why don't we start with you?''

''I don't know,'' she said slowly, gathering her thoughts. ''There's not much to tell.''

''Try me.''

Nadine lifted her hands and then, with a laugh, started. ''I was born here in Derwin, went to school here, left for about a year to take some journalism classes, came back when my father died and my mother became ill. Got a job at the *Derwin Times*, moved from reporter to editor where I am now.''

''That was a concise résumé.''

''I've had a concise life.'' Nadine shrugged. She took a sip of her tea as she looked past him, just in time to see Clint Fletcher get up from the table where he had been sitting. Did he come here all the time?

Clint glanced up and caught her gaze. Disconcerted, she watched as he paused, then sauntered over.

"Hello, Nadine." He turned to Trace, and Nadine had no choice but to introduce them.

"Trace, this is Clint Fletcher, my boss. Fletcher, this is Trace Bennet." She forced a smile. "Trace is starting an implement dealership in town."

Trace stood and held out a hand to Clint. "Pleased to meet you," Trace said. "Would you like to join us?"

But to Nadine's relief Clint shook his head. "No. I have to be on my way." He looked back at Trace, his mouth curved in a polite smile. "Thanks for the offer, though."

"I'll have to make arrangements to talk to you sometime," Trace said, sitting down again. "You can tell me all about Derwin."

Clint glanced at Nadine. "Nadine has spent her entire life here and can probably fill you in better than I can on the goings-on of the town."

Nadine bristled. He made it sound as if she had never been anywhere but Derwin and had no life whatsoever. "Not all of us have rich uncles who can afford to send us off to Europe, Fletcher," she snapped.

"I realize that, Nadine." He held her angry gaze, his own unflinching.

Nadine felt a moment of confusion at the understanding tone of his voice, the sympathy she saw reflected in his hazel eyes. Uncomfortable, she looked away.

Clint jingled the change in his pocket a moment. "I hope you two have a pleasant evening."

"And I hope it is to be the first of many," said Trace, a touch of humor in his voice.

"The first?" Clint asked. Nadine's gaze flew up to his, then she looked away. He paused a moment, then turned and walked away.

She turned to Trace, who was watching her intently. "Your boss has quite a forceful presence, doesn't he?" he remarked.

"When he wants to," she said, her tone abrupt.

"Has he lived here long?"

"No. He moved here when he was in grade twelve and came to live with his uncle, Dory Strepchuk. My old boss. He used to own the paper, and Clint took over from him." Nadine took a sip of her tea, now cool, and set it down with a grimace. She didn't want to talk about her boss. She could still feel his eyes on her, assessing Trace. For some reason she didn't want him to see her and Trace together.

"But you seem to know him well."

"I should." Nadine laughed shortly. "He went out with my older sister and flirted with the younger one."

"You have sisters?"

Nadine spun her teacup. "Two. Sabrina and Leslie. Both tall, blond, gorgeous."

"Why do you put yourself down like that?" he asked.

Nadine shrugged, uncomfortable with his scrutiny. "It's not a put-down. Merely the facts."

"Well, it sounded as if you were putting yourself down, as well." He sounded displeased. "You're a very attractive person." His gaze was intent. "You have such beautiful deep brown eyes, and such lovely hair.'' He paused as he looked her face over.

Nadine tried not to feel uncomfortable, tried not to let herself believe what he was telling her.

He sighed a moment. ''You have an earthy beauty....''

''Wholesome.'' Nadine couldn't keep the dour note out of her voice as she said that, nor was she able to stop the faint flush that crept up her cheeks at his kind words. ''You can stop now.''

''I will. For now.'' He winked at her. ''So now I know that you have two sisters and a grandma. How about your parents?'' he prompted.

Nadine looked down at her tea, curving her fingers around the cup as if trying to warm it up. ''My father was killed in a logging accident about six years ago. My mother died about six months ago.''

''I'm so sorry to hear that.''

Nadine lifted one shoulder negligently. ''She had ALS, Lou Gehrig's disease. It was better.'' She looked up at him, anxious to change the subject. Her mother's death wasn't news, but lately it seemed to bring up sorrow and regrets that she didn't want to deal with, not in front of a stranger, no matter how kind he might be.

Thankfully the waitress came with their food. Nadine automatically bent her head in prayer.

When she looked up, he was looking at her with a bemused expression. ''I think that's wonderful. Seeing someone who isn't afraid to show what they believe.''

Nadine didn't know what to say. Her belief was not something to take credit or be praised for.

"I'm glad that you aren't afraid to pray in public," he continued. He tilted his head as he looked at her, his gaze intent. "You are a very special person, Nadine. Your faith comes through in your writing, as well."

Nadine couldn't think of anything to say. His words spoke to her own longing for a soul mate, someone she could share her faith with. "I've been blessed with a believing family," she said quietly. "I know I want the same for myself."

"Not everyone gets that," he said, his voice tinged with pain. Then with a shake of his head he dispelled the mood. "And you have been blessed."

"And what about your family?"

And Trace told her about the Bennets. They still lived in the Fraser Valley and had a dairy farm. Trace had worked for a local implement dealer and from there had moved up. Now he was poised to start his own business. He had been scouting likely locations for the past year and had settled on Derwin.

"But I've been looking for more than just a place to build a dealership." He winked at Nadine. "I sure didn't expect to find such a good-looking date this quickly."

Nadine tried not to blush at how that had come about. It was still very embarrassing. "Let's not talk about that one, okay?" she pleaded.

"How many times do I have to tell you? I'm really enjoying myself." He shook his head. "Now you have to tell me more about yourself. What about your hopes, your dreams?''

Hopes and dreams? Had she even had an opportunity in the past years to articulate what she wanted, to figure it out?

''Stuck?'' he prodded.

She shook her head. ''It seems that I've spent so much time taking care of my mother and working that I don't know if I've even had a chance lately to hope and dream.'' She looked back at Trace and dismissed her melancholy with a light laugh. ''I guess I have to believe that God put me here for a reason and I'll find out what that is in His time.''

''God's ways are mysterious, that's for sure.'' Trace smiled as they shared a moment of accord.

The rest of the evening went by far too quickly and soon it was time to go. As he pulled up to her building, Nadine noticed one light burning in the living room of her apartment. Grandma was waiting up.

They walked into the building and Trace stopped at the door to her apartment, spinning out their farewell.

''Will I be able to see you soon, next time I'm in town?'' Trace picked up her hand, playing with her fingers.

''Sure,'' Nadine said, suppressing a trill of anticipation. ''Thanks for a lovely evening. I enjoyed it thoroughly.''

The door creaked behind them as it opened slowly. ''Nadine, are you still out there?''

Nadine stiffened at the sound of her grandmother's voice. ''Yes, Grandma.''

"Well, come in, right now." Grandma pushed the door open and stepped out into the hallway, wrapping her fleece robe tightly around her. "It's late."

Nadine glanced back at Trace, who, thankfully, hadn't changed expression at the sight of this diminutive woman.

"Trace, this is my Grandma Laidlaw. Grandma, this is Trace Bennet."

Grandma kept her hands around her waist and only nodded in acknowledgment. "So I finally get to meet you, Mr. Bennet."

"Pleased to meet you." Trace held out his hand to Grandma. She took it begrudgingly and quickly shook it. "And please call me Trace."

"I will." She looked him over once and then turned away as if he wasn't worth any more of her time. "I want you to come in, Nadine. It's late and I'm sure both you and Mr. Bennet have an early day at work tomorrow."

"I'll be in shortly, Grandma," Nadine replied in a warning tone.

Danielle was unrepentant. She glanced once more in Trace's general direction. "Nice to meet you," she said abruptly, her tone conveying anything but. As she left, Nadine turned apologetically to Trace.

"Sorry about her. She takes notions. And the notion she has in her grip tonight is that she refuses to like anyone she hasn't picked for me herself."

"That's okay." Trace slid his hands into his pockets, hunching his shoulders. "But I still want to see you again." He winked at her and straightened. For a moment Nadine thought he was going to kiss her, but he only touched her cheek with one finger. "I'll call," he said softly. Then, turning, he left.

Nadine watched him go, a sigh lifting her shoulders. She walked to the glass doors and watched as he drove away.

After she'd dropped Jack and come back to Derwin, she hadn't had time to date. Since her mother's illness she hadn't gone on a real date until tonight.

Nadine wrinkled her nose and laughed shortly. And even that date had been manufactured.

"Special delivery for you, Nadine." Sharlene breezed into Nadine's office two days later carrying a huge bouquet of white roses.

Nadine reached for the flowers, surprised, pleased. Flowers. "Who are they from?"

"That's what I'd like to know. Here, this came with." Sharlene handed Nadine an envelope. Nadine opened it and pulled out the small card, then smiled. Trace.

She went off in search of a vase, carrying the flowers with her. She found a jar and was returning to her office, her nose buried in the bouquet, when she literally bumped into Clint Fletcher.

He caught her by the elbows and steadied her, his eyes on the flowers.

"A secret admirer?" he said, his expression serious.

"This one's not a secret," she said with a smile. "They came from Trace."

He cocked an eyebrow at her, still not smiling. "The boyfriend?"

Nadine didn't like the ironic tone of his voice. "Yes. They were delivered here this morning," she answered.

"Well. He's certainly expressing his affection in an atypical fashion." Clint flicked a finger at the flowers. "I always labored under the impression that red roses were the flower of choice in a romance."

Where does he haul out that language? thought Nadine. "Well, labor no more, Fletcher. These days anything goes." Nadine took a noisy sniff of her flowers, her eyes on Clint.

"It would seem that way," Clint said dryly.

"Clint, can you come here a moment?" Wally, the other reporter, called out from the end of the hallway.

She turned and watched him go, puzzled at his comment and his attitude.

Shrugging off Clint's reaction, she returned to her office. She had a few calls to make, some follow-up work to do and had to go over her mail.

And it was Clint's and her turn to "Face Off."

The weekly column was Dory Strepchuk's legacy. Each week two of the staff of any of the three sister papers would take an opposing view on a controversial topic. This week, by some twist of fate, she and Clint had to go head-to-head on the topic "Should the Government Bail Out Large Companies?" Thankfully Clint had chosen the "yes" side.

And that would be okay with her.

Her phone was ringing as she stepped into her office. It was Trace.

"Get my flowers?" he asked.

"I did. Thanks so much. They're beautiful."

"Not as beautiful as you are." Trace chuckled. "I know that's a pretty corny line, but it's true. And you're simply supposed to say thank-you."

Nadine tried not to take his compliment seriously. "Thanks, Trace. They are very lovely."

"Got them just because. I miss you, you know."

"Now I know you're laying it on thick. We only met two days ago."

"I don't feel like that, Nadine," he said, his tone suddenly serious. "I feel like we've met years ago... like I've been waiting for someone like you...."

For once, Nadine didn't know what to say. Trace almost seemed too good to be true.

"I'm coming back to town on Thursday. I know there's a new movie showing in Eastbar. I thought we could go out for supper and then hit the movie. Just like we did last week." He laughed. "Is that okay with you?"

Nadine couldn't help the smile that curved her lips. "Sounds wonderful."

"I'm looking forward to it, Nadine." He was quiet a moment. "I know this sounds silly, but I really feel like we're meant for each other, Nadine. I'm looking forward to getting to know you better."

"Me, too," was all she could say. "Me, too."

"'Why do we allow our government to bail out megacorporations who have not shown themselves to be responsible corporate citizens,'" read Nadine out loud, "'and ignore the daily bankruptcy of any number of small, home-based businesses, owned by families and in financial difficulty because of circumstances beyond their control? Many large corporations are not even North American owned, but are subsidiaries of companies whose ownership is lost in a morass of paper shuffling and numbered companies. Is their plight more important than that of native North Americans?'" Nadine folded the papers with a grin and set them on the table at the Downtown Deli. "And my column goes on to make many more very scintillating points."

"Very well done," agreed Donna, pulling a sprout out of her bagel. "Emotional, but well done."

"Of course it's emotional. It's an editorial."

"Well, you tend to be more shrill whenever you write about anything even remotely connected to Skyline."

"No, I'm not."

Donna shrugged away the objection. "Anyway, it's good."

Nadine smiled. Encouraging words to a writer were food and drink. "Thanks. I think it's going to be a great match for the Skyline article I pulled out of the computer."

Donna examined her bagel more closely, her expression suddenly serious. "You still going to run that?"

"Probably."

"I thought Clint asked you to back off."

"He did. But I'm not going to. This is too important."

"Why are you deliberately antagonizing the poor guy? Clint's going to end up in trouble over it."

"I had an empty spot I needed to fill," Nadine said defensively. "With the column it's a perfect fit. Skyline has been on the receiving end of a few kickbacks and government grants." Nadine winked at Donna, trying to alleviate her serious mood. "Besides, no one had anything else besides photos of beaming farmers holding up monster vegetables."

"Why don't you leave poor Clint alone?" Donna continued. "He's got enough on his plate."

"What do you mean by that?"

Donna took the last bite of her bagel, frowning. "A nagging partner, a potential lawsuit and a stubborn employee who won't listen. That's more than enough," she mumbled. She finished her bagel and wiped her fingers off with a napkin. "But you don't want to talk about Clint, so tell me about your date with Trace instead."

Nadine knew she was touchy on the subject of Clint Fletcher and gladly took up the change in topic. "He's very nice. He's funny. He's good-looking."

"And Grandma?"

Nadine blew out her breath. "She's coming around." Which was stretching the truth about 175 degrees.

"So now that she's met your boyfriend, is she going to give up? Move out?"

Nadine picked up her sandwich, avoiding Donna's questioning look. "She hasn't said."

"I gather he doesn't meet with her full approval."

Nadine shook her head and took a bite of her sandwich.

"So what are you going to do?"

"I don't know." Nadine studied her sandwich.

"I don't know why you have so much trouble with her." Donna leaned forward, smiling. "Goodness knows, she's smaller than you."

"She's also incredibly stubborn and obtuse. And when I try to get really definite, she gently reminds me of all she did for me and my mom." Nadine picked at her bread. "That's where I usually cave."

"That's easy enough. Take some of the stuff you dish out to Clint and save it for Grandma. Might work."

"What is with you?" Nadine asked, surprised at the return to her boss. "I don't know what comments you're talking about."

"Those snide comments you're always tossing at him. You could use them on Grandma."

"I wouldn't do that. I love my grandma."

"And you dislike Clint?" Donna shook her head as she wiped her mouth.

"I don't dislike him. We just seem to strike sparks off each other." Sparks that made her remarkably uneasy.

"I think you do more striking than he does."

"Where does that come from?" asked Nadine, uncomfortable with what her friend inferred. "How come all of a sudden you're on his side?"

Donna sat back and dug in her purse for some change. "I'm not on anyone's 'side.' I've just been watching you and him, and if I didn't know any better—" she got up and dropped a dollar coin on the table "—I'd say you had a crush on the man."

"Are you crazy?" Nadine scrambled to her feet, dragging her camera bag along with her. "Where in the world do you come off saying something like that?"

Donna glanced at her irate friend as she waited for change from the cashier. "If you don't like him, why do you pay so much attention to him?" She held out her hand for the change. "Thanks, Iris. And you have yourself a good day."

Donna sauntered out of the Deli, leaving behind a confused Nadine and an obviously interested Iris.

Nadine paid the cashier as well, then caught up to her friend.

"Okay. What were you talking about back there?" Nadine jogged up beside Donna.

Donna stopped. "I was talking about the way you treat Clint. You can't seem to resist any chance to give him a dig or some kind of snide comment."

Nadine frowned, trying to think why Donna would say that. "I don't treat him that bad." She thought back to comments she had made to Clint, trying to see them from Donna's viewpoint. "I mean, I needle him, but that's just for fun."

"You may think so. But it doesn't come out that way."

"Well, he's just as bad."

Donna crossed her arms and looked her friend directly in the eye. "How?" she asked quietly.

Nadine looked away, rubbing her hand along the strap of her bag, trying to remember. "Give me a couple of days. I'll come up with something."

Donna nodded knowingly. "The truth is you can't come up with any one incident. And if you can't think of any time he's been miserable to you, maybe you might want to spend that time wondering why you pay so much attention to him." She winked at Nadine and stepped into the office.

Nadine leaned against the window. Clint was always ragging on her, always trying to find a way to make her flustered.

Wasn't he…?

Nadine bit her lip, convinced she could find *something*.

But after a few minutes she came to a disarming realization.

Clint had never talked to her the way she talked to him. And Donna was right. It was no way for a Christian to treat another person.

Chapter Six

"You're wearing a skirt to work, Nadine?" Grandma set her cup of tea down and stared at her granddaughter as she stepped into the kitchen.

"Trace is picking me up right after work for a date tonight."

She had topped the skirt with a loose sweater and, in a fit of whimsy, wound a gauzy patterned scarf around her neck, tucking the ends in. She had curled her hair and taken time to brush her eyelashes with mascara and her eyelids with a faint dusting of gold eye shadow. She couldn't recall when she'd purchased the rarely worn makeup—maybe for Leslie's wedding? Or was it Sabrina's? Nadine was surprised that the old mascara hadn't dried up.

"You look very nice," Grandma said approvingly. "The makeup looks good, as well. Sets off your pretty eyes."

"Thanks, Grandma." Nadine laughed as she bent

over and kissed Danielle's cheek. "It's been so long since I wore makeup, I'm trying not to feel like a store mannequin," she admitted, sitting down to her breakfast. She also wondered if she was going to make it to the end of the day before the hair hanging around her jawline drove her nuts.

"Well, you're going to turn a few heads, I'm sure." Grandma smiled her approval and Nadine felt a little better. "Clint Fletcher won't recognize you."

"I didn't do this for my boss," Nadine said more sharply than she had intended.

"Of course not." Danielle smiled. "I'm sure Trace will like the way you look."

Nadine was somewhat mollified by her grandmother's encouraging comments. "Thanks, Grandma."

They ate their breakfast in silence, Grandma reading the paper and Nadine going over her notes for the interview she was going to do tomorrow. When Nadine left the apartment she felt ready to face the world.

"Good morning, Sharlene." Nadine breezed into the office, pausing at the mail drop to check for any mail or messages.

Sharlene looked up from an ad she was writing out with a smile that froze on her face when she caught sight of her editor. "Nadine?" she said, her voice weak with surprise.

Nadine grinned back and flipped a hand through her hair. "Do I look *that* different today?"

"Different enough." Sharlene shook her head. "The Nadine I know wouldn't wear a skirt except to church, and she certainly would never put on makeup.''

Nadine smiled as she looked down at the envelopes in her hands. "People change," she murmured.

"Do they ever." Clint's disbelieving voice behind her made her head snap up.

Nadine kept her eyes straight ahead, feeling suddenly self-conscious about her clothes, her makeup, her hair.

What does it matter what he thinks? she reminded herself. He's just your boss. She curved her lips into a smile and turned to face Clint, who stood in the doorway of his office, one shoulder propped against the doorjamb, his eyebrows raised in surprise.

A sharp retort to deflect his comment came to mind, but on its heels, Donna's admonition from the day before. She hesitated, catching his eye. Clint's expression became serious as the moment stretched out. He straightened, his eyelids lowering slightly, his lips softening. She couldn't look away and, for some puzzling reason, didn't want to.

Flustered, she shuffled through the envelopes, dropping a couple. As she bent to pick them up, other hands beat her to it. Without looking up at Clint, she took them from him and escaped to her office.

What is wrong with you? she chided herself as she dropped her knapsack on the floor beside her desk. She shook her head as if to rearrange her thoughts and dropped the mail onto her already overflowing desk. Clint Fletcher is your boss, you are Nadine Laidlaw and you dressed up for your date with Trace.

She walked around her desk to turn on her computer. She had set today aside to clear off some paperwork and do some more work on some of the columns she had written. With a little luck she would be finished by the time Trace came tonight to pick her up.

She looked over her articles, skipped lunch and headed out to do an interview.

Trace phoned while Nadine was away, and left the message that he would pick her up from the office a little later than he had originally planned. Nadine didn't mind. It gave her a little more time to finish off some stories.

She spent the better part of the afternoon looking over the résumés of people who had applied for the other reporter's job. She desperately needed someone to help out. She and Wally were each doing a job and a half to make up for the vacancy, and it was wearing both of them down. Clint helped out where he could, but the workload was still too much.

The day seemed to fly by. When Nadine finally pushed herself back from her computer, she was surprised to see it was almost five-forty.

Blinking tiredly, she lifted a hand to rub her eyes. Just in time she remembered her mascara and stopped herself.

Nadine clicked her mouse to save the file she was working on and then shut down her computer. She didn't want to work anymore. Trace would be coming for her any moment.

She rolled her neck, looking with satisfaction over

her desk, pleased with the empty spaces she could now see. She had another interview to do tomorrow and Saturday a volleyball tournament to cover. Thankfully this one was in town, so she wouldn't have to travel. Trace wanted to take her out Saturday, as well.

She went to the bathroom and checked her makeup, brushed her hair and tried to still the butterflies in her stomach.

A date. After all these years, she was going on a date. She grinned at herself in the mirror. And not a date of Grandma's doing. A date with someone who wanted to be with her. Nadine tilted her head as she studied her reflection. She wasn't a vain person, but the fact that someone wanted to be with her made her take a second look at the young woman in the mirror. She winked at her reflection and walked out.

Half an hour later, Trace still hadn't come. Nadine had busied herself with odd jobs, cleaning out the coffee room, gathering a few mugs from different places in the office, trying to quell her nervous tension. What if he wasn't coming?

She tried not to, but periodically she walked down the hall to the front door to see if Trace was waiting outside. He wasn't, and Nadine wondered how long she should wait.

She made a fresh pot of coffee and leaned against the counter, waiting for the machine to finish dripping, an unwelcome feeling of melancholy coming over her. She decided she would give Trace another fifteen minutes and then she would...

She would what? she thought, her stomach tightening at the thought of facing her grandmother, telling her that she had been stood up.

The soft hiss of the coffee machine broke the stillness of the room. Nadine used to dread this time of the day. For the past year any free evenings she had were spent at the hospital. The last few months of her mother's life were fraught with tension and wondering. Each time the phone rang, Nadine and her grandmother wondered if this time it was the hospital. Her sisters came whenever they could, but Nadine knew they didn't have the time she had. That meant the bulk of the visiting and doctor's consultations fell on Nadine's shoulders.

The memories always brought tears, and tonight was no exception. Nadine felt the nudge of pain and closed her eyes as it drifted over her. She tried to fight it, but couldn't.

I miss her, Lord, she prayed, pressing her hand against her mouth, tears sliding down her cheeks as the pain increased. *I know she's better off where she is, but I still miss her so much.* She drew in a deep breath, wishing she could stop the tears.

A noise behind her broke abruptly into her sorrow. She whirled around, her heart pounding.

"Sorry." Clint stood in the doorway of the coffee room, his tie loosened, his cuffs rolled up. "I didn't know you were still here."

Nadine turned away again, surreptitiously wiping at her cheeks. "That's fine," she replied, looking around for a napkin, anything to get rid of the mortifying tears.

"Nadine." He came toward her, his deep voice tinged with concern. "Is something wrong?"

She snatched up some napkins and hurriedly wiped at her eyes. "Do you want some coffee?" she asked, her voice muffled by the napkin.

"I can get it," he replied, stepping past her, thankfully not glancing her way. He stood with his broad back to her, his shirt pulling across his shoulders as he reached up for a cup. He poured himself some coffee and then glanced over his shoulder at her.

"I'm sorry if I embarrassed you." He turned to face her. "I don't mean to intrude."

Nadine looked down at the crumpled napkin, now smeared with mascara. She shook her head at her own clumsiness. "I'm fine" was all she could manage.

"Has something happened?" he persisted.

Nadine hesitated, her previous encounters with Clint creating a barrier. She remembered once again Donna's admonition. He had been a visitor in their home any number of times, had met her mother and knew Grandma. He had been a large part of her life for a time. He was kind of an old friend, she had to concede. He could be told the truth.

"Nothing happened," Nadine said with a shaky smile. She took a deep breath to steady her voice. "I just…miss my mother." She bit back another soft cry and could speak no more. Another set of tears drifted down her cheeks.

Clint said nothing, and for that Nadine was thankful. He stood, quiet, waiting, listening. His gaze serious, interested. Sympathetic with no trace of pity.

Nadine took another deep breath, studying the smeared napkin. "Silly, isn't it? She's been dead six months and it seems like I'm sadder now than I was when she died."

"Six months isn't that long," he replied softly. "I would think it takes years to get over the death of someone you love."

Nadine nodded. "I remember my mom crying over my dad even just until a couple of years ago."

"I don't know if you ever get over the death of someone you care for. I think it's quite something that your mother loved your father like that." Clint laughed shortly. "You were lucky to see that while you were growing up."

Nadine paused, looking at him, surprised at this admission. "You were never close to your parents, were you?" she asked.

Clint shook his head, smiling sadly. "Hard to be close to a couple who seldom talked to each other, let alone their son." He looked up at Nadine, his gaze sincere. "I used to hate them, but I realized that it only drained whatever joy I could find in my life. I'm thankful that I found a loving Father who cares for me with a strength and sincerity I haven't found on earth. I learned that and much more from Uncle Dory and am thankful for more reasons than one that I was sent here to Derwin."

Nadine was taken aback at his admission. Clint had never been very forthcoming about his spiritual life.

"I always admired your mother's strength," Clint continued, setting down his coffee cup. "She did a good job raising you girls, teaching you the right things, encouraging you in your relationship with God. I'm sure she must have been proud of you.''

Nadine shrugged. ''Well, at least Sabrina and Leslie managed to get themselves married.''

Clint said nothing to that and Nadine sniffed once again, wiping at her eyes.

''You have nothing to be ashamed of,'' Clint said finally. ''Jack was a fool to let you go.''

Nadine looked up at that, blinking away more tears as she caught Clint's steady gaze. She looked at him again, as if seeing him with new eyes.

A sudden knocking on the front door startled them both. ''Hello, anybody there?'' Trace's muffled voice drifted down the hallway.

''Well. Looks like your date is finally here,'' said Clint, his voice dry.

Nadine turned to leave, but was surprised when Clint caught her arm to stop her. ''Just a minute,'' he said, picking up a napkin. He tugged on her arm to bring her closer. ''Your mascara is smudged,'' he said.

Nadine felt a most curious sensation as she looked up. His hazel eyes seemed to draw her in, pull her toward him. She felt the warmth of his hand encircling her arm, his fingers brushing her cheek as he wiped a smudge away. She raised her hand to rest it on his shoulder as she felt herself drift toward him.

Another loud knock on the door broke the moment.

''You better go before your ardent suitor breaks down the door,'' said Clint dryly, letting her go.

Nadine nodded, feeling suddenly breathless. She

stopped at the doorway, looking back. But Clint had his coffee in his hand and was sipping it, his eyes downcast.

Shaking off the feelings he had aroused in her, she turned and ran down the hallway.

"Wow. Do you ever look terrific," Trace greeted her appreciatively. "I didn't think you could get even more gorgeous."

Nadine smiled, passing off his compliments with a dismissive gesture.

Trace caught her hands. "I know exactly what that means, you silly girl. Hey, sorry I'm late," he said. "I got stuck at the bank." He pulled her closer and kissed her lightly on her cheek. "Forgive me?"

"I was wondering if you were going to stand me up."

"Are you kidding?" Trace pulled her close to him. "A guy would have to be crazy to do that to someone like you." He kissed her again. "The movie just started. We can grab supper later."

Nadine ran back down the hallway and got her purse from her office. She stepped out the door and, pausing a moment, walked back to the coffee room. Clint still stood at the counter, his coffee cup in his hands.

He looked at her. "Still here?" was all he said.

Nadine bit her lip, unable to pass off what had just happened, unsure of what to make of it. "Thanks," she said finally, hoping he understood what she meant. "For everything."

Clint nodded. "Any time, Nadine," he replied softly. "Any time at all."

"C'mon, gorgeous," Trace called. "The night isn't getting any younger."

"See you Monday," she said, then turned and left.

Nadine cranked on the film rewind as the noise of the celebrating team roiled around her. It was Saturday night. The home team had won their invitational volleyball tournament and were celebrating in the true manner of high school champions.

They were screaming their fool heads off.

Nadine popped open her camera, pulled the film out and, crouching down, dropped it into an empty canister and popped the top on. She was finished for the night.

"There you are." Trace's voice behind her made her whirl around in surprise. He wore a denim jacket tonight, blue jeans and cowboy boots. He looked like a rodeo poster boy, rugged and almost too handsome.

"Hi." She smiled up at him and he reached out and tucked a strand of hair behind her ear. "You're early."

"I'm even earlier than you think. I watched the final game."

"They're pretty good, aren't they?"

"I wouldn't know." He took her bag from her and pulled her close. "I kept getting distracted by this cute reporter on the sidelines snapping pictures."

Nadine just shook her head at his lavish compliments. As they passed a group of celebrating teenagers, a few of the girls cast admiring glances Trace's way. Nadine knew she shouldn't feel proud, but she did. Nothing boosted a girl's ego more than knowing that other women, no matter how young, thought your escort was good-looking.

She looked up at him and caught him smiling down at her. He dropped a quick kiss on her forehead and drew her closer. "I missed you, Nadine," he said.

Nadine looked away, her feelings uncertain. On the one hand she felt inundated with his charm, his obvious attraction to her, yet she couldn't help but feel uncomfortable with how quickly he'd seemed to lay a claim to her. This was only the second time they had been together, not counting their first "date." His intensity didn't seem right, for a reason she couldn't put her finger on.

They walked out to his truck and as they did, Nadine's cell phone rang. She pulled it out and answered it. It was Grandma.

"I'll be home in a while, Grandma. Don't wait up for me." Nadine rolled her eyes at Danielle's response, then ended the phone call.

"Handy things, aren't they?" Trace said with a grin as he unlocked the door for her.

"Not really. I wish I didn't have to carry it around, even though it is a great tool for a reporter." Nadine got into the car and laid the phone on the seat as she buckled up.

"Where do you want to go tonight?" Trace asked as he started up the car and reversed out of the school parking lot.

Nadine shrugged, stifling a yawn. She had been busy all day and hadn't given a thought to dinner.

"You look tired," Trace said as he pulled into the street. "How about someplace quiet?" He grinned at her and, gunning the engine, headed down the street.

Nadine felt a little better once she'd eaten supper. Trace was stimulating company and he made her laugh. The talk stayed light, something for which Nadine was grateful. She was tired and was also thankful when Trace said that he had to leave early.

"Looks like your grandma is still up," he commented as they walked up to the apartment.

"She likes to stay up until I'm home. Says you never know what might happen." Nadine shook her head. "I'd invite you in, but with Grandma still up…"

Trace shrugged. "I don't want to bother her. Besides, I'll be coming here tomorrow after church. If that's okay," he added quickly.

Nadine smiled back, a feeling of well-being bubbling up in her. "I'm looking forward to it."

Trace caught her close, and just as he was about to lower his head to kiss her, a cough sounded in the hallway behind them.

"Nadine, are you coming in?" Danielle demanded, her gray head poking out into the hallway, her voice querulous.

Trace pulled back and winked at Nadine. "I should let you go." He ran a finger lightly down her chin and then looked past her. "Hello, Mrs. Laidlaw. How are you?"

"Tired," said Grandma succinctly.

"I'm sorry." He looked back at Nadine. "I guess this is good-night?"

Nadine nodded, curiously glad Grandma had shown up. She felt once again that Trace was moving too quickly. Too quickly for her, anyway.

Trace ran a finger gently down her cheek. "I'll see you at church tomorrow?"

"I'd like that," she said softly.

"Good." He winked at her and then, with a quick wave at Grandma, turned and left.

Nadine watched as he pulled open the doors and sauntered down the walk. He got in the truck, waved at Nadine and drove away.

"So," Grandma said from behind her. "Why didn't he come in?"

Nadine sighed and turned to face her grandma. "Because I think he's a little afraid of you."

Danielle "humphed" at that. "He looks a little too polished for my liking."

"How can you say that? He wears blue jeans and cowboy boots."

Danielle just shrugged and sat down on a kitchen chair. "It's just an impression."

Nadine turned on the tap and filled a glass with cold water. "I don't know why you don't like him."

"I don't dislike him, Naddy. What a thing to say." Danielle sounded hurt.

Nadine gulped down the water and set the glass on the sink. "You don't treat him very well. The last time he stopped by here, he asked me what I had told you about him.''

Danielle fingered the belt of her housecoat, her eyes downcast. "I don't trust him, Naddy," she said softly, her voice suddenly quiet. She looked up, her blue eyes softened with concern. "I'm just not comfortable with him. I would much prefer it if you were to go out with…''

Nadine held a hand up. "Stop right there, Grandma." She tilted her head sideways, studying her grandmother as realization dawned. "I think you don't like him because you didn't handpick him for me yourself."

"I already said I don't dislike him," protested Danielle.

"Well, then, treat him better tomorrow, because he's coming over," Nadine announced, a warning note in her voice.

"I will, Nadine. I'm not rude."

"No, you're not," conceded Nadine. "But I know how you can smile and sting at the same time."

"I'll be very kind and considerate."

But Danielle didn't have to exert herself to that extent, because Trace didn't show up at church the next day and consequently didn't come to the Laidlaw residence for the Sunday lunch Nadine had risen so early to prepare.

Nadine tried to hide her disappointment and Danielle tried to hide her triumph. Neither were very successful. As a result, Sunday was not the blessing it should have been.

Chapter Seven

Nadine spread the latest edition of the *Derwin Times* out, propped her elbows on the desk and began her Tuesday-morning, once-weekly hunt for typos. It didn't matter how up-to-date the technology or how eagle-eyed their copy editor, on a good day only one typo slipped through, on a bad…

Nadine sighed, pulled out her red pen and circled the spelling mistake that jumped off the page at her.

She glanced over a few more articles, turned a few more pages, then stopped at her article on Skyline. She skimmed over it, then reread it to make sure she had been balanced and fair.

Nadine frowned, trying to read it critically, always difficult when the words were so familiar. It had taken her a couple of drafts to get it just right.

''Their labor practices are questionable, and when they were asked for a copy of their safety code, this reporter was brushed off. What do they have to hide?

And why do they continue to obtain government grants by fair means or foul…'' Nadine read. And it got stronger after that.

Because when it came to Skyline, she had emotion to spare. Nadine sat back and closed her eyes, reliving once again the helpless anger and frustration and grief of her father's life wasted by a company that lied. So much had been taken away from them, with so little explanation.

I want to bring these guys to justice, Lord, she prayed, as she so often did when she thought of Skyline and all the sorrow their actions had caused. *Show me the right way, show me how to do this.* But the prayer brought no peace, no answer. She knew only that she felt better doing *something* instead of merely sitting back, a helpless David facing down an indifferent Goliath.

"Call for you on line one, Nadine. Oh, and some woman phoned a few minutes ago. Didn't leave her name.''

Drawing in a deep breath, Nadine picked up the phone. "Nadine Laidlaw here.''

Trace greeted her cheerfully. In an hour he was going to be meeting her at the restaurant, and from there he would accompany her to the school meeting she had offered to cover. Nadine would be the happiest when they found a new reporter. Covering for a missing reporter kept her and Wally busier than she liked.

"How are you?'' she asked.

"I had to run into Edmonton to meet with one of

the company execs that I'll be working with. I won't be back on time, so keep your cell phone handy.''

Nadine hated taking her phone into meetings. It was disrupting, and it annoyed her to be at her phone's mercy. ''So what time will you be back?''

''I have a better idea. I'll meet you at the inn after your meeting, say, nine-thirty?''

Nadine sighed her disappointment. ''Okay,'' she said softly.

''Hey, sweetie, I'm sorry.''

''Of course you are.'' She tried not to remember Sunday and his broken promise then, as well. It shouldn't matter as much as it did. She still wasn't sure how she felt about Trace, but it was so wonderful to be wanted, to look forward to being with someone. ''I'll see you later, then.'' At least coffee with him was better than nothing.

She hung up the phone and fell back against her chair. Not an auspicious start to the week, she thought.

An abrupt rap on the door made her sit up. ''Come in,'' she called, folding up the newspaper.

It was Clint.

He dropped the newspaper on her desk and stood in front of her, his eyes narrowed.

''I thought you weren't going to run the article,'' he said tightly.

Nadine looked at the paper, folded open to her story on Skyline. ''That was your idea, Fletcher, not mine.''

''I called you into my office last week and asked you not to run the story.'' His voice was even, but Nadine could hear the suppressed anger.

Nadine steeled herself to look up into Clint's irate eyes so close to hers, trying not to remember their time in the coffee room. "The article is correct, and the facts have been verified by enough people that I feel more than justified in running it," she replied, her own anger building. "I also told you that we could call an editor's meeting and make a diplomatic decision on whether to run it or not."

Clint looked down at her, his hand resting on her desk. "It shouldn't have to come to a showdown of authority, Nadine."

"Maybe not," she acknowledged, "but an editor of a paper should be just that. An editor. Last I checked, that gives me certain authority and say in what goes into the paper."

"And last I checked, my name is on the masthead, as well." He straightened. "As the owner." He looked down at her, holding her challenging gaze. "I wish we could work together on this, Nadine," he said with a sigh.

Nadine watched him, her heart doing a slow flip. He suddenly looked vulnerable. And for a brief moment she felt a stirring of pity, mingled with attraction. It bothered her more than she cared to admit. It hearkened back to numerous daydreams she had spun over him years ago—and if she dared to admit it, even more recently.

And now, to her dismay, it seemed as if all those dreams and emotions were threatening to undermine her. Taking a deep breath, she concentrated on Skyline and the pain they had caused her family. "I don't know if we can,'' she said, her voice more sharp than she intended. "Skyline has blood on their hands. Men have died working for them. We have a responsibility to stop them.''

"Your father among the lives lost,'' he said quietly.

Nadine nodded.

Clint blew out his breath and rubbed his neck. "And this is going to help?'' he asked, indicating the open newspaper.

Nadine stood up and drew in a steadying breath. "I intend to serve notice to them that we report on more than just local sports and library board meetings.'' She leaned forward as if to emphasize her point. "We have a God-given duty to expose companies like Skyline. They're crooks and liars, and if they did the same thing in Calgary or Edmonton, they'd have a pack of reporters on their back.'' She drew in a breath, afraid she was beginning to sound shrill. "I really need to do this, Clint.''

Clint looked across the desk at her, his features softening. "I understand why…''

Nadine waited for him to say more, but he didn't. Their gazes met, locked, and it seemed that all else, for that moment, drifted away. Nadine felt gripped by the same curious feeling she had felt the other evening in the coffee room. Once again she felt the tug of attraction, the pull of his personality, and she knew that the feelings that were surfacing were the same ones that had plagued her so long ago.

She forced herself to look down, to break the intense connection with his eyes, busying herself with the newspapers on the desk.

She refolded his newspaper and handed it back to him, her eyes going no farther than his dark tie cinched around the collar of his gray shirt. "Here's your paper," she said.

Clint cleared his throat. "Thanks," he said as he took it. He tapped the paper against his thigh, still towering over her.

He hesitated, then finally left.

When the door closed behind him, Nadine pressed her fingers to her eyes as once again she felt a rush of tears. She dropped her face into her hands, and in the privacy of her office allowed the confusion of her emotions to overwhelm her.

She missed her father, she still grieved her mother. She felt alone, though surrounded by people who cared for her. She had been put off by Trace for the second time in two days.

And now she was falling for Clint Fletcher all over again.

How do these things happen, she wondered. How can a heart work so totally independent of a mind?

Was she an idiot? How could she fall for a man whose presence intimidated her so much that she resorted to deflecting his attention with cutting comments?

She looked heavenward. *Why, Lord? Why am I falling for this man? He doesn't like me that way, never has. Please take away these feelings. Please.*

She stopped, as if waiting for something, anything.

A feeling of reassurance, a still, small voice guiding her, helping her. But she felt nothing, heard nothing. Nadine felt as if her prayers went only as far as the ceiling above her.

And later that evening, as she sat alone in the inn, waiting in vain for Trace, she wondered what she had done to deserve the loneliness that seemed to surround her.

"Two cameras, film, notebook." Nadine scooped her hair away from her face and retied her ponytail as she took a quick inventory, pencil stuck firmly in her mouth. She looked up at Wally as he rubbed his forehead, looking a little pale.

"I think I still got the flu," he mumbled.

"I thought you were finished with that."

"Maybe it was your article on Skyline that brought it back on," he joked weakly.

Nadine didn't think that was funny. She and Clint avoided each other, but the tension in the office between them was palpable.

Wally groaned again and doubled over. "I think I better get back home," he said as he clutched his stomach.

"Okay," she grumbled, annoyed at him for still being sick, and feeling guilty at her reaction. "I'll drop you off on my way. Can you make it to my car?"

He nodded and slowly got up.

Nadine zipped her bag shut. "I need more film. I'll meet you outside."

Wally only groaned in reply and stumbled out the

door. Nadine followed him down the hall, making a quick stop at the darkroom to grab her film.

As she closed the door behind her she met Clint walking up the hallway, a frown on his face. "What's with Wally?" he asked.

Nadine swallowed and willed her beating heart to slow down. This was the first time since yesterday morning that they had spoken. "The f-flu…I think," she stuttered.

"Didn't you need him today?" he asked with an impatient frown.

"I guess I'll have to do without him."

"You were headed out to the Foodgrains Project, weren't you?"

Nadine only nodded, wishing she could just leave. It was bad enough she had had moments of discomfort around Clint before the Skyline article. Since yesterday and her own awakening feelings, it was harder.

Clint tapped the sheaf of papers he was carrying, his lips pursed. "Do you want me to help out?" he asked, his voice casual.

Nadine's head shot up. Why would he want to come? "No, no," she said hurriedly. "I'd just as soon do it on my own."

Clint nodded and Nadine realized that it sounded as if she was brushing him off. Donna's reprimand warred with her own confusion around her boss as she forced a smile at him, and she amended her statement. "I mean…that's okay. I don't want to bother you. You've covered for Wally enough the past few days."

"I don't mind. I could stand to get out for a bit."

Nadine glanced at his clothes, and he looked down himself.

"Don't worry. I'll change," he said.

Nadine chewed her lip, wondering what it would be like to have him around an entire morning, wishing he'd be called to a sudden emergency. Then, feeling distinctly un-Christlike, she nodded. "Sure," she said, forcing a cheerful note into her voice.

"Okay." Clint nodded without smiling. "I'll meet you at Nanninga's quarter in about an hour."

Nadine's eyes met his and once again she felt a pull of attraction. Their gaze held and then she glanced away. "Sounds good," she said quietly, then turned and went out to her car where Wally was waiting.

Clint got to the town limits and pushed the accelerator on his sports car to the floor. He felt boyishly excited and knew he shouldn't. Nadine had made it fairly clear that she allowed his presence on sufferance. He wondered why he kept harboring some faint hope that she would soften toward him. Two things precluded that—her boyfriend and her opposing stance on Skyline. He had gone to her office on Tuesday morning hoping he could try yet once more to talk her out of the latter, and if not that, at least try to get her to tone down her rhetoric.

His partner had called today with predictable news. He had just come out of a meeting with Skyline's lawyers. Another lawsuit was pending.

The newspaper was making a comfortable living for

all involved, but not a huge profit. And it got less with each court challenge Skyline mounted.

Nadine put him in an awkward situation. He lost no matter which way he turned.

Because for better or worse, he was unable to change his feelings for Nadine Laidlaw. Deep feelings. Serious feelings.

He had always been attracted to her, but she'd often made it fairly clear what she thought of him. However, she had slowly warmed to him the longer he went out with Sabrina. Though even after spending half an evening laughing and talking with him and her sisters, Nadine had always kept a reserve about her.

But lately he had caught a hint of vulnerability, a softening that drew him, made him want to peel away the sarcastic outer shell.

He knew what he would find beneath that. He read her articles, sensed her deep, unwavering faith, caught the wry humor that permeated her writing. When she wrote, she showed a side of herself that she seemed wary of showing to him.

Clint turned down the tree-lined driveway leading to his home and couldn't help but smile.

When he had moved here as a sullen teenager, Uncle Dory had put him to work, planting, mowing, weeding and in general maintaining the large yard and surrounding pastures and outbuildings. Growing up in the city, he had never had to do any physical work.

His parents were both professionals who were never home, and when they were, they fought. Clint was an only child who had turned into an ornery teenager whom his parents didn't know how to handle. When he was caught shoplifting they shipped him off to Uncle Dory with the hope that this calm, straightforward man would be able to turn their son around. What Dory did was keep Clint very busy.

As well as three newspapers, Dory owned eighty acres, ten cows, three horses, chickens, rabbits, pot-bellied pigs and about six dogs. Clint was responsible for feeding and cleaning the barns and stalls.

In time he began to enjoy the horses nuzzling him as he doled out their grain ration, nickering to him when he came to fork hay for them. He began taking more time with his daily chores. Working with the animals brought about a sense of satisfaction that had been missing from Clint's life in the city.

He and his patient uncle worked well together. Soon Clint helped with other jobs. Together he and Uncle Dory finished renovating the comfortable story-and-a-half home, and Clint took as much pride in it then as he did now.

Clint slammed the door of the car and strode up the gravel path to the house. He skirted the bushes nestled against the front entrance and unlocked the heavy wooden door, then shed his suit jacket and loosened his tie as he ran up the carpeted stairs to his bedroom. He turned to his cupboard to dig out more suitable clothes for a trip to the harvest project.

Jeans, T-shirt and an old corduroy shirt that was a carryover from his backpacking days. He slipped on the worn clothes, feeling as if he was going back in time. He generally favored suits and a more formal look for work, completely opposite to his uncle. It was his way of making a statement. Ties and crisp monochrome shirts as opposed to the worn sweaters and corduroy pants of his uncle. Tight writing with newsworthy stories instead of breezy, loosely written articles that meandered all over the map.

And Clint had begun to put his own stamp on the newspaper. It took time to clean out the deadwood and make the changes, but on the whole things were going well. His biggest problem was also his biggest asset.

Nadine Laidlaw. His editor and, it seemed, constant critic.

He wished he could understand his changing feelings for her. He reminded himself that she had a boyfriend. Trace Bennet.

But for some reason that Clint couldn't pin down, he didn't quite trust Mr. Bennet. Jealousy, perhaps. Certainly a smoothness on Trace's part that he couldn't see Nadine being attracted to.

He wondered if he should just give up. But in his heart he knew he simply couldn't.

He dug through the cupboard for his own camera and bag. Even though Nadine would be taking most of the pictures, he liked to keep his own skills up. He checked through it, making sure it was loaded, packed up some extra lenses, then slung it over his shoulder. He walked down the stairs, pausing at the bottom as he wondered once again, what had made him offer to help.

Was it her obvious frustration as she stood contemplating a sick reporter? The fact that she had been working extra hard the past few weeks covering for a reporter who had suddenly quit?

Or the notion of spending a morning with her away from the office and the politics of manager and editor?

Clint shook his head. It didn't matter. He had offered and now he was committed. If he had learned anything from his newfound faith, it was that there were times to work, times to pray and times to let things flow on their own.

Five combines lumbered down the field, the roar of the large diesel engines thundering through the peace of the surrounding countryside. Chopped straw spewed out of the back of the machines. Choking grain dust swirled upward and the sun shone like a benediction in a promising blue sky.

Nadine glanced once more over her shoulder at the gravel road, mentally calculating how long it would take Clint to get here.

The combines had already made one full round and she was itching to go. She couldn't wait for him, and didn't want to admit that she was.

Finally she grabbed her camera bag and jumped out of her car, jogging over to one of the grain trucks that stood ready to relieve the combines of the harvest.

The driver was leaning against the truck. "You're from the paper, aren't you?" he asked, pulling on the bill of his cap.

Nadine nodded as she pulled her camera and light meter out. "And I'm going to take your picture." She took a quick reading, adjusted the settings on her camera, focused on the driver and snapped her first picture. Nadine guessed from the bright logo emblazoned on his obviously new cap that the hat had been a freebie from one of the various implement dealers in the area.

Trace's competition, she thought. Once more she wondered what had happened last night. Or for that matter, Sunday. He hadn't called to explain and she wasn't about to chase him down.

A small red car pulled in behind hers. She couldn't stop the gentle lift of her heart, and when Clint stepped out of the vehicle, it was as if time had turned back.

He wore a brown corduroy shirt that hung open over a plain white T-shirt. Jeans hugged his long legs and sneakers finished the look totally at odds with his usual tucked-in shirt and tie.

Nadine felt her heart slow, then begin a dangerous thumping. He looked like the old Clint Fletcher she used to dream about.

He sauntered over, notebook and pen in one hand, his camera slung over his shoulder. The wind lifted his hair, softening it and making it fall carelessly over his forehead.

Nadine couldn't keep her eyes off him.

He stopped beside her. "How long ago did they begin?"

Nadine swallowed and returned her attention to her camera, fiddling uselessly with the lens. "Just started," she muttered.

She looked at the camera slung over his shoulder by its strap, and her discomfort made her take refuge in her usual caustic comments. ''Took your own camera in case I muck up?''

Clint shook his head ''It's just for myself.''

Nadine opened her mouth to apologize, then looked up at his handsome features. A soft smile played around the corners of his mouth, making him even more attractive than usual, and she changed her mind. Her sarcasm was her only defense against him.

''I should get going. I just got here, and need to get some pictures. Haven't taken any yet....'' And now you're babbling, you ninny, she reprimanded herself. Just because he shows up dressed in jeans looking like the old Clint Fletcher doesn't mean you need to make a fool of yourself.

''Talk to you later,'' she said, then turned and ran down the field toward the combines, her heart banging against her chest. You idiot, she fumed, he's just Clint Fletcher, the man you love to torment. You don't need to torture yourself by falling for him all over again.

Nadine took a steadying breath and lifted the camera to her face. Five combines crested the hill, their bulky shapes silhouetted against the sharp blue sky. The thunder of their engines gave Nadine a thrill.

The combines roared toward her, gobbling up the thick, fragrant swaths that lay in readiness on the golden stubble. The grains of wheat spun through various screens inside the combines. The straw was spewed out the back, mulch for next year's crop. The wheat was stored in temporary bins inside the combine. Once they were full, the trucks would pull up alongside and the hopper of the combine would spill out its bounty in a fountain of grain destined for people who had so much less.

Behind the combine, the field looked swept clean. All that was left was stubble strewn with finely chopped straw, looking like a buzz cut on a young boy.

"He will clear his threshing floor, gathering his wheat..." The quote from Matthew came to mind as Nadine walked, staying just ahead of the massive machines lumbering down the field.

She had done a lot of harvest pictures over the past couple of weeks, but this particular annual harvest held a special place in her heart. The Foodgrains Bank Project was a cooperative effort of the community. A large map of the quarter section or sections was displayed in the local co-op store and divided into parcels. Anyone who wished could purchase a parcel to help pay for the costs of seeding and fertilizing. The use of the land was donated, then the land was planted, sprayed for weeds and harvested by volunteers.

The grain went to Third World countries, where it was "paid" out in exchange for work from the people of the country they were assisting.

Nadine had done a piece on it each year since she first heard about it and felt as much a part of it as any of the organizers. She always bought her own acre and helped keep track of the progress of the combines, cheering when "her" part was done.

The Foodgrains Bank Project always had an air of celebration about it. Local implement dealers donated combines, members of the local church prepared a lunch for the volunteers. And some people came just to be spectators. The project became a way of recognizing the good things God had given the farming community around Derwin and a vehicle for farmers to share their harvest with much needier people.

One by one the five combines mowed down wide swaths of grain. Once filled, they spilled out the wheat, filling the huge truck. The truck pulled away and the combines returned to their swaths.

Nadine took many shots of the entire process. Then she glanced over at the group of people standing around the huge map of the quarter section. Clint was talking to a few of the volunteers, smiling, nodding. He held a cup of coffee, his notebook stuffed in his pocket, camera now hanging around his neck. Someone spoke. He laughed, his eyes bright, the deep timbre of his voice warming her soul like sunlight.

Nadine felt time still, pause and turn back. She hadn't seen this side of Clint since he had returned to Derwin a couple of months ago. Always he insisted on a measure of aloofness, always he held his emotions in reserve. But the Clint who mingled and mixed with the group of people on the edge of the field was so much like the Clint who had lived in Derwin those many years ago that her step faltered in reaction.

She was falling for him all over again.

She knew that as a Christian woman she could find contentment in service, in the myriad of things the church offered. She knew that serving the Lord should be her first priority.

But now, as she saw Clint, she realized yet again

that a gaping emptiness in her life remained. It didn't matter how many lectures on the joys of single life she attended, or how many times she read the apostle Paul's passage on being unmarried, she still struggled with a need for human contact—and affection. For someone's eyes to light up when they saw her, for someone to miss her when she was gone. A parting kiss in the morning, a hand to take her own as she walked down the street.

Nadine squinted at the men standing against the white grain box of the truck, their multicolored hats a bright contrast. It would be a tricky shot with the sun glaring off the white background. She raised the camera, analyzing the composition with one part of her mind even as the other tried to analyze her own life.

It was self-preservation that kept Trace at a distance, she concluded, snapping a few pictures, zooming in closer. It was the same thing that kept her sniping at Clint Fletcher. Trace she let get a bit close because she knew she could deal with him.

Clint was another story.

Nadine repressed her thoughts, concentrating on her job. She moved the camera along the group of men. They were the implement dealers and would appreciate having their picture in the paper, so she got a few more frames of them.

Then she stopped as Clint's face came into view. Nadine held her camera steady, unable to move it on. She adjusted the zoom, pulling the picture in, adjusting the focus. Clint's mouth was curved in a crooked smile, his eyes squinting against the bright sun. A soft breeze teased his hair, softened its usual crisp style. Unable to stop herself, Nadine snapped a few pictures. Then he turned her way and through the eye of the camera she saw him look at her, his gaze so intent, it seemed as if he was directly in front of her instead of fifty feet away.

Nadine felt her breath slow. She lowered the camera, still looking at him. Then she turned away and with shaking hands wound the film, wondering if the pictures would even turn out.

Nadine had intended to spend about an hour there, but was chivied by the organizers into staying for lunch.

"There's more than enough," said Freda Harper, wife of one of the implement dealers. She almost pulled Nadine over to the table that was set up in the shade of a grain truck. "Besides, I understand elk burgers are on the menu."

"Sounds intriguing." Nadine felt her stomach clench with hunger as she caught a whiff of the food on the barbecue. She glanced over the table spread with salads, buns, a few vegetable platters and squares. "And it sure looks good."

"Well, dish up." Freda smiled at Nadine as she helped herself to some potato salad. "We've had such a beautiful fall," Freda continued as she worked her way down the table. "I'm so glad the weatherman cooperated today, too."

"It sure has been a blessing for all the farmers," replied Nadine with a smile.

Freda nodded, her red hair glinting in the sun, a

bright contrast to the yellow sweatshirt she wore, then leaned closer. "You know, I've always meant to write you a letter, but I'm not much for doing that." She smiled apologetically. "But I've always wanted to say that I sure appreciate all the support you give this project. Douglas, my husband, got involved because of an article you wrote. How it's a chance for us, who have so much, to share." Freda scooped up a spoonful of salad and paused a moment. "But even more than that, I appreciate the way you always bring your faith out in the editorials you write. It's very encouraging to other Christians." Freda stopped, as if slightly embarrassed by her admission. "Anyhow, thanks."

Nadine felt a spiral of warmth curl up her heart. "Thank you," she said. Freda Harper's encouraging words were a gentle reminder to Nadine that her job was important and that it was used by God. "That's good to know. I guess it's one of the few places that I express my own faith."

Freda grinned back at her. "I imagine it's a little harder to show it in volleyball scores and hockey summaries."

"Your daughter plays volleyball, doesn't she?"

Freda nodded, and the talk moved to sports and children. Nadine found out that Freda had two girls in volleyball, one in senior high, one in junior high. They also had one foster child and one adopted child. The Harpers were a giving, loving family and Nadine had lots of questions for Freda.

By the time they got to the end of the line, they

were chatting as if they had known each other much longer than the ten minutes they had spent together, and Nadine's busy reporter's mind had another idea for a feature article.

Chapter Eight

"Sorry Nadine, but I told you I was stuck in a meeting...."

Nadine tried to smile. "You have quite a few meetings, Trace."

"It's this new business. It's a lot of work to set up."

"Whatever." Nadine tucked the phone under her ear and squatted by her filing cabinet. She tugged it open with an angry jerk.

"Really, Nadine. I'm not trying to put you on. I'm going to be in town in the morning. Can I come then?"

"No. I've got to interview a reporter for the opening here."

"What about Thursday night?" She hesitated, not entirely sure she wanted to chance another date with Trace.

"C'mon," he said, his voice wheedling. "Don't make me suffer."

"Why do I have such a hard time believing you?"

"Nadine. I really wanted to come last night."

Still she hesitated, unable to shake the feeling that he had been avoiding her.

"Once things slow down, I'll have way more time. I've got a few loose ends to tie up, and once that happens, I'm all yours. You have to believe me."

Nadine didn't know if she was imagining the pleading tone of his voice, but he sounded genuinely upset. She thought of Clint and the time they had spent together today. Going out with Trace would give her the emotional distance she needed from Clint. Trace was becoming less important to her, while she knew what she felt for Clint could hurt her more in the long run. "We'll aim for tomorrow night," she said with a sigh. Would she regret this? she wondered.

"Great, that's just great," he enthused. "I'll pick you up at five o'clock. I can hardly wait to see you."

She fiddled with the phone cord, frustrated with herself for her wavering attitude. "I'll see you tomorrow, then, Trace."

"For sure, Nadine. I won't let you down."

"I hope not," Nadine said. She ended the call and dropped the phone in the cradle, pulling a face at it as she did so. My life and welcome to it, she thought.

With a shake of her head, Nadine picked up some papers from the desk and shoved them into the appropriate folder in the file cabinet. She was acting in such a typically feminine fashion, even if she didn't dress the part. She glanced down at the blue jeans she wore today—and most every day. Running her finger over them, she remembered Clint's reaction when she'd worn a skirt. Remembered the surprised look on his face, the way his eyes had seemed to linger.

So different from his usual penetrating look. When he dropped that aloof manner, his eyes could sparkle, his usually firm mouth would soften and he was suddenly charming, infinitely appealing.

She called back this morning, how the wind had teased the groomed line of his hair, how his eyes had crinkled up as he smiled. Her hands dangled uselessly between the file folders as she relived each time their gazes had locked, each time they'd seemed to make a connection.

The tinny ring of the phone broke into her thoughts and Nadine pulled herself up short, mentally giving herself a shake. What in the world was wrong with her? she wondered. Getting all dreamy over Clint Fletcher.

She was losing it, she thought as she got up and picked up the phone. "Hello," she said curtly, pushing shut the door of the filing cabinet with her foot.

"Is this Nadine Laidlaw?" a harsh voice asked on the other end of the phone.

"Yes." Nadine frowned as she tried to place the caller.

"I sent you a letter. The one about Skyline. Did you get it?"

Nadine felt her own breath leave her as she fumbled behind her for a chair. "Okay. I remember now. You said you knew something and wanted to talk to me."

"I can't tell you over the phone. I want to meet you

somewhere. Are you going to be at the volleyball tournament next week?''

Nadine hoped a new reporter would be hired by then and the new person would cover the game. But she couldn't chance this. Not after all this time. She had to meet this woman wherever and whenever she asked. ''If you are talking about the one at the high school, the answer is yes.'' She scribbled a note on a pad, her hands shaking.

''Good. I have a son on the team. I'll be there.''

''And who is this?''

''It doesn't matter.'' The woman sighed. ''It doesn't matter who I am. I'll be wearing a green sweatshirt and gray pants.'' A pause. ''I don't want to do this, but I really have to.''

Nadine swallowed, her own heart pounding with a mixture of excitement and fear. ''I'm glad. I'm glad you're willing to talk to me.'' Nadine wiped a damp hand on the leg of her jeans. ''I'll see you at the tournament, then.''

A sharp click in her ear signaled the end of the conversation. Nadine slowly replaced the handset, her heart refusing to slow down, her thoughts spinning. Six years she had speculated on the circumstances surrounding her father's death. Six years she had asked questions and received no answers.

And now.

Now she was so close, so close.

Thank you, Lord, she prayed, clasping her hands in front of her mouth to stop the trembling of her lips. *Thank you for keeping faith. Thank you that I will finally be able to bring that company to justice.* The thought might be premature, but she felt a deep conviction that now, finally, she would find out the truth.

"And the truth shall make you free."

It was what Nadine had been striving for. She longed to be finished with the struggle. While as her grandmother and Donna chided her for her near obsession with Skyline, a small part of her knew they were correct. She had prayed, grappled with the comfort offered her in the Bible. Even while her mother was alive there were many times she had been tempted to quit, let it all go and realize there were going to be questions that would just not be answered. Then she would come home or visit her mother in the hospital. Brenda would be lying in her bed, barely able to speak, but always able to make it understood that she wouldn't have peace until Skyline was exposed.

Once she talked to her mysterious tipper, she might discover something she could work into an article. She knew Clint would hit the roof. She didn't want to deliberately antagonize him, but she knew this letter and the new information was a chance for her to assuage the guilt that clung at each thought of her mother's death.

But for now, she had pictures to develop and a few articles to write up.

Nadine reached over and unzipped her camera bag, pulling out the rolls of exposed film. If she didn't develop the pictures now, her time would get eaten up with phone calls and paperwork. She gathered up the film and walked down the hallway.

She knocked on the darkroom door. No one replied, so she pushed the heavy door open. Stepping inside, she closed it right away, giving her eyes a chance to adjust to the darkness. It was supposed to be absolute, but she was blessed with good night vision and could make out the vague outline of the workbench and sinks. She had spent countless hours in here when she first started, fascinated with the procedure of developing film. Thankfully this was one place Clint had not changed. Things were in exactly the same place they always had been. She walked slowly over to the bench and found the equipment she needed. With quick, sure movements she laid out her rolls of film and pried up the tops of the canisters with an old can opener, careful not to dent them too much. They were reusable and could be filled again. Using her memory of the room, she easily located the plastic developing reels and with quick movements worked the exposed film onto the reels and readied the graduates that would hold the film and developing liquid. These she filled with developer and then carefully lowered the reels into the containers. Snapping the lid on, she began slowly agitating them, inverting them repeatedly for the first thirty seconds.

She had about ten seconds to go on this stage of the developing when she heard a hesitant tap at the door.

"It's okay to come in, but do it quickly," Nadine called over her shoulder. She agitated the graduates one last time, wondering who else wanted to use the darkroom. The door opened and was quickly shut again. "Be warned," she said. "You're stuck in here until I'm done." She poured the developer into the sink, rinsed the graduates and snapped the lid back on. She switched on the red light above the counter and measured the stop bath into the container.

"That's okay," an all-too-familiar voice replied.

Clint.

Nadine swallowed and clutched the containers to stop the sudden trembling of her fingers. "What..." She swallowed and started again. "What do you want?"

"I had some film to develop."

With a flick of her hand Nadine switched off the red light. She opened the graduates and poured the stop bath over the negatives and snapped the lid on. She felt, more than heard, Clint walk over to the sink beside her. In the dark her other senses became heightened. She could hear his breathing, sense his presence. His proximity gave her a sudden jitter. Her heart beat heavily at the base of her throat. She agitated the containers, reminding herself to move slowly. After dumping out the stop bath, she poured the fixative onto the film and reached for the timer again. As she did so her arm brushed against Clint's.

"Sorry," she mumbled, finding the timer, only to drop it on the floor. Chiding herself for her clumsiness, she bent over trying to find it.

She felt the timer, but as she reached to pick it up, she felt other fingers encircle hers. Startled, she almost dropped the mechanism again, but Clint's hand held hers and the metal clock.

Nadine's hand refused to respond. She felt the

warmth of Clint's fingers covering hers as his other hand gently took the clock away from her.

"How long should I set it for?" he asked.

Nadine told him, then took a hurried step away from him and the feelings he generated in her. She didn't want to be so aware of him. She didn't want Clint, of all people, to have that kind of control over her. *I don't want this to happen, Lord,* she prayed fervently. One deep breath, then another and thankfully, she felt her equilibrium returning.

But she could stay in the one small corner of the darkroom for only a couple of minutes. She had to finish the last stage.

Thankfully Clint had moved and she could grab the canister and retreat to the opposite counter.

The silence in the room grew with each minute the timer ticked off, each "swish" of the developing tank. Nadine felt she should say something, anything, but it was as if her mind had shut off.

She could hear by his movements that Clint was finished rolling his film onto the developing reels. He would have to wait until the timer was finished to immerse his film in solution, and Nadine mentally hurried the minutes on.

"I thought today went well," Clint said, breaking the silence that seemed even more intense in the small, dark space.

"Yes, it did."

"You're keeping quite late hours today, aren't you?"

"Have to." Her voice sounded small in the darkness; his seemed to take it over.

"I imagine your grandma will be waiting."

"Yes." Brilliant conversation, Nadine, she scolded herself, trying to come up with anything that she could say to him.

"She's quite the go-getter."

"She can be a little overwhelming."

"She was always really friendly when I came over," Clint said quietly.

"Yes, she was." Nadine almost groaned at her lame response, resisting the urge to smack herself on the forehead. What's the matter? she thought. You spend the morning with him, then he corners you in the darkroom, tosses a few lame questions at you and you freeze up.

But even as she formulated the thought, she knew why. It had to do with the daydreaming she had indulged in a few moments ago in her office, with seeing him all morning. It had to do with a sudden and unwelcome awareness of Clint as an attractive man. It had to do with old emotions and old feelings. With new emotions, too. And she didn't like it.

The silence lengthened. Then Clint cleared his throat. "I never did give you proper condolences with the death of your mother. I can tell it's been hard for you."

Once again Nadine felt her chest tighten as still-painful emotions clenched her heart. She nodded, then, realizing he couldn't see the movement of her head, said softly, "Yes it has." She sniffed and reached into her pocket for a tissue, but her pocket was empty.

"Are you okay?" Clint's voice was a soft, rich sound, disembodied in the darkness.

"Yes." She wrapped her arms around her stomach, simply allowing the tears to fall unheeded down her cheeks. She ceased caring. Clint couldn't see her, anyway.

Through the darkness, she could make out Clint's tall figure taking a step closer. His hand reached out as if to find her. Nadine couldn't move, didn't want to. Then warm fingers lightly touched her cheek. A rustling sound, and once again he was carefully wiping her eyes with a handkerchief.

Nadine felt her stomach drop, her heart slow. She could feel his breath on her hair, the warmth of his fingers through the thin material of his handkerchief. She wanted him to stop. She wanted him to continue. She felt herself swaying toward him, was aware of every movement he made. It was as if an uncontrolled magnetism slowly drew them closer...closer. His breath was on her face now, her mouth. She tilted her head up toward him, feeling more than seeing his presence, and slowly their lips touched with tender hesitancy.

The clang of the timer shattered the moment. Nadine jumped and pulled back.

"I've got to get my film out of the solution. It's...ready...." Nadine turned away from him, her heart pounding. Fumbling with the containers, she yanked the tops off. She rinsed the negatives, her

hands shaking, and soon had the strips of film hanging
up to dry from the line strung along one end of the
darkroom. Then she whisked the residual moisture off
them with her fingers, not bothering to get a squeegee.
All she wanted now was to finish and get out. After
rinsing her hands under the tap, she quickly stepped
to the door.

"Let me know when I can open the door, please,"
she asked Clint, her voice breathless.

"Sure," he answered, his tone brusque.

Nadine could hardly wait until he told her she could
go, unable to speculate on what he had done—and her
response. When he finally gave her leave, she tugged
on the doorknob, and when she was out into the bright
light of the office, she felt like a prisoner escaping.
For a moment she stood by the darkroom door, catching her breath. Don't be silly, she chided herself. Clint
was her boss. All he did was...

Touch her face with his hard, strong fingers. Wipe
her tears...

An unwelcome weakness pervaded her limbs as she
remembered again his gentle touch, his nearness. How
tempted she had been to drift against him, to be enfolded against that broad chest, to close her eyes as
he'd kissed her.

Nadine allowed herself one moment of fantasy, a
few seconds of daydreaming. Then with a short laugh
she returned to reality.

She was Nadine Laidlaw. Editor of the *Derwin
Times*. She was attaching too much importance to a
few moments of sympathy.

She was supposed to be dating Trace Bennet. Had a date with him tomorrow night, in fact.

But for a reason she didn't want to examine, she hoped he wouldn't show.

"The job is yours if you want it." Nadine smiled at the young girl sitting across the desk from her.

Allison Edlinger grinned, leaning forward, her long blond hair slipping over her shoulder. "This is great. Just great. Thanks so much. When can I start?"

"Yesterday?" Nadine joked at Allison's enthusiasm. There had been six applicants for the job and only two were interview material. Of the two, Allison had the more impressive credentials—three summers' work for a weekly paper in southern Alberta and two years at another. Nadine had also been impressed by Allison's clips. "Actually, you can start as soon as possible. We've been just swamped." Nadine indicated her desk, which was full again in spite of a few long evenings. "If you want, I can show you around today. We've got deadline on Monday. Our paper comes out on Tuesday."

"That's a little unusual for a weekly," Allison commented.

"Yes. Most come out on Monday, but our new general manager changed the date so that we didn't have to work Sunday anymore. At least, not as much."

Nadine rose and ushered Allison out of her office. They walked to the back of the building where the two typesetters worked at their computers. She poked her head over Wally's cubicle on the other side of the large, open room, but he was gone. "This is where you'll be working," Nadine said, pointing to the cubicle that abutted Wally's.

They walked past the darkroom and Nadine introduced Allison to Cory, whose office was across the hallway.

"Cory is our ad person. She usually words the ads, helps set them out," Nadine said, indicating the older woman. They walked past Nadine's own office, and Donna's across from hers was also empty. "Empty building today," Nadine commented as they walked to the reception area. Nadine leaned on the counter. "And this is Sharlene, our receptionist, ad taker, sometimes copy editor..."

"Date with Trace tonight?" quipped Sharlene, reaching across to rearrange a fold of Nadine's scarf, which draped across her brown blazer.

"I guess we'll see. We were supposed to go out a couple of nights ago, but he cried off."

Nadine pushed away from the desk and walked over to Clint's office, effectively cutting off conversation with Sharlene. She felt uncomfortable talking about Trace. She had told herself she had dressed up for her date, but she was secretly hoping Clint was around, as well.

Nadine turned and gestured to the door that faced the open foyer. "And this, Allison, is our boss's office. Thankfully he's gone for the day, so I'll just let you have a peek into the inner sanctum."

Nadine opened the door.

"No, he's not—" Sharlene interrupted, but she was too late.

Nadine almost jumped at the sight of Clint working at his desk. He looked up and Nadine backed away. "Sorry. I was just showing our new reporter around." She reached over to close the door, but Clint was getting up from his desk.

"It's okay."

"I d-didn't want to interrupt you," Nadine stammered, suddenly feeling self-conscious of her skirt, her hair, her makeup. She remembered all too vividly the time spent together at the harvest and the episode in the darkroom.

"It doesn't matter," he said, glancing at Nadine, his eyes flicking over her clothes, a smile curving his mouth. "I wouldn't mind meeting her."

Of course he wanted to meet a new hire. How dumb of her. Nadine stepped back, taking a breath to compose herself.

Nadine made the introductions, and Clint reached out to shake Allison's hand. Allison smiled up at him, her blue eyes shining with appreciation. It seemed to Nadine that the light from the front windows caught Allison's blond hair, making it sparkle. Her dress emphasized her delicate shoulders and skimmed her narrow hips.

"Allison is starting today," Nadine announced, her voice sounding falsely bright. "She's originally from Vancouver, but has lived here for a couple of years already."

Clint glanced at Nadine, acknowledging her comment with a hesitant smile, then looked back at Allison. "Nice to have you with us, Allison. I hope you'll be working with us for a while."

Allison fairly simpered, and Nadine resisted the urge to roll her eyes. "I hope so, too," she said almost coyly.

"We should go back to my office," Nadine said to Allison. "There's a few things I want to go over with you—camera allowance, travel, that kind of thing. And then Donna will need you for the payroll forms."

It looked to Nadine as if Allison had to tear her gaze away from Clint's. "Sure," Allison said vaguely. "We can do that." She hesitated a moment, then followed Nadine back down the hall. When she opened the door to her office, Nadine was not surprised to see Clint still standing in the doorway of his office, watching them.

Always was partial to blondes, she thought as she closed the door behind Allison.

Nadine walked around her desk and slipped into her chair, pulled an empty pad of paper toward her and found a pen that still wrote. "First I need to get your address and phone number."

Allison said nothing and Nadine looked up.

"Earth to Allison."

Allison jumped. "I am so sorry," she apologized. "I have to confess that I'm still a little surprised."

"At what?" As if she didn't know, but politeness dictated that she had to ask.

"At how handsome the boss is." Allison shook her

head as if she was still trying to absorb it. "He's so good-looking, and what dreamy eyes."

Nadine stopped, her pen poised over the pad of paper. "He *is* your boss, I'd like to remind you," she said, her tone more sharp than she had intended.

Allison sighed, then smiled at Nadine. "Sorry. I didn't mean to sound like some drippy teenager, but I sure never imagined meeting someone like him in a town like this."

"Well, these unfortunate incidents happen," replied Nadine dryly. "Now. I'd really like to get on with this."

Someone rapped abruptly on her door and Cory stuck her head in. "Accident just came in on the scanner. Truck rolled over on the highway."

"Where's Wally?"

"Can't raise him on his cell phone. I'm pretty sure he's at the opening of the museum."

Nadine jumped up and grabbed her camera bag, checking it for the necessary supplies. She glanced at Allison. "Well, are you ready for your first assignment?"

Allison looked surprised, then nodded. "Sure."

"Great." Nadine looked back up at Cory as she zipped up her bag. "Where are we headed?"

"Secondary highway, 498, north toward Riverview."

"Leaving now. Any more info on who's involved?" Nadine asked as Cory stepped quickly aside for her.

"The trucker involved..." Cory hesitated as Nadine

headed out the doorway. Nadine stopped and glanced over her shoulder.

"What?"

Cory bit her lip. "He was working for Skyline."

Chapter Nine

"I couldn't believe how ticked that one guy was when you started taking pictures," Allison said to Nadine as they returned to the office. "I thought he was going to pull your camera out of your hand."

"There's more to that story," Nadine said grimly, stopping at the darkroom. She was surprised herself at how quickly some of the administrative people from Skyline had come to the scene of the accident. Nadine got some pictures of the paramedics working on the injured truck driver before she was blocked by the workers from Skyline.

"I'm going to have to wait and see what happens to him before we run these pictures, though," Nadine continued, dropping the canisters on the counter. "We have a standing rule not to print pictures of actual fatalities. If he doesn't make it, we're going to have to make an editorial decision as to which pictures we'll run."

"I'd say run the ones of the Skyline people trying to block the picture," Allison said as they walked out of the darkroom, stopping at Nadine's office.

"Not a bad idea." Nadine glanced at her watch. "I guess you've just put your first day's work in." She smiled up at Allison. "Do you have a place to stay for the night, or are you going to go back home?"

Allison shrugged. "I'm staying at a friend's tonight. She promised she would help me find an apartment if I got the job."

"Looks like you'll be hunting." Nadine let her camera bag drop to the floor. "You'll be covering a livestock show in Eastbar in the afternoon. I suggest pants."

Allison looked down at her dress. "We sure looked a pair, rushing out of your car, both of us dressed to the nines." She glanced at Nadine's legs. "I don't know how you managed to keep your hose from running."

"Me neither," confessed Nadine. She had discovered that she liked Allison. She was helpful, enthusiastic and a good sport. It hadn't taken her long to figure out what she needed to do at the accident scene. Her guileless smile and breezy manner had caught a lot of people off guard and they were, therefore, more forthcoming to her than they ever would have been to Nadine. "Just as well. I'm supposed to be going on a date tonight."

Allison frowned. "If you'll excuse me, you don't sound too enthusiastic."

"Probably not," she admitted.

"I'd ditch him and make a play for the boss," Allison said with a grin. "I haven't been here long, but if a guy looked at me like he looks at you, I wouldn't waste my time on someone I didn't like."

"Time out," Nadine said firmly. "First of all, he's your boss and *mine* and secondly, Clint Fletcher looks at me like he'd like to fire me but doesn't know how."

"Sorry," Allison said, suddenly contrite. "I didn't realize you felt that way about him."

"I don't feel any 'way.' I see him as my employer, and that is the only relationship we have." And don't we sound prim, Nadine thought.

"I'm sorry. Not exactly a good footing to start out on, is it?"

"No, I'm sorry," Nadine reassured her, frustrated with her lapse. "I always get uptight after covering an accident." Nadine glanced at her watch. "Well, I have to do some work yet and you should head out to your friend's place." She looked back at Allison and held out her hand. "Thanks again. I think it will be a good article."

Allison smiled in relief and shook Nadine's hand. "I hope so. And thanks again for the job." She tucked her notebook in her purse, turned and walked down the hall, her blond hair swinging with each step.

Nadine watched her go. So Allison thought Clint looked at her a special way. Did he really?

Nadine shook off the thought and went into her office. Pulling her chair up to her desk, she flipped through a pile of message slips and began answering them.

A while later she had finished up the calls and she turned her computer on, ostensibly to work on a story, but instead she ended up playing a computer game. Entirely appropriate, she thought. Once again, it's just me and my computer.

With a sigh, she clicked the Close button, jabbed at the power button on the monitor with one finger and the tower with another. The screen flicked off and the fan on the computer died down, leaving the office in total silence.

Trace had told her he would pick her up at five. The last time Nadine had checked her watch, it had been five-thirty. She refused to look at it again.

She lifted her bag onto the desk, shoved some papers into it that she would look over at home and zipped the bag shut, gritting her teeth as she felt the unwelcome and all-too-familiar prickling in her eyes. She had never been the weepy type, but since her mother died, her emotions were so close to the surface. Tonight was nothing to cry over, she castigated herself. Trace isn't that important to you.

But it seemed that she was crying more and more and she disliked it intensely each time it happened.

Except once, she thought. In the darkroom. When Clint had dried her tears.

Nadine felt her stomach clench at the remembrance of Clint's hands on her face, his gentle comfort. For a brief moment she allowed herself the luxury of remembering his touch, the scent of his aftershave, his hovering nearness.

Then with an angry shake of her head she dismissed

the memories. He felt sorry for her and had said as much before he dried her tears.

Nadine hefted her bag onto her shoulder and got ready to leave, yet hesitated as she turned the door-knob.

Going home meant Grandma and her unsubtle "I told you so" looks. It would be too humiliating to have Grandma see her come home from another canceled date.

So then what? Another solitary movie in Eastbar had no appeal, and eating alone had even less.

Nadine dropped her bag in frustration and started unbuttoning her blazer. She wouldn't go out by herself, yet she wanted her grandma out of her house. She wanted to be alone and when she had the chance, she felt lonely.

Wishy-washy. That was what she was, she thought as she hung her blazer over the back of her chair. She was easily pushed around and easily taken in. Trace was a case in point. How many dates had he kept as opposed to the ones he had broken?

Not that it mattered that much, Nadine thought, dropping into her chair. She had felt uncomfortable with Trace from the start. The whole relationship was contrived, almost like an arranged marriage.

Trace wasn't important to her. She still felt uneasy about him. Something about their relationship just didn't seem right. Yet, in a way she was loath to call it off altogether. What would she have then?

And what do you have now? she reminded herself, rocking back in her chair. You're all alone in this office. You were supposed to go out with him. Nadine blew her breath out in a sigh and pushed her chair away from her desk. She didn't feel like writing up the Skyline story and didn't want to go home.

She got up and wandered around the deserted office. Even Clint was gone. The thought made her feel unaccountably lonely.

Each step seemed to drag, each step echoing in the empty building as if mocking her own lonely state.

I've tried, Lord, she prayed, stepping into her small office. *I've tried to be happy with what I have. What's wrong with me?*

Wasn't she supposed to be a liberated woman? Hadn't she shown that she could compete with a man, could do the same job? Wasn't that supposed to be enough for a woman these days?

Nadine sat in her chair, letting her head fall backward, her eyes close. Deep down she wanted what her friends had. A husband, children. A home. She wanted to sit in church and frown at fidgeting kids, sing with her husband. She wanted to have windows to sew curtains for, laundry to wash. She wanted a house with an office that she could work out of, part-time. She wanted to hear a door open and close, feel a lift of her heart as her husband came into the house, feel the same sense of completion she had felt when her own father would come home and fill up the man-space that had been empty since he had left that morning. And she wanted that man to be Clint.

And who did she think she was fooling? she thought, frustrated with where her own thoughts so easily went. She remembered all too well the contrast between her and Allison this morning, how Clint couldn't seem to keep his eyes off the blonde.

Clint wasn't for her. Nadine figured she was destined to become one of those old newspaper ladies who ended up heading out to South America doing features on Mayan temples for travel magazines.

Or maybe a dedicated single missionary who would work in faraway mission fields. Then come back and do church tours and slide shows, drumming up support for evangelism in exotic locales far away.

With a wry smile at the mental picture, Nadine bent over, pulled open one of her drawers and found her Bible.

It had been a long time since she had read it at work. In the early days, shortly after her father died and her mother became ill, Nadine kept one Bible at work, one at home. She read both frequently, drinking from the well that never ran dry. She needed God so much then. Needed answers to questions that she couldn't seem to puzzle out on her own.

Each day had begun with reading and prayer…then. And now?

Lately she felt events slipping out of her reach, deadlines always looming. They had been shorthanded too long and it had drained her.

The sorrow she felt at her mother's death was still too fresh, and her guilt over being unable to find more about her father's death still haunted her.

Nadine pressed her hand against her chest as if to

keep the sorrow contained. She pulled the Bible out of the drawer and laid it on her desk.

She drew in a deep breath, then another. God had answered her scattered prayers about her father. God had been faithful. The phone call yesterday was confirmation to her that she was given another chance.

Nadine opened the Bible, leafing through the worn book, margins marked with notations from various Bible studies. Almost lazily she flipped through pages. "Grazing," her mother used to call it almost contemptuously. Brenda, in true accordance with her own strict upbringing, had insisted that the Bible be read from front to back.

It was thanks to this disciplined reading that Nadine had worked her way a number of times through the entire Bible. She had learned to appreciate the sorrows of the prophets watching their people turn away from God, to lament with them at the hardness of hearts.

But when her own heart was sore, when her own anger seemed to overwhelm her, she found herself turning to either the Psalms or the letters Paul wrote in the New Testament. It was there she found comfort for her anguish, balm for her sorrow and reminders to forgive.

But tonight she felt like lamenting, and turned to Isaiah.

She flipped through the chapters, reading imprecations of woe to those who turned away and yet finding at the same time the promises that Isaiah gave of the comforter.

Isaiah 55.

Nadine stopped, carefully running her fingers along the familiar lines. "Come all who are thirsty, come to the waters.... Why spend money on what is not bread and your labor on what does not satisfy?... Seek the Lord while He may be found.... You will go out with joy and be led forth with peace." As she read, the words slowly wound themselves around her worn and weary heart and she laid the book open on her desktop, hunching over it much as a cold person would over a glowing fire. Drawing in a slow breath, she read on, reading warnings and comfort and promises.

After reading for a while, Nadine bent her head in prayer, asking for wisdom and discernment and strength. She knew she didn't have to count on the men of the world for her happiness. God would give her what she needed.

Encouraged, Nadine slowly closed the Bible and placed it on one corner of her desk, ready for tomorrow.

Smiling lightly, she pulled her blazer off the back of her chair and slipped it on. With her scarf draped around her neck, she was ready to walk out of the office when the phone rang.

For a moment she was tempted to let it ring, but her innate curiosity led her back to her desk to answer it.

Trace was full of apologies and promises to come over right away, but Nadine cut him off. "Doesn't matter, Trace. It's over." As she spoke the words she felt a momentary shaft of panic. Was she crazy? Was she deliberately trying to sabotage any chance she would have at a life's partner?

But as she heard his protests, listened to his excuses, she realized that the longer she allowed the relationship to go on the worse it would get. Trace simply wasn't reliable, wasn't the kind of man she wanted for herself.

"No. I've thought it over," she interrupted. "You're just too busy and I don't like being stood up."

"Nadine, don't do this. Tonight was a blip, unexpected."

"Like your visit with your banker?" Nadine put heavy emphasis on the last word as if to tell him that she didn't believe his excuse of the other day, either.

"Her name is Margaret Toornstra. Give her a call." Nadine heard him take a breath, then another as if he was running. "Please, don't do this, Nadine. I'm begging you."

Nadine had heard his begging before and found it a little embarrassing. But she knew she had to end it. If she was to have a meaningful relationship, she wanted it with someone dependable and trustworthy.

If she was to have a relationship. She closed her eyes as the words taunted and echoed in her mind. She knew she had to trust. Being married wasn't everything. She had a challenging job and lived in a good place. She had her faith and her church community. As lonely as she sometimes felt, she wasn't desperate enough to settle for a man who showed her such little respect. She respected herself far too much for that.

She listened to more of his protests, his promises, waiting for a suitable time to end the conversation. It was a relief when she could finally say, "Goodbye, Trace," and hang up the phone.

As she did so, she shook her head. For a brief moment she felt a pang of sorrow, but then, behind that, a feeling of empowerment. She, plain ordinary Nadine Laidlaw, single woman of twenty-seven, had broken up with a very handsome, eligible man. She had made the choice, no one else.

And that thought, more than anything else, put a smile on her lips.

She walked down the hallway toward the front of the office. She might regret the impulse in the morning, but for tonight she felt as if she was in charge. She turned on the security, locked the main office door, then went back down the hallway to the back of the building turning lights off as she went.

Maybe Grandma would have some fresh muffins made, Nadine thought as she pulled out the keys to her car. To sweeten her I-told-you-so's.

Headlights swung down the alley and momentarily blinded her. Nadine stepped back toward the newspaper office. A car pulled up beside hers, and with a start, Nadine recognized Clint's vehicle.

The car stopped and Clint got out, walking around to meet her. "Hi, there," he said. "Going out?"

Nadine shook her head, a sense of shame mocking her newfound confidence. "No, just home."

"But I thought you had a date...."

"I did." Nadine shrugged, fully aware of her boss standing beside her, his height overwhelming her. His hair looked tousled, and his tie was gone, causing Nadine to recall the way he'd looked the day they'd covered the Foodgrains Project together.

"And…" he prompted, "he broke it?"

Nadine shook her head, fiddling with the end of her scarf. "No. I did. I didn't feel like waiting anymore." She looked up at him, only to catch his gaze on her. She looked down again. "What are you doing here?"

"Forgot some papers I needed." He jingled the change in his pants pocket. "So what are you going to do?"

Nadine shrugged. "Go home. See if Grandma has any supper left for me."

"I see." He made a move to leave, checked himself and came back. "I, uh…" He stopped and cleared his throat. Nadine glanced up at him, puzzled. He seemed hesitant, unsure of himself. "I haven't eaten, either. We could grab a bite at the inn."

Nadine paused in surprise, her hands no longer fiddling with her scarf. "Okay," she agreed, hardly knowing what else to say.

"Good." Clint took a step backward and whacked his leg against the fender of his car. He steadied himself, straightened and held his hand up to Nadine. "Sorry."

She didn't know what he was apologizing for, but his unexpected—and uncharacteristic—clumsiness gave him a sudden vulnerability.

"So. Do you want to ride with me or take your car?"

"I'll drive my car." She wanted the option of being able to leave on her own. "I'll meet you there."

He nodded, took another step back. "Okay. I'll see you later." He turned and jogged up the walk to the office, leaving Nadine to wonder what had come over her usually calm and collected boss.

Briefly she recalled his touch yesterday, his concern. Then with a laugh she dismissed her foolish thoughts. He just wanted company and she just happened to be handy.

But as she backed out of the parking lot behind the *Derwin Times,* she couldn't help remembering his grin when she'd said yes.

Clint settled himself behind the table and glanced across it to where Nadine sat. Her gaze roved around the restaurant, as she looked everywhere but at him. For a moment he regretted asking her. She seemed ill at ease, even though she had agreed to come.

He couldn't get her off his mind lately. It seemed that each day he tried to seek her out, tried to find out where she was.

That moment in the darkroom when he had kissed her. He still didn't know what had come over him. She had a boyfriend.

The guy who had stood her up tonight.

Clint took the menu from the smiling waitress and looked once again at Nadine.

Her thick brown hair shone with reddish highlights and hung loose, framing her face, softening her features even though tonight she looked a little tense.

Not at all unusual, he reflected. Nadine never seemed comfortable whenever he was around. And that in turn created a measure of tension within him. He didn't like it. He wanted her to be as relaxed around him as she had been around the people the afternoon of the Foodgrains Project. He wanted her to look up at him with a smile brightening her eyes, the way it had that day.

"What are you going to have?" she asked.

He wasn't really hungry, and had asked Nadine out for supper on an impulse. He had two issues to confront with her, and he guessed she would dislike dealing with one as much as the other.

One had to do with his changing feelings toward her. The other with Skyline. And for the first time in his life he didn't know how to proceed with either.

"The chicken burger and potato salad," he told the waitress, handing back the menu.

Nadine smiled at him. "Sounds like a good balance between health and convenience."

Clint just nodded, his heart skipping a beat at the sight of the smile he had wished for.

"I'll have a bowl of beef barley soup." She laid her menu down and folded her hands on the table in front of her. "Not really hungry," she explained, tapping her thumbs against each other, then looking around the restaurant.

They sat in a strained silence until the waitress left, and then Clint knew it would be up to him.

"How are your sisters?" Not that he really cared, but he had to start the conversation somehow.

Nadine smiled. "Fine. I haven't been to see Sabrina's daughter for a couple of weeks, but she's cute. Leslie is also expecting a baby.''

"Wow." He shook his head. "Seems hard to imagine either of them married.''

Nadine tilted her head in acknowledgment, glancing at him, then away. "I always knew both of them would get married before I did.''

Clint didn't know if he imagined the hint of pain in her voice and wondered if she was jealous. "Why did you know that?''

"You of all people can answer that.'' She lifted her eyebrows at him. "After all, you went out with one of them.''

But really only wanted to be with you, he thought. He was quickly losing ground with her. He needed to change the subject, and grasped at the first thing that came to mind. "How long was your mother sick?''

Nadine pursed her lips, picking up her napkin, playing with it. "Most ALS sufferers live anywhere from one to three years after diagnosis. In mother's case it took a little longer.''

"How come?''

Nadine carefully pleated the napkin as if weighing her answer. Then she looked up at him, holding his gaze. "My mother's mission kept her alive longer. And that mission was to see Skyline Contractors brought to justice for my father's death.'' Nadine stopped abruptly and bit her lip.

Clint absorbed this piece of news with a heavy heart. How could he do what he had to after what she had just told him?

He reminded himself that he was her boss, that his partner was practically screaming at him to rein her in. That another lawsuit would cost too much and that this time Skyline would do more than threaten.

"I know that your father died while working for Skyline, but I've never heard how it happened." Even as he spoke the words Clint wondered if he was fashioning his own noose. But he wanted to know. Wanted to find out what it was that drove her to keep up the battle after all these years. Wanted to discover what he could about her.

"Didn't Sabrina tell you?"

"She only told me that he died at work."

"Do you want to hear the official line we got, or do you want to hear what I think?" She looked away, then at him, her expression troubled.

"Tell me both." He leaned forward, wishing he could forget about his paper, wishing he dared give in to a sudden and intense need to protect her, to support her.

She carefully unfolded the napkin again. "The line we got from the company was that my father was out in the bush by himself. He was using a felling practice calling domino falling. What you essentially do is drop one tree so that it hangs up on another, cut that tree until it leans against another and so on. Then you get one main tree that falls all the way, taking all the others with it. It's highly illegal according to labor standards and extremely dangerous. Lots of fallers get killed that way. According to Skyline, this is what my father did, and he was killed by a hung-up tree coming

down on him.'' Nadine stared up at Clint, her brown
eyes intense. ''My father was the most careful man I
know. He would never do anything as dangerous as
that.''

''So what do you think happened?''

Nadine held his gaze a moment, then looked down
again. ''That's what I've been trying to find out. I've
talked to as many employees that will talk to me, other
subcontractors. I've heard rumors that my father went
in behind another young guy to clean up the mess he
made. I've heard that he was working in tandem with
another faller. And I've heard that it was just fluke.''
Nadine held up one hand, ticking off her fingers with
the other. ''I haven't gotten any names, any times, any
sign of other vehicles, no verification of any of the
rumors, at least not anyone who was willing to commit. Nothing.''

''The bush is a pretty wild place.''

Nadine almost laughed. ''Not when there's a logging show or two in an area. You go out there, it's
like a little community. If my mom wanted to bring
my dad supper, and we made a wrong turn, all we'd
have to do is drive until we saw a skidder or Cat op-
erator. They always knew who was working where.
But in my father's case…nothing.''

Clint didn't know what to say. Nadine's voice took
on a note of authority that showed him clearly that she
knew of what she spoke, and how important it was to
her.

''How did you find out?''

''My father didn't come home that night and my

mother called my dad's supervisor. He went back to the bush looking for my father. It took a while because he wasn't working in the block he had been assigned to. At least, not according to the supervisor's information.'' Nadine folded the napkin again, her eyes intently focused on it. ''He was found lying underneath a tree. Dead.''

Clint gave in to a sudden impulse. He reached across the table and covered her hands with his, squeezing them, wanting to pull her close, to comfort her. ''You must have cared for him a lot.''

Nadine looked down at their hands and tightened her grip on his. ''I did. I loved him a lot.'' She bit her lip, but when she looked back up at him, her eyes were clear but pensive. ''Seems kind of wrong,'' she said with a soft laugh. ''I had my mother around longer than my father, but sometimes it's as if I miss him more.'' She shrugged, then pulled her hands away from him.

''Your mother was a lot of work for you and your grandmother, wasn't she?''

Nadine waved the comment away with a graceful turn of her hand. ''I resented it at first, but then I wondered if it wasn't God's way of giving me a chance to get to know her better. I always spent so much time with my dad.'' She smiled, her eyes looking over his shoulder as if she had disappeared into another place and time. ''We would go out to the bush on Saturdays to cut firewood. The other girls stayed at home with mom.'' She smiled softly. ''He called me his little tomboy.'' She shook her head and looked back at Clint.

"I always remember him as a very kind man." Clint folded his arms, leaning his elbows on the table. "He would always ask about Uncle Dory and what we were working on at the acreage."

"He liked you."

"I liked him. He was a man of integrity who was content with his life." Clint couldn't keep the bitter note out of his voice. "Unlike so many others."

"Others being…" prompted Nadine.

Clint rubbed his thumb along the inside of his opposite arm, concentrating on the tabletop. "My parents."

"And…" Nadine prompted. "What about *your* parents."

Clint shrugged, hesitant to tell her even after all these years. "They both worked very hard to collect enough money to buy more things. They were going to give me a car when I graduated high school."

"But you didn't get it."

"No. I blew it. That's how I ended up at Dory's. I was caught stealing a flashlight from a hardware store." He looked up at her, his mouth curved in a wry grin. "My parents didn't understand what was happening. Neither did I."

"You wanted them to notice you."

Clint caught Nadine's intent look, surprised at her expression. As if she had just discovered something new, and, he conceded, she probably had. At that time he hadn't told too many people how he had ended up in Derwin. It was embarrassing to admit to anyone he wanted to impress that he had only stolen a flashlight. As he got to know the Laidlaws he said nothing—more because of his shame over the ease with which his parents had sent him away that far out shadowed any guilt he felt over a mistake. "That's exactly what Uncle Dory said," he said softly.

"And where are your parents now?"

"Dad's in Rome and Mother shuttles between Toronto and New York." Clint smiled at her as if to negate the bitterness that crept into his voice. He had forgiven his parents the same time he had become a Christian, but he still struggled with it.

"I take it they're divorced."

"You take it correctly."

"But it still bothers you."

Clint lifted one shoulder in a negligent shrug. "It doesn't matter what the marriage counselors say, it's always hard on kids when their family breaks up. At any age." Clint looked back up at Nadine, pleasantly surprised to see a gentle understanding in her expression. "Your family was one of the first ones I saw that worked. A family that cared about each other. A family that loved God. I've always wanted that for myself."

Nadine looked down and Clint thought that maybe he had overstepped some unknown boundary. One never knew with Nadine and he had been talking more in the past few minutes than he had in days.

But the moment was interrupted as the waitress returned with their order. She laid the plates down in front of them. Clint smiled his thanks at her.

The waitress left and Clint hesitated and then, without looking at Nadine, bent his head to say grace. He raised his head precisely the same time as Nadine. Their eyes met and held, a feeling of accord springing up between them.

It felt right to be sitting across a table from her, to say grace together. To be joined in a communion of spirit and mind.

Clint smiled carefully at her and when she returned that smile, he felt his heart lift.

He winged another silent prayer heavenward. A quick prayer for patience on his part and understanding on hers.

He just wished for exactly the right moment to bring up what he knew he had to talk to her about.

Chapter Ten

Nadine stirred her soup, trying to adjust to her new feelings about Clint. She felt as if all her defenses against this man had suddenly melted away, and she wanted to know as much as she could.

She glanced up at him, surprised yet again to see his eyes on her. Looking down, she busied herself with unwrapping her cracker from its cellophane wrapper. "When you left Derwin you went to Europe, didn't you?" As if she didn't know. Against her own will she had known every movement he made, thanks both to Sabrina and her own unquenchable interest in his whereabouts.

"My parents had a collective attack of guilt over their divorce, and sending me away on that trip was their way of making up for it."

Nadine felt her cheeks warm, remembering all too well a snide comment she had made in this very place when she had sat here with Trace.

"That trip was one of the really good things that happened to me." Clint was quiet a moment, his finger tracing idle circles on the tablecloth, his supper forgotten. "I traveled through places of extreme wealth and extreme poverty. I learned that what had happened to me was fairly small in the larger scheme of things. I stopped in churches that were older than any book I had read, I visited castles and museums and toured countryside that had been home to generations of families. And in a busy square in Jerusalem it was as if all the history I had seen in Europe, everything I had witnessed with your family, the myriad times I had sat in church with Uncle Dory and even my own parents, all coalesced. I realized that I had been given a precious gift not only of life, but of death. Christ's death. And that people all over the world and all through history had believed that and clung to it through all the happenings of their life." Clint looked up at her, his mouth quirked in a gentle smile. "I changed, I accepted all those promises that had been handed to me in so many ways. And then I had to come home." He hesitated a moment, as if he wanted to say more and was unsure of how to proceed.

Their waitress came by asking if either of them wanted more coffee. Nadine nodded and held out her cup, as did Clint.

When she left, Nadine leaned forward, full of questions, yet unsure of where to go. Clint's confession had created a sudden openness, a place to begin to get to know each other in new ways. He told her more of Europe, spoke of his work in the city and of his desire to one day come back to Derwin and take over his uncle's paper. A desire that had begun as a random thought and had changed into a real need as his own life changed.

The waitress had taken their plates and bowls away and poured another round of coffee. Clint leaned his elbows on the table, sipping as he asked her questions, responding easily to hers.

She idly fiddled with her spoon, answering his own soft-spoken questions, telling him about the precious few things that had happened in her life since he had left Derwin. A few times she glanced up at him to find him looking at her, his expression serious.

At those moments she felt her own heart quicken.

It wasn't until their waitress had come around for the fifth or sixth time with coffee that she realized how long they had sat there. She snuck a quick glance at her watch.

"My goodness," she exclaimed aloud. "It's eleven o'clock."

Clint frowned as if disbelieving her. He glanced at his own wrist. "You're right." He looked up at her and smiled. "I can't believe we've been sitting here that long."

Neither could Nadine. "I should get going. Grandma will be worried."

"But you were supposed to be out tonight anyway, weren't you?"

"Yes, but I never liked to stay out too long. I usually made Trace take me home before ten."

"Well, then, we had better leave." Clint pulled a

few dollars out of his pocket for a tip and dropped them on the table. He also took the check before Nadine had a chance. ''I'll get it,'' he said in reply to her protest. ''I've never had a chance to take you out and have often wanted to.'' He winked at her and got up. ''Be back in a minute.'' Bemused at his parting comment—and his wink—Nadine watched him walk confidently across the deserted restaurant.

She gathered her discarded scarf, purse and knapsack and got up herself, following more slowly, wondering what he meant, and wondering if she was reading more into the casual comment than he implied. By the time she came to the front desk, he was pocketing his wallet and turning back to the dining room.

''I'd offer to drive you home, but I imagine you'll want to take your car home?''

Nadine nodded, sorry now that she had taken it, wondering what would have transpired if he had driven her home. ''Thanks so much for dinner,'' she said, pulling her keys out of her purse.

Clint nodded, then, walking ahead, he opened the heavy glass door for her. They walked in silence through the parking lot to her car. Nadine fumbled through her purse for her keys. When she finally found them, she felt awkward and foolish.

''Here, let me,'' Clint said softly, taking the keys out of her hand. He opened the door and helped Nadine into the car. He held the keys, studying them. The lights of the parking lot cast his face in shadows. All evening he had looked relaxed and comfortable, drawing her out, smiling. But now his lips were clamped together, and a frown drew his dark eyebrows together.

"Nadine, I need to ask you something."

Here it comes, she thought. The real reason he asked me out. "Go ahead."

He took a deep breath. "I understand that you covered the accident at Skyline."

"What about it?" She stiffened in reaction, afraid of his answer, his somber tone.

He held on to the door and looked away, as if unable to face her. "I would like it if you could assign the story to Wally. Or better yet, Allison."

Nadine closed her eyes and resisted the urge to cry, scream, anything. You naive child, she chastised herself. This was why he asked you out. How could you think that Clint Fletcher would, for one minute, forget his precious newspaper?

"Can I ask why?" she said, her voice low, controlled.

"Objectivity."

"Which you don't think I have."

Clint shook his head. "I think you're too close to it, emotionally."

"Which you conveniently found out tonight," she said sharply. "It would have been cheaper for you to just tell me tomorrow at the office." She held out her hand for her keys. Why are you doing this? a more objective part of her mind cried out. Relax. Talk to him. But echoes of her own insecurity seemed to drown out common sense.

"You don't need to put yourself through all those emotions of your father's death again."

"Spare me the false concern," she said angrily, reaching up to take the keys from his unresisting fingers. "I've been a reporter long enough. I know how to cover a story."

Heartsore and angry, she gave the door a tug and managed to pull it away from him this time. She started the car, gunned the engine, reversed out of the space and tore out of the parking lot. The streetlights flashed past the window, blurred by her tears. She palmed them away as she steered her car past familiar houses and streets.

She hit the brakes and rocked to a halt in front of her apartment, then dropped her head on the steering wheel. Don't you dare cry, she told herself.

But somehow part of her didn't heed the voice, and the tears that slid down her face were hot with recrimination and sorrow.

Nadine booted up her office computer, pulled out her keyboard and, once she got into the office's word processing program, opened the Skyline folder.

She had been on the phone all morning and had a stack of notes from Allison as well as the pictures. This time she had made contact prints, or proofs, of the negatives. The story was too important to leave to chance and she wanted exactly the right shot.

She rearranged the hastily scribbled notes on one side of the U-shaped computer desk, reviewing the information that she had just about committed to memory.

As Nadine wrote up the story, weaving in the statistics, one part of her mind analyzed the flow, the other kept her emotions in check with difficulty. She had to prove to Clint that she could write this story objectively.

She was immersed in her work when she heard a tap at the door. "Come in," she called out without looking up.

"What's up, Allison?" she mumbled, pulling a pencil from behind her ear. She marked off one of the papers and turned back to the screen.

She frowned, her fingers flying over the keyboard. She was about to hit the backspace key to correct an error when she realized that whoever had come into the office still had said nothing. She glanced over her shoulder, and found her vision blocked by an expanse of white shirt, bisected by a brown tie.

Flustered, she turned back to the screen, conscious of Clint's hovering presence behind her. Her fingers stilled and she could say nothing, all too aware of what had happened last night.

He still said nothing. Instead she saw his hands come down on either side of her computer desk, surrounding her as he read over her shoulder. She could feel the faint warmth of his breath on her neck, could feel his presence around her, behind her, above her.

What was he trying to do? Intimidate her? Frighten her?

Taking a steadying breath, she typed a few more

words. She tried to keep her eyes straight ahead and away from his large hands on either side of her, but she couldn't. Her fingers slowed.

"Please, Clint," she said, her voice breathless, "if you're trying to intimidate me, you're succeeding."

Her hands froze on the keyboard as she felt his chin lightly brush the top of her head. "What do you want?" she asked finally.

"I don't know," he replied, his throaty voice soft in her ear.

Nadine swallowed as her breathing sped up, her heart in sync. She could feel the warmth of his body behind her. He was close enough that all she had to do was lean her head back and she would touch him.

"Please stop doing this." She had no defenses against him. He had been too much a part of her day-dreams, her longings, and she didn't know anymore where one left off and the other began.

He moved one hand, his weight shifted and Nadine thought he was going to straighten. Instead she felt his fingers lightly brush her hair aside, sending shivers skittering down her spine. And then, impossibly, she felt warm, soft lips touch her neck. They lingered a moment, their touch weakening her. She couldn't move, couldn't breathe, wished he would continue, prayed he would stop.

"Nadine," he whispered against her neck, his breath caressing it with a soft warmth. Then, finally, he straightened. He lightly touched her hair. "I need to talk to you...." His voice was subdued. Nadine bit her lip, half turning toward him, her vulnerability there for him to see.

The sharp ring of the phone broke the moment. Sharlene's voice came over the intercom. "Trace is on line one for you, Nadine." The door burst open and Donna strode in carrying a pile of computer printouts that Nadine had requested.

Nadine pressed her hand against her face, confusion warring with a hysterical urge to laugh. She hit the button that connected her to Sharlene's speaker phone. "I don't want to talk to him," she said sharply.

"Sure, hon." Sharlene broke off the connection.

Nadine turned to Clint, ignoring Donna, who stood in front of her desk, holding out the papers for Nadine to take. But Clint was already backing out the door, his eyes on hers, his face mirroring the confusion in Nadine's.

Why was he leaving? What did he mean by what he had done? Nadine followed Clint's exit with her eyes, still ignoring Donna. Finally she pulled herself together and took the documents from her.

"What did Clint want?" Donna asked. "You look like you're in shock."

"I am," she said in a faraway voice, her fingers brushing over the place where he had, just seconds ago, kissed her. She shook her head and, ignoring Donna's curious stare, dropped the papers on her desk and turned back to her computer, trying to collect her thoughts, her wits and all the other things Clint had scattered with his casual caress.

"So what happened?" Donna asked, leaning on Nadine's desk as if to get a closer look at her friend.

Nadine only shook her head. "I don't want to talk about it."

"You look like you should."

Nadine tried to type a few more words, then stopped and turned. "Clint…he just came in here…I think he wanted to talk." Nadine lifted her hands helplessly and shrugged.

"He looked about as stunned as you did. What happened between you two?"

What indeed, thought Nadine. She could still feel the soft warmth of his lips on her neck, hear the tenderness in his voice as he spoke her name.

"Earth to Nadine. Come in, *please*."

Nadine jumped at the sight of Donna's hand waving in front of her face. "Sorry." Flustered, she turned back to her computer, unwilling to face her friend's curious gaze. "I…don't want to talk right now."

"Sure," Donna straightened. "If you want to come over tonight and tell me then, we're doing the usual Friday-night thing," she offered as she backed out of the office.

Nadine nodded and smiled her thanks. Donna was a true friend. Knew when to ask questions and when to back off.

When the door closed she looked back at the screen, trying to read the words she had typed just moments ago, trying to understand what she had said.

But she might as well have been reading Chinese. She let her eyes close, her hands idle on the keyboard.

In the space of a day she felt as if her entire world had rearranged. Yesterday at this time she was contemplating a date with Trace. Now...

Trace was out of the picture and Clint had taken her out and, today, had kissed her.

And that gentle caress had moved her more profoundly than anything that had happened to her before. What was he trying to do? Was this just another way of getting her to change her mind? Would Clint resort to such measures just to keep his paper safe?

Even as she asked the questions, she knew that more was going on between them than manipulation.

Clint carefully closed the door to his office behind him, leaned back against the wall and dragged his hands over his face, wondering what had come over him.

He had gone into Nadine's office hoping to talk to her about a compromise regarding Skyline. But when he entered her office and saw her, it was as if something else moved his feet, his hands. He started reading over her shoulder, remembered what she had told him yesterday, heard the puzzled sorrow, felt her anguish at the loss of her father. Then suddenly he didn't want to talk anymore.

Clint shook his head. He was acting like a high school kid. He had a paper to run. He couldn't afford to get Skyline's back up. He knew they had to run the article, but what he had read on Nadine's computer did not bode well for her emotional detachment.

The anger that flowed from her fingers into the article had as much to do with her own unfinished sorrow as the recent accident that, he had found out, was not Skyline's fault. The trucker was a subcontractor and therefore responsible for his own equipment and his own hours.

Ten minutes ago he had received this information from an old friend who worked with the trucker. The friend hadn't wanted to talk to Nadine about the accident because he was afraid it would come back to Skyline and he would lose his own contract with them.

But how could Clint tell her this without making it look as if he was on Skyline's side, which he wasn't? His friend had told him enough that Clint himself could fill an entire newspaper with stories of graft, misappropriated government funds and fudged records. Only, no one would willingly confirm what he said. Jobs were scarce right now. No one was willing to put their paycheck or contracts in jeopardy.

And to top it off, his partner had phoned him early this morning, reading out a letter from Skyline informing their publishing group of an intent to sue should any more defamatory articles show up in the newspaper on Tuesday. He was leaving first thing Monday for Calgary. Which meant he had today and the weekend to either tone down Nadine's crusade or get someone else to write the article.

Clint walked slowly over to his desk. He was stuck no matter which way he turned. If he let Nadine write what it looked as if she was going to, they would get sued for sure. If he asked her once again to back off, he knew she would freeze him out just as she had yesterday evening.

Clint sat in his chair, rested his elbows on his desk, dropped his face into his hands.

Okay, Lord, he prayed, *show me what to do with Nadine. Show me how to manage this paper so that You are shown to a world. Help me balance what I want with what I need. Show me what to do with Nadine, Skyline, my work.* He prayed to let go, to trust that God would provide him with what he needed.

He wanted Nadine, he wanted his newspaper, and unless things changed, he wasn't about to get both.

Nadine rolled over and glanced idly at the clock by her bed. He heart plunged. Eight in the morning! In a panic, she shoved the tangle of blankets aside. She was supposed to cover the high school volleyball tournament in Edmonton in half an hour.

Nadine stopped herself midstride, and with a satisfied smile crawled back into bed.

She had forgotten about Allison Edlinger, their new reporter. She would be doing the sports beat from now on.

Nadine snuggled farther into the covers, relishing the fact that she could lie there for another hour if she wanted.

She hadn't told Grandma about her breakup with Trace, and there was no way she'd tell her about her dinner with Clint.

Sunday came with a sudden drop in temperature. Nadine spent an extra half hour in an agony of indecision choosing what to wear, how to do her hair, what to say when she saw Clint again, what he would say, but to no avail. Clint wasn't in church. The heaviness of disappointment wouldn't ease. Back at home, Nadine prowled around the apartment, restless and uneasy, all the while berating herself for acting like a teenager in the throes of a crush. By afternoon she changed into blue jeans and a sweater and retreated to her bedroom-cum-office. Once there she pulled up the Skyline file. She hadn't gotten anywhere the day before, and the story would have to be done by Monday morning to be able to be put in place in the paper. She had it in mind for a front-page story, though she knew Clint wanted it second or third page.

She could give in on that, she conceded as she pulled up the file.

Ignoring the guilt that accompanied working on Sunday, she typed a few words, deleted them, rearranged some of the copy, but it didn't seem to help. Somehow the words sounded stilted, harsh. She didn't know if it was Clint's words haunting her, or reality.

Had she lost her objectivity in regard to Skyline?

Frustrated, she fiddled with the words again. Nothing would come. She decided to check some of the previous stories, to see what she'd done with them.

A few clicks got her into her Skyline folder and then into all of the previous stories.

She highlighted them and opened them all at once. The first one came up on top and Nadine skimmed it, trying to read her reporting from a third-party point of view. It was easier to do now, this many years after the fact.

It had been written five years ago, a year after her father died and she had started working at the paper. She wrinkled her nose at the setup, the flow of the story. Obviously written shortly after her one term of journalism school.

And obviously written from the perspective of a very angry and bitter young woman. Nadine sighed as she read through it, realizing how this must look to Clint and anyone else who read it. Long words, lots of rhetoric and sprinkled with exclamation marks. With a click of her mouse button she closed it and skimmed through the next one and then the next.

Clint was right. Her emotions had guided her writing. When she compared it to other stories she had done, the Skyline articles held a measure of shrillness.

On a hunch, she printed them all out, including her most recent story, and brought them to her grandmother, who sat on the couch knitting socks, humming along with the CD of hymns playing softly on the stereo.

"Can you do me a favor, Grandma?" Nadine asked, handing her the rough draft of her most recent article. "Can you read this and tell me what you think?"

Danielle took the paper and slipped on the reading glasses hanging from a delicate chain around her neck. When she was finished she looked at Nadine, then back at the paper.

"Tell me the truth, Grandma," Nadine urged, sitting down on the couch beside her.

Danielle pursed her lips, glanced over it again and then handed it back to Nadine. "It sounds very angry. You make it look like the accident is all Skyline's fault, without coming right out and saying that, of course."

Nadine bit back a rebuttal. She had asked for an objective statement and she had gotten it. That her grandmother's words mirrored so closely what Clint had said was not collusion or a conspiracy.

"Okay. What about these?" Nadine handed her a few of the other articles she had written. "These are some old articles I've written over the years."

Danielle looked them over as well, her frown deepening with each one. "Funny that I don't remember reading them." Danielle shook her head and pushed her glasses up her nose again as she continued. The room was silent except for the rustling of papers as Grandma laid each one down beside her. When she was finished, she looked up at Nadine. "Why did you want me to read these?"

"I wanted a second opinion." She looked away, choosing her words carefully. "Clint is having trouble with Skyline Contractors. In the past few years, each time I've written an article about them, they've threaten to sue us."

Danielle gasped. "What? I don't remember reading anything about it in the 'Court Docket.'"

Nadine resisted the urge to laugh. "It wouldn't end up in there, Grandma. That's for minor stuff. The major stuff gets handled very neatly and tidily between lawyers who charge an arm and a leg to write threat-

ening letters and file important documents back and
forth.'' She picked up the articles, riffling through
them absently. ''They always threaten, but never follow through. The trouble is that it costs the newspaper
each time this happens.''

''And this latest story...''

''Is newsworthy. I don't know if they'd sue over
it.''

''So why did you want me to read it?''

''Because I wanted to know if my boss was right.''
Nadine hesitated. It was difficult to admit that she
might have been wrong. ''I wanted to know if I've let
my emotions rule my reason.''

''I think where Skyline is concerned, you have
never been able to be completely objective.'' She
stopped, picking up her knitting again.

''And...'' prompted Nadine.

Danielle finished off the stitches on the needle and
lowered the sock to her lap. ''I know there was more
to the story of your father's death than what we were
told. There was never a more careful and cautious boy
than Jake Laidlaw. When that—'' Grandma pursed her
lips angrily ''—that slimy little man came to the door,
trying to tell me that my son had done something un-
safe and illegal...'' Danielle glared at Nadine. ''I was
ready to go into battle. To prove them wrong. And I
know you felt the same.''

Nadine nodded, surprised at this side of her dear
Grandma. Meddling, yes, but confrontational?

''But,'' Danielle continued, picking up her knitting
again, ''going into battle wouldn't bring your father

back, trite as that may sound. Perhaps it was God's will. No one can say for sure.'' Danielle knit a few more stitches, her needles flashing. ''Your mother wasn't content to let things lie. She fought, battled, argued, spent hours on the telephone. When she got sick, she needed someone to continue, to be her hands and eyes, and the job fell to you.'' Danielle paused, frowning at her needles. ''I think your mother filled you with anger toward this company.'' Danielle looked up at her granddaughter with a sad smile. ''I think your mother took all the anger from her grief and poured it into you. I know you had your own anger, but you have never been one to mope and feel sorry for yourself.'' Danielle shook her head. ''Your dear mother had a tendency to cling to righteous wrath. And when I read these pieces, I hear her anger, feel her pain.'' Danielle reached over and squeezed Nadine's shoulder. ''I want to know, too, the circumstances surrounding my son's death. But it happened six years ago, Nadine. I've seen you spend a lot of time on the phone, writing letters to the government, talking to government officials, the police, other Skyline workers. It was easing off just before your mother died, but I sense that you think you've failed her by not finding out after all this time.'' Danielle slid over and slipped an arm around Nadine's waist. ''Don't take on a burden that isn't yours to carry. You really have to let God take care of this one. Let Him comfort you, let Him carry that weight.''

Nadine closed her eyes and let her grandmother hug

her. At the moment, Nadine felt as if Danielle Laidlaw was taller and stronger than she could ever hope to be.

She straightened and picked up the papers. Shuffling them into a neat pile, she stared at them without really seeing them. "Was I wrong, Grandma? Was I wrong to write this? Was this a wrong thing to do?"

"I don't think so, dear." Danielle patted her on the shoulder. "You are a very good writer, very eloquent and very emotional."

Nadine laughed shortly.

"I think it might be wrong to have kept your anger going so long." Danielle stroked Nadine's hair tenderly. "You are a wonderful, caring girl. I've never heard you complain, or grumble, even though I know you've had to carry some heavy burdens." Danielle smiled at her granddaughter. "I've always been proud of what you have done in your life. Proud of the things you write, the way your faith shines in your stories and articles. Maybe what you need to do is read over what you have written once again, for yourself, and see if what you know of God's love is shown in these articles."

Nadine nodded, realizing that no matter how much she thought she knew, she could always learn something from her dear grandmother.

Her grandmother stroked her hand carefully. "But more than that I want to say that I love you, Nadine."

Nadine looked at her grandmother and caught her soft, wrinkled hand in hers, pressing it to her cheek. "I love you, too, Grandma. I love you, too."

Chapter Eleven

Nadine gathered up her papers, stood and bent over to drop a kiss on her grandmother's head. "Thanks, Grandma," she said softly as she straightened. Her fingers feathered over her grandmother's gray head affectionately and, smiling, she turned and walked down the hallway.

Inside her bedroom she stopped beside the computer, tapping the sheaf of papers against the top of her desk, chewing her lip. She still had all her notes at the office. Most of the groundwork had been done. The story had to be told.

But not by me, she reasoned, looking down at the articles she had poured so much emotion into. Too much emotion. Her grandmother was right.

Allison could do it. It would be a good lesson in working under the pressure of a deadline.

Nadine dropped into her chair, pulled out the keyboard and with a few quick strokes, deleted the story she had just finished. For a moment she stared at the white screen, wondering what she had just done.

As the cursor blinked silently back at her, she sat back, a sigh lifting her shoulders and dropping the weight she had been carrying since she had first heard of the accident a couple of days ago. Her anger had been ignited, and all the stories of Skyline's misdeeds had swirled around her head. She wanted to right what she saw as a wrong.

But now it was as if the anger had been swept away, the burning need she felt to see justice done quenched under a blanket of peace that surrounded her. She bent her head, her fingers pressed against her face.

Thank you, Lord, she prayed softly, *thank you for my grandmother and what she teaches me, thank you for my job and what I can do in it. Help me to make wise decisions. In all of my life.*

Then, as she lifted her eyes, she felt a smile tease her lips. It was going to be all right. She knew she didn't need to be the one to personally see that Skyline was brought to justice as she remembered a poem that Grandma was fond of quoting: "Though the mills of God grind slowly, yet they grind exceeding small;/ Though with patience He stands waiting, with exactness grinds He all."

She didn't need to wield her words to take on what God could easily do himself and in his own time.

Nadine got up and stood by the window, her hands in her pockets as she stared out at the darkened street. The town looked exactly the same as it had a few minutes ago, but now it seemed to Nadine that she could look at it with more benevolent eyes.

A car drove slowly down the street, its headlights swinging around as it turned into their driveway. Puzzled, Nadine leaned closer, drawing aside the light curtain to see who it could be.

The car stopped and the driver got out. Trace.

What was he doing here? What did he want?

She dropped the curtain and, turning, ran out of her room, determined to get to the door before Grandma. But as she got to the kitchen, she realized she still wasn't as fast as her grandmother.

"Come in, Trace," Grandma was saying. "I'll tell Nadine you're here."

I should have told her, thought Nadine, but now it was too late.

She stepped into the kitchen just as Grandma came in from the entrance. "Oh, there you are, Nadine. Trace is here." Grandma wasn't smiling and neither was Nadine. No help for it, she thought. She was going to have to do this with witnesses.

"Hi, Nadine." Trace stood framed by the kitchen door, his eyes on her. He held out his hand as Nadine unconsciously stepped back. "You left this behind a couple of days ago," he said, showing her a cellular phone. "I thought I would return it."

"Thanks," Nadine said, reaching past her grandmother to take it from him. "I was wondering where it was."

Trace glanced over at Danielle, but when she made

no move to leave, he squared his shoulders and faced Nadine. "I'm really sorry about the other night."

Nadine shook her head. "Don't bother, Trace," she replied. "We don't have anything to say to each other."

"But we do. I need to talk to you. I have something to tell you that changes everything." Trace plunged his hand through his hair, his expression pleading. "Please, Nadine. I was hoping to come to church this morning and then come here after, but something came up."

As it always did, thought Nadine.

"Please come with me. Please hear me out," he continued.

Nadine didn't answer, but she suspected that if she didn't go with Trace he wouldn't leave until she heard what he had to say. And she didn't want to cause a scene in front of her grandma. She turned to Danielle. "I'm going with Trace for a short drive." She put heavy emphasis on the word *short*. "I'll be back in a while."

Her grandmother frowned up at her, as if questioning her wisdom, but Nadine shook her head.

As she walked past Trace, she caught a coat off a hook in the entrance and stepped out the door before he could open it for her. She was at his car before she realized she still carried her cell phone. Shoving it in the pocket of her jacket, she opened the car door and got in.

Trace started the car and drove slowly down the street. In the dim glow of the streetlights Nadine could see that he hadn't shaved, his face looked haggard, heavy shadows circled his eyes.

"Where are we going?" she asked as he turned left toward the highway instead of right toward downtown.

"I just want to get away from town, just go for a drive," he replied. "I have a lot to tell you."

"Can you start?"

Trace glanced at her, biting his lip. "I don't know where to."

She frowned at that. "What do you mean?"

Once he turned onto the highway, he sped up. The lights of town receded behind them and Nadine felt a moment's apprehension. Trace seemed distraught, and she wondered at the wisdom of going with him in his car.

"I've had a lot on my mind lately," Trace said after a while. "I've had to make some hard decisions and I haven't been able to tell you about them." He looked at her again, reaching out for her hand.

But Nadine shook her head and kept her fingers wrapped around her jacket. A week ago she would have responded, but that was before Clint had comforted her, had taken her out, had been there when Trace wasn't.

Had kissed her.

"What haven't you been able to tell me about, Trace?" she asked.

Trace hesitated, his hands wrapped tightly around the steering wheel. "When we met, there was an emptiness in my life that I couldn't fill."

His words echoed thoughts that had tortured Nadine

as well, and for the first time since he had started the car, she looked at him fully.

He glanced at her and smiled carefully. "I really care for you, Nadine. I do. I've never met anyone like you, someone I could laugh with..." He paused and looked ahead again. "Someone who has a strong faith. Someone I could admire and love."

"But..." she prompted, sensing that there was much more that needed to be said.

Trace shook his head as if to deny what he had to do. "I'm married."

Married. She had been going out with a married man, spending time with him, laughing with him, keeping him away from a wife, maybe even children. "How..." she began, then stopped, unable to articulate her confusion, her anger. "How could you do this?" she whispered, clenching her jacket. "Why didn't you tell me?"

"My wife and I have been living apart for a few months already." Trace laughed shortly. "I had left Tina a couple of months earlier and moved into a hotel in Derwin. I started buying the paper regularly, and would read your articles. I could tell that you had a strong faith, that you had a strength that I was looking for. When I read the article about us I knew I had to come to the office. Then when I saw you sitting there, I was stunned. You were, are..." he corrected "so beautiful."

"Why were you and your wife separated?" Nadine interrupted him.

"Tina and I are incompatible. She didn't want to

go to church and I did. She didn't want to raise our children to go, either...."

"You have children?" Nadine asked weakly. She dropped her head against the back of the seat, a nausea filling her stomach. How could he not tell her?

"That's why I haven't always been able to keep our dates. 'Cause of my kids. But it's not as bad as it looks," he continued hastily. "I'm getting a divorce. I'm going to try for custody of the children. Tina and I have already been living apart. I came to Derwin to make a new start, and then I met you." He sped up. "Can't you see? It was meant to be."

"No, it wasn't," she said vehemently. "It was a very bad mistake." Nadine felt like screaming. "You have a wife, children..." She couldn't get past that. "You went out with me when you should have been with them..." Nadine couldn't continue, couldn't think. "Turn around," she said suddenly.

"Nadine, you don't understand. I did visit them when I wanted to be with you. But once the divorce is final and we're together, with the kids..."

"Stop the car. I want you to turn around and take me back home. We have nothing more to talk about."

"I won't, Nadine, until you listen to me." Trace twisted his hands on the steering wheel, his jaw clenched. "My marriage to Tina was a mistake..."

"Don't even start trying to explain away what you have done. You made vows and promises. You broke them each time you went out with me, and I helped...." Nadine couldn't help the catch in her voice as she thought of the time they had spent together.

"You made me an unwitting part of that, and I can't forgive you. Not now." She bit her lip, unable to articulate the anger and frustration that flowed through her. "I want you to turn around and bring me back home, Trace. Now."

He slowed down, and Nadine breathed a sigh of relief. But when he pulled in to a field and stopped, she became frightened. Trace turned the car off and turned slowly to her. Panic shot through her as she kept her eyes on him while fumbling for the door handle. "What are you doing?"

"You don't have to be afraid of me, Nadine." He shook his head, reaching out to touch her hair. "I'm not going to hurt you. I wouldn't do that to you."

Her fingers scrabbled at the handle. *Please open, please open,* she prayed. With a quick jerk she yanked on the handle. She jumped out of the car, stumbled as her coat fell out of the car and tangled around her legs. The interior light of the car shone feebly on the freshly plowed field. She tried to run, tripped on a lump of dirt and regained her balance.

Trace got out of the car, and she tried to increase her speed.

"Nadine, don't run. You'll hurt yourself," Trace warned.

She kept moving awkwardly, her feet unable to respond to her head. Hurry, hurry, she urged, her ankle twisting as she hit another furrow, unable to find even ground.

"I'm not coming after you, Nadine. Just stop." His

voice came from farther away and she spared a glance over her shoulder.

The car was well behind her, and she could see Trace's figure silhouetted against the open door of the car.

"Come back, Nadine. I'll drive you home."

Still she hesitated. She was too far away from town to walk back, especially in the dark. But she had to get one thing straight before she would sit in the vehicle beside him. "What about your wife?"

"What about her?" he called back, his voice impatient. "We've been over that already. I'm getting a divorce. I told you it happened before I met you."

Nadine couldn't believe he could be so obtuse. "Doesn't matter," she replied, still facing him, the lights of the vehicle shining in her eyes. "I won't go out with you, Trace."

Suddenly he banged his fists on the roof of the car, startling Nadine. "You have to change your mind, you have to," he yelled. Nadine took another step back, ready to run again. Trace sounded out of control, and she was frightened.

"Trace, calm down. You don't know what you're saying," she replied. *Please, Lord, keep me safe. Send him away,* she prayed.

He jumped into the car and slammed the door shut. He started it up, threw it into Reverse and gunned the engine. Dirt flew as he backed out onto the road. Her prayer was about to be answered.

Nadine watched the glow of his taillights as they receded in the distance, the roar of his engine slowly growing fainter as the chill of the evening finally made itself known.

What had she done? What had she prayed for? He was gone and she was alone.

But even as the quickening breeze sucked warmth away from her, even as she looked around growing more and more confused and frightened, even with that, she had the conviction she had done the wiser thing. Trace was out of control, totally unreasonable.

Her eyes slowly became accustomed to the dark. A pale crescent moon hung in the sky above her, shedding a faint illumination on the land.

For now, all she could see was that she was walking in an open, plowed field. Across the road, another open field. To her left a row of trees marking the quarter line, and beyond that some more bush.

"Don't panic, and don't cry," she told herself as she carefully picked her way along. The furrows were deep and hard and the lack of light made it doubly difficult to walk. *Now what do I do, Lord?* she thought. *I know I did the right thing. I know I did. Please help me out of this.* She closed her eyes and continued her prayer for courage, strength and wisdom and anything else she might need to figure out how she was going to get back home.

She shivered in the chill wind and wished she had her coat on. Then she remembered that it had fallen out of the car when she opened the door.

Nadine hurried as best as she could to the place the car had been parked, and in the thin light she saw a lump of material on the ground. "Thank you, Lord," she said, gratefully picking it up. Something heavy flew out of the pocket and clattered on the hard ground.

Her cell phone. "And thanks again," she prayed with gratitude. She picked it up and shrugged into her coat.

When she opened the phone the display showed three bars, indicating barely enough reception to make a call. And the Battery Low sign was on. "Okay, Lord. I guess it's just little miracles tonight."

She punched in the numbers to her house and lifted the phone, wincing as the static crackled in her ear. The phone at her home rang again and again. "Please answer it, Grandma, please," she pleaded. Finally she heard "Hello?"

Nadine sagged in relief. "Thank goodness you're still up, Grandma. It's Nadine."

"Nadine?…are you?" Crackling static broke into the conversation.

"I'm close to the lake." Nadine clutched the phone with one hand, her thin jacket with the other. The wind was picking up, and already her ears were getting cold. "Trace dropped me off somewhere in the country."

"Where?"

"I'm not sure." Nadine almost screamed the words, panicking as she looked around for any kind of landmark. "I'm at least half an hour's drive out of town."

"Which—" her words were drowned in a roar of static "—direction?"

"West. We drove west out of town, then he turned north." The static crackled louder. She turned back the way she had come to see if the reception got any better.

She was now walking into the chilly north wind. Her fingers were getting numb and her ears ached. But at least the static had died down.

"Is there anything that you recognize?"

Nadine hunched her shoulders against the wind and turned a slow circle, fear clutching her heart. Then she saw it. "I see a gas flare. I'm exactly east of it." Nadine relaxed somewhat. "Praise the Lord," she shouted. "I know where I am—up the Fraser road. Can you come and get me?"

"Yes. Of course. Just stay where you are." There was a moment's pause. "You are okay, aren't you?"

"Yes," Nadine replied, her voice unexpectedly shaky. "Yes, I am."

"Okay. I'll be…soon…" Grandma's voice faded away and Nadine lowered the now-dark handset. The battery was dead.

She flipped it closed, dropped it into her pocket and turned her back to the wind. Nadine wrapped her coat closer around her, tucking her hands into the wide sleeves. It was probably her least practical coat, a thin corduroy barn jacket she had picked up at a garage sale a few days ago because it was red.

Trace said she looked good in red. Trace, who was married.

Nadine sniffed, swallowed, determined not to cry. She felt cheap, humiliated and vulgar. She hadn't known he had a wife, children. He hadn't given her an inkling during their many conversations.

Nadine stopped walking, squeezing her eyes shut against the sting of tears. *Forgive me, Lord. I didn't know what was happening. I didn't know.*

Nadine looked up at the stars that spread away from her, feeling small, unimportant, disposable. She was walking along a dark, empty road, a tiny figure on a huge globe populated with many other tiny figures, each with their own sorrows and problems. What made her think her problems were so much worse than many others?

But then, even as she formed that thought, she knew that the same God who had created all of this from nothing also heard her prayers, whether softly whispered or shouted aloud.

And now, as she walked along the road, she prayed. As she prayed she felt God's peace wash over her, comfort her, strengthen and forgive her.

But her hands were still cold.

She shoved her hands farther up her sleeves and walked quickly, hoping the movement would get her blood flowing and warm her up. Behind her the bitter wind pushed itself through the thin material of her jacket, whipped her hair around her face and seeped into her bones.

Please, Lord, let Grandma's car start. Please let her drive quickly. I'm cold. Really cold. She shivered and pulled one hand out of her sleeve and pressed its meager warmth against one aching ear. After a while she traded and did it with the other. It helped a small amount, but her hands would not warm up.

Please, Lord. Let my grandmother come soon, before I can't move anymore.

She had walked for a little way when a faint light shone above a rise in the road ahead of her. It got brighter and brighter and then, finally, headlights blinded her as a vehicle topped the rise and roared toward her.

Not Grandma, she thought with a sinking heart. Grandma's little car had only one headlight and about half the horsepower. She paused, clutching her coat, waving her arm. She didn't care who it was, she was going to ask if they could at least drive her somewhere warm.

But the car drove past her, then slowed and turned around. Hallelujah, she thought, turning her head to watch the car as it pulled up beside her. Nadine frowned as it stopped and the driver's door opened. She couldn't stop herself from taking a step back as a tall figure straightened.

Clint Fletcher.

Nadine felt shock slam through her. How did he know? What had made him come at precisely that moment?

Nadine hesitated, her heart beginning a staccato rhythm, her feet suddenly unresponsive. "How…"

"Doesn't matter." Clint moved around the car and opened the door for her. She took a few shaky steps, then got in, her heart racing. Clint slammed the door shut behind her and walked around the car, momentarily illuminated by the headlights. He got in on his side, closed his door and Nadine was surrounded by blissful warmth, blessed heat.

"Are you okay?" Clint asked, turning to her. He draped one arm over the steering wheel, while the other lay along the back of her seat.

She couldn't look at him, and only nodded. "My grandmother is coming...." She could hardly speak, her lips were so numb.

"Actually, she called me and asked me to come and get you."

The thrum of the engine and the gentle hum of the heater were the only sounds in the dark intimacy of the car. Nadine bit her lip, trying to stop her erratic breathing.

"Are you sure you're okay?" There was concern in his deep voice.

Nadine nodded, shivering as she began to warm up. She laid her head back, felt Clint's hand and sat up again. She swallowed, hardly knowing where to start. That Clint had come to get her, that he now sat beside her, concerned, caring, was more than she could comprehend.

His hand touched her head, curving around it, the warmth of his hand seeping through her hair making him very real.

"He didn't hurt you, did he?" Clint's fingers tightened their hold momentarily.

"No. No, he didn't."

"Good."

Silence again.

Clint shifted his weight, and then his hands engulfed

hers, warming them. "You're freezing," he said quietly, rubbing her hands with vigor. "How long have you been out here?"

"About an hour, maybe more." She still couldn't look at him, still trying to absorb what had happened, what was happening now.

"Trace just drop you off?"

She shook her head. "I could have gotten a ride back to town with him, but I didn't think it was wise to stay around him anymore. He was quite…upset."

"Upset? Why?" Clint rubbed harder, then stopped when Nadine winced. "Sorry," he murmured, pressing her hands between his large warm ones.

"He—" Nadine's voice caught on that and then the words came tumbling out. "He's married, Clint. He has two kids and a wife, named Tina. They've been separated for a while. He wants to file for a divorce." Nadine turned to Clint, her fingers entangling with his. "I didn't know anything about it. I couldn't believe he would do that to her, to me…." She bit her lip, holding back the tears. She had said she wasn't going to cry over Trace's duplicity, but it hurt.

Clint looked down, his thumbs caressing the backs of her hands.

"I broke up with him a few days ago, he came over tonight. He wanted me to come back," Nadine continued.

Clint raised his head at that, his eyes narrowed. "You broke up with him?"

Nadine nodded, feeling foolish. "It wasn't much of

a relationship. I don't think I really cared much for him.''

''Why not?''

Nadine could see the soft glow of his eyes, remembered the kiss he had given her, their conversation in the restaurant. He had come for her. Grandma had asked him to, but he still had come for her. She squeezed his hands as she took a deep breath and a chance. ''I like someone else better.''

Clint's thumbs slowed and he released her one hand, his coming up to lightly touch her cheek. ''That's good,'' he said softly. Their eyes met in understanding and Nadine felt her breath slowly leaving her body. His fingers stilled and moved from her face to her neck.

''What are you doing?'' she whispered inanely.

''Something I probably should have done years ago.'' He slid his fingers around her neck as his eyes held hers. Mesmerized, she drifted toward him. He drew her closer and then, finally, oh finally, their lips touched.

Hesitantly at first, as if the intimacy was too much to absorb at once. Then his hand tightened, pulled her nearer, and fitted his mouth closer, his other arm coming around to pull her against the solid warmth of his chest.

Nadine's eyes drifted shut, her hand slipped upward, across the breadth of his shoulder, around his neck. He was warm, solid, real.

She kissed him back, their lips moving carefully, exploring and discovering at the same time. This was where she should be. It was as if a mocking echo of her past had finally been stilled here, in Clint Fletcher's arms.

She drew slightly back, her fingertips lightly touching his cheek.

His features became serious then as his fingers carefully explored her face. "You're so beautiful," he whispered. "I can't believe you're here."

"I'm not beautiful," she said, her lifelong insecurity around this man making her unable to absorb the reality of Clint Fletcher touching her, kissing her, telling her these wonderful things.

He bent over and stopped her words with his mouth. "You are beautiful," he murmured against her lips. He kissed her again, making her insides melt with wonder. "I've always thought so."

She placed her hands against his shoulders, giving herself some room, barely able to take what he was giving her. "But you went out with Sabrina. You used to flirt with Leslie...."

Clint smiled a crooked smile and traced her lips with his thumb. "Once a reporter..." He let the sentence hang as he shook his head. "Okay, if we get this stuff out of the way, can I kiss you again?"

Nadine laid her head against the headrest, her hands enfolded in his, as she tried to let her mind catch up to reality. "I guess so," she answered, her voice shaky.

He brushed a strand of hair away from her temple. "I always admired you, liked you, thought you were beautiful. But I was always a little afraid of your quick tongue and those penetrating brown eyes that look right into a man's dark, black soul.''

Nadine frowned, her eyes traveling over his familiar features, his firm chin, his hazel eyes that now gazed intently at her. ''I wasn't like that,'' she protested lamely.

''I didn't mind, even though at times I resented the way you made me look at myself and my life. I went out with your sister because she was easy to be with. At first it was attraction. But later, as I got to know you, I came as much to have an excuse to see you and talk to you.'' He drew her closer, laying her head against his shoulder. ''I should have broken up with her sooner and I'm not proud of that part, but I liked your family so much. I liked coming over and talking to your father. I liked the way your family expressed their faith so easily, and I wanted a part of that.'' He paused a moment, his thumb making lazy circles against her temple. ''My mom used to take me to church once in a while, but God's name was never spoken outside of that building. Life just went on. Then I came here and started going out with Sabrina. I used to call, hoping you would answer and not Sabrina or Leslie, so I would have a chance to talk to you. You used to challenge me not only in my actions but in my faith. You made me realize that God was real and that we were accountable. You told me more than anyone ever did. Don't you remember what we used to talk about?''

Nadine closed her eyes, her cheek pressed against Clint's shirt, his warmth melding with hers. ''I remember. I liked talking to you. I liked you. I could never figure out why Sabrina broke up with you.''

Clint's thumb slowed and she felt his chest lift in a gentle sigh. ''She didn't break up with me. I broke up with her.''

Nadine stiffened in surprise, pulling away from him. ''You did?''

''When I was in Europe, I knew I couldn't stay with her. Then when I became a Christian I knew I had to be with you. I found out about your father too late. I wanted to be there for you. Then I came back and you were engaged to Jack.''

He spoke Jack's name with a soft contempt that made Nadine smile. She let his words wrap themselves around her, a balm to her wounded and lonely soul.

''I've always cared about you, Nadine.'' He pressed a kiss against her temple. ''I found out too late that you broke up with Jack. Then your mother was so sick. So I left you alone. And when I took over from Uncle Dory…''

''My mother had just died and all I did was snap at you.''

''I think I was always a little afraid of you.'' He laughed. ''Even when I saw you walking down this road, all alone, knowing you must be freezing, I wanted nothing more than to stop the car, run out and grab you, and I didn't dare.''

Nadine smiled, trying to imagine the picture. ''Why?''

''It's your eyes, remember?'' Clint laid his chin on her head, rubbing it slowly over her hair.

Nadine could only close her eyes and let herself be wooed by a voice she had so often longed would say the things he said.

"A lot of people knew that I envied my sisters a bit," she said, her hand playing with a button on his coat. "And they were right." She lifted her head and with a bemused expression touched his beloved features. "But only because of you, Clint. Only because of you."

He shook his head lightly. "You never had to, Nadine." He bent over and once again their lips met, their souls joined.

Chapter Twelve

Nadine didn't want to move, nestled in Clint's embrace—a place she never thought she would end up when she left the apartment a few hours earlier. Clint reluctantly loosened his hold and though they parted, his hand still held on to hers.

"I should take you home," Clint said with a smile as he tenderly brushed a strand of hair back from her face. "Your grandmother will be worrying."

"No, she won't. The longer I'm gone, the happier she'll be."

"Why is that?" Clint looked puzzled.

Nadine tilted her head to one side, a bemused expression on her face. "My grandma, the eternal matchmaker, has been trying to get us together since you went out with Sabrina."

He quirked his mouth into a crooked smile and touched her lips lightly with his fingers, tracing them almost reverently. "She's a pretty smart lady."

"I'm sure she'll be thrilled when we get back to the apartment."

"Then we had better get back and make her life a little brighter." Clint let his fingers linger on her face, then reluctantly dropped his hand to start the car.

Nadine sat back and watched him as he put the car in gear, glanced idly over his shoulder and spun the wheel with one hand to pull onto the road.

He glanced sidelong and as their eyes met, it was like a caress. Clint reached over and caught her hand in his own. Then he returned his attention to the road, leaving Nadine free to study him with a boldness she never had before.

His nose didn't have the long narrowness generally associated with "handsome" men, his chin jutted out just a little, his lips were full, not thin and aristocratic. Taken all together they created a face that drew eyes back to him for a second look. And when he smiled, his aloof demeanor melted into a boyish appeal.

But even as Nadine analyzed his face, she knew that his features were only the surface, a way of identifying Clint apart from other men. Beneath his handsome face lay what drew her to him, a man of faith in God, integrity and strong values. A man of substance.

He must have sensed her scrutiny, because he glanced her way, two small furrows creasing his forehead just above his nose like two parentheses. "What's the matter?"

"Not a thing," she said quietly, covering the hand that held hers with her other. "I'm so thankful you came for me. It was an answer to prayer." She traced the back of his hand and impulsively raised it to her face. "Thanks again," she said softly, pressing a kiss against it. His fingers curled against her face and Nadine winged a silent prayer of thanks heavenward.

Nadine wondered what it was going to be like to go to work tomorrow, knowing he would be there, just down the hall.

Tonight she had seen a part of him that still seemed unreal. It fit with what she had seen at other times—the evening in the restaurant, the day he had come to the Foodgrains Project. She had read his article from that day and seen yet another facet to his nature. His reserve hid depths that she looked forward to exploring. He was dependable, steady and true.

Clint slowed as he came to town, as if reluctant to bring other people into what was so new between them. He clutched Nadine's hand a little harder. "First thing tomorrow morning I have to go to Calgary for a meeting, and then I'm supposed to fly to Toronto from there." He turned to her, his eyes mirroring the regret that Nadine suddenly felt. "I won't be in the office this week, but I hope to be back Thursday. Can I call you?"

Nadine nodded slowly, the very newness of their being together precluding anything else from her. She felt a keen disappointment that she dared not express. Not yet. She had no intention of letting things move as quickly as she had with Trace, yet she had so hoped to have an opportunity to cement the fragility of their beginnings.

She wondered what God was trying to teach her with this. It didn't seem fair.

"I wish I didn't have to go," he said, holding her hand. "I wish we could spend some ordinary time together."

"I know" was all she said.

They drove on in silence as Nadine clung to the memory of what had happened tonight, hoping it would hold her through the week until Thursday.

When Clint dropped her off he declined a cup of tea with an exultant grandma. What had happened between them was too new and unformed, so when he left, all he did was touch her hand surreptitiously and send her a wink as he stepped into his car.

"So what do I do with this?" Allison stood in front of Nadine's desk the next day, her hands holding the sheaf of notes she had taken the week before.

Nadine looked up at her, gathering her scattered thoughts.

"I'm supposed to get these into a coherent article by this afternoon?" Allison lifted her hand as if in surrender. "I thought you were going to write it up this weekend. I don't have the background on this company that you do."

"That's why I asked you to write it up." Nadine smiled absently at Allison as her intercom beeped.

"You've got a caller on line one." Sharlene's voice came in over the intercom.

"You'll do just fine, Allison," Nadine said, waving her away. "Now get to work. I'll vet it for you once you're done." She punched the button and picked up the phone, effectively dismissing her new reporter.

Allison looked down at the notes again and then left.

"Hello," Nadine said with a grin at Allison's expression as she left. Nadine tucked the phone under one ear, cleaning up the papers on the desk and replacing them in a folder.

"Miss Laidlaw?"

"Yes."

"I'm the lady who's going to meet you Thursday."

Nadine frowned, flipping over the pages of her desk calendar. Nothing was written down on Thursday. "Can I ask who is calling?"

"I'm the lady who wrote the letter."

Nadine clutched the handset, her heart fluttering as it all came back. How could she have forgotten?

"Five o'clock work out for you?" the harsh voice continued.

"Yes," Nadine assured her, pulling a pen and a pad toward her. "I'll be there. How will I know you?"

"Like I said, I'll be wearing a green sweatshirt and gray pants. I know what you look like. Just stay in the main gymnasium and I'll find you."

"Okay. Five o'clock, main gym. Gotcha."

"No one else will know or be there?"

Nadine hesitated, wondering if she was getting set up. The lady sounded like a bit of a kook, but she didn't dare offend her. She had waited too long to find out what this informer knew. "No one else will know."

"Good. I'll see you there." And with that her mystery caller hung up.

Nadine laid the phone carefully in the cradle and, blowing out her breath, leaned back. There was altogether too much mystery surrounding this woman, and for a moment Nadine was tempted to let it all go.

But she knew she couldn't. She had gladly passed off the accident article to Allison, but this she had to follow up on.

The day slipped by. Phone calls took more time than they should and it was late afternoon before Nadine had a chance to go over the layout once more with the typesetter, double-check the articles for errors. Their ad accounts were up, thanks to a hardworking sales staff. Nadine could justify taking a two-page spread for the Foodgrains Harvest.

She had already selected which pictures they were going to scan in and how much space they were going to take up on the page. Now it was a matter of going over Clint's article one last time.

Clint's style was straightforward. He hadn't written many articles since he'd come here, but his professionalism showed in this one.

Clint wasn't a passionate writer, but a deep conviction showed in how he presented the project. He had distilled an entire afternoon of interviews and observation into a thoughtful treatment of giving and sharing. In a diplomatic style he pointed out a responsibility to share wealth with those less fortunate, but to realize that as the sharing was done, the giver was only passing on what had been entrusted by God. It was written as a news article, but it had glimpses of challenge to the reader.

Nadine felt a deep satisfaction well up in her as she read Clint's story. It had depth, it had a personal touch and it left the reader thinking. He presented his story in a way that made people stop and reassess their own lives and blessings.

She laid down the paper, her chin in her hand as she stared into space.

Was it possible that this articulate and careful man was the same person who had held her in his arms last night, had kissed her? She sighed as she thought of the days ahead, the office suddenly emptier with him gone, a space in her own life that had never been there before.

She often had to remind herself that he had come for her, that he had held her, kissed her. Without much effort she recalled their conversation in the inn. Their relationship had changed, had moved to a level she had dreamed of, but never dared see as reality.

She was seized with a loneliness that was even harsher and deeper than before.

She missed him.

Clint waited while Sharlene patched him into Nadine's office, feeling a moment's apprehension. He felt as nervous as a teenager and had to remind himself that he was Nadine's boss as well as...

He wasn't sure what, exactly. He only knew that he had no intention of letting Nadine slip out of his hands again.

"Hello." Nadine's hesitant voice made him smile.

"Hi, this is your boss. I was wondering if you have some important school-board meeting to cover on Thursday night."

"Wally's doing that." She sounded reserved.

"No volleyball games?"

"I've got Allison on them."

Clint leaned his forehead against the cool window of his motel room. He wished he was back in Derwin, back in his office just down from Nadine's. He wanted to hold her, remind himself that she had come willingly into his arms. He didn't know where to begin with this girl who had had him tied up in knots for so many years. "Then you can spare some time for me?"

"Thursday night? This Thursday night? What time?"

"I thought I could pick you up at about six from your apartment."

She was silent a moment, then said almost breathlessly, "I'll be meeting Allison at the gym before that, but that sounds okay."

"Okay, then. I'll call you once more, just to confirm." Goodness, he thought, sounds as if you're making hotel reservations.

And as he said his final farewells, sounding distinctly unloverlike, he thought that was what it had felt like.

He wished he could go back to Derwin right now, before Nadine changed her mind about him.

By Thursday afternoon Nadine was in such a dither, she couldn't concentrate on her work. She didn't know what to attribute which emotion to. Clint was taking her out that night and maybe they could start again. In a few hours she would, hopefully, find out the truth about her father. And after that…

She had committed herself to meeting this lady, yet she felt that she was betraying Clint.

You're not going to do anything with it! she reminded herself. It's just for information.

She tried to keep herself busy and her eyes off the clock, but it didn't work. Finally at about four-thirty she gave up. She didn't have to feel guilty about not working until five. Goodness knows she had spent enough overtime hours at the office.

She drove home, then showered and changed, her mind going back and forth between a loyalty to Clint, who wanted her to leave Skyline alone, and a need to find out what this lady knew.

Thankfully Grandma was gone, which meant she didn't need to explain her actions. She hadn't told Grandma about the mystery lady, just in case it turned out to be a hoax. Nadine didn't want to disappoint her.

A number of teams were warming up by the time Nadine entered the foyer, the shrill sounds of whistles echoing through the gym. She stood in the doorway of one of the gyms, but didn't spot a green sweatshirt. She wandered restlessly around the hallways, returning every few minutes to check.

Half an hour later Nadine's stomach was in knots. It was 5:20. Clint hadn't phoned before she left the office, so she assumed he would come to the house at six as they originally had planned. She tried to phone her grandmother, but there was no answer. From 5:15 on she had stayed in the main gym, thankful that no game was being played there. Allison was shooting pictures in the other gym.

At five-thirty she was pacing the hallway. She had maybe fifteen more minutes before she absolutely had to leave.

What if this was all a hoax? she wondered as she glanced at her watch. What if Skyline had deliberately planted this lady, was doing this just to sabotage her life?

Don't be ridiculous, she chided herself. You're getting paranoid because you're feeling guilty.

She was wondering if she should leave a note. Where? How? "Dear lady in the green sweatshirt and gray pants, I had to leave for an important date"? A date she'd been waiting for all her life.

Nadine almost laughed aloud. It was as if she had to choose between silencing the echoes of the past or grasping a hope for the future.

Nadine shook her head, glancing once more at her watch. Her stomach tightened as the hands moved steadily on to six o'clock.

Was she sabotaging a chance with Clint all for nothing? But no, she reminded herself. He had originally said six o'clock. Hopefully he would wait a little while.

She stepped back into the gym. She would make one more circle and then leave.

Right away Nadine saw a green sweatshirt. And

gray pants. Her shoulders sagging in relief, she ran around the edge of the court and caught up to the slight female figure.

"Excuse me," Nadine said, tapping her on the shoulder. "Were you looking for me? Nadine Laidlaw."

The woman turned around. Slight, fair-haired, streaks of gray glinting at her temples. Her eyes seemed weary, her smile forced as she looked up at Nadine. "I thought that was you." She shoved her hands into the kangaroo pocket of her hooded sweatshirt and indicated with her head that she wanted to talk outside.

Nadine followed her, trying to get her pounding heart to slow down. She's just going to answer a few questions, nothing major, she thought. Don't expect too much. But Nadine had to wipe her sweaty palms off on her pants as they stepped out of the noisy foyer into the relative quiet of outside.

The woman lit a cigarette and Nadine was surprised to see the flame of the match tremble. She pulled in a deep drag, blew it out and then looked at Nadine. "My name is Chantelle Hayward. My brother, Gordon, used to work for Skyline. He worked with your father."

This was it, Nadine thought. What we've been waiting for all this time. *Thank you, Lord. Thank you.*

"My brother was hired by Skyline almost seven years ago, just a month before your father died." Chantelle left the cigarette in her mouth as she dug into the pocket of her jeans. She pulled out an envelope and handed it to Nadine. "Six months ago he tried to commit suicide and failed. Before he tried he wrote a suicide note.''

Nadine glanced at Chantelle's face and then back at the envelope.

''Go on,'' urged Chantelle, shoving the envelope into Nadine's hands. ''Take it. It's just a photocopy. I read it already. Know what it says. He worked for that company for two months after the accident and he hadn't been the same since. I wanted to know what caused it.'' She laughed. It was a bitter sound. ''I almost wish I hadn't.''

''What happened?'' Nadine asked, her voice breaking. ''That he tried to commit suicide, I mean.''

Chantelle shrugged. ''Gordon wasn't what you'd call scholarship material, so we were really glad when he got this job.'' She took another drag from her cigarette. ''But he was there when your father died and he hasn't been able to forget it. He'd been threatened by unknown people to keep his mouth shut. But I knew you wrote articles about them and you're not afraid to call them what they are. Cheats.'' Chantelle waved the burning cigarette at the letter, the smoke wreathing between them. ''Your father didn't die because he was careless. He died because of my brother, but mostly because of Skyline.'' Chantelle dropped her cigarette and ground it out with the toe of her running shoe. ''The letter explains everything.'' She looked up at Nadine, her eyes almost glowing in the gathering dusk.

Nadine held up the envelope and looked at it once again. ''I'll read it. For sure I'll read it. Thanks.'' She was fully aware of the passing time, and now that she had fulfilled one obligation, she was anxious to get home.

"I want to see those guys pulled down for what they did to Gordon, to your family." Chantelle took a step forward, her eyes burning with intensity. For a moment Nadine felt afraid of what she saw in Chantelle Hayward's eyes. "You can show everyone what they are. Now you have proof."

Nadine swallowed. "I'll do what I can, Chantelle."

Chantelle stared hard at her. "I hate them, Laidlaw. I really hate them." She pulled out her cigarette package and withdrew another cigarette. "I hate what they do to the community, I hate what they did to my family. They're a pack of lying, cheating…"

Nadine frowned as she listened to Chantelle rant, her anger gathering momentum.

Nadine thought of her own anger, her own sorrow. Yes, she wanted to see justice done. Yes, she wanted to see Skyline brought down just as Chantelle Hayward did. But surely, Nadine thought, she didn't have the same deep, intense hatred that Chantelle did?

"So what are you going to do?" Chantelle asked, finishing another cigarette.

Nadine pocketed the letter. "First I'm going to read the letter and find out exactly what your brother knew. I'll take it from there."

"You're not going to wuss out on me, now, are you?" Chantelle glared at her. "It's all in there. In that letter. You read it." Chantelle walked backward toward the gym, still talking. "I'll call you in a couple of days and you can tell me then." She pulled open the door, a flood of noise spilling out.

"I will." The door slammed shut, cutting off the sounds of the tournament inside. Nadine leaned back against the wall, her insides trembling in reaction and a touch of fear. Chantelle had seemed almost fanatical, and Nadine wondered what in the world was in the letter.

She glanced at her watch. Six-fifteen! She turned and began running. It would take her ten minutes to get home. The thought that Clint might be waiting hurried her steps and lightened her heart. A date. A real date with Clint.

Her feet pounded out a steady rhythm as her breathing became more labored. Only a little farther, she reassured herself. Just a few more blocks. *Just let him be there, Lord. Let him be waiting.* She didn't dare stop, could hardly keep going and almost skidded around the corner to her street. When she saw only her grandmother's car and her old car in front of the house, she slowed her pace, clutching her side, her chest heaving.

By the time she got to the apartment, her breathing was slowing but her legs were trembling with a combination of the extra exertion and anticipation. She walked into the entrance, her heart still pounding.

"Hey, Grandma," she called out, kicking off her shoes and setting them neatly in the porch. "I'm home."

"Nadine." Grandma's voice chided her from the

end of the hallway just as Nadine hung up her coat. "Where have you been?"

Nadine stepped into the kitchen, her heartbeat finally slowing. "I had to meet someone for an interview at the school."

Grandma stood in the kitchen, her arms folded across her chest, her head tilted to one side. "Clint has been here waiting for you. He just left."

Nadine's heart stopped, beat once, then began racing again, this time in fear. "What—what did you say?"

"Clint just left."

"But I tried to phone you."

Danielle Laidlaw looked sheepish. "I wanted to have a nap, so I turned off the ringer. I remembered at six to turn it back on."

Nadine took a slow breath, willing her heart to still. "How long was he waiting here?"

"He came here at a quarter past five. Then someone named Allison phoned here at a quarter past six asking for you. I asked if she wanted to talk to Clint. She did and then he left." Grandma walked over to Nadine. "What is happening? Were you and Clint supposed to have a date tonight, and who is this Allison?"

"She's a new reporter at the *Times*." Nadine chewed her lip, remembering how she had told Clint that she was to meet Allison at the gym. Now it looked for sure as if she was hiding something. What should she do now? "Did Clint say where he was going?"

"He just thanked me for the tea and then left."

"I gotta go, Grandma." She turned and ran into the

entrance. ''I don't know when I'll be back. Don't wait up for me.'' As she grabbed her car keys off the hook, she flashed a nervous smile at her hovering grandmother. ''I'll tell you all about it later.''

Her stomach was churning by the time she pulled in to a parking spot. It would have been just as fast to run back from her house, but the stitch in her side gave lie to that thought.

As she strode down the sidewalk, she glanced at the vehicles. No sign of Clint's red car. She took a shortcut across the lawn and just as she came to the corner of the gym, she heard a vehicle drive out of the parking lot.

With a sinking heart she watched Clint Fletcher's vehicle slow and then spin around the corner and down the road.

Chapter Thirteen

Nadine leaned against the brick wall of the gym as she watched Clint's car leave. Only then did the enormity of what she had done hit her.

"You still here? I thought you were gone."

Nadine felt her heart stop at Chantelle's all-too-familiar voice. She turned. "I was, but I was hoping to meet someone."

"That new guy at the paper?" Chantelle rubbed one hand along the side of her pants. "You just missed him."

A coldness gripped Nadine's chest. "How do you know?"

Chantelle snapped her gum. "Talked to him. Told him some of what I told you. Figured it wouldn't hurt if two people knew the story."

Her hands felt like ice, her heart a heavy weight. Clint knew why she had come here, why she had missed him.

''He didn't seem real interested at first,'' warned Chantelle. ''But when I told him that it was about Skyline he looked as mad as I felt.''

Each word she spoke added to the heaviness in her chest. Nadine nodded quickly in acknowledgment, then turned, ran to her car and jumped in. Her head ached and her side still hurt by the time she pulled up in her driveway. But no sporty red car stood parked in front of the house.

Nadine laid her head against the steering wheel and allowed herself a few moments of tears. Was the letter worth it? She didn't know what was in it, but even if it proved that her father was completely innocent, would it change anything? She would probably not write the article. But would Clint know that?

Nadine remembered again Chantelle's bitterness and knew that once she herself had had the same burning need for revenge. But it wasn't solely up to her to bring justice into the world. She had done what she could and she now had to learn to let go. Justice belonged in God's hands, not her puny ones.

But Clint.

Her stomach plunged again as she thought of him sitting here at her house, waiting for her.

Can we back up and do this again, Lord? she prayed. *I'd like another try. I'll make the right choice this time.* But as she looked up, the lights of her apartment extra bright through her tears, she knew she'd had her chance and had made her choices. The letter in her pocket wasn't worth the opportunity she had thrown away with Clint Fletcher.

She bit her lip and indulged in a few more minutes of tears. Then, palming away the moisture from her cheeks, she opened the door and trudged back to the apartment.

Nadine slipped into the apartment and, with a tired sigh, kicked off her shoes for the second time in fifteen minutes.

"Is that you, Nadine?" called her grandmother from the living room.

"Yes," she called out, suddenly bone weary. She wanted to go to her bedroom, shove her head under a pillow and stay there until the spirit moved her to leave. Which, in her present state of mind, might be never.

"Come sit with me a minute and tell me what is going on."

Nadine stopped at the doorway to the living room. "Nothing is going on, Grandma. I missed Clint. I didn't know when he was coming, that's all."

Danielle turned to her granddaughter, her mouth drawn tight. "You leave the poor man sitting here for an hour and you say 'That's all'?"

"What else am I supposed to say?" grumped Nadine. She didn't need her grandmother's censure right now—she had enough self-disgust to spare. "I don't want to talk about it, Grandma."

"Well, I do. Clint Fletcher is a fine young man. He's handsome, smart and a sincere Christian. Quite a potent combination, I'd say."

I'd say, too, thought Nadine as she dropped into a nearby chair.

"Where were you, Nadine?"

"In the first place, I didn't know what time Clint was coming," she answered, ignoring her grandmother's question.

"He said he phoned the office. Where were you?" Danielle repeated.

In answer, Nadine slid her hand into her pocket and pulled out the envelope Chantelle had given her. "I went to meet with a lady who had some more information on how Dad died."

Danielle had opened her mouth to shoot another question at Nadine, but obediently closed it at what her granddaughter said.

Nadine waved the envelope back and forth, staring at it, wondering what it said and yet, somehow, not caring. It couldn't begin to make up for what she had passed up. Would she be able to explain? How would it sound? *"You asked me to lay off Skyline and then I keep you waiting while I go digging for more information to use against them"?*

"Is the information in the envelope?"

Nadine nodded, suddenly bone weary and exhausted.

"Aren't you going to read it?"

Nadine sat up, holding the envelope between her fingers. "I guess I may as well. Just so that standing Clint up wasn't all for nothing." She ripped open one end and pulled out the photocopy Chantelle had given her. Pursing her lips, she unfolded it and turned it over to read the tight, crabbed writing.

It felt eerie reading what was supposed to have been

read only after the writer had taken his own life. She skimmed over the references to personal events, events that would matter only to Chantelle. And then, half-way down, there it was. Her father's name. Nadine slowed her reading. As if to help, she traced the words slowly with her finger, her heart pounding with the words she read, her hands suddenly clammy.

"What does it say, Naddy? You look stunned."

Nadine finished reading, staring at the letter. Then she slouched back in the easy chair, dropping her head against the back of it. "It wasn't Dad's fault, Grandma," she whispered, letting the letter drop into her lap. "It wasn't his fault. Just like we figured. That poor boy."

Danielle got up and pulled the piece of paper easily out of Nadine's limp hands. She held the letter at arm's length, squinting irritably at it. She put on the reading glasses hanging around her neck. Her mouth moved slowly as she read the words, and when she was finished, she looked at Nadine.

"Who is this from?"

Nadine blew her breath out, her bangs fluffing up as she did so. "Believe it or not, it's a suicide note from a young man who worked with Dad the day he died."

"Suicide?" Grandma pressed one hand to her chest, the other reaching out blindly for some support. Nadine jumped to her feet and caught her arm.

"It's okay, Grandma. He didn't kill himself. And this is just a photocopy." Still holding the letter, Nadine led her back to the couch. She helped her grandmother sit down and then smoothed out the now-crumpled piece of paper. She glanced over it once more, rereading what he had said about her father's death.

Gordon Hayward had been training as a faller. He had been sent out into the bush totally green. He had made a mess of the trees, and a few days later Jake Laidlaw had come in to help. Jake had told him to wait in the truck where it was safe while he cleaned up. Then a Skyline foreman had come by and sent Gordon, over his protests, back to falling. Gordon had gotten too close to Jake, and a tree he was cutting went the wrong way and killed Jake. When the foreman came by again to check on Gordon he found him crouched in front of the pickup, crying. The foreman told Gordon that he was liable and could end up paying a fine. The Haywards were counting on his paycheck, and other jobs were scarce, so Gordon signed a written statement made out by Skyline saying that he'd heard the foreman warn Jake about his work.

Gordon worked for them until he found another job. But Jake's dying cries haunted him. The knowledge that he had implicated and killed an innocent man stayed with him and he couldn't bear the burden any longer.

"How did you get it?"

Grandma's quiet question jolted Nadine back to the present. She pulled her scattered thoughts together. "His sister Chantelle. I met her at the gym tonight." Nadine folded up the letter and laid it on the coffee table in front of the couch. "I got a letter from her a while ago, telling me that she had something I should see. We finally connected a few days ago and had made arrangements to meet tonight at the gym.''

''I wish I could say I was glad,'' whispered Danielle, her fingers resting on her lips. ''But to think of Jake lying there...'' Her words were choked off and she began to cry.

Nadine pulled her close, hugging her fiercely, her own emotions unstable.

Six years of speculation, finally answered. Her father, killed by the carelessness of an inexperienced logger, covered up by an irresponsible company. Nadine clenched her teeth when she thought of what Gordon had said about listening to the dying cries of her father.

Danielle straightened and brushed her tears off her wrinkled cheeks. She turned to Nadine and touched her cheek lovingly, her eyes still bright with tears. ''I'm sorry you had to be the one to find this out, Nadine. You've worked so hard on this, done so much.''

Nadine shook her head. ''I didn't do anything. Nothing has changed. Dad is still dead.''

''Yes, but it is comforting to know that he wasn't at fault.'' Danielle sniffed and then got up to get some tissues.

Nadine slouched back against the couch, her hands clasped over her stomach. Her mind drifted back over the years. She easily imagined her father sitting in his leather recliner across their living room in their old house, a wreath of aromatic pipe smoke surrounding his head as he worked his way through the *Derwin Times*. Her mother would be bustling in the kitchen, putting the final touches on the meal, and she and her sisters would be sprawled over furniture and floor, books spread around them as they pretended to do homework. Home was a comfortable haven then. What would have happened if he still lived?

"I have to write something up on this." Nadine snatched the letter off the table and strode past her grandmother. She had to do something, anything, instead of dwelling on might-have-beens. She hadn't intended to write a story, but now she realized she had nothing to lose that she hadn't already lost.

She switched on her computer, riffled through her computer diskettes until she found one labeled Skyline. Once the computer was booted up, she popped it into the drive, opened up a new file and began typing.

An hour later she looked up from the screen and rubbed her neck, now tight with tension. She saved the article on a disk and, just to be on the safe side, E-mailed it to the office, as well.

She leaned back in her chair, her eyes closed, wondering how she was going to work the article into the paper. Editorial? Tie-in with the accident of last week?

Why do it at all?

Nadine dragged her hands over her face and sighed deeply. Why do it at all? She leaned over and clicked the mouse on the Print command. She needed to see it printed out, needed to hold it in her hand.

She read the pages as they came out of the printer, the editor in her pleased with what she had written.

The article had bite, punch and flowed smoothly. It was the culmination of all the articles and editorials she had ever done on Skyline.

Nadine lowered the papers with a sigh. She had a wonderful article written with emotion and good cause. After six years her own instincts about her father's death had been proven correct. Tonight all the questions had been answered, all the *i*'s dotted.

But as she thought of Clint, she knew the price had been too great. Her heart felt like a square lump in her chest as she looked at her article once again.

It gave her no satisfaction.

What have I done, Lord, she prayed, dropping it on her desk and falling into her chair. *I gave up something precious just to prove myself right.* She spun her chair back and forth, back and forth, recriminations filling her head, fighting with memories of Clint smiling at her across a table, holding her, comforting her. All she had wanted as a young girl had been given to her as a gift, and she had just thrown it all away.

Chapter Fourteen

Clint wearily rubbed his eyes. This Thursday had been one of the longer days of his life. He had come directly to the office from the school, preferring to work rather than think about what had just happened tonight.

With a sigh he picked up the letter he'd received that morning from the newspaper's lawyer. Skyline hadn't filed anything yet, but their lawyers were still threatening.

He didn't know whether to ignore the threat or worry about it. The accountant's report and the lawyer's letter dealt with different aspects of the business, but they both said the same thing. A prolonged battle with Skyline would put the newspaper so far into the red that Clint stood to lose everything.

Clint dropped his head against the back of the chair, thinking of how quickly the evening had changed. He had left his meeting with high hopes and an eager expectation of seeing Nadine, of spending time with her. That she was gone when he came had been disappointing. But what that belligerent woman he'd met at the gym had told him had made everything turn completely around.

From the sound of the E-mail he'd just seen on the computer, Nadine was bound and determined to bring Skyline to justice, regardless of his wishes and needs. He thought he had laid out the consequences for the newspaper, thought he had given her enough reason to back off. But obviously it wasn't enough.

Did you think she was so terribly in love with you that she would give up a six-year battle just because you asked her to?

What could he possibly think he meant to her after spending a few evenings together? Nadine had made it quite clear what she thought of him, from the first time he stepped into this office.

Surely he hadn't imagined the way she'd looked at him when they'd shared a meal, the way she'd seemed to drift back against him when he came to her office? Too vividly he remembered how she had willingly gone into his arms that evening in the car. Surely her reaction was more than gratitude?

The timing of this week's meetings was terrible. How badly he had wanted to stay Monday and reinforce the fragile bond begun the evening before. He and Nadine had had no chance to solidify their relationship, if indeed they had one.

Clint got up and pulled his tie off, threw it into a corner and rolled up the sleeves of his shirt. Hands in his pockets, he walked to the window, staring past his blurred reflection to the meager light of the street-lights. Was it only a few months ago he had stood here with a sense of eager expectation, a realization that his life had come if not full circle, then at least to a point that he knew he should be? It was as if God had been slowly pushing him here by cutting off some opportunities and opening others. His job at the city newspaper had changed, become unsatisfying. Uncle Dory, out of the blue, had offered him his share of the business.

He had found out that Nadine was still single.

Clint leaned his forehead against the glass, the cool-ness soothing his tired head.

For a few days he'd thought his life was coming together, that it was finally getting some kind of co-hesion. He had a business he loved and the affection of a woman who had been on his mind for years, a woman who was a Christian, a soul mate. It was as if all the things he had been seeking were there in one neat package.

And now it looked as if he was going to lose it all.

The refrain of a song drifted through his head. "All to Jesus I surrender, all to Him I freely give..."

Clint rolled his forehead against the glass. Too sim-plistic, he thought.

Surely it wasn't wrong to want to run a healthy business, to take care of it, to take all necessary steps to make sure that his employees had a job? He had tried to keep the newspaper in perspective, to keep a balance with his faith and his work.

Could Nadine say the same thing?

He straightened, shoving his hand through his hair. Easy for him to judge her. He still had his father. He and Clint didn't speak often with each other and had never been really close, so Clint didn't know how he would have reacted had his own father died under questionable circumstances.

But revenge? If that indeed was what Nadine wanted?

Clint shook his head and rubbed the back of his neck. He didn't want to judge Nadine. He wanted to love her. He wanted to take care of her. He wanted to show her that love and he didn't know how to do it.

Yes, you do.

Clint paused, the voice pulling him up short. It had come from his own thoughts, his own conscience. On a hunch, he walked over to his briefcase and, hunkering down, opened it. He hadn't unpacked it after his meeting and had taken it into the office after his aborted date with Nadine tonight.

In one corner of it lay his Bible. Clint took it out, closed the briefcase and straightened.

Still standing, he thumbed through the New Testament until he came to Corinthians. Then, with one hand in the pocket of his suit pants, the other holding the Bible as it lay open, he began to read the words that had struck him so many years ago.

"Love is patient, love is kind, it does not envy, it does not boast, it is not proud. It is not rude, it is not self-seeking...." Clint paused at that one. Was it self-seeking to want to see his newspaper post a profit? His lawyer had consistently warned him against a battle with Skyline because of the cost, not because of the right or wrong of it.

Clint continued reading. "Love does not delight in evil, but rejoices with the truth. It always protects, always trusts, always hopes, always perseveres. Love never fails...."

Clint read on and then closed the book with a soft sigh. He ran his thumb over the worn edges of the pages, riffling them as what he had just read settled into his mind, finding the right places, a solution that would neatly fit.

And as he thought, Clint realized that in order for anything to fit, he would have to let go of some of the things he held too tightly. He would have to trust. It seemed too easy and it seemed too hard at the same time. Maybe it was a test, and if he passed, he would get whatever he wanted.

Clint laughed lightly at his own thoughts, at the idea of a small person like himself trying to find a way to entice God into giving him what he wanted, provided he played the game right. He laid his Bible on his desk, slowly sat down and closed his eyes in prayer.

Nadine sighed and rolled over. Six o'clock in the morning. The sun was barely up and she was wide-awake. Had been since five o'clock. And since five she had tried to find a way out of going to the office. It would be so much easier to stay home, avoid Clint, everything.

Again and again she relived the evening, imagining

different scenarios—cutting Chantelle Hayward off, coming home on time and sharing the letter with Clint. Or not showing up at the gym at all and spending a delightful evening with Clint.

Finally she threw the blankets back in frustration and stalked to the bathroom. She didn't care if she woke Grandma up. She had to do something instead of lying in bed castigating herself for being so short-sighted.

Her anger at herself simmered through her shower, as she got dressed. She took extra care, pulling out an outfit that Sabrina and Leslie had chivied her into buying last spring. Narrow gray corduroy pants, snug T-shirt also in gray topped with a collarless tunic in an unusual shade of apricot that complemented her brown hair.

Nadine finished toweling off her hair and blew it dry, deciding to let it hang loose.

The way Clint liked it.

The kitchen was still dark when she tiptoed into it. She pulled out an apple, poured herself a glass of milk and ate her breakfast leaning against the counter behind her. Nadine was thankful that Grandma still slept. The last thing she wanted right now was a postmortem on what had happened last night. Bad enough that she would be seeing Clint in a few hours.

She drove to the office, and as she parked her car in her stall in the back of the building, she noticed with a thump of her heart that Clint was at the office already. With a feeling of apprehension, she unlocked the back door and walked down the darkened hallway past the cubicles of the copy editors. One of the computers was on in a cubicle, the screen saver bouncing around on the screen. Frowning, Nadine walked over to it and hit one of the keys. The E-mail program was on, and Nadine saw that the article she had written last night was on the screen.

Clint must have turned it on, she thought, her heart sinking. She had forgotten she had sent it as a backup.

She looked around, wondering where Clint was now. Then she walked past the darkroom and down the hallway to her office.

Pausing at the door, she glanced up the hallway to the front entrance and Clint's office. His door was open, but the room was dark. Puzzled, Nadine took a few steps closer.

A figure was slouched over the desk, one arm flung out.

In the early-morning light filtering in through the window she could see it was Clint. His head moved slightly, disturbing the papers underneath him.

He was sleeping.

Clint shifted and Nadine turned to leave, but he only sighed and settled again. Feeling like an intruder, she stepped into the office, closer to his desk. She watched him a moment, his hair falling across his forehead, his soft lips slightly parted. His firm jaw was stubbled, the collar of his shirt open. His one arm was flung across the desk, his other hung down, inches away from her. He looked vulnerable and utterly appealing. Nadine felt a gentle ache in her heart as she thought of all that she could have had and then, without thinking, reached

over and carefully brushed his hair away from his forehead, her hand lingering on his cheek.

She didn't expect his eyes to open, and she froze as
the hand that hung down reached up and caught hers.

"Hey, Nadine," he murmured as he blinked and
slowly sat up, still holding her hand. He smiled blear-
ily. "Come here," he said, his voice husky from sleep
as he rose from his seat and tugged her toward him.

Surprise and shock threw her off balance and he
easily pulled her into his embrace. His arms came
around her, his chin rested on her head and she felt
his chest rise and fall in a protracted sigh. She couldn't
relax, knowing she needed to leave, not wanting to.

"Don't say anything," he murmured, holding her
close, rubbing his stubbled chin on her hair. "I like
this dream better."

You have to go, Nadine told herself, cherishing the
feel of his arms around her, being surrounded by the
warmth of him. You can't stay here, this isn't right,
she thought. But she closed her eyes, allowing herself
this one moment of wish fulfillment, this brief taste of
might-have-beens. She let her hand slip around his
neck, allowed her fingers to lightly touch his hair as
she finally relaxed in his embrace. She felt so secure,
so accepted, so cherished simply being herself.

She loved him.

The words began as a small thought but then, as she
closed her eyes, they grew until they were so close to
her lips, she had to say them. "I love you," she whispered in a voice so soft she wasn't even sure she had
spoken them aloud.

She swallowed the lump in her throat and then, turning her head away from him, slipped out of his embrace and stood in front of him.

But his hand still held hers. Puzzled, she turned, only to see him staring at her with perfectly focused eyes, no sign of sleep clouding their piercing gaze.

Unnerved, she pulled on her hand again, but Clint held fast.

"What's happening, Nadine?" he asked.

She could only stare at him, aware of what she had just done. "I'm sorry," she whispered finally.

"For what?"

His quiet question hung, echoing lightly in the silence of the office.

"Everything," she said softly, looking down at their intertwined hands, unable to pull her hand free and unwilling to as she realized he had been fully awake when he'd held her so close a few moments ago. "Standing you up last night, not being honest with you…" She stopped, unable to say more.

His hand lifted her chin, cupping it. His eyes met hers, his mouth curved up in a half smile. "You've done nothing to be sorry for." He stepped closer, then, without any warning, he bent down and touched his lips to hers.

Nadine felt herself sway toward him, and her hand came up and rested against his wrinkled shirt, as if to support herself. Then his arms were around her again, his mouth on hers.

It made no sense.

It made perfect sense.

Nadine let herself slip away to a place she had never imagined would be hers again to discover. A place where mind, heart and spirit were one with another, a place of surrender and strength, of peace and tumult; Clint's arms surrounding her, his body warming hers, his mouth caressing hers. She returned his kisses, clung to him, exulted in his strength.

But when he reluctantly pulled away, tucking her head once again under his chin, she did not dare think what it could all mean.

They were silent, as if each needed to absorb what had once again happened between them, as if each was afraid to voice what might change what had just happened.

Nadine suddenly pulled away, looking up at him. "I know you saw what I wrote last night. I'm not going to run the article."

Clint frowned, as if puzzled by what she said.

"I just wrote it after I got the letter from Chantelle." Nadine looked down, fingering the cuff of her tunic top. "I was upset. I had just found out the truth about my father. All those questions we've had about him were finally answered." She looked up at Clint, praying he would understand. "I found out how he died, what happened...." A wave of sorrow welled up as she remembered what Gordon had said about her father's cries. Her words were choked off and once again she was in Clint's arms. Hot tears slid past her eyelids and flowed down her cheeks.

"It's okay, Nadine. It's okay to cry," he murmured as he held her.

Nadine nodded. She drew in a steadying breath as the tears subsided. "I'm sorry. It seems all I do lately around you is cry," she said with a shaky laugh.

"I don't mind," he said softly, his hand on her shoulder. He angled his head, his hand squeezing her shoulder. "I want you to know, Nadine, that I think you should run the article on your father."

Nadine frowned at him, surprised. "What are you talking about? I thought Skyline was threatening the paper with a lawsuit?"

"So far it's just threats." Clint traced the track of a tear down Nadine's cheek, his eyes following the path of his finger. "I would be lying if I said I wasn't concerned about it. But your battle with Skyline has shown me something important. The reason I went into this business to start with. To print the truth. To expose wickedness and collusion." He smiled a wry smile, absently stroking her hair away from her face, tucking it behind her ear. "I learned something from you in all of this. You have shown me how a child should love their parent and how strong love can be. I never cared for my parents that way."

"Please," she begged, shaking her head. "Don't look to me as an example of filial love. My mother and I had a totally different relationship."

"Probably, but you did the same for her that you did for your father. You sacrificed much for her. A career, a marriage—"

"Breaking my engagement to Jack wasn't a huge sacrifice," she interrupted.

"That's good to hear." He fiddled with a strand of

her hair, sending delicate shivers down her spine at his casual touch. "You have always been someone who holds fast to what she believes. Your faith in God, your strength has always been an example to me. I've often wished for the same strength, the same ability to face problems head-on."

Nadine felt ashamed as he spoke. He was making her out to be so much better than she was. "Please, Clint. I'm not like that. I battled many times with God over my mother's illness. When she died I was relieved and had to ask God to forgive me that, as well."

"It doesn't matter, Nadine," he said quietly. "You have a beauty, a strength of character, a faith that has depth," he continued, his eyes on the hands that still played with her hair, as if unable to face her. "You're not the kind of person someone can get to know in one night, or one week, or month. You always intrigued me and scared me at the same time."

What he said began a faint stirring in the depths of her being.

"I think I've always cared for you. I know I have," he amended. "I don't know exactly how to say this except to be very honest." His hand stopped, resting on her shoulder, his finger caressing her neck. "I love you, too, Nadine."

She saw his lips move, heard the words as they settled into the empty, lonely part of her heart that she had kept blocked off for so long. As if in a daze, she slowly shook her head. "What did you just say?"

"I said I love you."

Nadine closed her eyes as if to hold the words in

her mind. Words that echoed and resounded, drowning out so many other tiny voices that she had stored away—voices that had humiliated and hurt, sometimes unintentionally. She opened her eyes again and then, surprising herself at her audacity, reached over and pulled Clint's head down to hers.

Their lips met, seeking at first, then moving more slowly as pain was eased and loneliness filled. Finally Nadine pulled away, her heart as full as when she had first fully experienced God's love for her.

"I love you, too, Clint. I have loved you for years," she said simply, her hands resting on his shoulders, his clasped behind her waist.

He drew in a deep breath, as if he had been holding it since he first declared himself to her. "So that means if I ask you to marry me, you'll say yes?"

"More than likely," she returned.

He pulled her close once again and as she rested against his heart, she let her arms slip around him, enjoying the solidity of him.

"It worked, you know," she said softly, rubbing her cheek against his wrinkled shirt.

"What do you mean?"

"My life." Nadine tilted her head so she could look up at him. "It seemed so unorganized, like anything I started would end up going in a different direction. Yet God took all those scattered pieces and made them work."

Clint smiled down at her. "I know we can't expect a life without trouble, but I still choose the kind of marriage your parents had. Their faith and their love.

They built on a strong foundation and I pray that we will, too.''

And as Nadine returned his smile she sent up a prayer of thanks.

And then she stood on tiptoe and kissed her man.

Epilogue

Danielle Laidlaw snapped open the newspaper, turning first to the "Court Docket."

"Can you believe this, Leslie?" she asked in a shocked voice. "Eva Nedelof was caught shoplifting at the Red Rooster. Poor soul." Grandma Laidlaw clucked in dismay as she turned the page. The kitchen was silent except for the soft tick of the clock and the breathy sighs of Leslie's baby girl.

"Oh, my goodness." Danielle adjusted her reading glasses and leaned forward. "Listen to this headline. 'Skyline Contractors Files For Bankruptcy.'" She frowned as she read on, mouthing the words silently. "They are such a big company. What happened?"

"I heard they did a lot of work for that oil company that was starting up. The oil company went broke and took Skyline with them."

Danielle shook her head. "I always wondered why they didn't sue the paper like Nadine was so afraid they would after they ran that piece on Jake. Just goes to show you, 'Though the mills of God grind slowly, yet they grind exceeding small;/Though with patience He stands waiting, with exactness grinds He all.' A German poet said that, and I agree.''

''When are Clint and Nadine supposed to be back from their honeymoon?'' Leslie asked, shifting her daughter to her arm, changing the subject.

Danielle shrugged. ''Nadine sounded anxious to come back. They've been gone for two weeks already.''

''Who's running the paper?''

''Clint's uncle Dory came back for a while.'' Danielle pursed her lips. ''How old is Dory Strepchuk?''

''Don't start, Grandma. According to Clint he's a confirmed bachelor.''

''I did okay with Clint and Nadine.''

''Clint had his eye on Nadine long before you came into the picture.''

''How did you know?''

Leslie laughed at her grandmother's expression. ''Don't pout, Grandma. I could see the way Clint looked at Nadine when he thought she wasn't looking.''

''I could do quite well for Dory.''

''Sounds like you have someone in mind.'' Leslie brushed a kiss across the top of her daughter's downy head.

''I do,'' Grandma said with a confident smile. ''Me.''

*   *   *   *   *

Dear Reader,

Whenever I tell a story, I start with my characters. What are their dreams, hopes and wishes? All of us have things that we want from life, yet prayerfully wonder if our motives are right.

Nadine wanted a number of things, but she had to learn to reevaluate her motives and her reasons for wanting them.

As we live our lives, our own wishes and dreams change with our situation. Sometimes we get what we want and then wish we hadn't. Sometimes we don't and are glad we didn't. I think the important thing is to remember that God uses all the good and bad things in our lives to shape and mold us, if we are willing.

I hope you enjoyed reading about Clint and Nadine. If you have any comments, I would love to hear from you. Please write me c/o Steeple Hill/Love Inspired, 233 Broadway, Ste. 1001, New York, NY 10279.

Yours truly,

Carolyne Aarsen

A MOTHER AT HEART

I have swept away your offenses like a cloud,
your sins like the morning mist. Return to me,
for I have redeemed you.
—*Isaiah* 44:22

This book is for my in-laws, the Aarsen family, and the practical love they share with the many people who have passed through their homes.

Chapter One

Miriam yanked open the hood of her small, black sports car, glared down at the smoking engine, then sneezed as the harsh smell of leaking radiator fluid assaulted her nostrils.

She pushed back her short hair and dragged her hand down the back of her head, rolling her neck to ease the kink in it. She was tired, cranky and worn out. For the past few days she'd been putting in twelve hours behind the wheel to get here. It was just her ill luck to break down only three miles from her destination.

With a sigh, she looked around. All she saw were rolling hills, and copses of poplar and spruce trees broken by fields ready for spring planting. Fields she had ridden past for most of her life on her way to school. Fields where she had ridden her horse before spring planting and after combining.

The county of Waylen. Her old home.

She hadn't been back since that horrible day, ten years ago, when she had walked down these very roads, tears blurring her eyes as she headed toward the highway, her possessions thrown together in a knapsack slung over her shoulder. She had never known why leaving abruptly was called "running away." She had walked every dreary and heartsick step on that early summer morning, her boyfriend's words ringing in her ears. Jake didn't love her anymore.

Halfway to town her mother had caught up with her, and high drama was replaced by her mother's usual carping and nagging.

Miriam sneezed once more, yanked back to the present by the stark reality that there was still no vehicle in sight. She had no option but to start walking down a gravel road in sandals far more suited to paved city sidewalks.

She pulled out the keys to the car and threw her cell phone in her large handbag along with a bottle of water she always had on hand. She was thankful that her cotton pants were thin. If she got too warm, she could put the cardigan she wore into the bag and risk sunburning her shoulders. She just wished she had a hat.

Shouldering her bag, she took a deep breath and started walking down the road. She pushed aside her irritation, reminding herself that she was on country time now. What would be would be, and fussing wouldn't change anything.

Besides, this was supposed to be a vacation. A time to catch her breath before she went back to try to save her business the only way she knew how.

Miriam pulled a face as she skirted a small puddle in the middle of the road. The idea of going back to the hurrying and waiting that characterized most of her modeling career held little appeal.

The sun shone down on her unprotected head, and not for the first time since she'd pointed her little car west did Miriam wonder why she hadn't sold her father's farm in western Alberta from the safety of New York.

As long as her mother had been alive the farm had remained unsold. It was where Edna had been born. Even after Edna had her stroke she made it quite clear the farm was not to be sold.

Now her mother was dead. Miriam needed the money to cover part of the debt she had amassed when a creditor defaulted on a large shipment. Her fledgling clothing company had been unable to absorb the huge loss.

Miriam had also fallen back on the one thing she knew. Modeling. She found a new agent. A good man and sincere Christian. Carl Hanson. It was Carl who had suggested this break. "Drive back to your farm," he said. "Don't sell it from here. Go back to your past. Catch your breath. Take a break from your trouble."

"If Carl could only see me now," she muttered, adjusting her bag on her shoulder.

She had gone only a quarter of a mile and her feet were already sore, when a sound behind her made her turn. But she saw nothing. Heat shimmered up from the gravel road, and below her the land flowed away.

Her eyes followed the brown hills, broken by groupings of poplar and spruce. The bare, lacy branches of the aspen trees held a hint of soft green that would be full when it was time for her to leave again.

Miriam eased out her breath, looked around. These rolling hills had occupied her mind many times, even in the most exotic of locales.

A yearning caught her unaware, reminding her of past events, still unresolved. Events that Carl knew occupied her mind. Events he had hinted that she should try to settle before she came back to a busy and time-consuming schedule.

Miriam stopped, her heart lifting at the sound of a vehicle coming.

She could hear it slow down by her car, then speed up again. A cloud of dust roiled behind it as it topped the rise.

The sun reflected off the glass of the cab so she couldn't see the driver. The truck skidded to a halt on the loose gravel, and the driver opened his door and got out.

She put on her most polite "I'm sorry to bother you" smile, as the man came closer and stopped in front of her, wiping his hands on his blue jeans, his white T-shirt already stained with grease and dirt.

Dark brown hair in need of a cut fell across his forehead. Heavily lashed brown eyes stared at her from beneath level brows. His full mouth was parted in a half smile. His strong jaw was dark with stubble.

Miriam acknowledged his good looks almost analytically. Her job as a model put her in the company of many good-looking men, but this man had an earthy appeal that spoke more strongly to her than did the clean, stylized looks she was used to. She was about to raise her hand to shake his when recognition dawned, and her stomach plunged.

Of all the people she would have to meet under these circumstances! Jake Steele. Next-door neighbor, one-time boyfriend and the man over whom she had shed a thousand tears.

She swallowed, her mouth suddenly dry, as she realized he didn't recognize her.

"I'm guessing that was your car parked back there. Do you need some help?" Jake said, his deep voice quiet. He looked down at her, his weight resting on one leg, his one thumb hooked on the belt loop of his jeans. The dusty white T-shirt and the faded jeans enhanced his masculine appeal. It wasn't lost on Miriam.

A girl can still lose herself in his eyes, she thought, remembering another time on this same road when she had done just that. When she and Jake had sat on the tailgate of his pickup, arms around each other, ignoring the moonlit landscape below them, lost in each other and the wonder of their love. A love Miriam had promised Jake would be his forever. A love he had quickly replaced—with her best friend.

What a fool she had been! Then came the anger. Again. She was surprised at its intensity, at the fact that after ten years she had any emotions to spare for this man. Taking a breath, she controlled herself. She hadn't come here to get even, just to find closure.

"My car broke down. I'm pretty sure it's the radiator. I was wondering if you could help me out."

Jake scratched his head, frowning, as if trying to place her. "Were you headed to my folks' place? There's no other place down this road."

Miriam swallowed down the unexpected hurt, readjusting her purse on her shoulder. "You don't know who I am, do you?"

Jake shrugged, the casual movement giving her a fresh pain. Once upon a time, years ago, she could have come up with some smart comment that would have made him smile, that would have eased away her own awkwardness. But life had been difficult the past few years, and laughter and joking didn't come as readily. Instead, she looked directly at him and simply said, "I'm Miriam."

She could tell from his expression the moment he finally recognized her. "Miriam Spencer?" he asked, his eyes narrowing.

Miriam made herself hold his gaze without blinking. "Not too many other Miriams around," she said, forcing herself to match his own even tone.

He nodded, his hands hanging loosely at his sides as he continued to look at her.

A soft spring breeze swirled around them, and the sharp trill of a red-tailed hawk shivered down. Anticipation hovered around them.

How many times had she relived this reunion in her mind? How many times had she imagined herself coming back, full of self-confidence, preferably on the arm of an equally self-confident and attractive man?

Miriam Spencer returning to the place of her humiliation.

"We've been hearing a lot about you," he finally said, his voice cool.

Miriam felt herself stiffen in reaction to his sudden reserve. She could see the condemnation in his eyes, feel the censure. She wondered which of the many false stories written about her in the tabloids he actually believed.

"I'm sure you have." She tilted her head, lifted her chin and held his gaze. "But you should know you can't believe everything you read." She turned to go, but Jake caught her by the arm, turning her back.

"I'm sorry," he said automatically, but she could see his apology lacked conviction. He was merely being polite. The way he always was. "Do you need a lift to your place?"

"That's okay. I don't want to put you out." Miriam shifted her bag, wishing she could just leave, but Jake still had his hand on her arm. Try as she might, she couldn't ignore the strength and warmth of it through her shirt. "And you can let go of my arm," she said, looking down pointedly.

Jake dropped his hand as if her arm were on fire. "Sorry," he muttered. Then he looked at her. "Look, it's a long walk back." He glanced down at the thin sandals on her feet, her loose-fitting linen pants that were already stained with dust from the road. "My truck is no limo, but it will get you to your place quicker than walking."

Miriam wished she could say no. She didn't want

his help. But a three-mile walk, on the sandals he had looked at so disdainfully, wasn't appealing. Accepting his offer was the mature thing to do. And that was part of the reason for this trip, wasn't it? To show herself that she had gotten past this part of her life?

So she nodded. "Thanks for the offer," she said, and she walked around to the passenger side of the truck.

He followed, saying nothing, and just as she was about to open the door, he reached past and did it for her.

Miriam glanced at him and nodded her thanks, then climbed up into the truck and settled on the seat.

Jake climbed in without saying a word, put the truck into gear, and they were off. A song blared from the radio, but Jake reached over and switched it off. Miriam wished he hadn't. The muted roar of the truck, the faint whiff of diesel mixed with dust that permeated the cab—both combined to bring back surprisingly sharp memories.

Memories of being scrunched awkwardly into a narrow tractor cab, riding along with Jake while he plowed, cultivated, seeded, sprayed, swathed or combined, singing along with songs on the radio, as they looked into each other's eyes. It didn't matter what job he had to do on his foster father's farm, she usually managed to finagle a ride with him.

Now, Miriam couldn't help but glance over at Jake. His dark hair still curled over the back of his collar, still invited a girl to run her hands through it.

Give your head a shake, Miriam chided herself,

sighing lightly. He's married, and even if he wasn't, you're not looking, remember?

She blamed her lapse on the surroundings. It was as if driving down these roads, seeing an endless sky, had immediately erased the past ten years in one quick swipe. It was as if being back here turned her from a woman, determined to keep her heart to herself, back into that young girl who gave it to the first boy she had been attracted to. Jake Steele.

Stick to the plan, she reminded herself. You're here to sell the farm, to put the past to rest. Then you go back east and keep struggling.

Miriam pushed the depressing thoughts aside and forced herself to ignore Jake, to look around. The road followed a ridge that cut alongside a hill rising above them on one side and flowing away from them on the other. Rock Lake was at the bottom of the hill, hidden by a large stand of spruce and aspen tinged with the pale green of new growth.

Ahead of them lay more fields, more bush, alternating shade and warmth as they drove along. Not much had changed since she left, she realized. The trees looked the same, the fields were the same.

It was like stepping back, and she shivered in reaction.

"Too cold?" Jake asked, finally speaking. He didn't wait for her answer but reached over to adjust the air-conditioning.

"Thanks." She fidgeted on the seat, the silence in the cab pressing down on her. "How's the weather been?" she blurted out, and then forced herself not to groan. What a cliché question. He would think she was a total airhead.

"Good."

"Seeding done?"

"Pretty much."

"How much land do you farm now?"

Jake shrugged. "About five quarters."

"Do you still have the cows?"

"Yup."

"How many?"

"One-hundred head. Just commercial."

"Wow. You and Fred have expanded."

Jake only nodded, and Miriam turned away in exasperation. He wasn't going to make this one bit easy for her. As if he had the right to be so taciturn.

Miriam wished she had never accepted his offer of a ride. Wished she had just started walking. Sore feet and overheating would have been preferable to this heavy atmosphere.

But she was a big girl now and determined to see this through. After all, he and Paula lived half a mile from her farm; she would be seeing them over the course of her stay. Better to try to get some of that first-time awkwardness out of the way before she met Paula, her old girlfriend—Jake's wife.

"So how is Paula?" she asked, pleased at the even tone in her voice. A tone that didn't betray the hurt that gripped her even now.

Jake's hands tightened on the steering wheel, and he threw her a quick glance, then looked away.

''You've really been out of touch, haven't you?'' he asked, his voice dangerously quiet.

Miriam almost pressed herself back against the seat at the anger in his voice. ''I don't understand what you're talking about,'' she said sharply. What right did he have to use that tone with her? He was the one who had gotten married barely four months after she left. She knew she had been out of touch, but what did she have to say to either him or her old girlfriend?

Jake stared straight ahead, his expression grim. ''Paula died three years ago.'' His words were clipped, his voice devoid of emotion.

Miriam stared at him, her hands numb, an icy cold gripping her temples as she tried to make sense of what he had said.

''What—Paula…dead?'' She struggled to find the right words, to find some meaning in his words. Why didn't she know this? How come no one had told her?

The questions dropped heavily, one after the other, piling up in her mind as she tried to get her thoughts around this horrible information.

''She rolled her car on a gravel road and wasn't wearing her seat belt. The doctor told us she died right away.'' Jake looked up again, his lips thin. ''I'm guessing this is a shock for you?''

Miriam shook her head, still struggling over what to ask, what to say, looking at him as if to find answers to the questions. ''I didn't know,'' she said weakly. She pulled her hand over her face and then bit her lip, as disbelief fled and sadness welled up. After all, Paula had been her friend, even though Miriam had not contacted her once she found out about Paula and Jake's marriage.

Miriam swallowed the sorrow, a belated sense of guilt washing over her. "I'm so sorry, Jake. This must be so hard for you." The words were inadequate, but protocol deemed they be spoken. "I'm sure it's been hard for Fred and Tilly, as well," Miriam continued quietly.

"Mom and Dad had a really hard time with it." His words were quietly spoken, and the silence of before settled once again between them.

"And how are Fred and Tilly?"

"Okay." Jake hesitated, as if to show her she didn't deserve to hear anything about his foster parents, the same people that had been second parents to Miriam, as well. "Dad had a heart attack a month ago. The doctor said he sustained a lot of damage so he's still pretty weak."

Miriam wanted to say that she was sorry. Again. How much apologizing was she going to be doing on this trip? she wondered. "Well, I hope he gets better."

"So do I," Jake said heavily.

In those three words Miriam could hear the love that she knew Jake held for his foster parents. Though he had moved to Fred and Tilly's place as a teenager, she knew that he had become like their own son.

Miriam swallowed again, staring straight ahead, battling the envy she felt. Jake, who once had nothing, now had everything—a family of his own, parents who loved him, a direction to his life.

Whereas she, who had once had it all...

The rest of the drive continued in silence, but now other emotions had been added to the mix, creating a tension in Miriam that built with each roll of the truck's wheels.

She was thankful when she saw Fred and Tilly's driveway, the same brightly painted horse-drawn plow at the end of it. Jake turned in.

"I'll just let Tilly and Fred know what's going on, and then I can bring you to your place," he said, his words breaking the long silence. "You may as well come in and say hello."

Miriam only nodded, clutching her purse as her own heart began to beat more quickly. It was a combination of nerves and fear and another kind of guilt at the thought of meeting Fred and Tilly again. She had spent many hours sitting at their kitchen table, had followed Fred around while he did his chores.

Miriam's father had died when she was ten and Edna had had to work. Saturdays had found Miriam either helping Tilly in the kitchen, or working alongside Fred—feeding cows, helping with the calves or helping with any of the myriad repairs required on the farm. The Prins's home became her second home, a haven from Edna's constant criticism and "big plans" for her daughter.

Miriam had had no big plans. All she had ever wanted was to stay in Waylen. When she was fourteen a social worker had brought Jake to Fred and Tilly's, and her plans changed to include marrying Jake.

When she first saw the dangerously good-looking teenager, she knew in her heart that she loved only him. Her mother, of course, made sure Miriam knew *her* opinion. "A foster child from who knows where." Miriam could still hear her mother. "You stay away from him, Miriam. Boy like him is nothing but trouble," Edna had said, contempt ringing in her voice.

Miriam had laughed at the notion. A girl who had been teased most of her school years for being skinny could hardly net the attention of someone like Jake.

But to her amazement, she had. Even Paula—beautiful, blond and curvaceous Paula—could hardly believe that Jake would prefer Miriam to her.

But he had. At least at first, Miriam reminded herself.

Miriam closed her eyes at a sudden surge of pain and sorrow. Paula, her one-time friend. Dead. She could hardly bear thinking about it.

Jake parked the truck and, without giving Miriam a second glance, got out. Miriam swallowed, rubbing her damp hands over her pants. What would she say to Fred, to Tilly? she thought, hesitating. Too much time had elapsed, and she had done nothing to bridge that gap.

Well, she was here now. She had to start this homecoming sooner or later. She slung her bag over her shoulder and climbed out of the truck.

"Thanks for the ride, and the help," she said to Jake, lifting her head to look confidently up at him.

"You're welcome."

He stood back, allowing her to go first. The yard was still muddy and wet in places, and Miriam had to pick her way across. Jake stayed beside her, probably to make sure she didn't fall, she thought wryly.

They had just made it to the cement sidewalk by the house when the door burst open.

"Daddy, Daddy, you're home." A little girl, her braids flying out behind her, came running up to Jake and launched herself at him. Miriam felt a lump in her throat.

A little girl. Jake had a little girl.

Jake caught the girl, swung her around. For the first time since Miriam had seen him, she noticed a heartfelt and sincere smile on his face.

"Hey, Pipper," he said, hugging his daughter tightly. He straightened, holding the little girl on one arm. Her arms were wrapped around his neck, and as they turned to Miriam, she felt a harsh clutch of jealousy. She could see Jake in the deep brown of the little girl's eyes, Jake in the thick waves of her hair—but Paula in the coy smile.

"Hi," the girl said. "My name is Taryn. What's yours?"

"This is Miriam," Jake interjected, settling Taryn on his arm. "Her car broke down on the road, and I gave her a ride here."

Taryn nodded, staring at Miriam as if studying her. "Has she been here before?"

"No, Pipper, she hasn't." Jake turned to Miriam. "Why don't you come in a minute? I'm sure Mom and Dad would like to see you."

Miriam nodded, feeling very much the outsider.

Taryn continued to stare at her, and Miriam couldn't keep her eyes off Jake's daughter.

She looked so much like her father, it made her heart hurt.

Miriam followed Jake up the walk, suddenly hesitant at the thought of meeting Tilly and Fred again. Guilt and shame vied with one another as her steps followed the old familiar pathway. She had skipped up this walk as a young girl, she had run up it as a teenager. She had always come here with a happy heart, the feeling that someone who cared for her lived here. This had been a home.

Jake pushed the screen door open and set Taryn down on the floor. "Take your socks off, missy," he said. "They're all dirty."

Taryn dropped down, and, lifting her foot, yanked off the once-white sock. "I was waiting for you," she said, grinning up at him. "You didn't have supper."

Miriam dropped her bag on the chair that had always been there, without even realizing what she was doing. She had to catch herself before she kicked off her sandals and ran past Jake up the steps to sit at the kitchen table. This porch was so familiar.

But the presence of a much older Jake and his daughter showed her all too clearly how much had changed.

Taryn got up, still looking at Miriam with a puzzled expression. "Did you know my mommy?" she asked.

Jake turned to his daughter, his surprise evident. "What did you say?" he asked her.

Taryn turned to him, still frowning. "I saw her picture in my mommy's book."

"What book?"

"The one with that Miriam lady's pictures in it."

"Is that you, Jake?" Tilly called from the kitchen, interrupting the moment. She came to the door, wiping her hands on a towel, smiling at her son. "How was your day, dear?"

Miriam felt her throat tighten at the sight of Tilly. The woman's face held a few more lines; her short, straight hair was now completely gray. But she wore the same glasses she had worn ten years ago, and the soft blue eyes were the same, the smile still welcoming.

"Good," Jake said succinctly. "I brought someone back." He stepped aside, gesturing toward Miriam.

Tilly lifted her hand up to readjust her glasses, and she squinted at Miriam, who tried not to fidget. "My goodness," Tilly said as she recognized who it was, her lined face breaking out into a large smile, her arms opening. "Miriam? Little Miriam Spencer?"

Tilly walked past Jake straight to Miriam, and enfolded her in a warm embrace. Miriam inhaled the familiar scent of Tilly's perfume, pressed her cheek against the well-known softness of Tilly's cheek. She swallowed a knot of sadness mixed with nostalgia. She had missed this, she thought, this enveloping affection that welcomed you back, that showed you were missed.

She hadn't felt a mother's arms around her since she had left this place, her home.

Miriam squeezed her eyes against the sudden pain as more memories returned, and hugged Tilly as tightly as she dared.

"Oh, little girl, we sure missed you. We did." Tilly rocked her lightly then pulled away, unabashedly wiping her eyes. "Look at you now. What a beautiful girl you've turned out to be." Tilly shook her head and reached up to wipe tears from her eyes. "You're so tall. So old."

Miriam blinked her own tears away, far too conscious of Jake watching them. It shouldn't have mattered, but she felt his disapproval as strongly as she felt Tilly's love.

She knew she had been in the wrong, keeping herself from this dear person. This dear second mother who had dried her tears and hugged her even more than her own mother had.

Miriam felt ashamed. She had known this was going to be a difficult trip. She just hadn't counted on the guilt that would come with it.

Chapter Two

"You smell like dirt, Daddy."

Jake smiled down at his daughter as he washed his hands, then bent over at the waist to wash his face and neck. "I was working in lots of dirt, sweetheart," he said, drying off. "I was working on the tractor."

"Your hair is dirty, too."

Jake glanced at his reflection in the mirror, shoving his hands through his thick wavy hair. It needed to be cut. He paused, looking at himself critically, trying to see himself through Miriam's eyes. Then he wondered why he should care.

Miriam Spencer. He drew a deep, tired breath, wishing away the jolt he had felt when he had first realized the identity of the very elegant woman standing on the side of the road. Now she sat in his kitchen, chatting to Tilly and Fred, who, even though she hadn't even bothered sending them so much as a postcard, were delighted to see her.

He felt like the prodigal son in the parable. He should be glad she was back, but he just wished he knew why she had come. He doubted it was to settle on the farm to raise wheat and barley. Miriam wasn't a country girl any longer. And it wasn't hard to see. Though her clothes were casual, they had an elegance that quietly stated their cost.

High.

He remembered the first time he had seen the new Miriam. Paula had shown him a fashion magazine, and Miriam was on the front—her tip-tilted eyes gleaming with gold eyeshadow, her full mouth glistening with coral lipstick. Her once unruly hair cropped and artfully tousled. Neither that person, nor the casually elegant girl now sitting in his kitchen were the Miriam he knew.

They weren't the Miriam who would sometimes wear a T-shirt backwards, who wouldn't care if her jeans were ripped or patched.

The Miriam he had once loved.

"What's the matter, Daddy? You look sad."

Jake pulled himself back to the present, and, squatting down, put himself level with his daughter. "I'm just tired, Pip. And hungry for some of Grandma's supper."

"That sure is a pretty lady that is here," she said solemnly, her hands on her father's shoulders.

Jake remembered a comment Taryn had made while they were standing on the porch. "What did you mean when you said you saw that lady's picture in Mommy's book? What book?"

"Mommy's book. You know." Taryn shook her head at her father's obtuseness. "Me and Grandma found it in the attic."

"Well, you'll have to show me the book when I tuck you in." He was curious, but knew it would have to wait.

Jake gave her a quick hug, and, holding her tiny hand, walked back down the hallway.

"Your supper is on the table, son." Tilly smiled at Jake as he sat. "Taryn, you should run and get your pajamas on. It's getting late."

Taryn dropped her head, her fingers fiddling restlessly with each other, her lip beginning to curl in a classic pout. "But I wanna talk to the lady," she mumbled, lifting her eyes briefly to her father.

Jake frowned at his daughter. She got the unspoken command, and, sighing, turned and left.

Miriam was already ensconced on the bench against the wall, a cup of tea in front of her. Fred sat beside her, bringing Miriam up to date on what had happened in Waylen while she'd been gone.

"Here you go, son." Tilly set a plate of warmed-up food in front of him—fried chicken, creamed peas, mashed potatoes, and applesauce on the side. His mouth watered at the sight. "And here are your messages." Tilly set an assortment of papers in front of him with scribbled names and numbers. "I should charge you secretarial fees," Tilly joked. "Melissa Toews phoned three times. Said it was important."

Jake stifled a groan. Melissa could never be accused

of being coy, he thought, flipping through the messages.

"Do you want the cordless phone?" Fred asked, reaching behind him to take the phone off the cradle.

"I don't feel like phoning anyone tonight." Jake set the papers aside. He often took care of his business during supper, but tonight he didn't feel like it. All of them could wait. Especially Melissa.

"Are you sure you don't want any supper, Miriam?" Tilly asked her, setting a cup of coffee in front of Jake.

"I'm fine, thanks." Miriam smiled gently at Tilly and rested her elbows on the table, avoiding Jake's look. "This kitchen looks the same as I remember it."

He wondered why she had come. Then, pushing aside his own thoughts, he bowed his head in prayer. He pulled in a slow breath, willing the negative thoughts away. He slowly let himself be open to God, thanking him for the food, for the day. He paused a moment, his thoughts turning to the girl sitting at the same table, and he sent up a prayer for Miriam, as well.

Praying for her put everything into perspective. Praying for her changed her from an old girlfriend whom he had often thought about to just a person from his past. And as he prayed for her, he felt peace.

He opened his eyes and unconsciously sought her out. She was watching him, her soft brown eyes full of a sorrow he hadn't seen there before. But with a blink of her long eyelashes, it was gone.

"And how is your mother?" Tilly asked, leaning

forward. "We haven't heard from her, either, since both of you left."

Jake stopped chewing, his own curiosity piqued by Tilly's straightforward, but softly spoken question.

Miriam looked down, running her finger along the handle of the earthenware mug in front of her. "She died six months ago in Toronto. She'd had a stroke and was just getting worse. I think death was a relief for her." Jake felt sudden empathy. He had never cared for Miriam's mother, but he knew that Miriam had loved her. He wanted to catch Miriam's gaze, to tell her he understood, but after his barely restrained hostility toward her in his truck, he felt he had no right.

"Oh, dear." Tilly reached across the table and caught Miriam's hand in her own. "I'm sorry to hear that. We never heard a thing…" Tilly let the sentence trail off. She paused, then asked, "How are you doing with it?"

Miriam reached up and carefully wiped her eyes. "It's still hard, but I think she was glad to go."

Jake heard the hint of sorrow in her voice and wondered who had comforted her when it happened. Was there someone important to her who had been with her? She was only twenty-seven years old. Old enough to be independent, yet quite young to be without either parent.

"So now you're here for a visit?"

Miriam nodded again. "I'm only here for a while, but it's nice to be back."

"And now your car is broken down." Tilly shook

her head, clucking sympathetically. "Well, don't you worry. Fred and Jake will make sure it gets fixed."

"What are you going to do about Miriam's car?" Fred asked, looking up from his paper.

"It's okay where it is right now," Jake said, pushing his potatoes around on his plate. "Tomorrow we can tow it into town and bring it to Denny's Auto Parts. All it needs is a new radiator, I'm assuming."

"It was leaking already in Winnipeg," Miriam said quietly. "I think all they did was put some stop-leak stuff in it."

"Do you want me to take care of it, Jake?" Fred offered.

Jake shook his head. "You're finally out of bed. I don't think you should overdo it."

"But you'll fall behind in the field work," Fred said. "You won't have time to run around."

"Look, I can call a tow truck," Miriam interrupted. "I don't want to put anyone out."

"It's not a problem," Jake said, trying to sound nonchalant. Actually it *was* a problem. He was nicely on top of the field work, and taking Miriam's car to the garage would use up a good half day. He didn't really have the time, but knew it would look churlish not to help. People called a tow truck in the city, not in the country.

He just prayed that everything would work out.

Miriam tried once more to protest, but Fred insisted that it would be no problem.

"Do you want any dessert?" Tilly asked, when Jake was done.

"No thanks, Mom. I'm full." He smiled up at her. "It was delicious, though."

Tilly stroked his hair the way she always did, and for a moment Jake was conscious of Miriam's deep brown eyes watching them. He felt a little foolish. Not too many twenty-seven-year-old men had mothers who still stroked their hair. But he had never protested, not even as a young man.

Whenever his brother Simon would come for a visit from the stricter home he'd been placed in, Tilly naturally treated him exactly like Jake. Like they were both Fred and Tilly's own sons. Neither he nor Simon had received much of a mother's love growing up. Their natural mother had given them up when he was five and Simon four after their biological father had died. They never did find out where she was, although Simon was now actively looking. Simon had been looking most of his life. He had run away from his last foster home at sixteen and wanted Jake to come. But Jake knew he was in a good place with Fred and Tilly and refused to go. Simon said that Jake would never hear from him again.

And Jake hadn't. Until five months ago when Jake got a phone call from a nurse named Caitlin Severn who had Simon as a patient.

Jake had overcome his own wounded pride at Simon's silence and traveled to Vancouver to see him. Now Simon was happily married. But he still wanted to find their mother.

Jake wasn't as interested. Each time he saw Taryn, he wondered anew how his mother could give up her own children and not even leave them with a name to track down. It was as if she wanted them swept out of her life.

"Hi, Daddy. Here I am." Taryn stood in front of him, her face shiny from washing, her hair still damp. She twirled around in her new, frilly nightgown, the ruffle on the bottom dragging on the floor.

"You look beautiful," Jake said, pulling her on his lap, tucking her under his chin.

"Not as beautiful as her—" Taryn pointed to Miriam with a giggle. Jake couldn't help but look at Miriam, who was now gazing wistfully at Taryn. He didn't acknowledge Taryn's comment—at least not out loud. And as he watched the play of emotions on Miriam's face, he wondered if she had any regrets. If the fame and fortune she had acquired satisfied her.

He turned back to his daughter, his heart full of gratitude, thankful that in spite of how things had turned out, he had this precious child.

"So, Pip, it's bedtime," he said quietly. "Kiss Grandpa and Grandma good-night, and I'll tuck you in."

"Okay," she said, lifting her shoulders in an exaggerated sigh. She slipped off his lap and walked around the table to kiss Tilly and then Fred.

For a moment Jake was afraid she was going to give Miriam a kiss, but shyness won out. Instead, Taryn just waggled her fingers at Miriam.

"Good night, Taryn. Sweet dreams," Miriam said softly, waving back.

"Okay," Taryn said with a smile. Then she turned

and flounced off through the hallways, toward the stairs, Jake right behind.

When Paula and Jake had first married, they had lived in a mobile home on the property. However, after Paula had died, Jake had brought Taryn here so often that she'd ended up getting her own room. Eventually Jake had started eating supper here, and soon the mobile home had been sold.

Now they all lived here in a house that was getting too big for Tilly to clean. But she refused to move to a smaller house in town, and Jake had to admit that it worked better for him, as well.

At the bottom of the stairs, Taryn stopped, holding up her arms for the first step in their bedtime routine.

He loved this house, he mused as he walked slowly up the broad stairs holding his little girl. As a foster child, he'd been blessed to end up here, and he knew it.

Though his mother had given Simon and Jake up, he was always thankful that they had been adopted by a single man, Tom Steele. He had given them a safe and secure home for seven years. His death had been a severe blow, and Jake knew that the loss of Tom tended to make him overprotective of Fred. He didn't want to lose another father.

"Stop, Daddy. I want to see the pictures."

Jake smiled and did as his daughter commanded. The Prins had a veritable gallery on the wall, and Taryn always had to stop. Jake didn't mind. He was so thankful for the legacy his daughter received through Fred and Tilly that it was doubly important to him that she knew where she came from. His vague memories of his mother didn't include a father, let alone grandparents. At times he still resented that, but realized that in Tom Steele, and later in Fred and Tilly, God had made up the lack.

"There's my mommy." Taryn leaned forward, pointing out their wedding picture. Taryn always lingered the longest here, even though she barely remembered Paula. Taryn had been only two when Paula died, and unaware of the circumstances surrounding her mother's death. Paula had been an inattentive mother at best, and hadn't spent a lot of time at home. Jake often regretted his marriage, but he had never, ever regretted Taryn.

"And this is Uncle Simon and Aunty Caitlin—" Taryn pointed with a pudgy finger to a smiling couple, their arms around each other. The picture had been taken outside against a backdrop of trees. The filtered sun highlighted their features and only seemed to enhance the love that radiated from them.

"When I get bigger—" Taryn stopped as her mouth stretched open in a big yawn "—I want to be a nurse, just like Aunty Caitlin, and help her in her hospital in Na...Nomimo," she continued, snuggling into her father's neck.

"Nanaimo," Jake corrected, giving his daughter a tight hug. "That's a good thing to be, sweetie. But if you don't get your sleep, you won't grow, and then you can't be a nurse." He jogged up the stairs to miss the rest of the pictures, aware of his daughter's penchant for dawdling. And tonight he didn't feel like indulging her. Much as he disliked to acknowledge it, he wanted to be downstairs with Miriam.

A night-light shed a soft glow over Taryn's room. Jake lay Taryn down on her bed, careful not to disturb the row of stuffed animals that sat along the side, next to the wall. He tucked her in and sat beside her, his arms on either side of her shoulders.

Taryn smiled up at her father, and a wave of pure, sweet love washed over Jake. He bent over and gave her another quick kiss. "Time for your prayers."

"We have to pray for Grandpa, don't we?" Taryn said, her soft hazel eyes shining up at him in the muted light.

"Yes, we want him to stay healthy, don't we?"

"Should we pray for Miriam?"

Jake felt his heart skip at her name. He took a quick breath, frowning down at his daughter. "What did you say?"

"I *asked*," Taryn began, putting emphasis on the last word as if to show Jake that he was being particularly obtuse, "if I should pray for Miriam."

"You barely know her. Which reminds me, what about this book you were talking about?"

Taryn sat up like a shot and, shifting around, pulled a worn scrapbook from under her pillow. She handed it to him.

"It has pictures of you in it." Taryn smiled, eager for the reprieve from sleep. "And pictures of my Mommy and pictures of the pretty lady. Miriam. I'll show you." Taryn reached for the book, and, reluctantly, Jake gave it back. He didn't like the idea of

Taryn living in the past, creating fantasies about Paula. But he also knew that it wasn't fair to take what little she had away.

Taryn flipped quickly through the pages of pictures from high school—a few of them of Jake—then she stopped and tilted the book in his direction. Jake felt his heart stop as he looked directly at a picture of Miriam.

In the picture she wore a mauve silk dress held up with narrow, jeweled straps. Diamonds sparkled at her neck, her ears, her fingers, all discreetly proclaiming money. Her mouth was quirked in what he knew was her cynical smile, her head tilted back as if she were laughing at some private joke. Her dark hair framed her face, short tendrils accenting her high cheekbones, the exotic tilt of her eyes. A slickly dressed man wearing a tuxedo stood beside her, his arm resting in a proprietary manner on her shoulder.

"Why did Mommy have pictures of Miriam in her book?"

Jake blinked, pulling himself back to the present. "She used to be your mommy's best friend," Jake murmured, turning the page to find yet another color picture of Miriam. It was a makeup advertisement. Miriam's face took up the whole page, her head angled slightly downward, her eyes glancing up, her shining mouth holding the hint of a smile. Jake swallowed as he stared at the picture. It was Miriam, and yet not. How many times had he seen that look on her face— across a classroom, in the hallways of school; whenever she would tease him, flirt with him?

"I want to show Miriam the pictures, okay?" Taryn gathered up the book and made to jump out of bed, but Jake stopped her.

"No," he said firmly, taking the book away from her and setting it on the bedside table. "I'm sure Miriam has seen these pictures herself. And you need to sleep." He pulled the blankets up around her and tucked her in. She said her prayers, and Jake said them with her.

Each evening he thanked God for the precious gift entrusted to him. And as he did most evenings, he promised he would do everything he could to make sure she would have a home as secure and loving as the one he had received through Fred and Tilly.

"...and be with Miriam, my mommy's friend." Jake felt a start at the sound of Taryn speaking Miriam's name, but he said nothing, not wanting to draw any more attention to Miriam.

He waited until she was done, then bent over and kissed her gently. He paused at the door to look once more, closed it behind her and went downstairs to face Miriam.

He heard them laughing, and stopped just behind the door, listening, remembering other times.

Like the first time he had seen Miriam.

He had been sitting on Fred and Tilly's picnic table, staring out at the view below—a young boy of fourteen, a foster child being brought to his third foster home in as many years and recently separated from his brother Simon. The social worker had been inside the house, talking to Fred and Tilly. He hadn't wanted to hear what she had to say.

So he had stayed outside, appreciating the flow of the land that stretched out below him, yet wondering how he was going to survive in a house with only two old people for company.

Then a skinny girl had ridden up on her horse and jumped off. She'd tied it to a post by the back gate and boldly walked up to him, retying the shoelace that held her ponytail in place. She'd asked who he was and what he was doing sitting at Uncle Fred and Aunt Tilly's picnic table.

When he ignored her, she just shrugged and waltzed on into the house, like she lived there. She came out a few minutes later and sat beside him on the table. She said nothing, this time. Just sat there.

Together they watched the sun going down, felt the soft chill that accompanied the fall evenings drifting onto the yard.

The social worker came out later, accompanied by Fred and Tilly. She stopped in her tracks when she saw Miriam, and spun around, asking Fred and Tilly who she was.

"Just the neighbor girl," they said. "She comes over a lot."

The social worker nodded and then stopped by Jake. Laying her hand on his shoulder, she bent down to his height—an older woman talking to an angry, young man. "This is a good place, Jake. Don't wreck things for yourself."

Jake had ignored her, staring past her at the setting

sun. Social workers were always full of advice and, as far as he was concerned, misconceptions. The fact that he had been in so many homes had more to do with Simon's constant running away than with his behavior. But he didn't want to get into that. It hurt to think of Simon. It was the first time they had been separated. So he only nodded and said nothing, wondering where his brother had ended up and when he would see him again. He knew it was a waste of time to ask the social worker. She would give him some vague answer about waiting to see if they settled in. Then she left.

Fred and Tilly went back to the house.

To his surprise and dismay, Miriam stayed beside him. He had wanted to be alone, but she wouldn't leave. After a while, though, it didn't matter as much. She had been pretty quiet.

Tilly brought them a glass of orange juice and then walked back into the house.

Miriam turned to him and started talking. He had known her silence was too good to be true. She asked questions, the basic ones—What's your name? How old are you? Where did you live before?

His replies were terse. He had answered enough questions before this placement to add twenty more pages to his already thick file. Everyone knew everything about him, so the trick was to hold back as much as he could for as long as he could.

Miriam chatted about the school, the town, Tilly and Fred. She said nothing about her own mother. In fact, at first he thought she didn't even have a mother.

Miriam came to Fred and Tilly's often. She sought

him out at school, introduced him to her many friends.
They spent a lot of time together. She had an easy
way with people, a self-deprecating wit and a love of
life that he found compelling and infectious.

He ended up falling desperately in love with her.
And she with him.

Miriam had filled the empty spaces that life had
carved out of him. Her unconditional love had shown
him that there were things worth making sacrifices for.
For the first time in years he had opened himself up
to another person, had made himself vulnerable. He
had trusted her.

She talked easily about her faith, and shared that
with Jake. They spent hours just talking, being together, sharing dreams and plans. Jake often felt unworthy of her.

Miriam often spoke of her mother and how important it was that they keep their relationship a secret.
And they did. Jake knew what he was: a foster child
with an uncertain future.

But they had plans. When they turned eighteen, they
would be adults, independent. They would declare
their love to the world, and then leave Waylen.

The longer Jake stayed at Fred and Tilly's, however,
the less he wanted to do that. While Miriam showed
him that pure love can exist between two people, Fred
and Tilly showed him the love of parents. They gave
him a home. Jake didn't want to leave anymore. He
talked of staying in Waylen, of getting a job in town.

Miriam grew frightened. Jake *had* to come with her.

She was counting on him to help her get away from her mother.

It hurt to think of what they had once had. To realize that the elegant woman who was chatting in his kitchen was even further removed from him now than she was then. So much had changed in each of their lives.

He stepped into the kitchen. Fred was describing an incident he had had with a bull, many years ago.

"...And Tilly thinks I'm waving to her to come closer, and she comes roaring up with the truck and scares the bull. He takes off past me down the road and with him went all the plans for the day. We finally got him corralled at midnight." Miriam had her hand over her mouth; her eyes sparkled and her shoulders shook in time to her chuckles.

Jake stopped, unable to look away.

This was the Miriam he had fallen in love with. *This* was the Miriam he had promised he would stay with forever. Not that overly made-up woman with the fake smile whom he had just seen in the photo. Not the defensive woman who had sat with him in the truck all the way here.

Then she glanced sidelong, her hand slowly dropped and her gaze skittered away.

He felt as if he had broken the moment.

"Taryn safely in bed?" Tilly asked, smiling up at him.

Jake nodded and sat at the table, suddenly feeling like the odd man out. He tried not to look at the clock, but couldn't help it.

Miriam caught him looking; she carefully put her spoon back in her coffee cup and folded the napkin Tilly had given her. Preparations for leaving.

"What's the rush, girl?" Fred asked, as Miriam eased herself from behind the table.

"I should go. It's been a long day of driving," she said quietly, picking up her mug. She brought it to the kitchen sink and set it down with a muted *clink*.

"Are we going to see you again?" Tilly asked as she got up herself.

Miriam turned to face Tilly and nodded. "Of course. Once I get my car fixed, that is."

"Oh, nonsense. I can come over." Tilly stopped, glancing at Jake, then back to Miriam. "What about your house? Is there any food there?"

"I bought some groceries, but unfortunately they're still in my car—"

"Don't be silly, girl, I'll give you some," Tilly interjected.

Miriam hesitated, and Jake sensed she was in a dilemma. Either she accepted charity from Tilly, or she put him out by asking him to return to her car.

"Did you have a suitcase?" he asked her, feeling foolish that he had never thought of that when he picked her up.

"It's in my car," she said, lifting her head.

"Well, it's not far down the road. I'll drive you back and you can get your other stuff."

"Thank you," she said with a gracious tilt of her head. She turned back to Tilly. "Thanks for tea." She stopped as if she couldn't say anything more.

Tilly walked over and gave Miriam another hug. "It's such a treat to see you again," she said, pulling back, cupping Miriam's young face with her old, lined hands. "I'm so glad you decided to come back."

Fred, too, walked over and gave her a hug. But Jake could see that even that small movement tired him out.

Miriam had noticed it, too. Her eyes were full of concern. "You make sure you get enough rest," she said to Fred, holding his hand between hers.

"You sound just like Tilly," he said with a shake of his head. "I'll be fine." He reached up and stroked her cheek, much the way Tilly had done to Jake.

In that moment Jake realized that, in spite of a ten-year absence, Miriam shared something special with Fred and Tilly. And for a moment he was envious.

Chapter Three

"So," Jake said vaguely as he spun the steering wheel. "What really brings you back here?"

His truck was halfway down the driveway before he asked the question Miriam knew had been burning inside of him. Miriam waited a beat, as if to establish some sort of conversational control. "I came back to sell my farm."

Jake's head snapped around and he stared at her, then looked quickly away. "This is a surprise."

Miriam didn't doubt it. Fred and Jake had rented it all these years. But all their dealings had been at arm's length through a lawyer Miriam hired to take care of her and her mother's business.

"I don't know if you're interested in buying it. I'm willing to offer you and Fred right of first refusal."

Jake blew out his breath and laughed shortly. "I would be. In a few years. Unfortunately, I can't afford to buy it now. Financially I'm stretched as far as I can go.''

Miriam felt a stab of dismay. She had hoped he would buy it, had hoped he could keep farming it, that somehow something that had once belonged to her would now belong to him, creating a vague kind of connection. Though she wasn't sure why. ''That's too bad,'' she said, threading her fingers together in her lap.

''At least we agree on that.'' His words were clipped, and once again Miriam sensed his anger.

But she was too tired to say anything back.

''What happens once you sell the farm?'' Jake continued.

Miriam took a slow breath, willing away her fatigue. She had walked down catwalks in Milan, had modeled famous designers' fashions with aplomb and self-confidence. Surely she could handle a farmer who needed a shave. ''I go back east and put Waylen behind me.''

Gravel rattled against the undercarriage as they drove down the road, the oppressive silence of two people unwilling to talk to each other filling the cab.

She was thankful that it was a short trip to the car. As Jake pulled up beside it, Miriam got the keys out of her purse. She climbed out of the truck and unlocked the car's trunk.

Jake was beside her, and reached in and wordlessly pulled out her suitcase. Miriam took out a small cosmetics bag and closed the trunk.

''This is it?''

Miriam nodded and walked around the car.

"You travel pretty light."

"I've made enough airline connections with my clothes headed off to Istanbul while I was going to New York. I've learned to take everything I need with me." Miriam juggled the grocery bags in one hand while she locked the door with the other.

"I don't think this car is going anywhere," Jake said suddenly.

Miriam frowned up at him. "What do you mean?"

"This is a dead-end road. You hardly need to lock the car."

Miriam tried not to smile, but couldn't help it. It did look silly to lock up a crippled car on a deserted road. "City habits, I guess," she said, chancing a glance up at him.

Mistake. He was smiling now, his features relaxed. He looked devastating.

She forced herself to look away. "Well, that should do it." Miriam straightened her shoulders and dropped her groceries in the back of Jake's pickup, frustrated at how quickly the old feelings she had had for him returned. It was as if she had never been gone. As if she had never spent time with any man other than this tall farmer of few words.

"You might want to put your suitcase in the front. I hauled feed with this truck the other day."

"A little extra oats and soy never hurt a girl," she said quickly.

Jake dropped the suitcase in the box. When he

glanced up at her, he smiled again, and Miriam's heart tripped.

Silly girl, she castigated herself. *You're wasting your time on this one.* She got in the truck, slammed the door and buckled up. The trip back to her house was as quiet as the trip to her car had been.

Dusk was gathering by the time they drove down the driveway. Miriam had so hoped to see the place in the light. But as they pulled into the yard, she caught darkened glimpses of overgrown grass, tangled shrubs and flower gardens full of weeds.

"My mother and I paid someone to keep this place up. What happened?"

"Velma Rogers? She only took care of the inside of the house. Said she wasn't paid for more. We tried to keep the outside fixed up, but we didn't have time," Jake said, his voice brusque. "We did check on the house every few months, just to make sure everything was still working. Your mother must have had the lawyer we paid to rent the land taking care of the power and gas bills."

Miriam nodded, then slowly got out of the truck, looked around. It was unkept enough in the half-light; she didn't know if she wanted to see it in the sunshine.

"Thanks for driving me here," she said, turning. Waves of exhaustion made her legs wobble. She clung to the open truck door. "Don't worry about the car. I can call a tow truck."

"That's okay," he said, turning and getting out of the truck. He pulled her suitcases out of the back. "I'll come by tomorrow, and you can help me bring it into town."

"No, really, I know how busy this time of the year is. I know the last thing you need to do is cart me around. Please." She felt a moment's warmth kindle in her heart at his thoughtfulness.

"And how are you going to call a tow truck?" Jake asked as he walked around the front of the truck. "The telephone doesn't work."

"I have a cell phone."

Jake nodded. "Of course." He strode ahead of her to the back door and stood aside so she could open it.

The sound of the door opening echoed hollowly through the house, and Miriam felt a wave of nostalgia. It was so familiar, so much a part of her youth. How many times had she opened this very door and come running in to throw her books down on the porch floor, asking if there was anything to eat?

Miriam flicked the switch by the back door, and light flooded the porch. There was a faint musty smell.

Miriam walked up the three steps into the kitchen, stifling a cry of dismay. All the furniture was draped with white sheets; pictures had been taken off the wall and stacked in corners of the room. It all looked desolate and distinctly un-homey.

Jake walked over to the taps and turned them. "Water's still okay, although you might want to drain the hot water out of the tank. I'm sure it's pretty stale. We did it at Eastertime, but that's the last time I went through this place. Velma had asked me to go over everything this fall again."

"Thanks, Jake. I'll do that." Her head was starting to buzz, and she wanted nothing more than to have a nice warm shower and crawl into bed. One look around the house, though, told her she had other things to do first.

"Do you want some help…" Jake let the sentence trail off.

"No, thanks. I'll be fine." She yearned for some time to herself, some time to gather her scattered thoughts. She wanted him gone. She wanted this cold formality between them to end, and it would only happen when he left.

Jake nodded, his one hand caught in the back pocket of his blue jeans. "I'll just walk through the house once, just to make sure everything's okay. Where do you want your suitcase?"

"Just leave it here, please."

The sound of his boots thumping through the house was muffled by the cloths draping all the furniture. Shivering, Miriam walked through the kitchen into the darkened living room, hugging herself against the chill of the house. The room here had a feeling of waiting.

With a muted rumble, the furnace started up.

Jake returned and paused in the arched doorway between the kitchen and the living room, looking around. "Well, I'll be going. Are you sure you're going to be all right?"

Miriam turned to him, nodding. "Thanks for everything. I'm sorry to be such a pain…" She let the sentence drift off as their eyes met.

The backlight from the kitchen silhouetted him, and

she couldn't help but acknowledge his appeal. He was taller, broader. Not the young man she had left behind, but a man who had had his own experiences. He had buried a wife, and now had a child, ran a farm and took care of parents that looked so much older to Miriam than they had when she left. He was a stranger to her. A stranger with his own heartaches and his own responsibilities.

"I'll be by sometime tomorrow to bring your car into town." Jake scratched his head as if he wanted to say more. Then with a shrug, he turned and left.

Miriam walked to the window of the darkened room and watched through the large picture window as Jake started his truck, the headlights stabbing the darkness.

She lay her head against the cold glass, letting the emotions of the day flow over her. Then, against her will, she felt tears gather. She didn't know precisely what she cried for; she only knew that she had felt a deep sadness closing in on her since she'd first seen Jake, then Fred and Tilly. All the memories of her mother's death returned, hard and fast. Telling the Prins had been like reliving that stark moment when she'd felt her mother's hand go limp in her own.

Once again she replayed those moments after the funeral, when all the temporary supports—the nursing home staff, the undertaker, the minister who performed the service—had slowly fallen away, and she'd realized she was all alone.

She had no one who cared. No one who mattered. The men she had met treated her like a trophy to be won and shown. Other men treated her like a commodity—a model, a face to sell their product.

There had been only one man in her life. Ever.

She felt another wave of sorrow thinking about Jake and his daughter. A daughter borne by her best friend.

She cried for the loss of the dreams that both she and Jake had spun during those innocent long-ago evenings, and for the lives that reality had changed.

The window was cool and soothing against her hot forehead, and slowly the tears subsided. They always did. And as always, reality returned. She had much to do if she wanted to sleep here tonight.

Jake turned into Miriam's driveway, the entrance of which was barely visible in the driving rain, unable to stop a gentle lift of his heart at the thought of seeing her again.

Yesterday, the surprise of her sudden reappearance after ten years had put him on the defensive.

And no wonder. She had kept herself away from people who cared about her, himself included, he reminded himself as his truck bounced through a puddle. She had told no one what was going on in her life.

But even as Jake mentally considered a litany of her shortcomings, he couldn't help but wonder how she had fared last night, her first night all alone in her childhood home.

He had thought about her in this empty house during the drive back home, then again as he lay in bed, staring up at the ceiling in his room. Surprising, how easily the memories had returned. The fun times they had had. The excitement of the first moment of discovering their feelings for each other. Yet Miriam had been more than a girlfriend. She had been his closest friend. There had been nothing going on in his life, past or present, that she hadn't known about.

Jake sighed lightly as he came to a halt in front of Miriam's house. Too much had happened between them, and the only way to get past it was to talk about it.

But why bother, when she was going to sell the farm and leave again?

Jake jumped out of the truck and ran up the walk to the house, rain slicing down on his head. He huddled deeper into his jean jacket and rapped on the door. The rain was really coming down now, a typical prairie rainstorm swishing and beating against the peeling woodwork of the house.

He rapped on the door again and then pushed it open, stepping quickly inside. As he closed the door behind him, he looked up to see Miriam come to the door. She was wiping her hands on a cloth, wearing an apron over a pair of loose cargo pants that hung low on her hips and a T-shirt that barely ended above the waistband.

"Hi, there," she said, her expression neutral. "Did you want to leave right away?"

"If you don't mind." Jake slicked his damp hair back from his face, wiping the moisture from his cheeks with the shoulder of his jacket, unable to take his eyes off her. Her hair looked tousled, her feet were bare and, unlike yesterday, today she wore no makeup.

The effect was captivating. She looked younger, fresher and more approachable. More like the Miriam he had once known.

He felt his heart stir in response, felt his pulse quicken. Then she lifted her soft brown eyes to his, and in that moment they seemed connected, pulled together by an invisible cord, by memories and old feelings that had never been resolved.

He blinked and forced his gaze away, breaking the tie. "I'll be waiting in the truck for you," he said, looking past her at the wall behind her. "You might want to wear some boots if you have them."

He saw Miriam nod and take a step back. "I'll be right out," she said quietly. When she turned and walked back, he couldn't help but watch her go, noting the graceful sway of her hips.

Pull yourself together, Jake, he berated himself. She's not for you and she's not sticking around. With a shake of his head, he left the house. I need to get out more.

Trouble was, he had no desire to date again.

He had a father who wasn't feeling well, an older mother who couldn't do as much as she used to, a small daughter he never felt he spent enough time with, and a large farm to run on his own. His love life had been luckless, to put it mildly. Women were a complication he could do without. He had Taryn. She was his first responsibility. Tilly and Fred were his second, and together that was more than enough for him.

He was glad he had decided at the last minute to

leave Taryn behind. The almost reverential tone she used when talking about Miriam made him uneasy. Besides, Taryn had lately taken to talking about getting a mommy, like this was an item Jake could take care of for her in a minute.

He knew Taryn, and he was afraid that her fascination would translate into simple math. Miriam was single, Jake was single. One plus one equals a mommy for Taryn. And in spite of the fancies of his own foolish heart, he couldn't imagine a more unsuitable candidate for the job than Miriam.

Jake watched as Miriam picked her way through the puddles on the driveway to the passenger side of the truck, clutching a bright red anorak tightly to her. To his surprise she had on a pair of sturdy hiking boots. He reached across the seat and opened the door. Miriam stepped in, a cloud of sweet-smelling perfume filling the cab as she shot Jake a grateful smile.

Jake twisted the key in the ignition and tried to ignore that irresistible smell that telegraphed her presence.

The only sounds in the cab were the hum of the heater fan and the slap of windshield wipers on the window. Just like yesterday, silence lay between them.

And suddenly Jake was tired of it.

"How long do you plan on staying here?"

"I figure about ten days. I was hoping to go to a real estate agent today."

"Do you think that's long enough to sell your farm?" Jake tried to inject a casual note into his voice. It made him angry that she could so easily talk of selling her farm. The idea bothered him for so many reasons.

"Probably not, but I could only spare that much time here. I have work to go back to."

"Modeling?"

"Yes."

Her quiet reply made Jake take a chance and look at her again. She was looking straight ahead, her mouth pressed into a firm line, her fingers wrapped tightly around each other.

"If you don't mind my intruding, you don't seem too eager about it."

Miriam laughed shortly, pressing her thumbs together. "It pays the bills."

Jake looked back at the road again. He was sure it did. Paula had often spoken with outright envy of how much she figured Miriam made, doing what she did.

He sighed, tapping his thumbs lightly on the steering wheel as he tried to find something to say. He felt awkward and gauche, and he didn't like it.

But she wasn't the Miriam he used to tease; she wasn't the Miriam who used to laugh at everything. In spite of his original antipathy toward her, he felt old feelings resurfacing, and through new-old eyes, he could see a sadness in her.

They turned a corner, and there was her car.

Jake stopped and frowned over a new problem. Town was west and Miriam's car was facing east.

"We'll have to tow it back to the house to get it turned around," he said, thinking out loud.

"Why don't you pull it to the next approach and turn in?" Miriam suggested.

Jake rubbed his thumb along his chin, shaking his head. "Then I won't be able to back out."

"How about pushing it around? It's just a small car."

Jake chewed on his thumbnail, considering.

"You still chew your nails?" Miriam asked, her voice tinged with laughter.

Jake jerked his head around, suddenly self-conscious. "I don't chew my nails," he said, dropping his hand.

"That's what you always said." Miriam smiled again at the shared memory, and once again their eyes met.

Why couldn't he look away? Why couldn't he just casually return the smile and turn his head? It was just mechanics—lift mouth in casual way; move neck muscles. Mission accomplished.

But other messages were ruling his head right now. Like how much narrower her face was than before, how the light caught her high cheekbones, accenting them. He suddenly noticed a delicate fan of wrinkles from her eyes, smudges of shadows beneath them. There was a weariness to her features that he hadn't noticed yesterday.

Jake took a deep breath, pulling himself back to the dilemma at hand.

"It's not a big car," she said again. "We could push it."

Jake considered this new suggestion, and then, with a shrug, said, "We can try."

Jake jumped out of the truck, shut the door and walked over to the car. Miriam was beside him.

"I could push, and you could work the steering," Jake said quickly. "The road isn't too muddy yet, so we should be okay."

"Let's try it." She pulled the keys out of her pocket and unlocked the car, then put the key in the ignition and put the car into neutral. She positioned herself, gave Jake a nod, and on his count they started pushing. The car was small, just as Miriam had said, but it was also low. Jake had to bend far down to get any kind of leverage, and going on his knees wasn't an option.

"Do they get any lower?" he grunted as he strained to move it.

"Not much," Miriam said.

"I'm surprised you didn't bottom out on these roads."

"You always—" Miriam took a breath and pushed harder "—talk this much…when…you're working?"

Keeps me from thinking, he thought.

The car was moving, slowly, but fortunately it was turning in the right direction. The road might just be wide enough.

Jake was bent over so far that he couldn't see what was happening, so when Miriam called out "Stop, stop," he didn't know why. He looked up just in time to see her jump into the car. He was totally unprepared for the jolt as the car came to an abrupt halt. His hands slipped up the trunk of the wet car, his feet slipped on the wet gravel. The next thing he knew, he was lying flat out in a dirty puddle of water, rain dripping down his neck.

He sucked his breath in and lay there a moment as if to assimilate what had happened, embarrassment and the icy water seeping through his clothes, each vying for his attention. The water won out as he shoved himself off the ground, getting his hands dirty in the process. Amazing how quickly one could go from feeling competent and in charge to humiliated and out of control.

"Are you okay?" Miriam poked her head out of the car and quickly put on the emergency brake. She got out, and as she took a good look at him, he saw her hand fly to her mouth. Her lips were pulled in and she glanced quickly down, then up again.

"You're laughing at me," he said, pulling his wet and dirty coat away from his chest, water dripping down his face. "I'm in absolute misery here, and you're standing there laughing at me."

"Sorry," she said, her voice muffled by her hand.

He saw her shoulders shake, and then, as he looked down at his soaking wet pants and coat, he started smiling himself.

Jake wiped the dirty water off his face with the cuff of his coat. He looked over at Miriam now, and saw her eyes dancing. "You better stop laughing, Miriam Spencer, or your hair won't look so clean anymore."

"I'm not laughing," she said, dropping her hand, forcing herself to look more serious.

But then he felt a clump of mud dislodge itself from

his hair and slide down his face. Jake swiped at it, but it was too late. Now Miriam was laughing out loud, her arms clutching her midsection.

"I'm sorry," she gasped, lifting one hand as if in surrender. "I'm sorry."

Jake laughed. Then, shaking his head, he walked over to the truck. "Well, you just stand there and giggle like a girl—I'm going to get the rope."

He pulled the tow rope out of the back of the truck and walked over to Miriam's car. His pants were wet anyhow, so he knelt in the gravel, staring under the car with dismay.

"Can I do anything?" she asked, squatting down beside him.

"Yeah," he said, glancing over his shoulder, forcing himself to look serious. "You can get that little body of yours under this car and hook this on."

Miriam looked taken aback. "Okay," she said quietly, wiping her hands on her coat as if in preparation.

"Kidding," he said, grinning at her.

"You rat." She gave his shoulder a push, almost knocking him over.

"Don't start anything you can't finish, Mims," he said with a mock warning tone and a wink. The nickname came easily to him and so did the wink.

Miriam's expression grew serious. "I haven't heard that in years," Miriam said, dropping her hand and straightening. Then she turned away. "Let me know if you need anything," she said quietly.

Jake looked down at the rope, shaking his head. Keep your mind on the job at hand, he reminded himself. He was surprised at how readily her old name had rolled off his tongue, surprised at her response to it. With difficulty he shrugged the memories away, and bent over to find a suitable place to hook up the rope.

"You'll need to ride in the car," he said to Miriam as he got up, pleased at how casual he managed to sound. "I'll go slow, and you'll have to brake before I do. I'll touch the brakes lightly when I need you to brake, okay? I'll give you lots of time."

"Where are we going?"

"Denny's Auto Parts. I'm sure they'll have something for you, or they'll find it. There's no dealer in town for that make of car."

She gave him a curt nod and got into the car. Jake hesitated a moment, then turned and walked back to the truck.

As he drove, Jake kept alternating between looking at the road ahead and at the car behind him, his mind on neither. He kept wondering why he had called Miriam "Mims." The name had come from a deep place he had forgotten about. He had used Mims only in times of affection.

He sighed and flicked on the radio, hoping the music would keep his mind occupied. But he couldn't forget the brief connection they'd shared when it seemed that all the ten years between them had never been.

Chapter Four

By the time they got to town, the rain had quit and the clouds above were starting to break. The weather-person had promised blue skies and wind tomorrow. Jake hoped that would keep up, so he could be in the fields again by Monday.

When they pulled into Denny's, he got out of the truck, undid the wet and dirty rope, and coiled it up, while Miriam went inside. He threw the rope in the back of the truck.

"You're lucky," he heard Denny say as he walked into the office. "We just parted out a car with a rad that will fit yours."

The young man at the counter sported a tattoo on each hand, a bizarre haircut and a full beard. Denny was a terrific mechanic, although a trifle tough—the complete opposite of his fellow worker, Ryan, who had short hair and was clean-shaven. They both wore grease-stained overalls and, right now, foolish grins. They were unable to keep their eyes off Miriam.

It irritated Jake for a moment. He didn't like the way they were looking at her, as if she were some exotic specimen they had never seen before.

"You done in here, Miriam?"

She glanced over her shoulder. "They said they'll have it done in a couple of hours."

"Funny. I never manage to get such quick service," Jake said, his voice laced with irony.

Denny shrugged, grinning. "You know us, Jake. We aim to please beautiful women." He leaned on the counter and glanced at Jake, his eyebrows raised at the sight of Jake's shirt and pants. "What were you doing?"

"I fell in the mud pushing Miriam's car," Jake answered tersely.

"Well, I sure appreciate the service." Miriam bestowed a polite smile on them. "Is there a place I can wait while you work on it?"

"You can sit here, or you can tell us where you will be and we can deliver it." Ryan smiled, leaning closer.

Jake resisted the urge to roll his eyes. These two were so obvious, it was sickening.

"I think I'll go to town. I have my cell phone. I'll let you know what's up." She smiled at them both and left, leaving two dazed men staring at her.

"She looks so familiar," Denny said to Jake as the door creaked closed behind her.

"She should. We used to go to school with her."

"That Miriam Spencer is 'Sticks' Spencer?"

Denny's mouth almost dropped open. Jake felt an unaccountable surge of anger at the memory of that hated nickname. Miriam had always laughed it off, but he also knew how it bothered her.

"Wow, she sure became babe material," Denny continued, stroking his beard.

"She is quite attractive," Jake said, cringing at his own prim note.

Ryan threw him a knowing smirk. "Oh, very quite," he said with a laugh.

Jake caught the door handle, feigning nonchalance. "Well, gotta run. Let me know if anything changes with Miriam's car," he said.

"She gave us her cell number." Denny craned his neck as if to get another look at Miriam, who was once again sitting in Jake's truck. "But I'll call you, too, just in case." Denny gave Jake a wink, as if congratulating him. "She back for a visit?"

Jake only nodded, uncomfortable with Denny's obvious assumption—that he and Miriam were going to try again. He knew he should correct the misconception, but he figured people would know for themselves, once Miriam was gone.

When Jake got outside, Miriam wasn't in the truck. He frowned, and then he saw her walking down the road toward town.

"Miriam!" he called out. "Where are you going?"

She stopped, glancing over her shoulder. "To town."

"I'll bring you," he said, stifling his exasperation.

Did she really think he would just go back to the farm, leaving her to fend for herself?

"That's okay. You don't have to."

"Come back and get in the truck," he said brusquely.

Miriam hesitated. Then, with a shrug, she turned and came back. He waited for her by the passenger side of the truck and held the door open for her.

Miriam threw him an oblique glance and got in.

Jake walked around the front and climbed awkwardly into his truck, the wet denim of his pants clinging to his legs and constricting his movements.

"Where do you want to go?" he asked as he drove out of Denny's yard.

"Doesn't matter. Is Raylene's place still around?"

"No. She moved to Denver."

"Denver? Why there?"

"I heard some cowboy in town for a rodeo caught her fancy, and she sold the place and left."

Miriam laughed at that.

"What's so funny? Can't you see old Raylene Dansers losing her heart to some old bull rider?" Jake said with mock dismay.

"Bull riders don't get that old," Miriam said, grinning.

"Actually, he was the header half of a calf-roping team. You can do that sitting down."

Miriam laughed again, and Jake felt a lightness pervade the once-heavy atmosphere. "I'll take you to the new place in town," he said impulsively. "You can see how much Waylen has changed."

Miriam looked sideways at him and, to his surprise, smiled. "Thanks, Jake. That sounds good."

A few minutes later Jake pulled up in front of a small café that Miriam remembered as having been a bakery.

"Where did the bakery go?" Miriam asked, getting out of the truck.

"Moved into a new complex downtown." Jake got out and stared down at his dirty pants. He really looked like a hick compared to Miriam.

He glanced up to see Miriam smiling at him. "Don't worry about your pants. I don't care if you don't."

He made it to the door ahead of her and opened it for her.

"Still a gentleman," she said lightly as she stepped through the door.

"Tilly raised me right," he returned, following her in.

"Hey, Jake." Peter Thornton, a farmer who lived down the road, waved to Jake from his seat as they came in. "The rain send you to town this morning, too?"

"Yeah," Jake said briefly. He didn't want to stop, but small-town protocol deemed that he do so. "You done seeding yet?"

"Got another 60 acres to do." Peter leaned back in his chair and looked past him, then back to Jake with a grin. "How about you?"

"Pretty close to done." He glanced back at Miriam, who stood just behind him, her hands clasped in front of her. He didn't want to keep her waiting through the usual give and take of farming talk. Besides, he wanted her to himself for a while. "Well, take care. Talk to you later." After a casual nod, he walked across the nearly empty café to the window.

He was thankful the café was quiet this morning.

Miriam sat down at the table and looked around with a smile. "Nice place."

"They opened about a year ago. They're doing quite well," Jake said, leaning on the table.

The waitress was already at their table, a pot of coffee in her hand. "Menus?" she asked.

Jake shook his head. "Just a cup of coffee for me," he said.

Miriam looked up. "Thanks, I'll have the same."

They watched as the waitress filled their cups, then was gone again.

"You didn't used to drink coffee," Jake said, pulling his cup closer.

"I started while I was modeling. All that waiting around." She took a careful sip from her cup, avoiding his gaze. Jake wanted to ask her more, wanted to know about her world—and yet didn't. He didn't know where to start asking about the life that had taken her away from him and Waylen. Yet he had to—it was who she had become.

"So what is it like—modeling?"

Miriam looked up past his shoulder and shook her head lightly. "Busy. A lot of rushing around because there's a ton of people involved in a shoot." She laughed, but it wasn't a pleasant laugh. "The work isn't so bad. It's how you get treated after a while."

"And how is that?"

"Like a thing—a centerpiece that gets pulled on, tweaked, changed and molded. Some girls love all the attention, but I felt like an object."

Jake heard despair in her voice. Despair and the same weariness he could see in her eyes. "So why are you going back to it?"

Miriam gave a graceful shrug. "The money is good."

It wasn't hard to tell that she didn't like the work. He didn't want to accept that Miriam Spencer—a girl who never seemed to care what she wore, who used to wear her long brown hair tied back with a shoelace—had turned into this elegant woman who spoke easily of doing work she disliked merely because the money was good.

"Well, you've done it long enough—you must have quite a bit of it by now," he said sardonically.

She said nothing, only lowered her eyes—but not before Jake saw the flare of pain in them.

He felt like a heel. He had no right to judge her. Not when he himself often wished for better crops, for higher prices. Money was important to him, too.

He wondered what to say next. Wondered what he could say to bring some measure of amicability back to the conversation. Because he discovered, suddenly, that he wanted to know more about her, to find out what had happened to her.

As he watched her carefully sip her coffee, he felt

a familiar stirring, an awakening of old feelings. She had been a friend—one of the first he had made here. Miriam had been the one who introduced him to other people, who included him in her circle, who made sure he was always socially comfortable. The friendship they shared had quickly changed and become more intense. Miriam was the first girl he had really loved.

And now, in spite of the complete change in her, and in spite of knowing she was going to be leaving, he was feeling attracted to her again.

Fool that he was.

He wanted to leave as if to outrun his own feelings, but there was no polite way to do so. He had invited her here.

The door opened and a woman called out a greeting to Peter, then walked over to their table.

"Hey, Jake, how are you doing?"

Jake looked up and met the smiling face of Donna Kurtz. "Doing good, Donna. How about you?"

"Busy. I just took a break from working at the church." She pulled at her paint-splattered T-shirt and flashed a crooked grin. "I thought you were going to come?"

"I'm sorry. I forgot they're painting there today." Jake felt guilty. "I'll be right over."

He turned to Miriam, who was looking up at Donna with a wistful expression on her face. "Miriam, you remember Donna, don't you?"

Donna's mouth fell open as she recognized her old friend. Then she was leaning over, hugging Miriam hard. "My goodness," she said breathlessly, "Look at you, Miriam Spencer.'' Donna clutched Miriam's shoulders, and shook her head in disbelief. ''Have you ever changed! What are you doing back here? How come I never knew?''

''I just came back yesterday,'' Miriam replied.

''Really?'' Donna glanced at Jake and then back at Miriam, her smile changing. ''And you and Jake already met up with each other.'' The innuendo in her tone was unmistakable.

Jake figured he'd better dispel that notion immediately. ''Miriam's car broke down not far from our place. I brought her into town to get it fixed.''

Donna nodded, but her smirk showed that she didn't quite believe it. ''It's just like old times, seeing you two together again.''

Jake wished she would stop assuming a relationship between them. It made him yearn for something that wasn't going to happen—Miriam's next stop was a real estate agency.

He glanced at his watch. He had other things to do, other obligations. If Denny was as fast as he said he could be, Miriam didn't have much longer to wait. ''I should go and help at the church,'' he said to Miriam, trying for a light tone. ''If you need anything, you can find me there.''

She nodded as her eyes met his, then looked back at Donna. He felt dismissed, and pushed his chair back.

''See you back at the church,'' he said, sending her a quick grin.

Donna nodded, then took his place opposite Miriam.

He stopped at the till and paid for their coffees, then walked to his truck. As he got in, he could see Donna and Miriam through the window of the café. Donna was leaning forward, and Miriam's face held that same wistfulness he had seen before.

As he started the truck, he wondered what was going on behind those deep brown eyes of hers. Once he would have been able to read the slightest nuance, but now she was as unreadable as a legal document.

He sighed and pulled away. As if he didn't have enough on his mind, now he had to go and complicate his life with this woman who was so different from the one he had once loved.

"I still can't believe you're here." Donna rested her elbows on the scratched red Formica tabletop, sipping her coffee, smiling across at her old friend. "It's been years and years. Too long."

Miriam acknowledged the comment with a nod, and kept folding the napkin on the table in front of her. More guilt. "I know and I'm sorry." She lifted her eyes to Donna. "I don't think there's anything I can really say to excuse or brush it all away."

"I heard a few bits and pieces from Paula just after you left, but that's about it."

"Paula and I stayed out of touch, as well—" Miriam stopped, sorrow over their mutual friend thickening her throat. "Sorry." She looked down, blinking quickly. "I still can't get past her death."

"It happened a while ago for me, but I can imagine it's a shock for you, just finding this out now."

Miriam drew in a long breath to compose herself and then looked up at Donna. "After she got married, the relationship faded away."

"I imagine." Donna took another sip of coffee, but held Miriam's gaze. "You know, when I saw you sitting here with Jake, it seemed just like old times."

"That's all they are, Donna—old times," Miriam said sharply. Donna's words struck too close to her own yearning. It had been hard to acknowledge Jake's marriage to Paula, but it was all the harder now that Paula had passed away. If Paula were still alive, Jake wouldn't be available.

Donna looked taken aback at Miriam's harsh tone. "I know that. It's just that we used to see you guys together all the time. That's all."

"I'm sorry, Donna. It's been so strange coming back here. Everything's changed so much."

Except that it was much the same, Miriam thought as she and Donna quietly sipped their coffee. Looking at Donna somehow made her realize what she had lost when she'd left. This place where she had grown up suddenly seemed secure, unchanging. Here were people who cared. She had been hugged more in the past two days than she had been in years. More people had asked with sincerity how she was doing.

For the past few years she had been only a face, a body, an object. No one seemed to care about her soul, her heart.

"You've changed, too. I remember the first time your face showed up on the front cover of a magazine. It was the talk of the town."

"I'm sure it was."

"Oh, don't get all huffy with me. That's what Waylen is like. People are nosy, but they care." Donna grinned at her. "And now, you owe me. Big time." Donna tilted her head, her tone full of meaning. "You don't write, you don't phone. So spill. What happened with you and Jake? What have you been doing? What is your life like? How's your mom?"

In spite of the sorrow raised by Donna's questions, Miriam felt an easing of the tension that had gripped her since she'd come here. Easygoing, straightforward Donna never pulled any punches, never minced words. Never judged.

"My mom died six months ago." Again Miriam stopped, swallowing hard.

"Oh, Miriam. I'm so sorry."

"I can't believe this," Miriam said, her voice shaky as Donna's hand squeezed hers tightly. "It's like each time I tell someone, I relive her death." She stopped, taking in a deep breath. "It was hard, but I think she was ready. She died quite peacefully."

"I'm so sorry," Donna said, stroking her arm with her other hand. "You've sure had enough to deal with."

Silence drifted up between them as Miriam wiped a fresh rivulet of tears, but this was the companionable silence of friends reestablishing their acquaintance.

"Sorry to dump on you like this. Hardly old home week, is it?"

"I'm your friend, Miriam." Donna smiled at her. "I'm supposed to help you, to listen to you."

"Thanks." Miriam felt another twinge of guilt that Donna should offer help and support when she herself had remained so distant.

"So what is modeling like?" Donna asked, changing the subject. "How do you feel when you walk out in front of all those people?"

Miriam didn't want to talk about modeling. She had fostered a foolish hope that when she came back here, she would be able to leave the other life behind her, if only for a while. But she had forgotten how intertwined lives are in a small town. Your news is my news.

"Actually, the majority of what I do is catalog work. I haven't done much runway work lately, and, to tell you the truth, it's fairly boring."

"Boring?" Donna said in a tone of disbelief.

"Yes, Donna. Despite what you see, it's dull, plodding work." She would have preferred to talk about her clothing retail business, but it was just another failure in her life. At least for now.

"Well, you still don't seem to have trouble keeping the weight off." Donna sighed, looking at Miriam. "I could never figure out how a girl so skinny could eat so much and not put on a pound."

"Always was a poor keeper. But enough about me," Miriam said suddenly. She didn't want to reexamine her life any more than she had to. She hadn't liked what she saw out east; she liked it even less here. "What about you? Married? Kids?"

"Yeah, I'm married. My last name is now Kurtz, and my husband, Keith, is an accountant. I've got two kids. One in play school, the other in kindergarten. I'm busy with church, school. The usual.'' Donna smiled a self-deprecating smile. ''My life must sound so dull.''

Miriam shook her head, a feeling of melancholy gripping her. ''It doesn't sound dull at all,'' she said quietly. ''It sounds pretty good to me.''

''Don't give me that.'' Donna held her gaze. ''As if beneath every glamorous outfit you've ever worn beats a heart that deep down would love nothing more than to be at home baking chocolate chip cookies.''

''I prefer macadamia nut, myself.''

''See? A gourmet. You don't belong in this little hick town anymore.''

Once Miriam might have scoffed at the idea, but as she had traveled these past few years, she had been able to look at Waylen from a distance. ''Waylen isn't as bad as you might think, Donna,'' she said.

''You sound serious.''

''I am. The fashion life reads well in short magazine articles. But a good photographer can make any-thing—and I mean anything—look good,'' Miriam said with meaning. ''I haven't met many sincere peo-ple in my business. They're either putting up with you because you might be useful to them, or they're suck-ing up to you because you are useful to them.'' She gave a shrug, knowing that she had already said too much. She hadn't come back here to show everyone how unsatisfied she was with her life.

''So no one important in your life right now?''

''Nope. Footloose and fancy free.'' Her wry grin

belied her casual tone. "My agent, Carl, is a darling, but he's married. I've not met Mr. Right yet."

"I can't imagine that. I always thought you would be the one who would get married first," Donna said with a grin.

There it was again: the soft pain brought up by the innocent comment. The reminder of how close she and Jake had once been. How had she thought she could keep herself aloof from that?

"I'm sorry," Donna said, shaking her head. "Me and my big mouth." She sighed. "I don't know what happened between you and Jake. I don't suppose it's any of my business, but it was as much of a shock to me as anyone when he and Paula got married."

Miriam sensed the opening that Donna gave her, but decided not to seize it. She had come to set the past to rest.

"Well, that's long over, and we've both changed a lot," Miriam said lightly. "Tell me about the rest of the people here. What's Linda doing? Still hoping to write that bestseller?"

They sat for another hour, chatting, talking, laughing. Miriam found herself drifting back into life in Waylen. It was familiar, and yet, listening to her friend talk easily about children and her husband, Miriam had a feeling that she had missed out on an important part of life. Her own life seemed shallow and frivolous by comparison.

Finally, Donna had to leave. "Why don't you come with me? Sondra is there. I'd love to see the look on her face when you show up."

Miriam shook her head. She would have liked to come, but Jake was there, as well. It would be better if she kept her distance. "I have a few other things to do. Thanks, though."

"You said you're staying around a while—we'll have to make sure to connect again. Otherwise the church is having a picnic a week from this Sunday. You should come."

Miriam paused again, considering. Memories of other fun-filled days flashed through her mind. "That sounds good."

"Great. Well, keep in touch. And we'll see you on Sunday."

They left the restaurant, each going her separate way. Miriam watched Donna stroll down the street, waving at one person, stopping briefly to chat with another. For a moment she wanted to go with Donna. She wanted to be a part of that community.

Don't be silly. You don't fit here anymore, she thought. She wondered if she should go to church on Sunday, if she wanted to risk the very stares and censure that Donna had hinted at. She had enough self-doubts; she didn't need to pile on any more.

But she remembered other times in church, other times when she had felt peace, and joy and love. She felt a yearning to experience that again, that healing, that feeling that someone did care about her, about her soul. That she was important to God.

She had strayed so far from that center of her life. She couldn't help but think of how easy it had been to drift away, to get caught up in the vacuousness of the fashion world. And she had been such a major part of it—dressing up, acting, being fussed over.

Seventeen years old, self-conscious, still smarting from Jake's defection. What girl wouldn't go a little crazy with all that attention, all those photographers telling her how beautiful she looked, all the admiration? But it was from people who saw her only as a face and figure.

Miriam spun around and strode away from the café, wishing she could as easily leave parts of her past behind.

Carl and his bright ideas, she thought. It would have been easier on her self-esteem and her conscience if she had just stayed out east and sold the farm from there. She never spent this much time moodling about might-have-beens. All her free time in the past few months had been taken up with bankers, phoning up suppliers to beg for extensions of credit, phoning up debtors to beg for payment.

When one of her biggest customers went bankrupt, it had caused her problems. She might have been okay, but for a crooked accountant. Now, thanks to him, she stood to lose her company, as well, unless she could come up with a substantial influx of cash.

That accountant, Miriam thought with disgust. Another man who couldn't be trusted. Her life seemed to be a series of men who didn't want to stay with her, be loyal to her. That's why it puzzled her that Jake could still tie her up in knots. He had only been the first of many men who didn't seem to need her in the long run.

She sped up, and this time made it all the way to the real estate office. She pushed the door open and stepped inside.

Half an hour later she was back on the street. The papers were signed and the machinery had been put into place.

Now what?

Miriam emerged from the office and sighed, looking down the street. A few trucks drove by, a couple of cars. People greeted each other as they passed on the street. Everyone belonged here. They fit.

She walked down the street until she found an empty bench and, wiping the moisture off it, sat down. She called Denny's on her cell phone and arranged for them to bring her car downtown. Then, just to make a connection, she phoned Tilly. Maybe she needed some groceries.

"That would be wonderful, Miriam. I don't dare leave Fred. He is feeling so listless, I don't want to leave him alone."

"He's still not feeling well?"

"It seems so up and down. If he doesn't get better, I'm going to have to bring him in to the doctor. But for now all is well, and God is good. We still have each other and Jake and Taryn, and for that we can be grateful, can't we?"

Yes you can, thought Miriam.

"Now, what groceries do you want?" Miriam wrote down what Tilly told her. They chatted a bit more and then Tilly said goodbye. It was like old times, Miriam thought with a smile as she closed the phone. Running errands, idle chat.

She missed it.

She was putting her phone and the list back in her purse when she saw a tall figure pausing at the traffic lights on the main street. Jake.

He was frowning. Miriam could see it from here. She swallowed down her quick response to him, frustrated with how easily old feelings came back. The light turned green and he crossed the street. He walked along the street opposite her, then looked up and saw her. His step faltered, then, after a quick glance both ways, he jogged across the street toward her.

Visiting with Donna this morning had recreated the past. Now, once again, as Jake sauntered up to her, she felt the same foolish thrill she always did when she saw him. It didn't matter that just this morning she had seen him with mud on his face and pants; he still seemed to tower above her, to dominate the area around him.

"Hello," she said evenly. "You finished at the church?"

"They didn't need me. So I had some business to do."

"I'm picking up some groceries for Tilly."

"That's not necessary," Jake said abruptly. He shifted his weight and slipped his hands in the back pockets of his blue jeans. "I can get them."

Miriam felt dismissed. Though she wanted to fight it, she realized that putting her farm up for sale pulled her back from their lives, as well.

She busied herself looking through her purse, found the piece of paper on which she had written the list, and handed it to Jake. "Are you sure? I don't mind doing it."

"That's okay. Thanks anyhow." He forced a smile as if to compensate for his brusque attitude, but Miriam wasn't fooled. She knew what Jake's sincere smile could do. And had he bestowed one on her, she wouldn't be standing here, seething over how easily he seemed to exempt her from his life.

She had hoped to visit with Tilly for a while, but she'd have to make time for that another day.

"Well, I guess I'll see you around." She was about to turn.

"Did you want me to give you a ride to Denny's?"

"That's not necessary," she said mimicking his words of a few moments ago. "They said they would deliver the car to me."

"Okay. I'll see you around then." And he turned on his heel and walked across the street again.

Miriam watched him go, her emotions narrowing down to anger. She felt as if she had been judged and found wanting. As if Jake Steele were above reproach, she thought angrily.

By the time Denny brought her car to town, she was tired and glad to see him.

She followed him back to the office, paid for the repairs done on her car and then drove home.

The road back was still wet from the rain of this morning and the car was difficult to handle, but that didn't stop Miriam from going too fast. She fishtailed a couple of times, and after the second time, forced herself to slow down. The last thing she wanted was for Jake to have to rescue her. Again.

By the time she got home she wasn't quite as angry as before. Instead, a peculiar hurt overlaid her earlier emotions. A painful realization that she didn't fit here anymore.

Well, it was a good thing she had realized that as soon as possible and hadn't pinned anything on this place.

She spent the rest of the day and most of the night cleaning up and making the place look a little better.

Saturday dawned warm and bright and Miriam headed outside to clean the yard. She went through the old shop on the place, a fresh wave of nostalgia washing over her at the still strong scent of diesel and oil that seemed to have soaked into the very timbers of her father's shop.

She remembered happier times when her father had helped her put the chain back on her bike, helped her with a science fair project that her mother didn't want done in the house. She remembered "helping" her father by handing him tools from the chest-high toolbox that still stood in one dark corner.

Miriam looked around her with a measure of anxiety. Yesterday, when she had signed the sales agreement, she hadn't realized the magnitude of her actions. She would have to have a farm sale to get rid of all these things.

The thought depressed her. She had been to enough farm sales as a young girl. She remembered how uncomfortable she had felt, poking and prying through other people's things, listening to disparaging comments made about some of the items offered for sale.

But imagining the contents of the house going up for sale bothered her less than the idea of seeing her father's tools lined up and auctioned off.

She wandered through the shop, surprised to see so many tools still here. The lawn mower and garden tiller stood in their usual corner. Her father's table saw and drill press stood opposite, coated with a layer of greasy dust. Buckets and pails of bolts and nuts were lined up on shelves above the workbench. Mouse droppings were thick on the floor and an old leather carpenter pouch that had fallen off its hook had been fair game for them: it was full of holes.

For the rest, it was all intact.

With a mental shake, Miriam walked over to the lawn mower and pulled it away from the wall. She opened the gas tank and frowned. Empty, of course. And she knew there was no gas in the gas tank in the yard.

So much for mowing the lawn, she thought.

She could ride over to the Prins's farm and borrow some gas; her father had enough jerry cans she could carry it in.

But after meeting Jake in town, she was reluctant to go over there when he was around.

Monday, she could. Jake would probably be working in the fields then.

She pushed the lawn mower into its spot and walked back to the house, wondering how she was going to fill the rest of the empty evening.

Chapter Five

Miriam flipped down the visor in her car and checked her lipstick. She unconsciously ran her hand over her hair and glanced down at her clothes—black blazer over dark, narrow fitted pants. Conservative enough for church, she figured.

Yesterday she had spent half the day trying to talk herself out of coming, but when she woke up this morning, she knew she didn't feel right staying home.

She pulled the key out of the ignition and took a deep breath. Taking a walk down the country roads might have been a better idea. Standing here in the shadow of the church—the shadow of seventeen years of sermons, obligations and Sunday School lessons—she felt as if she were looking at her life with new eyes.

The parties, the late nights, the friends she had spent time with, the endless traveling from one exotic location to another, the many, many times she had thought she should visit her mother, and hadn't—all seemed so shallow. She had stopped attending church when her co-workers teased her about it.

I was just young, she appealed to a distant God who was tied up with this church and her past. *I was finally free from obligations and a mother who never approved of anything I did.* She clutched the keys tighter, their sharp ridges cutting into her palm, as if the pain would serve as penance for what she had done.

"I don't need this," she said to no one in particular, leaning back against the seat. "I didn't have to come today."

But she had.

She had come seeking peace, but instead she was being faced with her past at every turn.

Miriam had never been a quitter, and she wasn't about to start now. She knew that people, once they found out she was back, would wonder why she hadn't come to church the way she always had when she and her mother had lived here.

So, straightening her shoulders, taking a deep breath, she stepped out of the car to finish this.

She walked slowly up the front walk to the church. A flat, wide sidewalk led to two sets of double doors.

Inside, a group of people stood in the foyer, chatting. They glanced at her, then smiled a polite smile before moving toward another set of stairs beside an elevator. Miriam didn't recognize them and was sure, from their reaction, that they didn't recognize her, either.

The doors behind her opened again, sending a shaft of light into the foyer. Miriam took a step away, making room for the people.

"Miriam," a sweet young voice called out, and Miriam spun around.

"Well, hello, Taryn." She smiled at the young girl who came running up to her. Taryn wore a yellow dress covered with an old-fashioned pinafore. Her hair was braided this time and tied up with two white ribbons. One, however, had come loose and was trailing down her front.

"You came to church." The statement was made without guile, and Miriam couldn't help but smile down at the adorable little girl. "Are you going to sit with us?"

"Maybe Miss Spencer wants to sit with someone else," Jake said to his daughter as he walked up to stand beside her.

Miriam reluctantly turned her gaze to him. His white collarless shirt was a bright contrast to his tanned complexion. His dark, wavy hair was brushed away from his face, bringing his features into stark relief.

Handsome as ever, thought Miriam with a stab of regret. His smoldering eyes, his full mouth. It was as if the man she had seen the other day, mud covering his face, his eyes sparkling—the man who had called her "Mims"—had been just a figment of her imagination.

Taryn looked up at her father, then back at Miriam,

her eyes sad. "Do you want to sit with someone else?"

Miriam looked down at the little girl, her heart softening at the appeal in those eyes. Avoiding a reply, she squatted down and carefully retied the bow that hung loose. "There," she said, giving the bow an extra tug. "I made it nice and tight. It won't come loose again."

Taryn lifted the bow, tucking her chin in and almost crossing her eyes to see it. "That looks nice. Daddy can't tie these very good. He says he has farmer hands." She grinned up at Miriam. "Can you fix the other one, too?"

Miriam didn't dare look at Jake. She could sense his displeasure, yet something stubborn in her nature made her bend over and quickly tie up the other bow, then fluff it out.

"Thanks, Miriam," Taryn said, unabashedly catching Miriam's hand in her own as Miriam straightened.

Fred and Tilly were coming toward her, walking slowly to accommodate Fred, Miriam surmised.

"Hi there, Miriam." Fred walked up to her and patted her on the shoulder. "So good to see you here."

Miriam smiled at the approval on his face. At least in Fred's eyes she had gotten things right.

Tilly bustled up, greeting her with an enthusiastic hug. "I was so praying you would come today." She smiled, stroking Miriam's cheek.

Miriam felt another knot of emotion at the sincerity in Tilly's voice.

"I'm glad I came, too," she said softly, swallowing. She avoided looking at Jake, but was conscious of him watching them, fully aware of his disapproval. It shouldn't have mattered, but Miriam felt it as strongly as she felt Tilly's love.

She wished she dared confront him, to try to explain, but her own emotions over Jake were too unstable, too vulnerable. She hated it, but it was a reality she had to accept. Once she was gone, it would go away, she figured. Once she was back at work, remaking her life.

"You can come with us, Miriam. Please sit with us." Taryn caught her hand. "Can she sit with us, Grandma?"

"Of course." Tilly smiled down at her granddaughter. "Will you, Miriam?"

Once again, Miriam felt stuck. She knew Jake was not pleased, yet couldn't find it in herself to pull her hand away from Taryn, or to say no to her old neighbor.

"Sure. I guess I can."

"Goody." Taryn caught her father's hand in her other one and started pulling the two adults toward the stairs leading to the sanctuary. "C'mon, Grandma and Grandpa," she called over her shoulder. "We have to sit down."

Miriam felt the small, soft hand in hers, and something inside her melted. Suddenly she didn't care what Jake thought, didn't care what anyone else thought. This precious little girl wanted Miriam to be with them, and it felt wonderful.

She tried not to read too much into the child's actions. Taryn seemed naturally precocious, but as they walked up the stairs, two adults joined by a young girl, Miriam felt her throat thicken.

She remembered walking precisely in the same formation with her parents. Her father on one side, her mother on the other, and little Miriam safe and secure in the middle.

The memory was so vivid that she bit her lip, fighting an unexpected sorrow, the stairs wavering in her vision. Ducking her head, she quickly wiped her eyes, hoping Jake wouldn't see.

But she didn't have long hair to hide behind anymore. And as she straightened, she felt Jake's eyes on her. She couldn't stop looking at him any more than she could stop Taryn's excited bouncing.

Once again, their eyes met and held. Once again, Miriam felt as if she were drifting toward him, unable to stop herself.

But Taryn gave them both another tug, and the moment was broken.

"Daddy has to get the bulletin," she announced to Miriam, swinging her hand. "You stay with me and Grandma and Grandpa."

Miriam looked down at the crooked part in the little girl's hair, and resisted the urge to run her hand over Taryn's head, to bend over and gather this little girl in her arms.

Instead, she blinked once more and looked ahead to the sanctuary, already three-quarters full.

She knew the instant Jake returned. Out of the corner of her eye she saw him take Taryn's other hand, almost felt his sidelong glance. She kept her eyes ahead, however, looking at the congregation, wondering where they would sit. A couple of people had already turned, then spun back around to whisper to a neighbor. This created a small ripple of movement among the people sitting in the back.

"Well, Miriam. Ready to face your past?" Jake's deep voice seemed to mock her, but when she turned to challenge him, she saw his soft mouth curved up in a hint of a smile. "You're quite notorious, you know."

"Notorious?" she repeated, trying to inject a note of humor in her voice. "Disreputable notorious or distinguished notorious?"

"Probably a bit of both," Jake said, looking away.

"Let's go sit," Taryn urged, looking up first at Jake and then at Miriam. "They're going to start singing, and then everyone will look at us."

Judging from the number of backward glances they were getting, that was going to happen anyhow, thought Miriam. She squared her shoulders and looked down the long, carpeted aisle of the church.

Just another catwalk, she thought, and a different audience. She rolled her shoulders, straightened her clothes and reminded herself not to strut.

Tilly and Fred went on ahead, followed by Jake, Taryn and Miriam. The aisle was wide enough for the three of them. She was thankful, however, that Tilly stopped halfway to the altar.

They settled in the pew—Miriam, then Taryn, then Jake; and beside him, Tilly and Fred. Fred calmly picked up the bulletin and started reading. Tilly leaned forward and started talking with the person ahead of them. Jake just crossed his arms and looked straight ahead.

Taryn sat between them, her hands folded demurely in her lap, her short legs sticking almost straight out in front of her. She tapped the toes of her shiny black shoes together, then looked up at Miriam with a huge grin. Miriam felt an answering tug of emotion. Taryn was so accepting, so open. Miriam didn't feel worthy of the obvious adoration that showed in the little girl's eyes.

The music from the organ stopped, then the organist struck the opening bars of a hymn. With a rustle and murmur, the congregation rose to sing.

Miriam took her cue from Jake and pulled a hymnal from the pew in front of her. The song sounded so familiar, but she couldn't place the title and didn't know where to find it. She tilted her head to see if the number was printed on the song board at the front of the church, but the board was no longer there.

She felt a hand on her arm, and, turning, saw Jake's book tilted toward her; he was showing her the number. She nodded, a faint blush warming her cheeks when she saw the title. It *had* been a while since she had been in church, she thought with a measure of shame as she flipped through the pages. Too long, when she couldn't even find one of her one-time favorites in the hymnal.

The words sifted down through the past ten years of her life, through all her other experiences, the multitude of Sundays she had either been working or sleeping in because of a terribly late night. They pulled up old thoughts, old memories that Miriam had slowly buried under a deluge of new experiences that at first seemed exciting, and now seemed cheap.

She stopped singing.

Once again she felt as if she were a young girl standing beside her mother. A young girl whose every action was criticized and discussed at length within her hearing.

Miriam closed the hymnal and dropped it back into the holder, ignoring Jake's quick glance and Taryn's puzzled one. Instead, she stared straight ahead, waiting for the song to finish, hoping she would make it to the end of the service. She had thought she and her mother had laid these regrets to rest. Yet how quickly the feelings came back with the sound of an old hymn.

The song finally ended, and the minister strode up to the front and greeted them, his voice encouraging and hearty. He welcomed visitors, and Miriam noticed a couple of faces glance furtively at her. She ignored them.

Then everyone sat down, and Taryn looked questioningly up at her. Miriam smiled down, then looked away. She hoped she could just get through this service without making it too obvious to the little girl beside her that she suddenly wished she were anywhere else but here.

The organ struck up the first notes of the postlude, and Jake glanced at Miriam. She stood holding the pew, looking straight ahead, her short dark hair shining under the overhead lights. She hadn't sung any of the songs and had sat through most of the service with her arms crossed tightly over her stomach, looking as if she'd sooner be anywhere else.

She turned her head and caught his eye, her expression composed. It was as if the woman who had wiped her eyes a while ago didn't even exist. He held her gaze, unable to stop his own reaction. This beautiful woman was a stranger, yet as he looked into her eyes and remembered her tears, he caught a glimpse of the girl he had once loved.

He turned away.

Taryn was chattering to Miriam behind him; Tilly was talking to someone else, signaling for him to go ahead. Jake ended up walking out alongside another farmer, chatting about the weather and the condition of the pastures. He tried not to be aware of Tilly introducing Miriam to her friends, not to listen to Miriam's calm voice replying to breathless questions.

Sunday was always a quiet day, a true day of rest. And usually he looked forward to it, but not today. He didn't know if he wanted Miriam sitting across the table from him.

"Can you walk with me to the car, son?" Fred laid his hand on Jake's shoulder to get his attention.

Jake glanced down at his father. Fred's lips were edged with a thin white line and his complexion held a faintly grayish tinge.

"You okay, Dad?" Jake asked, alarmed at how his father looked.

"Just a little out of breath."

"I'm going to take you to the hospital."

"No, Jake. Don't. The doctor told me this would happen once in a while. I want to get out of here. Fresh air is all I need."

"Okay," Jake said, taking his father's arm. But all the way to the car, he kept his eyes on the older man. It was hard not to look as if he was hovering. But by the time they reached the parking lot, Fred already looked a little better.

At the car, Jake helped his father inside. Then he got in himself. "You're sure you're okay?" Jake asked one more time.

"I'm just tired." Fred laid his head back and then rolled it sideways to face Jake. He smiled and took a slow, deep breath. "And how are you? Are you okay?"

"Yes." Jake frowned, wondering what his father was getting at.

"Doesn't bother you to see her again?"

"Her?"

"Miriam. You used to like her quite a bit, didn't you?"

Jake raised his eyebrows, surprised at how percep-tive his father was. "Yes, Dad. I did."

"And now? She's still single, I gather."

"She's also come to sell her farm and then go back east."

Jake glanced at Fred again, trying to gauge his reaction.

"You going to put an offer in on it?"

"I don't know. I really don't know." Jake knew he wouldn't be able to bluff his father. Fred knew the precise financial situation of the farm.

"It would be a shame to lose it."

"But I would be doing it with your money. I'm not a risk-taker."

"The price of cereal crops will go up again," Fred reassured him. "You'll make your money on the land. Sometimes you have to take risks, Jake...in various parts of your life."

Jake knew Fred alluded to more than just the farm, but decided to leave it be.

"You might want to consider it. Have something to maintain, to pass on."

"I don't have a son, Dad," Jake said with a smile.

"That's okay, Jake. Neither did your mother and I." Fred returned Jake's smile. "And look what happened to us. God brought us you."

Jake felt a surge of tender warmth at his father's comment. "And I'm so glad he did."

Fred only nodded and then laid his head back, closing his eyes again. Jake could tell he wanted to go home, and he got out of the car to find his mother and Taryn.

Just as he did, he saw them with Miriam, walking over to the graveyard.

Jake watched, realizing what they were up to. Tilly had Miriam's arm tucked in hers and was talking, her head bobbing. Taryn skipped ahead of them, her braids bouncing with each step, her arms held out straight from her sides.

They walked directly to Paula's grave, and Taryn bent over to trace her mother's name. Running back to Miriam, she caught her arm and pulled her along.

From his vantage point, Jake couldn't read Miriam's expression. He wondered what she was thinking. Miriam and Paula had been friends for years, yet Paula had never seemed to have the same devotion to Miriam that Miriam had held for Paula. Of course, thought Jake, Paula always took care of Paula first.

Miriam stopped in front of the stone and clasped her hands in front of her, her head bent.

Jake felt a stab of guilt at the sight. Taryn and Tilly occasionally went to Paula's grave. He never did. When Paula had died, his sorrow had been tempered by a guilty measure of relief. Paula had been difficult to live with. In the last years of their marriage, she had hardly been around. Even after Taryn was born, Paula had managed to find all kinds of reasons to be gone. It was on one of her many trips away that she was killed.

The little group stood still for a moment, and Jake was surprised to see Miriam reach up to palm her cheeks.

Taryn, never able to stay still too long, started running to other stones. Tilly and Miriam tarried a mo-

ment, moved on, then stopped again. Jake guessed
they were looking at her father's grave.

Once again Miriam paused. Tilly put an arm
around her shoulder, and for a moment Jake felt sorry
for Miriam. He had stood beside the grave of a beloved foster father. He knew what it was like to lose
a loved one. Miriam had no parents at all, now. Her
father was buried here, and her mother out east.

At least he still had parents whom he loved. And
somewhere on God's good earth, a biological mother
whom his brother Simon was determined to find.

For a moment Jake wondered about his mother.
Wondered if she was still alive, if she ever thought
about them.

Then he dismissed the thought, feeling as if he
were betraying Fred and Tilly. They were enough
family for him.

Taryn saw him and came running over. "We saw
my mommy's grave," she called out cheerfully. Tilly
looked up and saw him, then said something to Miriam, who nodded and then left.

As Tilly walked across the parking lot, she waved
at a few people, called out greetings to others. Then
she saw that Jake and Fred were waiting, and hurried
her pace.

"Sorry," she said, puffing as she opened the back
door of the car for Taryn. "Miriam wanted to visit
the graveyard."

"She was sad again," said Taryn, scrambling into
the back seat.

"Seat belt," warned Jake as she settled in.

"That poor girl. I'm glad she agreed to come over now," Tilly said, cinching her own belt. "She can seem so strong, but inside she's hurting. She used to be so strong in her faith—I just pray she finds some peace here."

Jake started the car, his eyes on Miriam, who now walked back to her car, alone. For a moment he, too, prayed for her.

Chapter Six

❦

"So you went to your aunt and uncle's place, and then what?" Tilly asked Miriam as they cleared the table of dishes. Jake and Taryn were playing a game on one corner of the large oak table. Fred was lying down in his bedroom.

Miriam watched Taryn for a moment, remembering the many times she had sat in the same place Taryn now did, playing a game with Fred or Tilly, and later on, Jake. The sun poured in through the same flowered curtains. On the wall above the table, ticked the same blue clock. The figurines in the window were the same as she remembered, and the sets of salt and pepper shakers still sat on the shelf that hung on one end of the wooden cupboard. It was home to her.

Miriam turned back to Tilly. "We only stayed there a couple of weeks. Then we found our own place. I finished high school and shortly after I turned eighteen I was scouted by a modeling agency."

"And what did your mother think of this?"

Miriam drew in a slow breath, reliving the roller-coaster events of her life at that time. "Mom had a debilitating stroke just before that. She was fully dependent. I knew I wouldn't be able to go to college or university. I needed to support the two of us. So I started modeling."

She declined to tell Tilly that she had also found out about Jake and Paula.

"Where did you go?"

Miriam shrugged. "The coast, California at first, then Europe," she said, deliberately ambiguous. She didn't want to admit that she couldn't remember a lot of those years. One place melded into another in her mind—planes, hotels; up early to catch good light, up late to catch the best party. Then doing it all over again the next day or week.

"My goodness, what a life for a young girl," Tilly said, gathering the rest of the pots and bringing them to the counter. "Well, I'm glad you're back here. We've missed you."

"Why did you miss her?" Taryn interrupted, looking up from her game.

"Because she was a good friend. She used to come over here all the time," Tilly replied, turning to her granddaughter.

Miriam fended off another attack of guilt. And Miriam didn't tell her mother much either. She figured it would be better for her mother if she didn't know all the details of Miriam's life. The years she had spent traveling had left her rootless, living a life that had no

adults in it to call her to account for what she had
been doing. There was no voice of reason in her life,
no guidance. Her mother could barely speak, let alone
counsel her. She realized now how important even a
quiet word of caution or chastisement would have
been at that time in her life.

"What's the matter, dear? You look troubled."
Tilly laid her hand on Miriam's arm.

She shook her head and curved her lips into a smile.
"I'm fine."

"I win, Daddy. I win," Taryn crowed. She gathered
up the pieces of the game, then leaned her elbows on
the table and looked at Miriam. "You want to play
with me, Miriam?"

Miriam smiled at her as she picked up the cups from
the table. "I should help your grandmother with the
dishes."

"Oh, nonsense. You go and play with her. It takes
nothing to load up this dishwasher." Tilly took the
cups from Miriam.

Jake was still sitting at the table, leaning back in his
chair, watching her through lowered eyes.

"I'll be blue, you can be red," Taryn suggested,
handing Miriam a playing piece. "You know how to
play Snakes and Ladders?"

"I think so," Miriam said, smiling.

Taryn grinned back. "I can start, okay?"

"Fine by me." Miriam settled beside her, directly
across from Jake. She chanced a glance up at him,
lifting her chin as if to say, *What is your problem?*
Throughout dinner she had felt as if he'd been watch-

ing, measuring. At first it had made her feel uncomfortable; now it was getting annoying. He tilted his head a bit, as if to see her from another angle, then dropped his chair with a *thunk* on the floor.

"I should go and check the cows," he said tersely to anyone who was listening.

"I have to shake the dice and then count," Taryn explained to Miriam, ignoring her father.

"Miriam, did you put that pot in the sink?" Tilly asked, looking up from the dishwasher.

Miriam felt a bit sorry for Jake. No one seemed to have heard what he said. She was about to ask him about the cows when Taryn poked her in the arm.

"Miriam, it's your turn."

"Taryn," Jake said, his tone hard. "Don't be rude."

Taryn looked down, immediately contrite. "Sorry, Daddy."

Jake looked around the kitchen, blew out a sigh and left.

Miriam watched him go, unable to keep her eyes off him. They hadn't spoken more than two words to each other since he had opened the meal with prayer. She had caught him looking at her, but had tried to act casually. It was difficult. She had thought their time spent in town might be a melting point. But she had been wrong. He sat across the table as disapprovingly as he had the first day she had come here.

She yearned to fix what hovered between them, even though, if she thought about it logically, it seemed pointless. She wouldn't be staying, and once she was gone she wouldn't be returning.

She turned back to the game and Taryn.

Twenty minutes later, with the dishwasher humming in the background, Tilly sitting at the table reading some material she had gotten from church, Miriam figured it was time she left.

"No. Stay a little longer," Taryn said. "We can play another game."

"We've already played four games," Miriam said with a smile, getting up from the table. She laid a finger on Taryn's nose and walked over to Tilly, dropping her hand on her shoulder. "Thanks for dinner. I really appreciate it."

"It was nice to have you." Tilly got up and pulled Miriam close. "It has been too long." She held Miriam by the shoulders, looking at her with her penetrating blue eyes. "You won't let that happen again, will you?"

Miriam bit her lip and shook her head. "No. I'm sorry." Apologies again, she thought. "Please give my regards to Uncle Fred for me."

"I will. I'll stop by sometime this week, when Fred's a little better. Are you going to be around?"

"For a while yet."

"Good. We'll have time to catch up." Smiling, Tilly walked with Miriam to the porch.

Miriam pulled her coat off the hanger and turned once more to Tilly, her heart softening at the sight of the older woman standing in the doorway the way she had so many times when Miriam had come over as a girl. "Thanks for having me over," she said quietly. "It meant a lot to me."

"I'm glad. You come again."

Taryn had followed them and now leaned against Tilly. Tilly absently stroked the little girl's head, and once again Miriam felt a clutch of envy. Taryn didn't know how fortunate she was, she thought—to be loved so unconditionally by so many people.

Miriam tossed them a quick wave and then, turning, left. She hurried down the sidewalk, wrapping her coat around her against the cool wind that had sprung up.

She pulled her car keys out of her purse and was about to press the remote starter when she heard her name being called.

Stopping, she lifted her head to see where the voice came from, then saw Jake come striding across the yard, his hands in the pockets of his denim jacket, collar pulled up against the chill.

Miriam watched him approach, allowed herself a moment to appreciate his height and the easy way he carried himself. Jake had always had a quiet maturity, a steadiness that had appealed to her own young, flighty nature. And once she got to know him, he had a surprising vulnerability. But the Jake Steele she'd known was but a boy compared to the man who now came toward her. This man was harder, more reserved. Each time their eyes met, it was as if he were appraising her. She never felt as if she quite measured up.

She wondered what he wanted to say to her now. Throughout the meal he had been quiet, watching her with those deep brown eyes that at one time had melted her heart, but now seemed as uncompromising as the Ten Commandments she had heard this morning.

"Out checking the cows?" she asked as he came closer. She was determined to treat him the same way she would treat any man she had just met—to be chatty and interested in what he was doing, but keep her emotions firmly intact. Ten years was long enough to move on, and it was time she did.

He stopped beside her, his shoulders hunched against the wind. "Yes. I'm moving them out to pasture tomorrow."

She was doing an admirable job of slipping back into her "country" persona. Next thing, she'd be asking him how many acres of canola he was going to plant and what kind of weed spray he was going to use.

She fiddled with her key chain, trying to think of something casual to say.

"Miriam."

Jake spoke her name quietly, almost in entreaty. Miriam couldn't stop looking up at him, couldn't stop her heart from pounding. To her shame, hearing him speak her name made her feel as breathless as a young girl in the throes of her first crush.

Which Jake had been.

He was standing quite close to her, his hands in the pockets of his coat, holding it open. Their eyes met, and Miriam forced herself to try to breathe normally at the connection. "Yes?" she asked.

"I, uh, was wondering if you..." He paused again,

and Miriam felt a foolish lift of her heart. He sounded the way he had the first time he'd asked her out on a date.

Don't be utterly foolish, Miriam reminded herself. You are both older and wiser. He's a father, a widower. She forced herself to keep silent, to wait to see what he wanted.

Jake shoved his hand through his hair and held her gaze, his own steady, relentless. "I was wondering if you would mind waiting a while before you put your farm up for sale."

Funny how quickly a heart could plunge. How quickly breathless hope could be replaced with harsh reality. She slowly drew in a breath, then another. "I can't. I already went to the real estate agent on Friday and listed it."

Jake blinked, his expression unchanging. "I see."

Miriam wanted to tell him that if he wanted it, he could have it. But she couldn't give him anything. Not her heart, not her land. And she couldn't tell him how badly she needed the money to satisfy her creditors. It was too humiliating.

"How long did you say you were going to be here?" he continued.

"I was going to stay until next Tuesday. Then I have to leave."

He nodded again, biting his lower lip. He wanted to say something else to her, she sensed.

"I, uh, don't know how to say this," he began. "But I get a real feeling that Taryn is becoming quite attached to you."

Miriam shrugged the notion off. "I'm just someone different. That's all."

"I hope so. I don't want her to be hurt."

Miriam felt his words as much as heard them. "I understand exactly what you are getting at, Jake," she replied, her anger rising. "I can't imagine what you think I would do to her."

Jake looked down, digging the toe of his boot in the ground, then glanced back up at her. "Taryn forms attachments very quickly. I once made the mistake of taking a girlfriend home to meet her. When we split up, Taryn was more brokenhearted than either me or the girlfriend. I don't want to see that happen to her again."

"I'm hardly a girlfriend, Jake," she said, the words sounding harsh even to her.

"That's true. I'm sorry if you misunderstood me, but I have to take care of her."

Miriam unclenched her fists and forced herself to relax. "I realize that, Jake."

"Well, I better let you go then." He took a step back, turned and walked away, his head bent to the wind.

Miriam clutched her own coat closer to her, swallowing down resentment over her life situation and anger over Jake's. He was only doing what he had to. He was taking care of his family first. She couldn't blame him for that.

But it still hurt.

In Jake's life, Taryn was first.

She acknowledged the rightness of it even as she

felt an alarming jealousy that this girl was now the most important person to Jake.

Even if there was a slight chance, even just a hint that Jake was interested in her, Miriam knew that she wasn't a suitable person to be Taryn's mother. Between her life-style and this one was a rift that couldn't be crossed. Her life was just a wasteland of broken dreams and promises. She really didn't have anything to give anyone. She wouldn't know how to be a mother, how to be a wife. The reality was that she was broke, out of work. She had a debt load that overwhelmed and frightened her any time she thought about it. Even with the work Carl promised, it would take a long time to repay.

She was no longer an asset to a man, to someone like Jake. She would be more of a liability. In many ways.

Miriam got into her car, put it into gear and backed out of the driveway, wondering how she was going to last her allotted time here.

On Monday afternoon, Miriam pulled into Fred and Tilly's driveway. From what she could see, the big tractor Jake used for field work was gone.

Safe, she figured. She needed some gas to fill up her lawn mower, and there was none at her place. She had spent most of the day sorting through the stuff she and her mother had packed up and moved to the basement. After her "talk" with Jake, she had been so upset that she had had to keep busy, to keep her hands and mind occupied.

After about seven trips to the community landfill, she had substantially reduced the number of boxes left over. What was left could be put up for sale, and most of these she had moved to the shop.

So now the outside needed to be cleaned up. The real estate agent had said she would be coming either today or tomorrow to take a picture, and Miriam figured she might as well make it look as good as possible.

Stepping out of the car, she looked around the yard. Beyond the huge barn, she could hear cows bellowing. She wondered if something was wrong.

Curious, she walked past the barn and to the corrals beyond. Climbing up on the fence, she saw the herd of cows hanging around the two huge metal feeders—they were empty.

Cows probably need to get fed, she thought, stepping down. She walked back to the house and knocked on the door. No answer. Puzzled, she pushed open the door and put her head in.

"Hello, anybody home?"

"I'm in the living room, Miriam," Tilly called out. Miriam stepped inside, kicked her shoes off and walked in.

Tilly was sitting on the recliner, reading. She looked up when Miriam came in. "Hello, dear. So good to see you again." She put the footrest down and got up. "Come in, sit down."

"I can't stay long. I was just wondering if I could get some gas. I need to mow that lawn."

"Oh, I'm sure you can. Do you remember which

tank is diesel and which one is regular?'' Tilly asked with a frown. "I know I don't.''

"I can probably figure it out." Miriam glanced around. "Where are Fred and Taryn?''

"Taryn is at play school, and Fred is sleeping. He took a bad spell right after Jake left. Do you want something to drink?''

"No. I should get back to the house. It looks like there's a rain shower coming, and I want to get the lawn mowed before that. I'll probably stop by tomorrow.''

"You do that, dear.''

"What's wrong with the cows? They're sure making a lot of noise. Are they hungry?''

Tilly's hand flew to her mouth. "Oh, no. Fred was supposed to feed the cows this morning. Jake told him not to, that they could wait, but Fred was insistent. Now he won't be able to.'' She shook her head. "I guess they'll have to wait until Jake comes home. And he'll be so tired.''

Miriam hesitated. It was none of her business what happened to Jake's cows. Yet, she could see how genuinely distressed Tilly was.

Tilly got up and put her book down. "I'll just have to feed them myself. I'll have to phone the school to tell them I'll be late picking up Taryn.''

Miriam had to smile at the thought of Tilly sitting in a tractor, wearing her ever-present skirt and blouse.

"Don't be silly," she said suddenly. "I remember helping Jake feed the cows. I can do it.''

"No, dear. You don't have to do that. You're here for a holiday."

"Feeding the cows is hardly a huge chore," Miriam said with a laugh. "It will be a nice break for me."

"Are you sure?"

Miriam could see obvious relief on Tilly's face, and nodded. "Think of it as payment for the gas I have to borrow."

"Hardly seems fair. But as long as you don't mind. It will work out really well for me. I have to pick up Taryn in half an hour, and I know Fred can't do it. Not now."

"Then that settles it. We don't want her waiting for you." Miriam patted Tilly on the shoulder. "You just sit down and take it easy. I'll get those cows fed."

An hour later, Miriam jumped out of the gate and closed it behind her. The tractor with the bale forks had no cab, and she was still picking hay out of her hair and wiping dust out of her eyes. She figured she looked a fright, but didn't care. It was fun driving the tractor, dumping the huge round bales into the feeder and trying to avoid running over cows or calves. After depositing the last bale, she had backed up and simply sat and watched the calves racing around, their tails up in the air, then stopping suddenly and coming back to check out who this strange person was.

She still had to smile, thinking of how clean and fresh they looked compared to the cows. She had forgotten how cute they could be and how much fun they were to watch. For a moment she was the Miriam of old, helping Jake with his chores, hoping her mother wouldn't find out.

She walked back to the tractor and climbed on, put it in gear and then drove it to where it had originally been parked. She had to stand up to turn the wheel; the steering was tight and the front-end loader made it that much more difficult to maneuver.

But she'd done it, she thought proudly as she shut off the roaring engine.

She blinked some more and then climbed off. Before she'd fed the cows, she had filled her jerry can with gas, and Tilly had now left to pick up Taryn. Miriam could leave right away.

With a smile, she turned—and almost ran smack into Jake.

Miriam swallowed and took a step back. "Hello," she said quietly, wiping her hands on her pants. "I fed your cows for you."

"I see that," he replied, not moving. "Thanks."

"I came to get gas for my lawn mower, so I figured I would do it. Tilly seemed quite worried about them."

"I was just coming home to do it."

He sounded defensive, and Miriam felt that once again she had done the wrong thing.

"Whatever," she said, dismissing his comment. She went to walk past him, and as she did, he caught her arm.

She turned to him and unconsciously pulled her arm back.

"Sorry," he said, dropping his hand. "I just wanted to say thanks. I really appreciate the help."

Miriam sensed a discord between them that came up with each encounter. She knew it had as much to do with their past as their present, but she didn't know how to work through it.

Or even if she wanted to. What would it accomplish?

"You're welcome," she said. Then she turned and left.

Back at home Miriam threw herself back into her work. She mowed the lawn, trimmed the hedge, pruned the apple trees; and when the shower she'd talked of came, she found other things to do.

The next morning, the sun was shining and birds trilled their songs, calling her out.

She had a few other things to do, and then planned to go over to Fred and Tilly's. It was beautiful weather, so she could probably avoid Jake. Most likely, he was out in the field.

She had spent most of last night and part of this morning sorting through things, deciding what she wanted to keep and what to throw out.

She managed to put aside about two boxes' worth of keepsakes and mementos for herself—the photo albums, a few old books and records, a set of baby booties her mother had saved.

Miriam turned her head to look out the living room window, smiling at the sight of the lawn. It was a neatly clipped sweep of green, broken by a single maple tree dominating the front yard. Tall aspen trees, holding a hint of spring green, surrounded and protected it. Beyond them a double row of spruce trees stood guard, sheltering the yard on all sides from wind.

Outside had always been Miriam's sanctuary. Outside was where she went to get away from her mother and her constant demands.

Miriam pushed herself off the couch and got up. She needed to get away from the house…and the memories.

She found her jacket, zipped it up and stepped outside with the same sense of freedom she had felt as a young girl whenever she managed to get away.

Inhaling the warm scent of spring, she started walking briskly down the driveway. She didn't have any destination in mind, just a desire to get away from the cobwebs, the dust and the past.

The driveway was shielded by double rows of trees, and by the time Miriam saw the road, she felt better. As she walked down the familiar route, she felt the peace that had seemed to elude her in the house float down over her weary soul.

The land was open here, rolling and friendly. She let her eyes drift over the fields, the trees. Memories of her life in New York became overlaid with the combed-looking fields that had already been cultivated, the pastures that were already green. The soft, spring wind sifted through the trees alongside the road, and from the power line above came the sweet song of a sparrow.

Spring in the country.

Miriam felt a gentle stirring of her heart as the

atmosphere surrounded her, drawing out happy memories, moments of utter abandon and freedom.

How often had she and her friends sat, hunkered over the ditches, floating sticks and leaves in the spring runoff? How often had they taken her horse and, doubling up, ridden off in whichever direction the day took them?

Paula's face came to her mind, and Miriam bit back a sudden cry. Paula, her good friend. Paula, who had listened to Miriam's adolescent complaints about her looks. Paula, who had been her confidante when Miriam had discovered her growing love for Jake Steele, the boy so many girls liked. Paula, who had ended up with the prize, after all.

Now Paula was dead. Sorrow tightened her throat, pressed on her heart.

Miriam couldn't stop the tears drifting down her cheeks, cooled by the spring breeze. She couldn't help but remember the sight of Taryn pointing out her own mother's gravestone. Seeing Paula's name etched in the granite slab had made her death so definite, so real.

She wondered if Paula and Jake had been happy for those few years they had been together. She wondered if Jake mourned her very much.

Once again Miriam felt jealousy.

Shaking her head, she tried to pull herself away from these maudlin thoughts. "Just enjoy the day," she said aloud. "Just enjoy the day."

A thicket of spruce and aspen trees beckoned, and as she walked through the moldering undergrowth, the spicy scent of freshly opened aspen leaves teased her nose. Willow branches caught at her, but she finally found the game trail that led her deeper into the bush.

And there it was, high up in the boughs of a large pine tree—the remnants of her old tree house. A few boards speckled with lichen and moss hung from a couple of nails, and the platform was still in place. On the tree beside her were nailed the single boards that provided a shaky ladder to her old retreat.

She smiled, remembering how many fantasies had been spun here. When she was older, she and Paula had come here...until Paula declared herself "too big" for games like this.

Then when she and Jake started dating, this fort had become a haven for them. Here they could sit and talk of the future, make plans, dream.

Miriam smiled lightly, then turned away. It seemed memories of her past romance with Jake would come to her no matter what she did or where she went.

She walked back the way she had come and returned to the road. Once there, she set out for nowhere in particular. She just wanted to walk and to enjoy the fact that today she had no other obligations, no concerns.

As she walked, she looked around, seeing the spread of the land, the various hues of green that told her summer was almost here. Soon the cows would be out on pasture.

"And all the trees of the field will clap their hands..." The quote came to her lips as she paused, looking out over the land. She couldn't even remember where that was found—only that it came from the Bible.

She stood, looking out and smiling, and for the first time since she had come, felt peace. A soft breeze swirled around her like a benediction, rustling through the leaves of the trees above as if they were indeed clapping their hands.

There was joy in the air, and Miriam pulled it to herself and let it flow through her.

She tried to memorize each line of trees, each glade, the flow of the fields, the pastures, the farmyards she could see and the barns and grain bins that filled them. This was where she had come from. She wanted to remember this moment, this very place. In future, when she was stuck in the oppressive heat of summer in New York, when she sweltered outside or shivered in air-conditioned cool inside, she would return to this place in her mind, and know that somewhere life flowed instead of jerking and jumping around.

Miriam hadn't prayed in years, but now the words came to her lips unbidden. "Thank you, Lord," she whispered. "Thanks for this moment, for this part of the world."

She waited a moment as if to acknowledge a certain holiness to the moment.

Then she began walking again.

She had walked for about fifteen minutes when she heard a car coming up behind her. She moved to the side of the road, hoping it would slow down. The road was still wet in spots, and she stood a good chance of getting splashed.

The car slowed, all right, and then came to a complete halt, the engine running. Miriam turned to see Tilly Prins rolling down the window of her midsize car, smiling at her. Fred was on the seat beside her, Taryn in the back.

"Hello, Miriam," she called out. "Out for a walk on this beautiful day?"

"Yes, I am." Miriam couldn't hide her smile as she walked over. "How are you doing, Uncle Fred?" Yesterday he had looked a little better.

Fred opened his eyes and smiled wanly at her, and then closed them again. Tilly shook her head, her lips pursed. "He's running a high fever, so I'm bringing him in to the doctor. Fred fell when he got out of bed this morning, he was feeling so weak," Tilly added, turning back to Miriam, her head tilted up to look at her, her blue eyes looking tired. "Jake was gone. Otherwise, I would have asked him to take Taryn."

Taryn leaned forward, a frown puckering her forehead. "I can't go to play school 'cause there's not play school today."

"That's too bad," Miriam said, giving her a gentle smile. Today Taryn wore blue jeans and a pink windbreaker. Her hair was pulled back in a ponytail high up on her head, tied up with a matching pink ribbon. She looked adorable.

Tilly paused, glancing sidelong at Taryn, then back up at Miriam, beckoning to her to come closer. Tilly lowered her voice. "I know you're on a holiday, but I was wondering if you would be willing to take Taryn for the day."

"Please," Taryn pleaded, her hands curled into fists pressed under her chin. "Please let me come to your place."

"It would really help me out a lot," Tilly said.

Miriam looked down at Tilly, noting the wrinkles around her face. Yes, Tilly had grown older while Miriam had been gone. She looked tired and careworn.

She bit her lip, remembering countless times she had sat in Tilly's kitchen, eating cookies and talking. Countless times she had complained to Tilly about her mother's unfair treatment. Hugs and kisses she had received from this dear woman who was as much of a mother to her as she had been to Jake. Helping her out now would be but a drop of kindness compared to the gallons of love Tilly had given her.

"Sure," Miriam said, unsure of what she was expected to do with a little girl all day. "I'll take her."

"Thank you so much," Tilly breathed, and as Miriam saw some of the strain leave Tilly's face, she knew she had done the right thing. She would just have to take her chances with Jake.

"Oh goody, goody." With quick movements, Taryn unclipped her seat belt and jumped out of the car.

"You behave, now," Tilly said with a warning frown. Of course Taryn nodded. She turned back to Miriam. "Thanks again, my dear. You've really helped me out a lot." Tilly smiled with relief, put the car in gear, then paused. "I don't know how long I'm going to be, but if I'm not home by suppertime, can I ask another favor of you?"

"Anything, Tilly," Miriam said with heartfelt sincerity.

"Jake is going to be working your fields sometime today, and I usually bring him supper so he can keep going. If I don't come back on time, I made a casserole for him. Can you see that he gets it?"

Miriam felt her heart slow at the thought of seeing the very man she hoped to avoid.

"I'll probably be home," Tilly said, acknowledging her hesitation. "But just in case."

"If you're not around, I'll see that he gets something to eat." Miriam shrugged fatalistically. *What would be would be.*

"Thanks again, Miriam." Tilly smiled at Taryn, then back at Miriam, and with a wave, drove away, dust billowing up behind her.

Miriam and Taryn stood on the road, waving back as the cloud receded farther and farther, until it disappeared around a curve.

Miriam felt Taryn slip her hand into hers. She couldn't stop her own from tightening around the smaller one as she looked down at Jake's daughter. For a moment she indulged in a dangerous "what if."

What if…she and Jake had stayed together? What if…this precious child had been hers and Jake's?

"Do you want to keep walking?" Taryn asked, grinning up at her, swinging her hand. "I like walking."

"Then let's keep going." Miriam gently eased her hand out of Taryn's. She felt uneasy pulling back from

Taryn's obvious affection, but knew it was better if she didn't allow this young child to get too attached to her.

Just as Jake had warned.

Chapter Seven

"**M**y daddy is workin' on the tractor today and then he has to move the cows." Taryn hopped across a puddle and flashed a grin at Miriam. "He's gonna be busy, he told me. But when he's done, we're going to go to the city and buy me some pretty gloves. He promised me."

"You really love your daddy, don't you?" Miriam asked as she strolled along, hands in her pockets. She knew she shouldn't pry, but some part of her wanted to know more about Jake and his relationship with his daughter.

"I love my daddy the bestest. I love my mommy, too, but she died," Taryn stated in a matter-of-fact voice. "My friend Suzy Adams has two mommies and two daddies."

"That's a lot of mommies and daddies," Miriam said with a shake of her head, wondering how often poor Suzy Adams was shunted from place to place.

"I just want one mommy," Taryn said, as if this were the most reasonable request in the world.

Miriam instinctively knew she had to change the subject. "Do you want to make a water wheel?" she asked, scanning the area for some cattails. She saw some on the other side of the road, their brown heads tilting slightly in the breeze.

"What's a water wheel?"

"You make it out of two cattail stems." Grinning, Miriam walked over to the cattails and reached into her back pocket for a pocketknife.

"Oops," she said, laughing and looking sheepishly back at Taryn. "I don't have a pocketknife." Funny that she would do that, she thought. "I forgot I don't carry one anymore."

"That's okay. My daddy always has a pocketknife. It has a tweezer and a scissor. It's a red pocketknife and has J.S. on it. That means Jake Steele. He told me that. He got it as a present from someone special— not from my mommy though." Taryn chattered on as she bent over to look at a rock, poking it with one finger.

Miriam's feet slowed, a spark kindling within her. After all these years, Jake still had the pocketknife she had given him, the one she had saved up her meager allowance for. She allowed herself a moment of wondering why.

Don't be silly, girl. Miriam pulled her thoughts up short. He's always been careful with the things he has, that's all.

"We should probably go back. It's quite some ways

to walk yet,'' she said to Taryn, who now had three rocks clutched in her hands.

Though Miriam didn't encourage her, Taryn chattered while they walked, bringing Miriam up to date on what was happening in her life, her father's life and Tilly's and Fred's lives. It was a bittersweet pleasure to Miriam to hear about Jake—how much he was at home, how often he slept in the recliner in the evening, how he liked to read Taryn stories.

They had come to the top of the hill, just a few hundred feet from her driveway, when they heard the familiar growl of a tractor coming down the road. Her heart skipped. Tilly had said Jake was coming to work the fields by her house. It was probably him right now.

"My daddy," Taryn called out as soon as the tractor topped the hill. She grinned up at Miriam. "That's my daddy. Let's run and we can catch him."

Still clutching her rocks, Taryn took off, her ponytail bobbing with each step. She was heading straight for the lumbering tractor.

Miriam's heart jumped, and she sprinted after the little girl, catching her by the shoulder. "Don't, Taryn. What if he can't see you? He'll run right over you."

Taryn frowned up at Miriam. "Not my daddy. He sees everything."

As the tractor came closer, Miriam realized from Jake's glower that Taryn was right.

Jake slammed the throttle lever back, hit the clutch and braked. Why was Taryn with Miriam? And where was Tilly? He put the tractor in park, took in a deep breath and climbed out of the cab.

"Daddy, Daddy, look at the rocks I found." Taryn came running up to him, waiting, as he had taught her, a safe distance away from the wheels of the huge tractor.

He walked closer, pointedly ignoring Miriam as he took a moment to squat down and look at the rocks in his daughter's dirty hands. "They are very nice," he said, turning one over in his hand, then handing it back to Taryn.

"And Miriam was going to make a water wheel, but she didn't have her pocketknife." Taryn bestowed an innocent smile on him, clutching her rocks back to her chest. "I said you have one. Can we use it?"

"Sure you can," Jake said absently as he straightened, finally looking over at Miriam, who stood a distance away. A safe distance away, he thought, reaching automatically into the front pocket of his jeans to pull out his pocketknife. He walked over and handed it to her. "Taryn said you needed this?"

Miriam took it, avoiding his gaze. "We were going to make water wheels just after Tilly met me on the road." Miriam looked down at the knife, then up at him. "Fred isn't feeling good, and Tilly had to bring him into town. She asked me to watch Taryn for her."

Jake heard Miriam's words, his heart tightening. Fred, sick again? It must be serious if Tilly was taking the time to bring him in, and Fred was letting her.

He closed his eyes briefly, sending up a quick prayer. *Please, Lord. Don't let it be serious.* He opened his eyes and caught Miriam looking at him with that same wistful expression he had seen before. He felt a sudden desire to touch her, to reassure her himself. He had to stop himself from pulling her into his arms.

"You still have this," she said quietly, holding up his pocketknife. She looked up at him again, the spring breeze lifting strands of her hair.

"Yeah. It was the first birthday present I had gotten in a few years." He shrugged, willing away the attraction he felt for her.

She smiled then, running her thumb over the worn red plastic. "I remember saving up to buy it for you."

Once again Jake suppressed the urge to touch her hair, to curve his hand around her neck. To pull her close.

He took a step back, as if afraid he had already done so. "I better get back to work," he said abruptly. "Did Tilly say what time she would be back?"

"I'm not sure," Miriam said. "She asked if I could bring you supper if she didn't get back on time." She chanced another glance up at him, adding, "If you don't mind, that is."

Jake felt a nudge of sorrow at the uncertainty on her face. It made her look vulnerable. Not an emotion he would have associated with her at any time in her life. Not as a young girl, not as a woman. "No, that's okay." He waited as time seemed to drift away. Once again they were young and in love. Once again she smiled up at him, her eyes shining.

But he remembered the pictures in Paula's book: a

girl made up and expensively dressed. He could pretend all he wanted, but this Miriam was far removed from him. He called a quick goodbye to his daughter and climbed back in the tractor.

Then he put the tractor in gear and turned into the field. Dropping the cultivator down, he adjusted the depth and half turned to look behind him.

Miriam and Taryn stood on the road, watching him.

His past and his present, side by side.

For a moment he wondered what his life would have been like had he and Miriam stayed together. Would that little girl have been theirs? Would they have had more?

"Don't be ridiculous, Jake," he said, switching on the radio. "She's in another realm now." And her leaving meant this land he now worked would be sold.

His day chugged along, punctuated by hourly news and weather reports. The songs melded one into the other, country songs usually, or classical music when he bothered to change the station. Jake worked his way up and down the quarter of land, each time on his return watching out for Miriam and his daughter. He caught sight of them once, walking down the road, heading out, he suspected, to make the water wheel Taryn had spoken of. The sun gave off a sharp spring brightness, creating a feeling of expectation and promise, and he wished he could be with Taryn and Miriam, diking up the spring runoff, doing little family things.

He tried to concentrate on his work, but found his eyes straying to the two figures as they made their way down the road, looking for all the world like a mother and daughter.

The next time he came back to the road Miriam and Taryn were gone, and he felt as if the day had lost a measure of that brightness and expectation.

The sun moved inexorably across the sky. By 5:30, Jake once again began watching the road for Miriam. It was because he was hungry, he told himself. But when he thought of spending another mealtime with her, he felt a burst of pleasure.

"You're a strange man," he said aloud, turning the wheel of the tractor at the end of the field. "And a very stupid one." He got the tractor straightened around and lined up, then dropped the cultivator again. The roar of the tractor's engine was the only sound he heard as he worked his way down the field. He was up and over the rise when he saw a car parked on the road. His spirits lifted in spite of his previous castigation.

He could just make out Miriam's slim figure, her hand up, shading her eyes against the lowering sun, watching him, waiting for him. It felt good to know she was there.

He parked the tractor and walked over. "Where's Taryn?" he asked as he approached.

"Playing in the ditch. We ate already. I've got your supper in the car," she said, walking over to it and opening the door. "I hope it's still warm." She pulled out a hamper.

Jake walked around the car, and when she straightened, he was there to take the hamper from her. Star-

tled, she took a step back and almost lost her balance.
Jake caught her by the shoulders, and her head came
up. Once again their eyes held. Awareness arced between them. Jake didn't let go of her shoulders, and
she didn't let go of the hamper.

Her eyes were the same deep brown that he remembered, fringed with silky lashes, tilted up at the corners
exotically. She still had a tiny mole at one corner of
her eye; her cheek still sported the barely discernible
scar from the time she bumped it on his truck door.
The same light freckles were sprinkled across her forehead, and her lips still held...still held... Jake couldn't
keep his eyes off her mouth. The way she nervously
wet her lips. The way she swallowed. The way they
parted slightly as her breath quickened.

"Please, Jake," she said quietly.

Jake looked up into her eyes again, his fingers tightening, his thumbs caressing her arms through the thin
material of her sweater. Then, with a deep breath, he
dropped his hands. What was wrong with him? He was
acting as if they were both still teenagers. Still in love.

"Sorry," he said, taking the cooler from her. There
was a moment of awkwardness as their hands meshed;
she tried to let go and he tried to take hold.

"Look at what Miriam made me," Taryn trilled,
skipping up to his side.

Jake put down the cooler, thankful for the diversion.
"Wow. A willow whistle."

Taryn nodded. "Listen." She put it in her mouth
and blew lightly. It gave a definite *tweet* and Taryn
grinned her pleasure. "Miriam made it for me outa

piece o' wood from the bush. She just cut it and made it. She said when the bark dries it won't work anymore. You try it now." Taryn handed it to him, and Jake dutifully blew on the willow whistle.

The spicy smell, the smooth texture of the bark and the faint bitter taste all took him back to other springs.

Other springs with Miriam. She was the only one he knew who could make these. He had asked her to teach him once, but she had played coy, telling him that it was one of her few talents and that she needed to keep some secrets.

He had never learned how to make them. He had one he had kept but as Taryn said once they got older they didn't work. He hadn't blown on one since then.

Miriam was setting up lawn chairs beside him, and he handed the whistle back to Taryn, who gave it another *tweet* and ran off back to the ditch for more treasures. Jake shifted to face Miriam.

"You still remember how to make those."

Miriam nodded. "I didn't think I'd remember, but once I started, it all came back. My dad taught me well."

Jake watched as she snapped open her chair and set it on the gravel. "I've never heard you talk about your father."

Miriam bent over the cooler again. "I don't really remember much about him. I was only ten when he died. But I do have a few good memories." She looked up at him, and ventured a half smile.

Jake felt it again—the awareness, the realization

they had known each other in a different time and place, as different people.

They shared a past, memories and an intimacy that he had never really felt with anyone else, even Paula.

And for the first time since Miriam had come, he wondered if she had ever cared for anyone else. Had ever been close to another man.

He realized in the next moment that he didn't want to know.

Jake bent his head and slowly relaxed, letting his thoughts rest, settle and separate from the awareness of the girl sitting beside him.

Thank you for this day, Lord, he prayed, *for my daughter and my family. Please let Fred be okay.* He stopped, almost afraid to pray too hard for Fred, to acknowledge too deeply his own fears about Fred's health. It was as if he didn't quite trust God to take care of him. *Help me to let go, Lord. Help me to know that You love us perfectly. Help me not to build my life on my family.* He stopped again, thinking of Taryn, Tilly and even the girl sitting beside him. *I give them all to You, Lord. I give You each member of my family. Take care of them.* Then he asked for a final blessing on the food and lifted his head, a gentle peace surrounding him.

"I should tell you, Tilly phoned," Miriam said quietly.

Jake lowered his fork, almost afraid to hear what she had to say.

Miriam frowned lightly. "Fred is still running a high fever. If it doesn't go down, they're going to send him to Calgary for some more tests. He's a strong man, Jake,'' she said reassuringly. ''I'm sure he'll be okay.''

''I pray he will,'' Jake replied, toying with the rest of his casserole. He took a few more mouthfuls, then set it aside, his hunger gone.

''Tilly told me that Fred had a heart attack a while ago.'' Miriam's comment broke the silence. ''I'm sure you're quite concerned about him now.''

Jake leaned back in the chair, nodding. ''I get afraid when I think about his health. Anything could happen.'' He looked out over the field, his legs stretched out in front of him.

''How old is Fred now?'' Miriam asked.

''About sixty.'' Jake sighed lightly. ''Which used to seem very old when I was younger.''

''Parents aren't supposed to get old or sick.''

Jake glanced sidelong at Miriam, who leaned forward on her chair, elbows on her knees, her chin resting on her hands. She was staring out over the field, but Jake suspected she was thinking of her own mother.

''I'm sorry about your mother.'' Jake shifted to face her, resisting the urge to touch her, to comfort her.

''It's been difficult....'' Miriam stopped, her lower lip pulled between her teeth.

Jake didn't know what else to say so went back to his meal. He had never cared for Miriam's mother, but he knew that Edna had been a strong force in Miriam's life. Now Edna was dead, and what had happened was long ago.

There were questions he wanted to ask Miriam, things he wanted to know.

And what would that accomplish? he thought, turning away again. Do you want to find out how quickly she forgot you? Do you really want to know? His ego was as fragile as the next man's. Better let it sit. Once she left, and the farm was sold, he would probably never see her again.

He finished his meal and got up, setting the plates inside the hamper. "Thanks for supper."

Miriam nodded and got up, as well. She had been quiet, very unlike the Miriam he knew. Once again he wondered what had happened to her and whether he would find out while she was here.

Miriam closed the lid of the hamper and turned, just as Jake moved to pick it up. She stepped aside and watched as he put it in the car. He came back, and she turned to politely thank him, only to find him staring down at her, his expression unreadable.

"Have a good evening, Miriam," he said quietly.

His deep voice touched a memory. He towered, overpowering, his eyes delving deep into her, searching. He shifted his weight, coming closer to her. For a heart-stopping moment, Miriam thought he might kiss her, the way he would have ten years ago.

Then he stepped back, making way for her to pass. She felt an illogical twinge of disappointment, then walked past him to Taryn.

"I'll be home in about an hour," Jake said behind her. "If Tilly isn't there, do you mind waiting?"

"No," she said without turning. "I don't mind."

A beat of silence, then, "Thanks so much. For everything."

She chanced a look over her shoulder, but avoided his eyes. "You're welcome," she returned, just loud enough for him to hear.

"Bye, Daddy. I'll see you later," Taryn called out.

By the time they got in the car, Jake was in the tractor. As they drove away, Taryn turned around to watch her father as they drove away from each other.

Tilly wasn't at the farmhouse by the time they got there, so Miriam ran the bathtub for Taryn and helped her get ready for bed, listening to the child chatter about the cows, the baby calves and how much she loved her daddy.

A few minutes later, Taryn was kneeling on her bed, pulling a scrapbook from under her pillow. "This is my mommy's book," Taryn said, eagerly holding it out to Miriam. "You want to look? There are pictures of you in it."

Miriam hesitated.

"Please look," Taryn said, pulling Miriam down onto the bed. She set the book on her lap and started turning the pages.

Miriam watched Taryn's small fingers quickly flip through until she found the place she wanted. Miriam wasn't eager to see what Paula might have put in the book, yet it held a strange fascination. Why did Paula want to know what her friend was up to? Why did she go to the bother of cutting out pictures of her husband's old girlfriend? Miriam wasn't naive enough to think that Paula kept them because of some sentimental attachment. The last phone conversation they had ever had was full of Paula's crowing over the victory she had achieved.

She had gotten Jake to take her to the prom.

"Here. They start here," Taryn said with a note of triumph.

Miriam looked down at a picture of herself on the arm of a well-known actor. She was leaning against him, clad in a shimmering sheath she had taken on a loan from a struggling designer.

Opposite it and on the next page were advertisements she had done. These were followed by more of her at a charity function escorted by a well-known fashion designer.

Miriam felt a moment of shame, thinking that Taryn, this sweet innocent child, had seen this part of her life. A part that Miriam wasn't proud of and had spent the last few years trying to live down.

"You had lots of boyfriends, too," Taryn piped up. "You still have lots of boyfriends?"

"Not friends," corrected Miriam sardonically. She closed the book and placed it on the side of the bed. "You don't need to keep this, do you?" She hated to think that Taryn had been exposed to a part of life that no girl of five should know about.

Taryn looked up at her, her expression hurt. "It was my mommy's."

Miriam felt instantly contrite. "Of course. That makes it special, doesn't it." Miriam sat on the bed beside Taryn, determined to prove herself worthy of this young child. "But you know what? Those pictures of me aren't who I am. And they aren't the kind of pictures a little girl like you should see. They are all pictures of big people doing silly things. Things you don't need to see."

"Is it a sin?" she asked, her eyes wide.

Miriam repressed the urge to laugh, yet realized she had never considered her life in such a harsh glare before. Was it "sin"?

She wasn't sure that she was ready to categorize it so bleakly. It certainly was far removed from the life she had lived here in Waylen—that much she was willing to concede.

"It isn't a sin to look at those pictures," she said, neatly sidestepping Taryn's question. "But maybe we could take these ones of me out. Then it can be just a book about your mommy."

Taryn considered this a moment. "But I like you. And I want a picture of you."

"You know what?" Miriam said. "I have other pictures of me. I could send you some of those." She had enough comp cards—surely, she could find a recent one that made her look like a normal person instead of the party-hardy girl she used to be.

"Okay." Taryn smiled and snuggled down into her bed. "Now you have to say my prayers with me." She closed her eyes, her hands folded on her chest, and began singing.

The young voice breathlessly singing the familiar words of "Jesus Tender Shepherd" touched a chord deep in Miriam's heart. If she closed her eyes, she could remember the smell of fresh laundry, and her mother sitting beside her on the bed, singing the song that asked Jesus to stay with her through the darkness, thanking Him for His care during the day.

Miriam swallowed a lump of emotion, suddenly unable to sing along.

Taryn finished on her own and peeked up at Miriam. "You have to help me."

"I forgot the words," Miriam fibbed, sniffing lightly. "Now say the rest of your prayers."

Taryn closed her eyes and launched into a list of "please be with," and named Fred, Tilly, Jake, a few friends from play school, and then, to Miriam's surprise, Taryn asked God to be with Miriam, asked Him to make her happy and not so sad.

Miriam bit her lip, struggling against an unexpected wave of sorrow. To be prayed for, to have someone concerned about her—when had that last happened in her life?

Stop being so maudlin, she told herself.

Ah, the strong voice of reason. Miriam surreptitiously wiped her eyes, took a steadying breath and waited for Taryn to finish her petitions.

When the child was done, she grinned up at Miriam again. "I always pray for you."

"That's nice," Miriam said with a smile. "Now go to sleep."

"Are you going to kiss me good-night?"

Miriam saw a danger in that. As Jake had said, Taryn too easily became attached to people. In spite of Tilly, Fred and Jake's unwavering love, Miriam could see Taryn was hungry for the affection of a mother.

She knew this was her chance to let Taryn know her stay was temporary and to reinforce what Jake had asked of her. ''You know what I'll do instead,'' she said, her heart aching at the poignancy of the moment. ''I'll give you a kiss in your hand and you can use it whenever you want. Okay?'' Miriam didn't wait; she lifted Taryn's small hand and carefully placed a kiss in it. Then she curled her fingers around it and laid it beside the child on the bed. ''There. Now you have a kiss from me that you can use when I'm gone.''

''Where are you going?''

''I don't live here. I'm only staying for a few more days. Then I have to go back to New York. That's where I live.''

''But couldn't you stay? I want you to stay. I want you and my daddy...''

''Miriam doesn't live here, Pip.''

Jake's deep voice from the doorway made Miriam jump. How much had he heard? She glanced up at him, unable to stop her reaction to his presence.

He stood, leaning in the doorway, his hands tucked in the pockets of his jeans, his shirtsleeves rolled up, his shirt open at the neck. The light from the hallway threw his face into silhouette. In that moment Miriam could see so clearly the difference between the young man she had loved and the man who now stood before her. His shoulders were broader, his chest deeper, even his relaxed stance showed her a level of confidence that only comes with age.

It also made him that much more appealing.

"She's only here for a little while, and then she's going back home." Jake pushed himself away from the doorway and walked over to the bed. Miriam jumped up and stepped aside. But the room wasn't very large, and they bumped into each other in the process. Jake caught Miriam by the shoulders, and their eyes met.

It was only a split second, barely measured in a heartbeat, but in that moment her awareness of him compounded. She almost stumbled but regained her balance, thankful for the subdued light in the bedroom. No one could see Miriam Spencer, one-time It Girl and cover model, blushing at the touch of a man who still smelled like the dirt he had been cultivating all day. A man whose chin was rough with whiskers.

A man who didn't really want her around.

Miriam said a quick good-night to Taryn, and then left. Once downstairs she couldn't decide whether she should leave right away, or stay. Politeness deemed that she at least say goodbye to Jake, but she didn't know if she wanted to face him.

She cleaned up the kitchen, glad to keep busy, and, before she was finished, Jake came down the stairs.

"She settled in now?"

Jake nodded and dropped wearily onto a chair, tunneling his hands through his hair. He looked tired. She was sure he was thinking of Fred.

Miriam felt a surge of protectiveness toward him, a desire to run her hands over his head, to tidy the unruly waves, to tell him that everything would be okay.

He looked up at her, his mouth curved into a wry smile. "I want to thank you for taking care of Taryn. I've had a lot on my mind."

Miriam clutched the towel closer, then walked over to the table and sat beside him, covered his hand with hers. She knew he was worried about Fred. She was, as well. "Fred is strong, Jake. I'm sure he'll be fine."

Jake took her hand between his, playing with it.

"I want to thank you for your help. I know I asked you to stay away from Taryn, but…" His voice trailed off.

She didn't want to feel a thrill at the warm touch of his hands, didn't want to look up into his eyes and feel lost again. But she did.

Her business debt seemed to hang over her head like an imprecation. It was wise to remember that. Jake was a good father, a sincere Christian, and she knew that she wasn't the kind of person he would marry. Not anymore.

Somehow the thought hurt beyond description. She didn't want to feel unworthy. She had spent enough of her youth carrying that stigma. Her mother unwittingly reinforced every teasing comment from schoolmates by criticizing her clumsiness, her inability to meet her mother's exacting standards. Miriam had managed to ignore her fellow students and to laugh off their comments, but her mother's had buried deep into her psyche.

Until Jake.

He had been the first man she had ever loved. The first person who had considered her beautiful.

Jake continued to play with her hand, his touch sending shivers curling through her. "I don't imagine you've had much chance to be around kids, yet you certainly have a way with Taryn." He smiled carefully and tilted his head to one side, as if studying her. "What you did upstairs with her was a lesson in diplomacy and tact."

Miriam shrugged the comment away, even as it warmed her to the very fingertips Jake now held. Praise from Jake always did that to her. Silly that even now, it could move her more than any compliment from a photographer or her agent. "She's a sweet child and very intelligent. I do find I have to be careful with her."

"And you have been." He held her eyes with his, his mouth quirking up in a half smile. "Thanks again."

Miriam couldn't have looked away if she'd tried. She wanted to say something to lighten the atmosphere, to give herself some emotional edge.

Instead she leaned forward, giving in to the attraction that was building within her, hoping she could pull this off. "Thanks, yourself," she said quietly, pressing a light kiss to his forehead. But then she inhaled the earthy, farmer smell of him, her confidence wavering, her senses heightened by the contact.

Jake snaked a hand around her neck, capturing her. "Why did you do that?" he asked, his deep brown eyes delving into hers.

Miriam allowed herself a small dream, a tiny reaching toward the unattainable, and stroked his thick hair away from his face, the way she always used to do. "For old times' sake," she whispered, her voice catching.

Jake's eyes seemed to darken as tension built, almost tangibly. Then, slowly, he pulled her head down and touched his lips to hers. It was the barest of caresses, his breath warm on her mouth. Their knees were pressed against each other, preventing closer intimacy.

His warm, soft lips moved over hers, entreating, compelling. Miriam's hands went slack, then she reached up, threading her fingers through his thick hair, anchoring his head as her own mouth returned his caress.

What are you doing? The thought cut through the soft, intangible cocoon of ardor they had spun. Miriam didn't want to acknowledge it, didn't want to pull away. Jake's hand on her neck, his mouth on hers— these were so achingly familiar and so dear. His touch answered a longing that no one else had or ever would.

But…he wasn't for her. She dropped her hand and lowered her head, breaking the contact.

Miriam saw his hand clench into a fist on his knee, and she wanted to touch it, to smooth away the tension she saw there. But she had caused it, she was sure, and would not be able to offer a cure.

"Why, really, did you come back, Miriam?" he asked, his voice hoarse with repressed emotion.

Miriam felt her heart skip, wondered what she dared tell him and still keep her heart whole.

"Did you come here just to sell the farm?" Jake

looked up at her. "You could have done that from out east. You say you came for a break, but I sense there's a lot of pain in your life. Was it a man?"

Miriam closed her eyes at how close he had struck with his comment, yet how far. She could tell him "yes," and she knew he would take it the wrong way. If she said "yes," he would assume she meant a man back east, and he would let go of her hand.

But their sitting here in this kitchen, his rough hand holding hers, brought back bittersweet memories. Memories of stolen kisses and whispered promises. Memories of a love that still haunted her.

And though what she had to say would make her vulnerable to him, she knew she had to finish this at this moment if she was to go back with any measure of peace.

"I guess I wanted to find out about you and Paula," she said quietly. "I had a foolish hope of reconciling with her and you. But I can't talk to her, so there's only you. I want to find out why you broke up with me. Why you married her."

Jake's head shot up and his hands tightened on hers.

As their eyes met, Miriam wondered if she had done the right thing.

Chapter Eight

Jake stared at her, trying to delve past her composed features, her shuttered gaze. "You were the one who wanted to run away," he said simply.

"Because you were talking about our giving each other space and time. And then when I was gone just a few months, I find out you loved Paula."

Jake straightened, realizing for the first time how it had looked from her side.

"Is that what you thought?" he asked.

"What else was I supposed to think?" Miriam's voice was heavy with sarcasm, and the mood in the room suddenly shifted.

"I left, and the next thing I knew you took her to the prom and married her," she continued. "What happened?"

"Why didn't you write me?" he countered.

"Are you kidding?" Miriam got up and shoved the chair back, and Jake saw a brief flash of the old Miriam. "You break up with me, and you expected *me* to write *you?*"

"I didn't break up with you, Miriam. I told you we needed to give each other some space, some time."

"So you could marry Paula."

He suddenly realized how the situation had looked to her, yet hesitated to explain.

"No," he said quietly.

"Then why?" Miriam's voice rose. "Why did you never write me. I was willing to wait. You promised you would love me forever. Why didn't you care—?" Her voice broke on that last word and her hands flew to her face, covering her shame, her pain.

Jake felt his own heart twist at the sound of her voice, the sight of her anguish. He was surprised at the strength of her emotions. Why should it matter after all this time?

He was unsure what to do. She stood, leaning against the kitchen counter, the muted sounds of her cries fastening on his soul like barbed hooks.

He got up, walked toward her and carefully, gently, took her in his arms. At first she resisted, her shoulders hunched, her hands still clutched over her face.

Then, slowly, as he continued to hold her, to stroke her back, the tension holding her in its thrall loosened, and she lay her head against his shoulder. Her slender arms slipped around him, and Jake let his eyes drift shut as she clung to him, his own arms tightening, holding her as close as he dared.

"I'm sorry, Miriam. I'm so sorry. What a mess this all turned out to be."

"Why did you want to break up with me?" she cried, her voice muffled against his shoulder. "Why did you marry Paula? Was she the one you loved?"

Jake didn't want to talk about Paula. Didn't want to bring her between them again. For now he was content just to hold Miriam, to imagine for a moment that she was in his arms because she loved him and because this was the only place she truly wanted to be. He sighed lightly, tucking her head under his chin. And he knew he had to tell her the truth. "No, Miriam. There was another reason I married Paula."

"First tell me why you broke up with me." Miriam pulled away, looking discomfited at her outburst.

"I didn't want to. Your mother had told me that she had all these big plans for you and that I was getting in the way." Jake's chest lifted in a sigh; he carefully reached up and stroked her silky soft hair, inhaling the scent of it. *Just for now, Lord,* he prayed. *Just for now let me pretend she loves me. Just for now let me pretend that she cares for me and that she has come here because she wants to stay.* "I knew what I was, what I didn't have," he continued. "I was turning eighteen in the summer. When that happened, Fred and Tilly would no longer be responsible for me. What could I offer you? When you came up with that half-baked scheme about running away—I have to confess, for a moment, I thought of it, too." He trailed a finger behind her ear and down her neck, remembering other times, happier times, when she was in his arms. "But I also knew that running away never solved anything. It only got Simon in trouble. I knew I had to wait and see what was going to happen in my life. Your mother..." He stopped. Her mother was dead. Bringing her up was unfair and didn't solve anything.

"What about her?"

"Doesn't matter," Jake said quietly.

"Yes it does, Jake." She brushed the remnants of the tears away from her face. "I know she had a lot to do with how my life ended up. When she was dying, I tried to ask her, but she couldn't tell me. You have to."

Jake drew in a deep breath and turned away from Miriam, his mind going back to that evening when he found out what Edna Spencer really thought of him. "She told me that I didn't deserve you, and she was right. However, she also warned me that if I continued seeing you, she would cause problems for me and social services. I was scared. I was afraid she would see to it that I was kicked out of Fred and Tilly's place, and I had no other place to go. I didn't want to talk to Fred and Tilly about it because I didn't trust them. But I also knew she was right. What she had planned for you was bigger than anything I could ever offer."

He shrugged, rubbing the back of his neck. "I thought the best thing for both of us was for me to let go of you and give you a chance at something else." He pulled his hand over his face and blew out his breath. "I thought that maybe someday, I could make something of myself and come and get you. Letting you go was one of the hardest things I ever had to do. Then you left, and I never heard anything more." He turned to face her, his eyes holding hers, his own questions demanding answers. "I guess the last thing I expected was that you would become a model."

"That happened after you married Paula. Please tell me why?" Jake heard the sorrow in her voice, and it echoed the pain in his heart.

He didn't know precisely how he was going to explain. "Paula was...aggressive."

He turned to face her. But Miriam was now pressed back against the counter, her arms wrapped around her waist. Definitely defensive.

"You mean she came on to you, and you couldn't resist?"

"Not exactly that." Jake reached out to touch her, and Miriam flinched away. He had hoped that what he had said would ease some of the tension, but instead it increased it. "I'm not proud of those few moments in my life. I was missing you. You hadn't written. I didn't know where you were. I tried to phone and got your mother. I was lonely, and I didn't know what to do anymore. Fred and Tilly had told me they were going to send me to agricultural college and that they wanted me to stay with them after that. Fred wanted me to run the farm with him." He laughed, a bitter sound. "If he had told me that a month sooner, things would have been different for us." He carefully pulled her hand away from her waist, taking it in his own, needing to make a connection with her while he spoke. "If I had known I had a future here, security, I would have stood up to your mother."

"Why didn't you, anyway?"

"I was a foster child, and I had lived in enough

foster homes to learn to keep things to myself. You don't ask about the future because no one can tell you. You have no legal rights, and your foster parents have no legal responsibilities. I had lived with Fred and Tilly for four years, yet I still hadn't learned to fully trust them.'' Jake stroked her fingers with his, his eyes on her hands.

"And Paula."

She was relentless. "Yes, Paula." He laughed shortly. "She asked me to the prom, and I said yes. I was lonely, and I missed you. Shortly after that we ended up at a party together. I thought you were living it up in the east, happy without me." He laughed shortly. "I thought this was the glorious future your mom had planned." He rubbed his neck, sighing. "At this party, I started drinking, and the next thing I knew I woke up in my truck. She was with me."

Miriam pulled her hand out of his, a soft cry escaping her lips.

"I know now that nothing happened," Jake said quickly, wanting to get past that part of the story and how it might look to her. "But at the time she had me convinced that we had been intimate. I had no other choice but to offer to marry her. I was young, scared and thinking I would lose my chance with Fred and Tilly. I didn't realize then that it wouldn't have, and that I'd always underestimated the power of their love for me. Always." He pulled in a deep breath. "Paula and I didn't have a great marriage. It was okay at first, but what she had done always hung between us. I tried, but I know I didn't try hard enough. She said she felt tied down by the farm. By Taryn. So she would leave. She always came back, and I would try again. It would be okay for a couple of weeks then she'd get antsy and pretty soon she'd be gone. The last time she left I begged her to stop doing this. She got angry and stormed out the door. Two hours later the police were at the door.''

"Oh, Jake. I'm so sorry."

"In spite of all of that, I have Taryn. I will always thank the Lord for her. The beauty that came out of the ashes.''

Silence again. Miriam sighed lightly, her hand rubbing her forehead, back and forth, back and forth.

"What a mess," she said softly.

Jake silently agreed.

They stood in silence, Jake trying to mentally meld what he knew about Miriam's life with what he had once believed; he prayed she was doing the same.

And what was going to come of this heart-to-heart? Love might conquer all in songs, but for him and Miriam, it seemed, there was too much history to get past. He had wanted to clear the air between them, to lay old ghosts to rest. She had come to do the same.

But now, after talking with her, he wondered if they would ever have a chance.

Miriam pushed herself away from the counter and stopped a moment in front of Jake. She laid her hand on his shoulder and looked up at him.

Jake knew he should let her go, but he couldn't. He looked at Miriam, letting his eyes linger on her face, the features that were so much hers and yet older, harder.

He reached out to touch her, just once. That was all he meant to do. Then, as his hand lightly cupped her cheek, she caught his wrist, holding his hand against her. She sighed lightly, turning her head just enough to kiss the palm of his hand.

Her gesture pulled him toward her. And once again he curled his hand around her neck, once again he dared to pull her head nearer. She didn't resist, and it was his undoing. Their breaths mingled for only a moment, then he carefully touched his mouth to hers, the familiarity of it rocking him.

Then he slipped his arms around her, pulling her closer, holding her tighter, as his mouth moved against hers. She clung to him, returning his kiss, her fingers threading through his hair, capturing his head.

It wasn't enough—it was just a teasing hint of what they had missed all those years apart. Jake kissed her again and again, his mouth on hers. Then he pulled away, ignoring Miriam's muted cry of protest, kissing her cheek, her forehead, her eyes, curving her head into his neck and holding her tightly against him.

"Oh, Miriam," he said. "I wanted to do this the first time I saw you on the road."

She said nothing, only clung to him, her movements almost desperate.

Then, suddenly, she pulled away, taking his arms and drawing them away from her. She touched his mouth with her fingers as if to capture the kiss he gave her, slowly traced the line of his lips, then, without saying another word, turned and walked out of the house.

Jake felt bereft as he watched her get in her car and drive away, dirt spinning, gravel flying out behind her. She fishtailed at the end of the driveway, then turned and drove away.

Jake took a long slow breath. *I don't know what just happened, Lord, but be with her,* he prayed quietly. *Hold her in Your hands, take care of her.* He drew in a deep breath. *Help me, as well.* He didn't know what he needed, but he knew that he had to swallow his own pride and go one step farther.

He had to talk with Miriam about the future—and that thought frightened him more than anything.

Miriam stepped on the accelerator as her car hurtled along. She drove without a destination, outrunning what lay behind her.

She felt as if her breath were still trapped in her chest, a heavy disquiet stirring deep within her. What she and Jake had shared in the past hour had completely switched and realigned her world.

All her perceptions, her ideas, had rearranged, and she had discovered one irrefutable fact.

She loved Jake Steele.

She slowed, wavering, her hand clenched to her heart. Oh, how she still loved him.

A deer, startled by her headlights, bolted in front of her. Miriam braked and swerved, narrowly missing it. She slammed on the brakes and rocked to a halt, dropping her head on the steering wheel.

She drew in a long, shuddering breath and slowly sat up. The quiet hum of the car and the glow of the dashboard lights created a safe place.

Just as it had been a haven to her as she drove to Waylen, this car was her escape now.

Miriam turned off the engine and the lights of her car. The moon was waning, a thin sliver of light in a sky scattered with crushed stars.

She stepped out and let her eyes adjust to the heavy darkness. The silence pressed in on her, broken only by the faint croaking of frogs in a marsh below her.

She was close to Rock Lake, she realized, slowly able to make out a few more landmarks. She crossed the road and scrambled through the ditch, still soggy from spring runoff. A fence blocked her way, but she climbed over it, disregarding the barbs on the wire.

Miriam walked slowly along the field, staying close to the edges, her eyes on the ground. By the time she got to the top of the hill her eyes had adjusted. The cool evening breeze was stronger here on the top of the hill, and she shivered, pulling her coat closer.

Below her yard lights winked, scattered across the landscape, each representing a farmer's yard. There were more than when she used to come up here as a much younger girl.

Miriam pulled her coat down and slowly sat down, pulling her knees close to her, dropping her head back.

Above her hung infinite stars like crushed diamonds flung across velvet, layer upon layer going far beyond what her fragile and mortal eye could see. Her mind knew what each of those tiny pinpoints of light represented, their size, their distance a number she couldn't get her mind around. And this was only a small part of our galaxy. There were as many galaxies as there were stars. She closed her eyes a moment, growing dizzy as she tried to fathom the depth of the skies around her.

Opening her eyes again, she easily found the Big Dipper wheeling slowly around the North Star; from there the Little Dipper Ursa Minor, then to Vega, Deneb, the constellation Cassiopeia. Her favorite, Orion the hunter, was a winter constellation and no longer visible.

She remembered lying out on sleeping bags outside with a flashlight and a star book her father had bought her. When she was older, she used to impress Jake with her knowledge of the night sky. She used to wish she could be an astronaut and fly, fly away from here, away from her mother's petty restrictions, constant criticism and carping.

Miriam bit her lip, guilt stopping her memories. Her mother was dead. In the weeks before she died, Edna had tried to apologize, had tried to explain why she pushed Miriam so hard. Miriam still didn't understand, and seeing Jake—the man her mother had so feared and disliked, the man she had once loved, the man whose life her mother had threatened to destroy—made Miriam feel as if, once again, she had to forgive her mother.

Seventy-times-seven.

The formula came back from old readings of the Bible. ''I've done this already,'' she said aloud, looking up at the sky as if speaking to God. "I've forgiven her again and again. Will it never be over? Will I never be finished with this anger, this feeling of unfinished business?"

She stopped as if waiting for an answer, her hands two tight balls of tension, her teeth pressed against each other. "I hated her so long—she took so much away," Miriam said again, her voice quieter.

The silent stars wheeled slowly on, unconcerned, timeless, vast.

She was just a small speck in this cosmos, unimportant, unnecessary. She had made sacrifices for her mother, and in the process had lost the one thing she wanted.

Jake's love.

She loosened her fingers and caught her knees, resting her chin on them, as she studied the vaguely lit land below.

Closing her eyes, she resurrected the touch of Jake's lips on hers, his hand on her neck. A thrill shivered through her at the memory. It had been so easy, so familiar.

There had been no awkwardness. No hesitation. No words spoken, no promises made. Just a memory for her to hold onto...for the next ten years. The emptiness of the life that lay ahead of her became suddenly unbearable.

"What am I going to do?" she cried out. "Oh, Lord, You've got to help me."

Her cry had become a prayer and she repeated it. "Please help me. I have fought being unworthy all my life. I've struggled with feeling unwanted, feeling ugly, feeling like a failure, feeling alone. I can't do that again.''

Each time she saw Jake pray, each time she saw him with his daughter and saw the absolute love he showed her, each time she saw his devotion to Tilly and Fred, it was a reminder of who he was. A man with a sincere faith, a devotion to family.

And here she was—a woman who lived a life of selfishness, of vanity. After her mother's stroke, Miriam had visited her only rarely, using her busy schedule as an excuse. Then even these few visits had become more sporadic. She had wasted money, time and much of her earlier years thinking only of herself. Self-preservation, she had called it, and it was necessary in the cutthroat world of high fashion.

Or so she had told herself.

Her clothing business was to be her escape from that world, a chance to slow down and enjoy life, to be her own person. But even that was struggling, and all she had to show for ten years of work was a car—paid for—a year's lease on an apartment in New York—paid for—and a closet full of clothes. And thousands of dollars in bills that lay on her shoulders like the weight of the world. Bills for which she was personally responsible.

It was then that she had met Carl. Or actually, he had met her. He had heard she was looking for an agent, had found her and had convinced her to let him become her new agent. Miriam had resisted going back to modeling, going back to becoming a thing, an object—but Carl was different. Carl had spoken of a God who cared. A God who saw her as valuable and wonderful, just as she was.

Miriam had spoken to some of his other clients, had run a check on him and found out that he was not only legitimate, but well-liked and respected in the fashion industry.

So she signed on with him. He got a few jobs, and one evening, as she sat in his office, fighting tears of weariness, still grieving for her mother and lost chances of reconciliation, he had told her to go home. To catch her breath, to sell her farm, and then, when all that was done, to come back. He had a line on a big job that would help her get through this financial crisis she was in right now.

So she came. She drove because it was a way for her to relax, to see the countryside and realize that there were other things going on, other jobs getting done.

But now, after being here a few days, she felt worse off than before.

Falling in love with Jake was all wrong. She was in no position to make herself vulnerable to him again. She was in no position to give him anything. Once he had said he had nothing to give her. Now it was she who not only had nothing to give, but came with a large debt. She was all wrong for him.

What she had discovered tonight had completely changed the way she thought of him: he hadn't married Paula out of love, but because he'd been coerced.

Miriam clenched her fists in anger, pressing them

against her forehead at the thought of her friend's duplicity, her mother's scheming and pressure. How could she and Jake ever hope to get past this? It seemed too big a barrier. How could God have allowed all this to happen?

She looked up, past the stars to where she figured God was, removed from the miseries of common people like her and Jake. *Please help me, Lord. I know I haven't talked to You a lot, but I don't know where else to turn.* She hadn't prayed for so long; she knew this wasn't precisely the way, but she didn't know how else to go about it. *Please help me. I don't know what to think, I don't know what to do.*

She reached out with her mind, stretching, pulling, striving, wondering if God heard or if He cared.

Chapter Nine

"I sure appreciate your taking time out to help me," Dane said to Jake. "For a while I thought I might have to feed the calves for another week or so until I found someone who could move them to pasture for me."

Jake glanced at his neighbor and shrugged. "No problem, Dane. Glad to help."

Dane Rogers was an older man who lived alone and had done so all his life. He was pushing seventy-five, yet he still farmed his own land, raised some calves and in general enjoyed his life.

"I heard Fred wasn't doing so good. How is he now?" Dane asked as they stood enjoying the sun, and the slight breeze that kept the bugs away.

Jake shook his head, watching the few stragglers pair up. "They kept him in the hospital overnight a few days back, just to keep an eye on him. He's home now, but still not great. We'll see what happens."

"Life sure keeps a man busy, don't it," Dane said. "I heard Miriam Spencer is back."

Jake gave the older man a sidelong glance. "You hear a lot for someone who doesn't get out much."

Dane grinned, hooking his thumbs in his wide suspenders. "The phone is a wonderful thing, but I sure miss the party line."

"I'm sure you do. Anything else you heard that you figure I need to know?"

"Well, I'm sure you know Miriam is still single." Dane elbowed him lightly, and Jake sighed. "She used to like you, didn't she? Surprises me that a girl that good-looking hasn't matched up with anyone. Makes you wonder, don't it?"

Actually, it hadn't made Jake wonder. Not until Dane mentioned it. He had assumed that Miriam had had boyfriends, that she had dated, but he had never wanted to speculate on why she was still single. He knew what Dane was hinting at, but since Miriam had come home, he hadn't dared let his speculation run that far.

"She's only here for a while. She wants to sell her farm and head back east to make more money." Jake couldn't keep the harshness from his voice. The other night, and the nights since, he had lain in bed, reliving every moment with Miriam, unable to come to a solution.

It seemed that too much hung between them, that the barriers were insurmountable. Yet he couldn't help but remember her response to him.

Her tears.

And the fact that she was still single, as Dane so thoughtfully pointed out. He had kept himself busy, had tried not to look too interested when Tilly talked of Miriam's visits.

"Oh, I'm sure you could talk her out of leaving. You're still a good-looking young man." Dane clapped a companionable hand on Jake's shoulder. "Give it a whirl. What have you got to lose?"

My pride, Jake thought. Yet even as that idea formed, he knew it was a small price to pay. Thinking about Miriam leaving gave him a hollow feeling that grew each day, each hour.

Jake shrugged as if to dispel the sensation. "I've got enough on my mind right now, Dane. I don't know if I have the will or energy to go courting."

"She lives just down the road. How much work could it be?" Dane chuckled. "Tell Tilly to have her over for supper. Take her for a ride in your tractor."

"And isn't that romantic," said Jake wryly, walking over to his truck.

"What I remember of you two, it used to be."

Jake smiled, remembering, too. "Right about now I've got to fix my tractor, get my crop in, check my own cows, and try to figure out how I'm going to replace the land she's selling. Seems like enough to keep me busy." He got into the truck and rolled down the window. "You let me know if you need anything else, okay?"

Dane leaned his arms on the window frame, shaking his head. "No time to court a pretty girl, but figures he has time to offer to help me. You got your priorities all mixed up, my boy.''

Jake laughed lightly. ''I've got to go, Dane. I'll follow you out and then shut the gate for you.''

''I can do that myself, you young punk.''

''Okay.'' Jake put the truck in gear and slowly pulled away. He swung the truck and the long fifth-wheel trailer around, then headed out the gate and down the road. He glanced in his side mirror and saw Dane pull out behind him and shut the gate.

Satisfied, he sped up. He had hoped to check his own cows this afternoon and then run back in to town for a part for his tractor. Maybe tomorrow he could get the Spencer field done. Then it would be Sunday again.

And shortly after that, Miriam was leaving.

He clutched the steering wheel, forcing himself to stay focused. They each had their own lives, he reminded himself. They each had their own responsibilities. She had been back barely a week. He must be crazy to think that just because mistakes of the past had been talked about, all was cleared away. Miriam had run away that night and stayed away. That told him, more clearly than anything she could have said, what she wanted.

She didn't fit, didn't belong.

Yet even as he thought that, he remembered how good she was with Taryn, how easily she seemed to fit in to the farm life. He remembered her feeding his cows. He still had to smile at the sight of her in her expensive clothes, manhandling that tractor around the yard; she was as small as ever, and still had to stand up to steer.

He had felt guilty that day. Felt as if he had abrogated his responsibilities and she'd had to cover for him.

Yet it made him feel like the two of them, for a brief moment, had shared this part of his life. He felt like what he did was important to her.

Get a grip, Steele, you really are delusional, he thought, gearing down as his truck powered out on the hill.

Miriam got out of her car and looked around the yard. It looked much neater than when she had first arrived. The progress should have made her feel good, but it didn't.

This morning she had gone to Waylen to check with the real estate agent and go over some details. Then she had met up with Donna and a few old friends.

Sitting around in the café had been fun, and she hadn't laughed that hard and long in months. It had been cathartic, and Miriam regretted the moment when each of them had to return to their own responsibilities.

Miriam and Donna had lingered, and Donna had reminded her that they were going to meet again at the church picnic tomorrow. Miriam had reluctantly agreed to go. She didn't know if she wanted to sit through church again, but was eager to meet up with her old friends.

And Jake would be there. The pernicious thought

clung to her subconscious, and all the way home she couldn't seem to dispel it. Since that evening when he had told her the truth about Paula, she couldn't face him, couldn't indulge in might-have-beens. The pain of regret cut too deeply.

She couldn't forget his kiss, his arms about her.

Physical attraction, that was all it was, her thoughts reminded her.

But she knew it was more. It was like coming home, like a safe place after fear.

You don't fit with him anymore, she thought. He's in a different place than you. Too much has happened that can't be changed.

Miriam tried to imagine herself with Jake again. Was it just nostalgia that made it feel so right? Would she be able to stay here, to be a wife, a mother?

It's a dream, she reminded herself. She had huge responsibilities waiting for her back east. The thought of staying here might be wonderful, but it was a luxury she had no space, no room to indulge in.

With a sigh, she walked into the house and looked around. As she dropped into her father's old recliner, her eye fell on a couple of boxes of books that she had set aside, unopened.

Miriam got up and pulled open the top of the first box. She supposed she could just have left them, but she hated the idea of unfinished jobs.

Some of the books were old storybooks of hers. She took them out, smiling at the pictures on the covers. They brought back pleasant memories of sitting on her father's lap while he read to her. Flipping through the pages she became once again that young girl who wanted to be anywhere else but where she was.

When her father died, it had gotten even worse.

Miriam quickly set the book aside and took out a few more.

In the next layer she found a Bible.

Sitting back on her heels, Miriam turned it over in her hand and then opened it. It was her parents' wedding Bible. Miriam smiled a soft, sad smile as she leafed through it. She had had such a convoluted relationship with her mother that she often wondered what kind of mother she herself would make.

She thought of Taryn's longing for a mother. For a brief moment, Miriam allowed herself to think of tucking in that dear child each night, while Jake stood in the doorway, or sat on the bed with her. Jake had said he loved her. Had never loved anyone but her.

With a soft cry, Miriam clutched the Bible to her chest, her head bent. Why had he said that to her? Why had he given her that shred of hope? She could do nothing with it.

She couldn't stay.

Miriam took a quick breath and got up. She wanted to get out of the house and away from its emptiness. This wasn't a home.

And neither is your eighteenth-floor condo, she thought, stepping outside. She had lived there for six years, often stopping only long enough to send her dirty clothes to the cleaners, sleep and then return to the airport for another flight to another destination.

Then the last two years, she had spent most of her

time at her office, or running around looking for suppliers and markets for her new clothing company. When she was trying to find a way to keep her company solvent, she spent many evenings in her office, as well, catching a few hours' sleep in her chair, or on the couch.

No, the condo wasn't home, either.

The only real home she had known was Fred and Tilly's. The truest love from a mother she had received was from Tilly.

Not from her own mother.

Her mother had cast a long shadow on her life, Miriam realized, settling down under the old maple tree. Her steady criticism, her constant griping about Jake, her threats to him…

Miriam's teeth clenched at the thought, and once again she wished her mother was alive so she could confront her with this.

And again Miriam struggled to forgive. Forgiveness was so difficult to grant when there was no physical person to talk to, to get angry with.

Just the memory of a broken woman who struggled to tell Miriam why she had done what she did.

Miriam laid her head against the rough bark of the tree, hearing once again her mother's halting words, reminding Miriam that even though her love as a mother was weak and impure, God's love wasn't.

But Miriam felt she had strayed so far from that love, it was no longer hers for the taking.

She flipped through the pages and found the silk ribbon at Ecclesiastes. ''Generations come and generations go, but the earth remains forever,'' she read. Miriam looked around at the land, ready for planting. She thought of Jake working it, and knew he counted on the revenue from her own land. The land would remain forever, but it would go to different hands. She wished she could change that, wished she could give it to him. A gift.

But she needed the money. She had obligations. Debts to pay.

She wished she knew what to do and wished this Bible would show her.

But she hadn't read it in so long, she didn't even know if the promises in it were for her. Once, she could have looked at her life and said, yes, this was a life sanctified by Christ.

She could say that no longer.

The sun beat down on Jake's head as he clucked to Pinto. The horse flicked its ears, looked back, and then started walking back down the trail to the road. He slowed the horse down, reluctant to be drawn back into the rush and pressure that exemplified planting season. Fred had often told him that somehow it always got done. Seed time and harvest, the ebb and flow of the cycle, always happened. And the few times it didn't, it was often because of measures beyond their control.

Jake drew a deep breath and sent up a prayer of thanksgiving for this beautiful day. Then, he came to Miriam's driveway.

He pulled his horse to a stop, his hands resting on

the pommel of the saddle, Dane's words ringing through his head. He was unable to dispel the memory of Miriam in his arms.

Courtship. He and Miriam had missed out on that when they started going out. They had had to keep their relationship a secret, and thus had never indulged in the fun stuff that came with dating.

Did he dare open himself up to her like that?

What would he gain and what would he lose?

Pinto shook her head, her bridle jangling, and snorted as Jake sifted through the reasons for and against.

It would be so much easier just to keep on going. But to what? He loved Taryn. He loved Fred and Tilly.

But he also knew that deep inside he yearned for a helpmeet. Someone who would be his partner in many senses of that word. Someone who would miss him and whom he would look forward to seeing at the end of the day. Someone who would sit with him on the couch and talk to him about her day. Listen to him talk about his.

All those roles were filled in one way or another by his daughter and his parents. Yet Tilly had Fred, and Taryn was slowly growing up and away from him. That was nature.

He was all alone in a family.

Yet, if he were to give in to the love he felt for Miriam, and she left anyway, how would he manage? He had been desolated when she left the first time. He was older and less flexible now. It would be harder this time.

Because whether he liked to admit it or not, his love this time around was deeper and stronger.

He closed his eyes, letting the memories of the other night drift around him, hold him, as Miriam's arms had held him. He knew that she cared. Something held her back, and the only way he would find out what, was to spend time with her.

Starting now, he thought, pulling Pinto's head around.

The horse trotted down the driveway. When they got to the maple tree, he stopped.

Miriam sat underneath it, a book open on her lap, her eyes shut.

Jake wondered if she was sleeping, but then he saw her shake her head. "Hey, there," he said quietly, hoping he wouldn't startle her.

Miriam looked up, her hand on her chest, her mouth and eyes wide open. "Oh, my goodness. You scared the living daylights out of me," she said weakly.

Jake dismounted and tied Pinto to a nearby tree, walked across the lawn to her. Miriam stayed where she was, her hand still on her chest.

"I didn't even hear you coming," she said, avoiding his gaze.

"I thought at first you were sleeping."

"No. Just sitting and thinking." She moved to get up, but Jake stopped her with a hand on her shoulder. He sat down beside her, his legs crossed. He pointed to the book on her lap. "A little light reading?"

"It's the Bible. Hardly light," Miriam replied, her fingers fiddling with the pages.

Jake watched her hands' restless movement, the way she looked as if she had pulled herself back and away from him. It was as if she didn't want him here.

He would have left, but the Bible on her lap kept him beside her.

Please, Lord, show me what to do. Give me the right words. I've never done this before. There's so much I want to tell her, but right now she needs to be shown Your love, as well.

He tried. "So what have you…" He hesitated, cleared his throat and tried again. "What have you been reading?"

"Nothing."

"What are you looking for?"

Miriam shook her head as she flicked through the pages. "I don't know," she whispered. "I used to read this more often. I remember at night, before I went to bed, I read a passage." She smiled a bittersweet smile and looked up at him. "I worked my way through the whole Bible that way. Even through all the laws and all those prophets. Now I realize they weren't just talking about Israelites. Those prophets were talking about me."

"What do you mean?"

Miriam shook her head. "Nothing. Sorry I brought it up." She made a move to get up, but Jake put a hand on her shoulder, stopping her.

"Miriam, you know I love you—"

"Don't, Jake," she said, holding out her hand to stop him. "Don't even bring that up—"

"I have to, Miriam. I don't have a lot of time with you, and you need to hear this."

"I want you to stop. You're making this too hard."

"What am I making too hard?" Jake let his hand linger on her shoulder, his fingers lightly caressing her neck. He didn't dare let go of her, but didn't dare make more than this light connection.

She drew in one shaky breath and then another. "I've fought this feeling of unworthiness many years. I don't like feeling this way, but I do. I do around you."

Jake heard her words, felt the pain pouring out of her. He didn't know what to say, or how to say it.

Gently he took the Bible from her lap and paged through it until he found what he was looking for. Romans.

"'There is no one righteous, not even one,'" he read. "'There is no one who understands, no one who seeks God. All have turned away, they have together become worthless; there is no one who does good, not even one.'"

"See what I mean?" Miriam said, pulling her knees up to her chest.

"That was written for me as well as you," Jake replied. "Let me keep going." As the soft spring wind caressed them, rustling through the leaves of the tree above, and as the sun filled the day with brightness and warmth, Jake read to her of the law, of judgment, then of Christ's intercession and love. Then he read, his own voice growing with conviction, "'For I am convinced, that neither death nor life, neither angels nor demons, neither the present nor the future, nor any powers, neither height nor depth, nor anything else in all creation will be able to separate us from the love of God that is in Christ Jesus our Lord.'"

Jake paused, letting the words diffuse through his own life, praying that Miriam would take them for herself.

"This isn't a battle you have to fight, Miriam. All you have to do is take what is given. God is waiting for you to stop the struggle, to let Him give." He leaned forward, touching her again, praying that his weak words would be imbued with power from God. There was only so much he could do; accepting God's love, accepting his love, was up to her.

Miriam laid her head on her knees. "It sounds too easy."

Jake heard her words and fought his own disappointment. He was just a messenger, he knew that, but he had hoped that the words that had given him so much comfort would do the same for her. He loved her deeply, but he also knew that unless she accepted and believed the same thing he did, it would come to naught.

"It is easy. God made it easy for us because we can't come to Him any other way."

Miriam said nothing, gave no sign that she had heard.

Jake lay the Bible at her feet, pausing a moment as he watched her sitting at his feet. He bent over and lightly touched his lips to her exposed neck.

"I love you, Miriam," he whispered. "Always remember that. And always remember that God loves you more."

And then he left.

Chapter Ten

Miriam waited until she heard the soft footfalls of Jake's horse receding down the driveway.

Only then did she dare lift her head. Jake's words resounded in her mind. God's love. His love. The two seemed intertwined.

And she still felt as if she couldn't accept either one.

Miriam saw the Bible lying at her feet and reluctantly picked it up. She could still hear Jake reading from it, his voice resonating with conviction.

She had known God's love, had sung countless times the song "Jesus Loves Me"—one of the first songs learned by children being introduced to faith.

But it was too much for her to accept. She didn't feel worthy.

She got up, still holding the Bible, and glanced at her watch. My goodness, she had been sitting out here for a couple of hours. She wondered how long it had been since Jake had left.

Jake.

Miriam's heart plunged, then began to race at the thought of him, at the memory of his lips touching her neck. The peace fled, replaced by confusion.

He had offered her his love. And she knew she couldn't take it. She had nothing to give him. Nothing.

She clutched her Bible closer. Then she went into the house. She wanted to talk to Tilly, but she had to make sure Jake wouldn't be there.

A quick phone call told her that Tilly was home. Jake was gone. Miriam jumped in her car and sped over. She could think of no one better to talk to than the woman who had been more than a mother to her.

Tilly was rolling out pie crusts on the kitchen counter when Miriam came into the house. Taryn was playing with scraps of leftover dough on the kitchen table—much as Miriam used to when she was younger. It looked so delightfully normal, and was a welcome contrast to the turmoil she had just felt.

"I made a duck," Taryn announced to Miriam, showing her a roll of dough. "And some snakes. They're easy."

Miriam stopped to admire the handiwork, unable to stop herself from stroking Taryn's head. She felt a connection with Jake when she spent time with his child.

Then she joined Tilly. "Need any help?"

Tilly smiled up at her. "You can get the filling ready. I'm making some lemon pies for the picnic to-morrow. Are you going to go?"

"Yes I am."

"I've got all the things ready for the filling. You can start making it for me, if you want." Tilly pointed with her chin as she formed the pie crusts.

Miriam pulled out a pot from one cupboard and a wooden spoon from the drawer. While Miriam worked, Tilly slid the pie shells in the oven, set the timer and began cleaning up.

"My goodness, I feel like quite the domestic," Miriam said with a grin, as Tilly wiped the counter. The filling was just starting to boil, and she turned the heat off.

"You know," Tilly said, turning and leaning back against the counter, "it seems like just a short while ago the last time you were standing at that stove, helping me make pie."

"I certainly came over here a lot," Miriam said, carefully licking the warm filling off the spoon. She set the pan aside for the filling to cool.

"Can I lick the spoon?" Taryn asked, looking up from her ducks and worms.

"Oops." Miriam looked at the now-clean wooden spoon and then at Taryn's crestfallen face. She had started licking the spoon completely out of habit. Turning, she washed the spoon, stuck it in the filling again, and brought it over to Taryn. "Be careful, honey. It's still a bit warm."

"Thanks, Miriam." Taryn took the spoon from her, touched her finger to it and put it in her mouth. "I love lemon pie."

"So do I. It's still my favorite, and your grandma makes the best."

When the crusts were done, Miriam poured the filling into them, while Tilly whipped up the egg whites. Soon the counter held four tempting lemon pies.

Fred joined them then, still looking haggard.

"How are you feeling, Fred?" Miriam asked, concerned at his lack of color.

"Not great, my girl. Not great." He eased himself into his usual chair and caught his breath. "Whew. I guess I won't be running any sack races at the church picnic tomorrow, hey, Pipper?" he asked Taryn.

"Oh, Grandpa, you're silly," Taryn said, lining up her dough ducks. She showed her grandfather what she had made, and he was suitably impressed.

Tilly had made tea, and soon they were sitting around the table, talking about all the wonderfully inconsequential things that make up a day.

Miriam felt herself relax in this comfortable home. It did that to her, she thought, taking a sip of her tea. Every time she came here, it was like coming home. She could pretend that Tilly was her mother, Fred her father.

And Taryn...

Miriam glanced sidelong at the little girl, who was busily playing with her dough animals. She resisted the urge to smooth the child's hair, to pull her close.

Jake's child.

Jake, who had told her he loved her. Told her that God loved her. And what was she supposed to do about that? What could she do? She had obligations, responsibilities.

Her debt on the business was adding up each month

as the interest mounted. She needed the work Carl had lined up for her. It wouldn't get rid of all the debt, but it would be a good start. The sale of the farm would make the biggest difference. But it didn't look like that was going to happen real soon. So, she really needed the work Carl had found for her and more, which meant she needed to be thinking about going back to New York.

Not yet. Not yet, she thought.

When it was time for her to leave, it was time for her to think about all of that.

"What's the matter, Miriam?" Tilly asked. "You look troubled."

Miriam glanced up at Tilly, surprised at her perception. "I'm okay," she said evasively.

She forced her thoughts to the present. Forced herself to ask Taryn if she learned anything new in play school. Forced herself to ask Fred how the seeding was coming, hoping that maybe they would talk about Jake.

They didn't disappoint her.

She knew it was foolish to put herself through this, but she couldn't stop herself.

Eventually, the gentle chime of the grandfather clock in the living room reminded her of the time.

"Stay for supper, Miriam," Tilly said, frowning at her. "You don't have to leave right away."

But she did. Because if she stayed, she would see Jake, and right now her emotions were too fragile to deal with him.

So she got up and promised Taryn again that she would come to the picnic.

"Can you take me in your car?" Taryn asked as Miriam was putting her shoes on the porch. "I never had a ride in your car."

"Yes, you did," Miriam said, pulling on her jacket. "I gave you a ride when we brought supper to your dad."

"But can I have another ride? Please?"

Miriam was about to say no, but could really find no reason.

"Okay. I'll pick you up in the morning. You be ready, missy."

Taryn frowned. "Missy? I'm not missy. I'm Pipper. *You're* missy."

Miriam felt her throat catch at that. It was true. Fred always called her Missy. It would be like Taryn to notice that.

"Okay, Pipper. I'll come tomorrow. On time."

"Okeydokey." Taryn flashed Miriam a grin, and Miriam couldn't help but smile back.

She stuck her head through the doorway to say goodbye to Fred—

He was lying back in his chair at the table, his eyes closed, his mouth slightly open.

"Are you okay, Fred?" Miriam asked, panic slicing through her.

"Yeah, I am. Just resting," he said, lifting his head. He gave her a smile, but it looked forced.

"You sure?"

"Yes. I'm fine."

Tilly came to the door and gave her a quick kiss. "You stop by tomorrow after the picnic, you hear?"

Miriam hesitated, unsure of what tomorrow would bring.

"You come now, Miriam."

"Okay. I will."

She could get through this. She could.

"Can my daddy have a ride in your car?" Taryn asked when Miriam came to the door on Sunday. She was sitting on a chair in the kitchen, trying to buckle up her shoes.

The thought of Jake sitting with her all the way to church was enough to make Miriam stop breathing. She tried to find a tactful way to forestall Taryn.

"I have to take my truck, Pipper," Jake said as he came into the kitchen. "I have to take some tables to the meadow."

Miriam looked up at him as he stopped by the kitchen table to take a quick sip from his coffee. His hair was still damp from his shower, shining in the lights from the ceiling. His cheeks were freshly shaven, and she caught the faint scent of his after-shave lotion. It made her stomach flip.

He caught her eye, lifted his mouth in a careful smile and walked toward her. She knew he was thinking of yesterday, of their time sitting together on her lawn, while he read to her.

She hadn't been able to get him, or the passages he read, out of her mind. Somehow, though, it all seemed too good to be true. She remembered what he had said about God making it easy to come to Him.

She wondered what she would learn in church today.

"Will I see you at the picnic, Miriam?" Jake asked, holding his mug, leaning one hip against the door to the porch.

She swallowed at his nearness and could only nod. "Yeah. I promised Taryn and Donna I would go."

"Lucky, Taryn," he said, and Miriam glanced up. She had intended to look away right away, but was unable to. Then Jake smiled again and turned to help his daughter.

"I'll see you at church, Pipper," he said, dropping a kiss on her head. "And I guess I'll see you, too," he said to Miriam.

Miriam nodded, caught Taryn's outstretched hand and walked out to her car.

Luckily for her, she didn't have to say anything on the way to church. Taryn supplied all the conversation.

They pulled up in front of the church. What a difference a week makes, she thought, slowly getting out of the car. Last week she had come here defensive, unwilling and unready to be a part of this community.

During the week she had met up with old friends, had reconnected with the community. Had spent time with Fred and Tilly. Taryn.

Had found out the truth about Jake and Paula.

She glanced over her shoulder at the graveyard, wondering about Paula. Wondering how Paula had thought she could build a marriage on a lie.

Miriam turned away from Paula and the past, and, pulling her long skirt close to her, closed her car door. Today was Sunday. A day of renewal and blessing. She wasn't going to let the past and its mistakes overshadow it.

Taryn bounced up the sidewalk, then, at the sound of a truck engine, stopped. Miriam turned around.

Jake pulled up beside her car.

Miriam waited, feeling slightly foolish, as Taryn went running back to her father, her cheeks flushed, her ponytail bobbing. "You have to sit with me and Miriam."

Jake smiled down at Taryn, then looked up at Miriam. He stood beside them, his expression enigmatic. Then, as their eyes met, she saw his mouth lift in a crooked smile.

And her heart did that funny little dance.

Taryn caught her hand and Jake's as they walked toward the church.

It felt right, Miriam thought with a gentle ache. It felt as if this was how it should be.

As they walked up the stairs, Miriam looked once again at Jake and was unnerved by his direct gaze.

"I didn't have a chance to ask how you are doing, Miriam," he said. His voice was quiet, but it carried a wealth of meaning. Miriam knew he alluded to yesterday, and was suddenly shy.

"I'm glad to be here," she said, looking away. Which was the truth. She was not entirely comfortable yet, but still glad to be a part of this.

Through the thin material of her shirt she felt the

warm weight of his callused hand resting on her shoulder. She swallowed at the contact, resisting the urge to lift her shoulder to hold his hand against her cheek.

"That's good," he said, squeezing ever so slightly.

"Daddy, why did you let go of my hand?" Taryn demanded.

Miriam felt her cheeks flush, and was surprised at her reaction. She hadn't felt this flustered around a man since—her heart lifted again—since she and Jake had first started dating.

"Where's Tilly and Fred?" Miriam asked, finally noticing their absence.

"Dad is really tired so Mom thought it would be better if she stayed home with him."

"I'm sorry," Miriam said, holding his gaze. She couldn't look away, couldn't break the contact.

"Miriam, good to see you." Donna breezed up beside her, and Jake drew away. Miriam tried not to feel disappointed, and turned to her friend.

Donna gave her a quick hug, smiling as she pulled away. "Hello, Jake," she said as her gaze flicked to Jake and then back to Miriam. To her credit, Donna's expression remained neutral, although when she looked back at Miriam she gave just a hint of a wink.

Donna smiled down at Taryn. "Bet your grandma made lemon pie again, didn't she."

Taryn nodded, beaming up at Donna. "We brought three. And Miriam helped make them."

"Three lemon pies? And Miriam helped make them?" Donna raised her eyebrows exaggeratedly. "My goodness. We are getting domestic, aren't we?"

Miriam laughed. The thump of many small footsteps coming up the steps behind them made Donna turn.

"Here comes my tribe, and there goes the peace. I'll talk to you later."

Miriam watched as Donna became surrounded by a noisy group of children. Donna licked her finger and smoothed down a cowlick on one, straightened the collar of another and picked up a little girl. Her husband joined her and took the girl from her. Then they all walked in to the church.

"Sort of makes you feel breathless, doesn't she?" Jake asked as they watched Donna's family walk down the aisle.

"She always had a lot of energy," Miriam said.

"I heard you had a girls' afternoon out with her."

Miriam glanced at him again. Again he was smiling.

"Yes. I had a nice afternoon catching up with old friends."

"I'm glad," he said, and Miriam wondered what he meant.

"Let's go," Taryn said, tugging on Miriam's hand.

They walked down the aisle of the church as a threesome. But this time Miriam felt less like a stranger and more like a part of things. One of her old friends glanced up as they passed and waggled her fingers at her. Another raised her eyebrows and winked.

Because the church was full, Jake ended up sitting directly beside Miriam, with Taryn on his lap.

Miriam tried to still the nervous thumping of her

heart at his nearness. This was foolish, she rebuked herself. A person shouldn't be feeling this in church.

She pulled a Bible out of the pew and started to read it, trying to concentrate on the words. But Taryn kept chattering to her, and Miriam had to respond.

Then the minister came in, the worship service began, and Miriam felt as if all the loose pieces of her life were being shaken around.

She paid close attention to the songs, searching. It was as if she were on the edge of something important, earth-shattering—but she couldn't quite grasp it.

This was a good place to be, she thought, as she sang along with the hymns. She had missed so much by staying away from church all those years.

And yet, as the service progressed, she knew there should be more. This wasn't just a comfortable tradition that made people feel good. There was a sense of worship and awe, and Miriam knew she hadn't quite caught it yet. It gave her a sense of disappointment, and yet at the same time an eagerness to find out for herself what was missing.

It seemed as if the service was over too quickly.

She had managed not to concentrate too much on Jake. Taryn had fallen asleep on his shoulder, and he had held her. Once he had laid his arm along the back of the pew behind her. It had been hard to concentrate then, but she had managed.

The organ burst into the postlude, and with a gentle sigh Miriam turned.

Jake barred her way, still holding a sleeping Taryn. "Enjoy the service?"

"Yes. I did," she replied, returning his direct gaze.

He smiled and nodded, touching her arm lightly. "I'm so glad."

Then Taryn woke up, someone jostled Miriam from behind, and the moment was broken.

Somehow they got separated in the flow of people leaving the sanctuary. Miriam met up with Donna and a few of her old friends. They told her where the picnic was, and when Miriam got to her car, she noted with dismay that Jake was gone. She had been kind of hoping Taryn would want a ride to the picnic in her car.

She felt a sharp stab of disappointment, then shook it off. She had just experienced a wonderful Sunday, and she was going to enjoy the church picnic, something she hadn't attended since leaving Waylen.

And she was looking forward to being with Jake, because she also knew that once they were there, he would make sure they would spend some time together.

Her heart hitched. She didn't want to think further than this afternoon. It was a special time, a gift. The future was for another day.

"Where's Miriam, Daddy?" Taryn tugged on Jake's arm. "She has to eat her pie."

"I'm sure she's here somewhere." Jake frowned as he looked around. He had left right after church and had insisted Taryn come with him. She had pouted, but had given in.

"I wanna play with my friends," Taryn announced

to Jake. He nodded, then looked around for someone to visit with.

He ended up in a group of men talking about the usual topics that take up a farmer's mind—the crops, the weather, the prices of their commodities. They stood around, a short distance from the tables being set with food, their stances identical—hands in their pockets, occasional comments punctuating the conversation.

Jake could hold his own in these situations. Once he had started farming, he knew it was the only thing he wanted to do. He loved the routine of the life, the ebb and flow of the seasons. It hadn't taken him long to establish his own position in the community. He often wished he had been able to go to school, to further his knowledge, but farmers were an independent lot, intensely involved in their own operations. There was always some seminar being offered at any given time, and Jake went to each one.

"Put any canola in this year, Jake?" one of the men asked him.

"No, Andrew. I seeded the Spencer quarter to it last year. I thought I would hold off this year."

"I heard the Spencer land is up for sale. Aren't you interested?"

Jake shrugged the comment away. "I'm stretched to the limit."

"Aw, c'mon. I know old Fred. He's got some stashed away, I'm sure." Andrew nudged Jake with an elbow, his eyebrows raised lightly as if to negate Jake's comment.

"I'm not taking any chances with money that isn't mine."

"Is it true Miriam's heading back east?" another asked him.

Jake loved this community, but privacy was a luxury not given its members.

"She has other obligations," he said casually.

"Too bad. Didn't the two of you have something going, once upon a time?"

Jake laughed lightly. "That was a long time ago, Andrew." For a relationship that was supposed to be a huge secret, a lot of people not only knew about it but also remembered it. Ten years later.

"Speaking of Miriam, there she is."

Jake tried not to turn too fast. Tried to keep his heart from jumping around like a frisky calf. He managed a semblance of nonchalance by waiting and then glancing over his shoulder.

She stood in the middle of a bunch of her old friends, talking animatedly. As she spoke, she gestured with her hands, graceful movements that emphasized her delicate bone structure. She wore a loose T-shirt and full skirt in vibrant earth colors that brought out highlights in her short brown hair, and set off the peach tone of her skin.

Her beauty made his chest tighten, and he wondered again how he could think she would even be interested in him.

An errant breeze lifted a strand of her hair and dropped it across her eyes. As she lifted her hand to brush it away, she looked up.

And straight at him.

Her gentle smile caught at him as a connection was made that excluded everyone else. There was no one around but the two of them. He saw no one but her.

We belong together, he thought, then remembered to breathe. The sound of laughter permeated the moment. Miriam's neighbor caught her arm. Andrew asked Jake another question, and the interval was swept away.

Jake felt his life shift, saw this possibility as attainable. Miriam here, with him. He knew that this moment was a hint of what could be.

He smiled as he thought of the rest of the afternoon. Taryn would be busy. Her friends would find other people to talk to. He hoped sometime, somewhere, he could get Miriam alone.

A truck pulled up, and Jake was coerced into unloading a few more tables for more food. He caught scattered glimpses of Miriam as the tables were organized—warm dishes, still-steaming plates of soft buns, bowls of colorful salads, pans of dessert.

Then, at an unseen signal, families began gathering, parents bending over to put food on their children's plates. Small hands pointing, heads shaking their emphatic ''no.''

Jake looked for Taryn and then saw her. With Miriam.

He smiled, watching as Taryn made Miriam lift lids off casseroles. It wasn't difficult to tell which of the dishes met with her favor and which didn't. Miriam patiently worked her way along the table, and once glanced up at Jake. She smiled, then looked down again.

Jake waited until the families had served their children, and took his own place in the lineup. When his plate was full, he looked about for his daughter. She and Miriam had found a place under a tree and were already starting.

Jake sauntered over, nodding his greetings to people who called out to him, but not allowing himself to get waylaid.

"We prayed already, Daddy," Taryn said, looking up at him with cheeks already smeared with tomato sauce. "And I found s'getti."

"I see that." Jake pulled out his handkerchief and squatted down, trying to wipe her cheeks with one hand, balance his plate of food with the other.

"Here. I'll do that." Miriam took the handkerchief from him and wiped the worst of the sauce off, while Taryn tried to help by licking her cheeks. "There. That looks a little better."

She frowned at Taryn. "Are you feeling okay? You feel a bit warm."

Taryn shook her head. "I'm not sick."

"I didn't say you were sick, just warm. You looked flushed, too!"

"Nope, I'm good," Taryn insisted. "I have to run races."

"It is warm out," Jake said, balancing his warm plate on his lap. Then with a quick glance at Miriam, bent his head.

He thanked the Lord for the beautiful day, for having Miriam and Taryn with him. He prayed for his father and his mother. Then, almost hesitantly, he prayed that Miriam would be willing to stay. That they could rediscover what they had missed all those years ago.

With a soft sigh, he looked up. Miriam was toying with her fork, pushing around some pasta, a light frown on her face.

"What's the matter, Miriam?"

She looked up at him, her eyes wide, then shook her head. "Nothing," she replied. "Nothing at all."

Jake ate slowly, surprised to find his appetite had decreased. He managed to eat it all, but by the time he was done, Taryn was restless.

"I wanna go with my friends," she said, standing up. "I wanna go in the races."

"You didn't finish your spaghetti," Miriam said.

"I'm not hungry."

"Let's go then," Miriam said, slowly getting up.

"We'll go together." Jake wiped his mouth, balled up the paper napkin and got up. They deposited their paper plates and plastic utensils in a garbage can and walked over to where young children were already gathering for the annual races.

Taryn pulled away from them, running over to be with her friends, leaving Jake and Miriam on the sidelines.

"I guess we'll have to cheer her on," Miriam said, glancing up at Jake with a grin.

"She expects it." Jake looked down at her, hoping he appeared nonchalant. She glanced up at him, then away, biting her lip. He wondered if she felt the same way he did.

Jake felt guilty, because much as he loved his daughter, right now he didn't want to stand beside Miriam and watch Taryn race. Right now he wanted to take Miriam to someplace private, pull her into his arms...

"You have to watch me, Daddy," Taryn called out.

Jake blinked, and shook his head to rein in his own drifting thoughts.

He looked at his daughter and couldn't help but grin. Taryn was bent over at the waist, her elbows up, fists balled at her sides, in an exaggerated runner's stance. Someone called out "Ready, set" and then "go," and Taryn was off, legs pumping, arms swinging, her face screwed up in a tight frown.

"Pretty intense, isn't she?" Miriam said, laughing.

"She stays focused."

Miriam nodded, crossing her arms over her stomach and shivering lightly.

"Cold?" Jake asked.

"No."

They were silent again, watching as Taryn came walking back to them, her head hanging.

"I didn't win, Daddy," she said with a pout. "I runned my fastest and I didn't win."

Jake crouched down and gave her a quick hug. "That's okay. I watched you run. You went real fast. You don't have to win for it to be fun."

But Taryn wasn't convinced by the platitudes. She stayed beside Jake and Miriam for the second race, complaining of a headache, but by the time they announced the sack race, she was game again.

This time she won. And this time she was all smiles. She came back with a red ribbon and a huge grin on her face.

"I wonned. I wonned." She waved the ribbon.

"Wow, that's a pretty ribbon." Donna had come up and was now crouched beside Taryn, admiring the ribbon. She glanced up at Jake with a knowing smile. "Do you mind if I take Taryn off your hands for a while? My kids are going to get their faces painted, and then we're going to do some old-fashioned apple bobbing."

Jake could have hugged her. "No. Not at all."

Donna winked at Miriam, then took Taryn's hand and walked away.

Jake felt as nervous as he had on his very first date with Miriam. He didn't quite know what to say, how to go about this whole dating thing.

"So, looks like she'll be busy for a while," he said inanely.

Miriam nodded, avoiding his gaze.

Jake tried to think of something else to say. Something that wouldn't sound fake, fatuous. Finally he decided the straightforward approach was the best.

"Let's go for a walk, Miriam. I want to talk to you."

Miriam glanced at him over her shoulder, her eyes wide. "Okay," she said.

Jake took her arm, and studiously avoided the glances of the people close by them. They walked up the hill, through the long grass, until they came to a quiet grove of trees. It was cooler in there, and Jake saw Miriam shiver again. He glanced over his shoulder, but they were still in plain sight, so they walked a little farther.

Finally, he couldn't stand it any longer. He caught her by the arm and turned her around.

"I think we're far enough now," he said quietly, pulling her into his arms as he leaned back against a convenient tree.

She came willingly, slipping her own arms around his waist, laying her head against his chest.

Jake sighed and pulled her close, resting his head on hers. He rubbed his cheek along its soft silkiness, over and over again.

"I love you, Miriam. You know that."

Her only reply was a careful nod.

"So now what?"

She didn't move, didn't reply, only held him more tightly.

Jake bent over and brushed his lips over her shoulder, then nudged her head aside with his chin. She looked up at him. Their faces were so close, he could feel her breath, could feel the warmth of her burning cheeks.

And then he kissed her.

It was like coming home after a hard day. It was like a drink of water after a long thirst.

They belonged together, and as he kissed her, it was as if she had never left. That familiar touch, taste and feel. She felt right in his arms, as no other girl ever had.

Her lips were cool and soft, and as his mouth moved over hers, he reached up to stroke her cheek, run his fingers through her hair.

She murmured his name, her own hands caressing his shoulders.

Reluctantly he pulled away. With his forefinger he traced the exquisite line of her eyebrow, the softness of her cheek, her lips.

She closed her eyes as he touched her, her hands tightening on his waist.

"What are you doing to me, Jake?" she sighed.

"Trying to show you what you mean to me." He pulled her close again, content just to hold her. He knew she hadn't made any declaration to him, and wondered if she would. He didn't want to force anything out of her, but his own heart ached to hear something—some kind of confirmation of how she felt. He knew she felt something. She wouldn't have let him hold her, kiss her, if she didn't.

He just wished he knew what.

"Jake, tell me. Tell me in words."

He heard a yearning in her voice and wondered if she was even aware of it. "I love you more the longer you stay here." He touched her hair, his fingers playing with the soft waves. "I'm not that good with words. But when you're with me, I feel like all the things that were missing are here. I feel like holding you is what I was meant to do from the moment I was born. That this is part of my purpose in life."

She moved her face against his shirt, as if caressing him with her cheek. "Jake," she said softly. That was all. Just his name, but it held much more. She drew back, still holding him. She looked deep into his eyes; then her gaze traveled over his face, as if memorizing it. "You're the only man I ever loved. Ever."

Her words rocked through him, taking his breath away.

"I know it sounds silly," she continued, "but it's true. I had to tell you."

"Oh, Miriam. Do you know how long I've waited to hear you say those words?" He wanted to kiss her again, wanted to shout the news to the world. "Miriam, I think I've waited long enough. I have to ask you. Will you marry me?"

He felt a tremor in her arms as she clung to him. Her eyes opened wide and then slowly shut. She shook her head.

"Not that, Jake. Not that."

"What do you mean?" He felt as if all the breath had been pressed from him. He had just opened his heart to her, made himself as vulnerable as he had ever done with any woman, and now she sounded as if she hadn't wanted to hear it.

She caught him around his neck and pulled his head down to hers, kissing him hard. For a moment he let her. For a moment he pretended that she returned his feelings for her. But then, sensing her confusion, he carefully drew away.

"Miriam, what's wrong?"

She said nothing, only laid her head against his chest again. "Nothing."

He knew better, but also sensed that, for now, he didn't want to explore her reticence. She was in his arms. She had said nothing about his proposal. It still hung between them, and he didn't dare bring it up again. He felt a shiver of panic, wondering if she was still figuring on leaving tomorrow.

He didn't want to think about it. He remembered how willingly she had come into his arms. Remembered that she had told him she loved him, too.

She shivered, and Jake straightened. The moment was passed and nothing had happened. Disappointment crushed him, and he could say nothing to her as they walked back.

People were grouped together, visiting. Some were watching the little children getting their faces painted. Somehow, on their way back, Miriam drifted away from him, and Jake let her go.

He was confused and hurt and didn't know where to go from here. *Okay, Lord. I opened my heart to her, told her exactly what my intentions were. Help me to understand what is happening. Work in her heart. I know she needs to be here. I know she belongs here. Help her to see that.*

Jake wanted to leave right away, but Taryn was getting her face painted, and he knew it would look very rude if he suddenly left. So he hung around, made meaningless conversation, and all the while tried not to look out for Miriam.

Chapter Eleven

"There you are."

Miriam turned with a start to face her friend, Donna.

"Taryn's not feeling well," Donna said, frowning. "She's been asking for you."

"Where's Jake?" Miriam didn't want to go. She didn't want to run the risk of seeing Jake so soon after turning down his proposal.

"I can't find him. I thought he'd be with you. Besides, it's you she wants. C'mon." Donna tugged on her arm and glancing around one more time, Miriam followed.

"But she was fine just half an hour ago." A lifetime ago, she thought.

"I wouldn't worry about it, Miriam. Goodness, you sound like a guilty mother." Donna nudged her in the side. "I know exactly what you were doing. You don't need to look so guilty."

Miriam couldn't stop the flush that warmed her

cheeks. It was as if everyone here knew exactly what had happened for that short while that she and Jake had disappeared.

She felt her stomach tighten at the thought of his proposal. What was she supposed to do now? How could she go back to New York, how could she continue a life that she disliked, knowing that everything she wanted was here—but how could she stay and accept Jake's proposal? How could she make her financial problems his? She couldn't.

"What's the matter, Miriam? You look so sad."

Miriam was tempted to tell her. But she had spent too many years taking care of herself, and confession didn't come easily to her.

"I'm okay. I'm just worried about Taryn," she lied.

"Well she's just over here, lying down." Donna brought Miriam to where Taryn lay, curled up on a blanket. She sat up when Miriam approached, and Miriam could see how flushed her cheeks were, past the bright flowers painted on them.

"What's the matter, Pipper?" Miriam asked, crouching down at the little girl's side.

"My head hurts again."

Miriam laid a hand on her forehead and was surprised to feel how hot it was. "But you seemed fine this morning," she said aloud. Then she remembered how the child had slept on Jake's lap in church. That wasn't normal for Taryn. That much Miriam knew.

"I'll go get Jake. He might want to take her home," Donna said, getting up.

Miriam sat down and drew Taryn onto her lap, cradling her warm body close. What had she done, leaving her like this, going off with Jake like some teenager? How could she be so irresponsible?

She's not my little girl, she thought. Miriam stroked Taryn's hair back from her face. It didn't matter. She shouldn't have left.

Taryn said nothing, just lay there, adding to Miriam's guilt. Then Jake rushed to her side, falling down on one knee beside them. He also laid his hand on Taryn's forehead, and met Miriam's eyes.

"I feel terrible," Miriam said. "She just doesn't feel well."

"Let me take her. I think she'd better go home."

Taryn protested as Jake tried to take her away from Miriam's arms. "No. I want Miriam." The little girl clung to Miriam, and there was nothing she could do.

Jake helped Miriam up and tried once more, unsuccessfully, to make Taryn come to him.

"I'll bring her to your truck," Miriam said.

"I wanna go in your car. You said so." Taryn lifted her head, her expression downcast. "I wanna go in your car."

Miriam didn't know why Taryn was being so stubborn. A combination of not feeling well and just plain Taryn, she figured.

"I used my truck to bring the tables here," Jake said as they walked down to where they had parked the vehicles. "I imagine they'll need it to bring them back to the church."

"I'll get my husband to bring your truck to your

place,'' Donna offered. ''Why don't you just get Taryn home. We'll make sure your truck gets back.''

Jake shot her a grateful smile and turned back to Miriam. ''So we'll take your car, then, if that's okay?''

''Fine. Of course.'' She shifted Taryn so that the child was easier to hold.

They walked slowly down to the car, Jake beside Miriam, supporting her as they walked. She hadn't realized how heavy Taryn was. When they got to the car, Jake took the keys from her, unlocked her door and helped her in.

Then he got in on the driver's side, and they were off. They drove in silence.

Miriam couldn't look at him, but she was remembering his declaration of love. His proposal. She closed her eyes, laying her head on Taryn's, unable to think of the implications of what he had said to her.

By the time they got to Fred and Tilly's house, Taryn was asleep again, her body burning up with fever. This time, Jake took her from Miriam and carried her into the house. Miriam followed behind.

Tilly was sleeping in the recliner when they walked through the living room on their way upstairs. She sat up with a jolt when she saw them.

''What's the matter?'' She got up, rubbing her eyes.

''Taryn's not feeling good,'' Jake said tersely as he strode up the stairs.

''She feels like she has a fever,'' Miriam added, waiting for Tilly to join her. Together they went upstairs.

Jake was stripping Taryn out of her clothes and putting her in her pajamas. "She's just burning up," Jake said, slipping the nightgown over her head.

"Let's take her temperature." Tilly walked to the bathroom and found a thermometer. She cleaned it, and shook it as she brought it back to the bedroom. Taryn was sitting up, her eyes looking glazed, her cheeks a vivid red.

"Here, honey, open up." Tilly put the thermometer in her mouth, and the three adults waited.

Miriam felt slightly out of place, standing here, but she didn't want to go. She felt partially responsible, even though common sense told her that Taryn had probably already been coming down with this bug last night.

Tilly took the thermometer out and tried to read it. She handed it to Jake, who read out, "One hundred and three."

"That's high," Miriam said, chewing her lip. "Shouldn't we give her something for that?"

"I have some children's medication we can give her," Tilly said, sighing lightly. "Jake, you go downstairs and get a spoon for me." When they left, Miriam sat down beside Taryn, who was fretting.

"My head is sore, Miriam. How come my head is sore?"

"You have a fever. That means there's something bad in your blood, and the good cells are fighting it. That's why you're hot."

Taryn nodded and curled up on the bed. "I'm tired."

"Your grandma is getting you something that will

help take down the fever,'' Miriam said, stroking her hair away from her forehead. Just then Tilly came in the room with a bottle and a glass of water, and Jake came with a spoon. Miriam took the bottle and measured out the dosage according to the instructions on the bottle. ''Here, open wide.''

Taryn obeyed and then pulled a face. She grabbed for the glass of water and gulped it down. Then, with a sigh, she lay down again.

Miriam adjusted the blankets around her, as Jake pulled the blinds down over the window. Miriam stroked Taryn's cheek once, and then left.

Tilly brought the medicine back to the bathroom then followed Jake and Miriam down the stairs. Back in the living room, she dropped into her recliner. ''Oh, Jake, Simon called. Said it was important. He'll call you again tonight.''

''What did he want?''

''Didn't say.''

''How's Dad?'' Jake asked.

Tilly just shook her head. ''Not good. I don't know what to do. I might have to take him to the doctor again, tomorrow.''

''You look tired, Tilly.''

''I am.'' She sighed and closed her eyes again.

Miriam sat down on the couch and couldn't help but glance at the clock. She was shocked to see that it was already five o'clock—almost suppertime. ''What did you have for lunch, Tilly?''

''I didn't feel like making lunch.''

Miriam glanced at Jake, then got up. ''I'll get some

supper together for you. I'm sure Fred should have something.''

''He says he's not hungry.''

Miriam heard the note of despair in her voice and walked to her side. She bent over and kissed Tilly lightly. ''I'll see what he wants, and I'll take care of it. You just sit here.''

Tilly smiled up at her and caught her hand. ''Thanks, child. You are special.''

Miriam doubted that, but the words warmed her heart, anyway.

Fred was awake when she peeked into his bedroom. He looked haggard and worn. When Miriam asked if he wanted anything, he said no.

''What about some soup?''

''I don't know.''

''I'm going to take that as a yes. And Jake is going to make sure you eat it all,'' she warned before she left the room.

Back in the kitchen, Miriam wondered what she had gotten herself into. She wanted to leave, but how could she with Fred and Taryn sick? So Miriam found a recipe that she knew was Fred's favorite. It was also easy to make. Quick potato soup.

Luckily there were some leftover potatoes in the fridge, and soon Miriam had the ingredients together and was adding them one at a time to the pot on the stove.

She was just stirring the grated cheese into the soup when she saw Jake leaning on the counter beside her. She didn't want to look at him, but couldn't stop herself. How easy it was to lose herself in those eyes, to let herself drift toward him.

His hand on her arm stopped her, and she turned her attention back to the soup, stirring it as if everything important to her was in that pot.

Then he left her, and she breathed a sigh of relief. This wasn't turning out at all the way she had planned. She was supposed to be leaving tomorrow, and each encounter with Jake tested her resolve. She had no right to encourage him. But she was weak, lonely— and in love with a man she couldn't have. Shouldn't have.

Miriam swallowed, praying for strength. *This isn't fair, Lord. This just isn't fair. To give him back to me and make him so unattainable at the same time.*

Jake sat with Fred while he ate, and Tilly and Miriam sat in the kitchen. Taryn was sleeping, still fitfully. She would until the fever broke, Tilly informed Miriam.

Miriam knew absolutely nothing about childhood illnesses and was worried sick. She couldn't understand why neither Tilly nor Jake were sitting upstairs with her at this very minute.

The dishes were done, Tilly had gone to bed and the medication Taryn had taken was starting to kick in when Miriam decided to go. She tidied up the living room, delaying the inevitable, yet knowing she was playing a dangerous game. She wanted to see Jake again.

He came downstairs after checking on Taryn, and

when he saw her in the living room he paused at the bottom of the stairs. "So, I guess you have to go?"

Miriam nodded, still clutching a newspaper she had found on the floor.

He shoved his hands through his hair and sighed. "I know this is going to sound terribly improper, but I have to leave early in the morning to finish seeding." He hesitated, biting his lip. "I was wondering if you would mind staying here tonight, just until Tilly gets up. I'm worried about Taryn..." He let the sentence trail off, and at that moment Miriam could see utter weariness in his eyes.

"I'll stay, Jake."

"Thanks." His eyes met hers and he slowly walked over.

He was going to kiss her, she knew that.

He didn't even touch her—just bent over, his lips lightly caressing hers.

"I still love you, Miriam. I want to marry you."

She laid a finger on his lips to forestall him, her heart contracting with pain. "Please, Jake. Don't make this any harder for me than it already is."

"Don't make what harder?"

"Leaving."

She saw the stricken look on his face. She lowered her gaze as if to erase the memory, then felt his hands on her shoulders again.

"Jake." She couldn't stop herself. "I love you, I do. But I can't be what you want me to be." She felt her face twist with sorrow. "I can't be the kind of mother that Taryn needs. I thought I could, but when

I saw Donna with her children I realized how little I knew. I don't fit here.'' She drew in a shaky breath, curled her fingers around each other. What she said was partly true. But she couldn't tell him about her debt.

''Where do you fit, Miriam?'' He asked the question softly as he drew her in his arms. ''If you don't fit here, why do you think you'll fit in a place that you don't want to go back to? I know you don't. I see the look on your face when you talk about your work.''

Miriam bit her lip, resisting the urge to lay her head on his chest, to let him take all her problems and fix them. But it would be putting even more on his shoulders than he already carried. It wasn't fair to him, and if she truly loved him she would leave. She knew it was the only way.

Jake tightened his hold on her, caressed her head with his chin. ''I won't stop loving you, Miriam. So where does that leave me?''

He took a step back, lifted her chin with his finger and laid a gentle kiss on her lips. ''Think about that when you're heading back east.''

Miriam swayed as he stepped back. She wrapped her arms about her waist again, her chin down. She couldn't look at him. Couldn't tell him. She knew how important his family was, this farm. It was the first place he had told her that he felt he belonged. She couldn't jeopardize that. If they were to get married, her debt would become his. It was too much.

Silence again. A dark, intense silence that kept them apart.

"I'll set out some towels for you," Jake said, then turned and left.

Miriam watched him go back upstairs, his tall figure disappearing from view. He didn't look back.

Confusion tortured her thoughts. She knew she had to stay. She couldn't leave tomorrow. Not with Fred so sick, Taryn not feeling well and Tilly so exhausted. There was no way she could simply drive away and leave Jake to carry this.

But how could she stay? How could she see him every day, knowing she couldn't have him?

She dropped her head in her hands at the thought of being around Jake that long. So close and yet so far.

This isn't fair, Lord, she thought. *I can't do this to him. The only thing I can do is leave. He will think I hate him, when I'm doing it because I love him.*

She didn't know what to say, didn't know how to pray. She thought back to this morning, to the service, to yesterday and what Jake had told her.

It was too bewildering, and it was too early to go to bed. She dropped into the recliner and, glancing to the side, noticed the Bible. She needed comfort and guidance, and in these lonely hours of the night she didn't know where else to turn.

She opened it and turned to Romans, the same chapter Jake had read from. Slowly she reread the words, clinging to one love she knew she was allowed to claim.

She had lived a life close to God before. Would He take her back?

Nothing could separate her from God's love. The Bible said so. The same Bible that had brought good news to millions of people for hundreds of years. So many people before her believed it; many after her would, as well.

Miriam closed her eyes, her thoughts becoming prayers. Nothing, she thought. No present or future. Her past, her mistakes, her mother's mistakes, the things she wished she could change—none of that would separate her from the love of God shown in Christ. He would take her no matter what she came with. His love encompassed her regardless of her debt.

She reread the words again and again, and slowly she felt power surge through her. This wasn't a battle she had to fight alone. She didn't have the strength. All she had to do was take what was given. The other night, on the hillside, she had struggled, had tried to find God, as Jake had suggested.

She had gone about it all wrong, she realized, tracing the words of the passage with her finger. God was waiting for her to stop the struggle, to let Him give.

Miriam clutched the Bible, her eyes closing as she opened her tightly held heart and gave it over to God. She felt a joy and peace flood her heart. Tears of cleansing thankfulness drifted past her closed eyelids and down her cheeks as she found herself quietly humming songs from her youth. Songs of praise.

She opened the Bible again randomly and started reading John. She stopped at John 16:24. "Until now you have not asked for anything in my name. Ask and you will receive and your joy will be complete."

I want to do something for Jake, she prayed. *That is all I ask. Something to show him I love him. Something he will remember. I know he loves me and I know that leaving will seem like betrayal, but I can't ask that of him. I can't.*

She read on, gaining strength and comfort. She knew she would need everything she could to get her through the next day—until she left.

"Thank you, Lord," she said quietly.

Everyone, except Jake, was still asleep by the time Miriam got up the next morning. She hadn't slept much. She was too aware of the fact that Jake lay only a room away from her. It made her edgy and nervous, and by the time she woke up again, she was sure she had gotten only a couple of hours' sleep. Jake's alarm woke her up. However, she waited until she heard the sound of the tractor leaving the yard before she rose.

She would have to wait until Tilly was up to run home for a fresh change of clothes.

She sat down in the recliner again and picked up the Bible. She read through some of the Psalms, again seeking and finding the comfort she had found last night. In the silence of the morning, she prayed again. Prayed for God's good and perfect will to make itself known to her.

Then, unable to sit any longer, she went upstairs and checked on Taryn. The child was still asleep, still feverish. But she didn't seem as warm as yesterday.

Miriam brushed the hair out of Taryn's face, lightly

touching her cheek. Taryn sighed and turned onto her back, still sleeping.

Miriam felt a rush of tenderness for this young child, and wished she could stay, prayed she could stay. *I don't want lots of money, Lord. I don't need to be rich. If I could stay here, it would be all I'd want.*

Miriam mentally pulled herself back from these lives that she had to leave soon. Turning, she left the room.

She cleaned up what she could and then went back downstairs to set the table for breakfast and possibly make a pot of tea for Tilly.

The shrill ring of the phone broke the silence of the house. Miriam almost ran to get it, snatched it off the hook. "Hello, Prins household," she said, breathless.

"This ain't Tilly, is it?"

"No."

"Don't tell me Jake got married without telling me?"

What a thing to say to a complete stranger! "I'm sorry. If you wish to speak to Jake, he's gone already," Miriam said, unable to keep the prim tone out of her voice.

"My goodness, you're a secretary. Since when does Jake need a secretary?" the man said with a laugh.

"May I ask who is calling?" Miriam asked.

"You may." Silence followed this comment, and then Miriam recognized the joke. And the voice.

"Hello, Simon," she said dryly.

"Wow. An amazing secretary who recognizes voices of someone she has never met. Who are you?"

"Miriam Spencer."

A pause followed that, as she sensed Simon trying to place her. "Okay," he said triumphantly. "I remember. You're that old girlfriend. The high school fling."

Miriam knew she had been more to Jake than a fling, but disdained to comment on that.

"Did he get my message last night?"

"Yes. Tilly told him you called."

"Well, this is kinda sudden, but I'm leaving right away for the airport. I'll be there sometime this afternoon. Do you know if he's done seeding yet?"

Miriam was confused. "As far as I know, he should be done by today."

"Great. My timing is, as usual, impeccable. I know this is short notice, but I'm hoping to get there by about three. If Jake isn't home, then you and me can sit down, have tea, and you can remind me what a jerk I used to be."

"Okay." Miriam tried to keep her voice cool, remembering his unmerciful teasing whenever he would visit, and how Jake had always intervened, standing up for Miriam.

"Well, take care," Simon said, his voice breezy, before hanging up.

As she hung up she glanced at the clock, and, as if to force herself to stay on course, phoned Carl.

"So, you heading out today?" he asked.

"Well, something came up here. I'm probably leaving this afternoon."

"That's cutting it a bit close, but I guess you know your own limits. How are you feeling?"

In love. Confused. Scared. Forgiven. "I'm okay," she said.

"You don't sound okay."

"I'm fine. I've got to go. Talk to you later."

"Hey. Hang in there, girl. We'll untangle this financial business once you start working."

Not quick enough to make any difference here, she thought wryly. She knew she was looking at a minimum of four years of heavy payments, if she got other contracts as good as the one Carl had gotten for her. Otherwise it would be longer. "Yeah. It'll be fine."

Chapter Twelve

"Smells good in here."

Miriam turned from washing the dishes in the sink to see Tilly in the doorway, yawning. The woman had dark rings under her eyes; her skin was blotchy and puffy with fatigue. She drew her light blue bathrobe around her and blinked. Without her glasses, she looked especially vulnerable.

And old.

"Not a good night, Tilly?" Miriam asked, pulling out a chair for her. She had been busy in the kitchen, baking Fred's favorite muffins, hoping she could tempt his appetite.

"I felt like I didn't sleep, but I must have." She smiled her thanks as Miriam poured her a cup of tea from a carafe. It was still steaming.

Tilly caught the mug close to her, as if to absorb its warmth. "Jake said you have to leave today?"

"Later on. I'm driving back so I can make up the time along the way."

Tilly took a careful sip of her tea and sighed. "How's Taryn?"

"She's sleeping well now. Not restless. She's still a bit warm. I don't know if she's feverish."

"The fever must have broken, or she'd still be hot." Tilly looked around the kitchen. "Thanks for cleaning up. And for making supper last night. You're a treasure, you know."

Miriam felt a surge of warmth. She knew, but only because Tilly had been telling her that all her life. "Thanks, Tilly. I love you. I hope you know that."

"I do, dear. I do."

The thump of footsteps on the stairs made them both turn around.

Taryn. Already dressed in her blue jeans, and a big smile on her face when she saw Miriam in the kitchen. She walked around the table and sat down on the bench behind it. "I'm hungry," she announced.

Miriam glanced at Tilly, who was trying not to smile. Taryn was obviously better. Miriam felt as relieved as Tilly looked.

"How about a muffin and some juice?" Miriam asked, pulling a pitcher out of the fridge.

"Two muffins." Taryn held up two fingers, her brown eyes gleaming.

"We'll start with one, I think."

Once Taryn was done breakfast, Miriam went to see how Fred was doing. He lay, still and quiet, in his bed, and Miriam became concerned.

She came back out of the room. "I think we should take him to the hospital, Tilly," she said.

"I thought so." Tilly pulled her hand over her hair, smoothing it back with a weary gesture. "I'll go get dressed and then I can bring him."

"You're not taking him. You're way too tired. I'll bring him in."

Tilly shook her head. "No. They always ask so many questions, and you can't answer them. Besides, I don't think Taryn should go out just yet. She may look perky now, but she'll be droopy again in a couple of hours."

"Well, let me come with you, at least."

"Okay," Tilly agreed. "And thank you."

Miriam parked her car back in the driveway and glanced over at Taryn who, just as Tilly had predicted, was sleeping again.

She felt a twinge of guilt, but then realized she would have felt worse if she had let Tilly go in all by herself. Each had taken her own vehicle, but at least Miriam had been with Tilly for a while.

Now she was back at home, with nothing to do but wait for Jake.

Taryn yawned and stretched, smiling at Miriam. "I'm hungry," she announced.

"I can't get over your appetite, little girl," Miriam said, getting out of the car. She walked around and opened the door for Taryn, who already had her seat belt undone.

Once inside the house, she rummaged through the

refrigerator and found some soup left over from yesterday. She heated it up, and Taryn ate it all.

"Now we need dessert."

"Not for lunch." Miriam cleared away the bowl and took it to the sink.

"Can we have a marshmallow roast? My daddy always has one with me."

Miriam knew that to be a bit of an exaggeration, but figured it was a perfect way to keep Taryn entertained for a while. She didn't know what else to do with the child, and it would probably be good for her to get outside.

Fifteen minutes later they were squatting in front of a low-burning fire, toasting marshmallows. Taryn's face was smeared with the remnants of her most recent marshmallow, and Miriam regretted not bringing out a wet facecloth for her.

"You look grubby," Miriam said, reaching across to carefully wipe off the worst of it with the cuff of her shirt.

Taryn tried to cooperate by licking her chin with her tongue and wiping her face with her hand, but only succeeded in making it worse. "I'm gonna need a bath," she said.

"Yes, you are." Miriam touched her nose lightly with her finger and smiled.

Taryn looked suddenly serious. "I heard Grandma say you're going away today. Why don't you want to stay?"

Miriam's heart sank at the sad look on the little girl's face and the plaintive note in her voice. She got up and, leading Taryn by the hand, walked over to the picnic table. They sat down together, and Miriam took a deep breath. "Remember the night I gave you a kiss on your hand?"

Taryn opened one sticky fist and looked down at it, nodding slowly, her ponytail bobbing.

"Well, that kiss was for when I'm going away." Miriam stopped as a lump in her throat cut off her speech. She waited a beat, then forced herself to continue. "I have to go back to work. I don't live here."

Taryn clenched her fist. "But I want you to stay." She looked up at Miriam, her soft brown eyes filling with tears. "Don't you want to stay with us? Daddy wants you to stay."

"I told you already, dear, I have to go back." Miriam stopped, then pulled Taryn against her, held her close.

Taryn wound her arms around Miriam in a tight hug. "But who is going to bring me to play school?" she cried, her voice muffled against Miriam's jacket.

"Your grandma will still be here. And your daddy."

Taryn sniffed loudly. "I want you to bring me."

Miriam pressed a kiss to Taryn's head, inhaling her smell. She felt a yearning toward her that she was sure had much to do with her own regrets, her own sorrow over lost opportunities.

She should have been mine, Miriam thought, closing her eyes. Remembering what Paula had written, she fought down a surge of anger, of hate over what her friend had done and the repercussions of it.

Once again she struggled to forgive her mother for taking her away, for blackmailing Jake.

Am I never going to be done with this? she prayed, rocking Taryn lightly, the hurt magnifying the more she thought of her mother, of her friend. *Dear Lord, must I go through this each time I think of them?* To forgive was difficult enough, but to forgive someone who wasn't even there seemed futile.

At the same time Miriam knew that if she was going to go back east stronger than when she arrived, this was precisely what she had to do. Forgive.

Please Lord, help me to get through this. Help me to forgive them. I can't do any less, because I know how much You forgave me. Miriam finally realized what she was saying in her own prayer. She *had* been forgiven. The guilt she felt over past sins, her feelings of shame, had all been forgiven, thoroughly and completely. Yet she still struggled to give that same forgiveness to her mother and her best friend.

As Miriam rocked Taryn, she smiled. *Thank you, Lord, for Your love, for Your forgiveness. Please be with this little girl and help her to understand. Help her when I go, because I know she is attached to me.*

Miriam took a slow breath, and another, and then gently set Taryn away from her. "Let's go in the house and get washed up, okay?" she said quietly, wiping away a tear from Taryn's cheek with her thumb.

Taryn sniffed, nodded once and jumped off the picnic table. She stopped, her head cocked to one side. "Do you hear that?" she asked, turning back to the farm driveway. "I hear Daddy's tractor." She grinned back at Miriam and began running toward the driveway.

Moments later, Miriam realized it wasn't a tractor, and felt a surge of disappointment.

The vehicle slowed by the driveway and then turned in. It was a silver sports utility vehicle, its shiny finish coated with a thin layer of dust.

The license plates told her that it was a rented vehicle. Simon most like, she assumed as she glanced at her watch.

"Come back here, Taryn. Wait until he's turned off his truck," Miriam warned.

Taryn paused as the vehicle parked beside Miriam's. Then as it came to a stop, she jumped up and down, clapping her hands. "It's Uncle Simon!" she shrieked.

A tall man got slowly out, stopped beside the vehicle and stretched. He wore a leather jacket and blue jeans. His face was half covered with a pair of brown-tinted aviator glasses, and as he turned to look at Miriam, his mouth curved into a distinct smirk.

"Uncle Simon!" Taryn called out, running directly toward him.

"Hey, squirt," he said, bending over to grab the little girl. "How's my favorite niece? And you must be Miriam," he said, turning to Miriam. He slipped his glasses off his face and tucked them in the pocket of his coat. His smile grew broad and more sincere. He held out his hand. "Nice to meet you. I don't know if you remember me. I'm Simon."

"Yes," Miriam said quietly, returning his firm shake with an equally firm one. "I remember you. I'm sorry but I haven't had time to run out to the field and tell Jake you were coming. I thought he'd be back by now."

Simon nodded. "Oh, well. I'll just wait."

"Do you want some coffee or tea?" she asked.

Simon grinned again. "Tea. That's what we drink in this house, isn't it, Taryn." He bounced his niece once and set her down. He turned to Miriam. "So we'll have a cup of tea and then you can tell me all about what's happened in your life since the last time I saw you."

Miriam doubted that she would, so she just smiled and walked ahead of him into the house.

Jake pulled up the seed drill and glanced at the gathering clouds. Normally the thought of rain would have made him antsy, but he was done, praise the Lord.

He drove the tractor to the road and got out to secure the drill for transport. Just as he was walking back to the tractor, the first few spatters of rain hit.

He had tried not to think about Miriam while he worked. Had tried not to think of her leaving today. But he had spent most of the morning reliving what had happened yesterday. What could he have done different? How could he have convinced her to stay?

But she was adamant, and no matter what he had said, he couldn't break through the barriers she had erected. He knew she loved him. Was sure of it. She had said it herself. So why did he have the feeling he was even worse off than before?

She was holding something back from him.

So he sat in his tractor, mulling and praying and wondering if he was going crazy all at once or if it had been coming on for some time.

He reached up and turned on the radio, hoping to find something other than the usual heartbreak and honky-tonk. He settled on a classical station, which soothed him.

By the time he returned home, he felt as if his emotions were finally under control—until he pulled into his driveway and, with a lift of his heart, saw Miriam's car.

Right beside it was a rental vehicle. Probably a salesman, he thought, with a sigh of frustration. The last thing he wanted was to go over the merits of one kind of spray over another or what kind of baler he should buy. Not with Miriam still in his house and getting ready to leave.

Please give me strength to get through this, Jake prayed, leaning back against the tractor.

Then he noticed that Tilly's car was gone, and fear gripped him. There was probably a simple explanation, but he was afraid.

He looked over the yard that his father had built up all these years. Other than his time with his first father, Tom Steele, Jake had spent some of his happiest years here. *Please let everything be all right with my dad. I love him too much. I know I should let go, but I'm*

*afraid to. I don't have the strength right now to lose
another father.*

He leaned against the tractor another moment,
knowing that whoever was in the house could wait.
He needed to draw on the strength that only God could
give him. He felt emotionally vulnerable and drained.
His father was ill, and he was in love with a girl who
he knew wouldn't be satisfied living here. Not after
the life she had lived. He had been utterly foolish to
even entertain that idea.

He turned to trudge across the yard. The rain was
coming down in earnest now, so he started to run.

As he opened the porch door, the sound of a man's
deep laugh greeted him. It sounded like Simon. Puzzled and apprehensive, he toed his boots off and set
them aside, then walked into the kitchen.

A tall man sat with his back to Jake. Taryn sitting
on the chair nearby, chattered away to him. She was
looking a lot better. The man turned as Jake entered
the kitchen.

"Daddy, Uncle is here," Taryn called out as soon
as she saw her father.

"Simon." Jake felt surprise as his brother stood up
to greet him. "What in the world are you doing here?"

Simon grabbed Jake in a most unmanly hug, then
pulled away, his expression serious.

"I took a chance," he said slowly, watching Jake's
face intently. "I talked to Miriam this morning, right
after I got a call from Jonathan. You remember him?
The Mountie?"

Jake nodded. Jonathan had been instrumental in bringing Simon and Jake together.

"You might want to sit a minute, and I'll tell you what I found out." Simon pulled out a chair and set it out for his brother. "It's about our mother."

Jake chanced a quick look at Miriam, who stood by the sink, watching him, her expression enigmatic. He looked away.

He didn't want to deal with this right now. He didn't want to think about a mother that he had never met, that he had no emotional attachment to.

Yet here he was, sitting at his own table, listening to what might be the final chapter in his brother's life-long quest.

"I found out our mother's name," Simon said quietly. He sat across from Jake, his hands folded on the table in front of him. "It's Joyce Smith."

Jake looked straight at him. "You're kidding."

Simon shook his head. "But I have an address…"

"So why don't you phone?"

"I don't want to do that. After all these years, I'd just as soon go up, see if it's true, and if it is—" he shrugged "—we'll take it from there. It's the closest we've come since I started looking."

And it had been a long search for his brother, thought Jake, remembering the number of homes Simon had run away from partly in the hope he would find his mother and partly to attain his independence. The whole point of the search was to reunite the family—Jake, Simon and their mother.

But Jake had found contentment and happiness with

the Prins family, and could not be convinced the last time Simon had wanted to run away.

So Simon had left. It was only in the past half year that they had found each other again. But even now, Jake wasn't sure he wanted to spend the time and energy that Simon did in what seemed like a fruitless search.

And his timing was atrocious.

"I can't go, Simon. Fred isn't feeling good. I've got Taryn to think of..." Jake's voice trailed off as he glanced at Miriam, unable to voice the rest of his thoughts. *I need to talk to Miriam before she leaves again.* "It's ridiculous."

"What's ridiculous about it, Jake?" Simon leaned closer. "What's so hard about wanting to finally meet your mother?"

"She's *not* my mother," Jake snapped, the tension of the past few days catching up on him. He pulled in a breath, praying again for patience and for the right words to explain to his brother. "We've never known her. She hasn't tried to contact us. She's not tried in any way to reconnect. She's out of our lives."

Even as he spoke the words, Jake thought of Miriam standing just a few feet away. Thought of her reasons for not keeping in touch, thought of the hard and difficult events of her life that had kept her away.

"I'm sorry, Simon," he added, dragging a hand over his face. "I'm tired. I've got a lot on my mind, and I just don't think I can do this right now. We don't even know if she'll be there when we get there."

"If we don't take this chance, we might lose her

again, Jake." Simon leaned back in his chair, his arms crossed over his broad chest. "I'm going, whether you're coming with me or not. I just thought it would be better if we both went."

Jake understood the wisdom of that and understood Simon's unspoken request for help and support. Simon never wanted to admit when he needed help. You just had to know.

And Jake knew. Right now what Simon wanted, as much as to find their mother, was for Jake to come along with him.

"I'm sorry, Simon. I can't see my way around this."

"I can stay, if that's a problem," Miriam spoke up.

Jake swung around. "What do you mean? I thought you had to leave."

"I can put it off a few days."

Jake held her eyes with his, as if to delve into her mind. "Why would you do that?"

Miriam didn't answer, and instead turned to Simon. "Can you take Taryn for a short walk outside, please?"

Simon looked at her and then nodded.

"C'mon, squirt. You have to show me your yard."

Taryn jumped off her chair, eager to go out with her uncle.

They left, and Miriam sat at the table beside Jake.

"Where's Tilly?" Jake asked, unable to keep the brusque tone out of his voice. He disliked the vulnerable feeling she brought out in him, he disliked how he kept making himself vulnerable and she kept being evasive.

"She brought Fred into the hospital. They want to keep him in for observation. They put him on an IV because he was so dehydrated. They figure it's just a flu."

Jake felt relieved. "Now...what did you have to say that Taryn couldn't hear?"

Miriam looked down at her hands, pressed her slender fingers together. "I think you should go, Jake," she said quietly. "I think it's really important that you try to find your mother. That you and Simon do it together."

Jake caught a whiff of her perfume, watched how the light of the window lit up her hair, placed hollows in her cheeks and the delicate bones of her shoulders. They were alone. How was he supposed to listen to her telling him to leave? How was he supposed to keep a clear head and have a sane discussion about a mother he never knew and hadn't thought much about in the past sixteen years?

How was he supposed to do that when the woman he had been thinking of all those years now sat across from him, so close and yet so distant? All he wanted to do was pull her into his arms and kiss her until she agreed to stay, until she agreed to become his wife.

But that's not what she wanted to talk about.

And he knew that was not how things were going to end for them.

He pulled his attention back to what she was saying. "Why do you want me to go?" he repeated.

"Because…" Miriam bit her lip. "I guess it's because I ignored my own mother's needs so long. I got caught up in the things I wanted to do. I hated her so long for taking me away from you. I hated her because you got married. I still struggle with forgiving her." Miriam stopped, pressing her hand against her mouth and looked away.

Jake fought a manly battle to resist pulling her to him; he could tell she wasn't done.

"Yesterday after you left, I kept reading the Bible," she continued. Miriam lowered her hand into her lap, scratched at the polish on her nails. "I haven't lived the best life since I started modeling. That was my own choice. No one forced me into that. I spent a lot of time taking very good care of myself and making sure I had fun. What you read in the papers wasn't entirely true, but it wasn't too far off the mark when it came to my selfishness. I hardly visited my mother, hardly spent time with her. I thought she had to be punished for what she had done to me."

Miriam paused again.

"Your mother was a difficult woman," Jake reminded her. "It wasn't all your fault."

Miriam smiled. "Thanks for that. But I never realized what I had been holding back. My mother became a Christian in the hospital. The past few months of her life, when I was struggling with trying to keep my business afloat, I used to visit her more often. She was hard to visit with—she talked so slow. But she kept telling me that I had to lay my burdens on the Lord." Miriam laughed shortly, glancing up at Jake, then away. "It seemed too easy. I didn't think God could bail me out of my business troubles."

"What business troubles?" Jake was a little lost.

Miriam shook her head, and Jake could tell that she was hesitant to tell him.

"Please, Miriam. I won't judge you."

Miriam smiled a sad smile. "That doesn't matter. It's not important. What I wanted to tell you was that when my mother died, I still hadn't forgiven her." Miriam looked up at Jake, her eyes steady. "The other day, sitting under the maple tree in our old front yard, you showed me something. And I discovered a few things about myself. I found out that I had no right not to forgive my mother when God had forgiven me so much. I accepted that forgiveness last night."

"Oh, Miriam." Jake felt his heart overflow. If God had done that in her life, he thought, what else might lie in store for them?

"I know I'm not done," she continued. "I know I have a long way to go. But what I wish more than ever is that I had spent more time with her. That I had taken the time to sit with her. To learn beside my mother's bed what I had to learn without her around." Miriam leaned closer, taking Jake's hand. "You have that chance. You have a chance to meet your mother, to find out why she gave you up. I'm sure you must wonder, just as I wondered why my mother did what she did to me. I still don't think it was right, but I've had to accept that she did it because, in her own way, she cared."

Jake wanted to deny what she was saying. What her

mother had done was selfish. Her threats had been cruel and frightening to a young boy who was so unsure of his own place in the family he had been placed in. But he knew he had to deal with this on his own.

Had things turned out differently between him and Miriam, he might have an easier time dealing with it. But Miriam sat across from him now, urging him to leave, urging him to pursue a different part of his life even though he was sure she knew there was something building between them.

What do I do, Lord? he prayed, his head bent. He clutched Miriam's delicate hand in his own and lifted it to his face, holding it against his rough cheek. *What do You want me to do?*

He felt her fingers curl against his cheek and he turned, pressing a kiss to its soft palm, breathing out in a sigh. Then he let go of her hand and got up.

"I'll stay and help Tilly and be here for her," Miriam said. "I know you're finished seeding. You shouldn't miss out on this chance. I don't think you should do this with a phone call—I think you need to do this face to face."

Jake stood facing her, his hands in his pockets. "Why do you want to do this for me?" he asked, still struggling to understand why she seemed so adamant. "I thought you had to go today."

"Don't worry about my life, Jake," she said. "It's not worth the effort." She looked up at him. "But you have a chance to meet your mother. To ask her important questions. Maybe it's a way of my own mother's death making sense...if someone besides me can learn something from it.''

Jake understood her need. But it didn't seem to fit with what he wanted to do. He prayed they would find a time and place where they could finally speak the truth to each other. "Okay," he said quietly. "I'll go. As long as you will be here when I come back."

"I will." She relaxed back in her chair.

"I'm pretty sure we won't be gone long. Probably two days at the most." This was not the conversation he had had in mind. He didn't quite know what he had expected. But for now, knowing she would be here when he returned was enough to cling to.

"Good" was all Miriam said. She got up, and for a heart-stopping moment Jake thought she was going to come up to him, wrap those slender arms around him, pull his head down to hers...

He forced the thought aside as she walked past him to the porch. "Where are you going?" he asked, his voice brusque with repressed emotions.

Miriam turned to him, her eyes hopeful. "I'm just going to get—"

"Taryn wants a drink." Simon's loud voice interrupted. He knocked on the open screen door. "Can we come in now?"

Miriam looked away. "Sure. We're done."

"Good." The door creaked as Simon pulled it open, and Taryn was chattering about the calves as she came in. She bounced into the kitchen and ran straight to her father. "I need a drink, Daddy."

"What do you say?" Jake and Miriam spoke at precisely the same time. Their eyes caught and held, and Jake could see Miriam blush.

"Sorry," she murmured.

"Please can I have a drink," Taryn said with studied impatience. "Then I want to go outside again."

"I'll go with you, Taryn," Miriam offered. "I have to clean up the picnic stuff anyhow."

"Okeydokey," Taryn said, then noisily gulped down a cup of juice that Jake had poured for her. She wiped her mouth and ran outside again.

Jake watched them leave, feeling as if an opportunity had passed.

"So," Simon asked, leaning against the kitchen counter. "I'm leaving in about fifteen minutes. Are you coming?"

Jake glanced out the window at Taryn and Miriam, who were cleaning up around the fire pit. He could see Taryn was excited, and once again he was struck with a sense that this was how it should be. A family—

"Jake," Simon called out with a laugh. "I'm over here, not out there."

"Sorry." Jake averted his gaze and took a deep breath. "I've decided to come with you," he said.

Simon was quiet for a moment, as if acknowledging the difficulty of the decision. "I know this is a hard time for you to leave. But I'm scared if we wait any longer, we'll miss her. I am really praying that it will work out in the end."

"So am I," said Jake fervently, thinking not only of Fred and Tilly, but of Miriam, as well. "So am I."

* * *

"I'm glad Jake stopped by the hospital on his way out," Tilly said as she sat back in her recliner in the living room. "Otherwise I wouldn't have known anything about him going."

"How do you feel about this?" Miriam asked, curling up in one corner of the couch.

Tilly shrugged as she picked up a magazine. "I think it's a good idea. Jake has never said much about his biological mother but I know, since he had Taryn he's been curious. I know he's wondered what would make a woman give up two boys like she did. I imagine she must have been in quite a difficult position to do that."

"I pray he finds her," Miriam said simply.

"I'm glad you could stay awhile longer," Tilly said. "Otherwise Jake couldn't have gone at all. This won't make your trip back too rushed?"

Miriam shrugged the comment away. Each minute she stayed here added driving time to the trip. It would be tense, but if Jake came back when he said he would, she could make it by driving and sleeping in her car. "I'll be okay."

"And when you do go back, we are going to hear from you again, aren't we? I don't want you to feel you're all alone."

"I'm not, Tilly. I know how wrong I was to stay out of touch…" Her voice trailed off as she thought of what she had deprived herself of—Fred and Tilly and the love they had for her.

"I care for you, girl, and I sense that you are uptight

about this job you have to do. Do you want to talk about it?''

Miriam gently shook her head. ''I can't. But I want you to know that I'm not going back because I want to. I have…obligations.''

''Well, I want you to remember that you can always talk to the Lord.'' Tilly leaned over and pulled out her Bible. She leafed through it and glanced up at Miriam. ''This is a piece I like to read when I worry about the future.'' She adjusted her glasses and began to read from Psalm 71. ''In you, O Lord, I have taken refuge; let me never be put to shame. Rescue me and deliver me in your righteousness; turn your ear to me and save me. Be my rock of refuge, to which I can always go; give the command to save me, for you are my rock and my fortress.''

Miriam listened to Tilly's soft voice, letting the words comfort her. Then Tilly read, ''Though you have made me see troubles, many and bitter, you will restore my life again; from the depths of the earth you will again bring me up. You will increase my honor and comfort me once again.''

''Can you read that again?'' Miriam asked, sitting up.

As she did, Miriam took a deep breath, as if to draw the very essence of the words into her. It was a promise. Did she dare cling to it? Did she dare think it would be true for her?

Tilly read on and Miriam listened, feeling strengthened and nurtured. Nothing had changed, but she felt as if she had been given a port in the storm. Somehow she had to trust.

Chapter Thirteen

"Let's stop here." Simon slowed down by the restaurant just off the main road going through town, then turned in and parked in an empty spot right beside the building. He turned off the engine and laid his head back. Neither he nor Jake said anything. They were tired and disheartened.

Jake was the first to get out. He wanted to stretch his legs. They'd spent the past two days driving, put on over a thousand miles and talked to a dozen people. Knowing they still had another two hours ahead of them before they were home made him feel exhausted. He hadn't seen this much of Alberta since he and Simon were getting shuffled around the foster care system.

"Well, that was a bust," Simon said, getting out of his side of the vehicle. "I'm sorry, Jake. I guess we should have quit at Riverview when we didn't find her, but I thought we were so close…'' He let the sentence drift off.

''It's not your fault,'' Jake said, as they walked past the huge windows to the entrance. ''Besides—'' he said as he pulled the double door open ''—it was a chance to spend some time together.''

''A lot of time,'' Simon said dryly, as they stepped into the restaurant.

''Are you going to stay the night when we get to the farm?'' Jake asked, settling into a chair behind a table. He didn't even bother consulting the menu tucked between the sugar container and the napkin holder. He just wanted a cup of coffee and a muffin.

''Probably. If that's okay with Tilly.''

''It'll be fine, and you know it.''

''Will it be fine with Miriam?'' Simon asked with a knowing smirk.

Jake ignored him. He didn't want to talk about Miriam with Simon. He didn't dare spend too much time even thinking about her.

''I remember a little pep talk you gave me one time,'' Simon continued, clasping his hands and resting them on the table, leaning forward. ''I remember your telling me not to underestimate what I had to offer Caitlin. I wonder if it isn't my turn.''

''What do you mean?''

''Look, I know as the big brother you're supposed to be the one who has his act together, and for most of your life, you have.'' Simon sat back as the waitress stopped at their table with a pot of coffee. After she'd filled their mugs and left to place their order, Simon poured sugar in his coffee and began to stir. "You've always been the one who knows where he's going."

"And your point is?"

"You don't want Miriam to go."

"I don't," Jake agreed, blowing lightly on the steam of his coffee. "I don't want her to go, but she has to. Or so she keeps saying."

"Have you asked her why?"

"I've tried to, but she puts me off, like she doesn't want to tell me." Jake shrugged and took a careful sip of the coffee. "She's hiding something, but I can't get it out of her."

"You kissed her yet?"

Jake tried not to, but could feel his neck grow warm. "Yes."

"Oh, goodness, my ever cool brother is looking a little sheepish." Simon grinned. "And?"

"And I can't believe I'm having this conversation with you, Simon. You sound like a teenager."

Simon laughed. "Caitlin always says I never really experienced childhood—that's why I won't grow up. So? Spill."

Jake sighed, knowing his brother wasn't going to quit. "I love her, Simon. Okay? I heard you say those words about Caitlin, and I remember feeling smug that I got you to admit it. So now I'm saying the same thing. I love her." He rubbed his eyebrow with his index finger and shrugged.

"And..."

"And nothing. She's lived a glamorous life, she's used to flying all over the world and making money.

You saw that fancy little car of hers. Can you imagine her living in Fred and Tilly's house, getting by on a farmer's income, shopping in a little Podunk town like Derwin?''

Simon frowned as if contemplating. ''You know what, Jake? I can.''

Jake snorted. ''You've only seen her for an hour. How in the world can you make that kind of assessment?''

Simon sat back with a self-satisfied grin. ''Because I've seen the way she looks at you, big brother. That's why.''

Jake heard what Simon said, his heart quickening. He thought of what Miriam had said just before he left, when she was trying to talk him into going to find his mother. How she had accepted what God had done for her. Why would she tell him that?

He clutched his coffee cup, hardly daring to imagine that it could be.

''I guess you've got things to talk to little Miriam about when you get home,'' Simon continued.

''I don't have much left to ask her. I've already proposed.''

''Then propose again. And again. Until she accepts.''

Jake heard Simon, and wondered. Simon had always been the stubborn one. Maybe his approach was better.

The waitress came with their muffins, and Jake, feeling suddenly benevolent, smiled his thanks. She paused, her brown eyes holding his, then smiled carefully back.

She set the muffins down in front of them before leaving.

"So now what do we do?" Jake asked Simon.

Simon shrugged, tapping the side of his mug with his finger. "I don't know. I could ask Jonathan, Caitlin's brother, to help. He could contact some of his fellow officers—they might find out something for us. I wouldn't know where to start looking for someone whose name is J. Smith." Simon sighed, and Jake knew how disappointed he was. He had thought they were so close. Looking back, it would probably have been wiser to phone ahead, but Simon had been so sure she would still be there.

"Well, one good thing came out of it all," Simon said with a weary smile. "We found out we have a sister. Cory Smith."

Jake returned Simon's smile. "That was a bittersweet discovery," he said. "I wonder if she's full or half."

"Does it matter?" Simon asked quickly.

Jake shook his head. "Not a bit. But it does make not finding Mom a little harder to take."

They were quiet a moment, each lost in his own thoughts. "I want to thank you for coming, Jake," Simon said quietly. "It meant a lot to me."

Jake merely nodded his acknowledgment. All the way to Riverview, he had doubted and wondered if he had done the right thing by going on this quixotic mission. But seeing the gratitude on his brother's face, and being there to find out for themselves from an old neighbor lady that they had a sister, balanced out the frustration. Somewhat.

"More coffee, sirs?" The waitress stopped by their table, holding a coffeepot in one hand.

Simon looked up and winked at her. "No, thanks, sweetie. We got a long ride ahead."

"Well, have a safe trip."

Jake felt Simon kick him under the table, and he looked up, frowning. Their waitress was looking directly at him, smiling. "Come again," she said, laying the bill on the table.

She had a throaty voice, compelling in its own way. Her cheerful smile seemed to light up a face dominated by deep brown eyes fringed with thick lashes. Her long hair, held back with a barrette, was a sandy shade of brown, curling down her back. Pretty, strikingly so.

Once she would have made him take a second look, but now she did nothing for him.

Jake returned the smile, careful not to look too welcoming. "We will," he said with false cheerfulness.

They walked out of the restaurant and into the warmth of the day, both anxious to get on their way.

The trip back to Waylen was quiet. Jake and Simon were each lost in their thoughts. The closer they got to home, the more uptight Jake got. In spite of his brother's assurances about Miriam, Jake knew that there was a lot that couldn't just be willed away. She had other obligations and was used to a life-style he couldn't begin to understand. And she had a secret she wasn't telling him.

As they pulled into the driveway, Jake sat straighter, looking for Miriam's car. He felt a clench of disappointment when he saw an empty spot where it had been two days ago.

"Looks like we're too late. Again," Simon said quietly.

"She might just be back at her house," Jake said, getting out of the vehicle. He almost ran to the house, anxious to find out where Miriam was.

Tilly was sitting in her usual chair in the living room, when Jake burst into the room.

"Well, hello, Jake," she said, setting aside the book she was reading. "So you're home. And right on time like you said." She got up, carefully watching his face, probably to see if she could find any hint of what had happened. "So how did it go? You didn't say much when you phoned to tell me when you were going to be home."

"We didn't find her."

"Oh, Jake." Tilly reached out for him and drew him into her arms. For a moment Jake allowed himself the comfort, feeling a little guilty that his mind was on other things—on Miriam, rather than on the disappointment of not seeing his biological mother.

Tilly pulled back, shaking her head. "That is too bad. Did you find out anything?"

"We found out we have a sister." Jake smiled at his mother and shook his head, still unable to absorb that piece of news.

"My goodness. That's interesting." Tilly clucked in sympathy.

"How's Dad?"

"He's much better. He's coming home tomorrow. It was just a flu he couldn't get over."

Tilly was about to ask something else, but after finding out that his father was going to be okay, Jake was done with amenities.

"Where's Miriam?"

Tilly pressed her hand to her cheek and sighed. "She's gone to her house. She got a phone call from some man named Carl. He called a couple of times. Once she knew when you were coming, she made arrangements. She's only been gone a couple of minutes. I was supposed to give you a message. It's on the kitchen table."

Jake felt his heart plunge into his stomach. A goodbye note, he thought. This time it was her turn. She had said she'd wait until he came back. Leaving just minutes before his return was cowardice. Miriam was avoiding him. And he was tired of it.

He ran into the kitchen, almost knocking over his brother in the process.

"What's up, Jake?"

"I don't know."

Jake bit his lip, almost swaying with weariness. If only he and Simon hadn't stopped in that restaurant. If only they had driven straight through. If only he hadn't gone with Simon in the first place.

If, if, if.

It seemed his entire life was punctuated with those words.

But he was tired of ifs. He wanted answers, and this time he wasn't going to let her go without his finding them.

"Simon, I want you to take my truck and park it on the road. Miriam has to come by here on her way out. I don't want her going."

"Sure thing." Simon threw him a mock salute and jogged out the door.

Jake felt a measure of relief when he heard his truck start up. First line of defense in place, he thought. He turned to his mother, who handed him the folded note. "Did she say anything to you? Give you any hint why she decided to leave all of a sudden?"

Tilly nodded, a sad smile curving her mouth. "Not really. Miriam had gone for a walk, and this Carl fellow phoned. He asked where Miriam was. I told him she was outside. Then he got angry and said something about her risking this job. I asked him to explain." Tilly looked up at him, touching his shoulder lightly. "Jake, she risked losing an important job just to stay here. To help us out. Now she has to drive day and night to get there on time." Tilly shook her head. "Jake, it's a six-day drive to New York, and she has only four days to get there. It's too dangerous. Don't let her go."

Jake heard his mother's words, trying to understand, realizing that Miriam had made a huge sacrifice so he could try to find his mother. He also realized that she wasn't going to leave until she gave him the reason why.

Jake's chest lifted in a sigh. "I'm going to her house."

Tilly gave him a hug. "I'll be praying for you both, son," she said, sniffing lightly.

Jake drew back, looked down at her softly wrinkled face, her bright blue eyes that shone with tears.

Son. He hadn't found his biological mother, but he had found a mother in Tilly.

Now all he had to do was find the other woman in his life.

He ran out to his truck. Simon was leaning against it, arms crossed, looking like a modern-day highwayman. "So far so good, brother," he said, as Jake came running up to him. "Don't come back without her," Simon warned.

"I won't." He jumped in, gunned the engine, spun around and headed down the road.

Miriam dropped the last of her clothes into the suitcase and zipped it shut. She couldn't help a quick glance at her watch, fear gripping her. Could she make it? Had she cut things too close? She pressed her hand against her stomach. "Please Lord," she prayed. "Give me strength. Let me get back safely."

It was going to be long hard driving. She would have to grab some sleep when possible.

She drew in another breath, wishing she had the nerve to stay and talk to Jake. But if she had, she might not have left. If she didn't do this job and the next and the next, her debt would keep building.

She had no choice.

Miriam thought of what Tilly had read to her while Jake was gone.

She walked out of the house and, without a second glance behind her, closed the door. The moon was out, and in its watery light she could see the maple tree. She set her suitcase down and walked over to it, touched it. While it wasn't difficult to say goodbye to the house, it was going to be hard to leave this tree. For it was here that she had first felt the healing power of forgiveness.

God's forgiveness.

She wondered if Jake could eventually forgive her.

She knew it was a cheap move, to write him a note. It couldn't begin to cover what she felt. She didn't even know what she dared tell him. It was as if she were sixteen all over again, head over heels in love with Jake and unsure of herself.

A cool spring breeze danced around her, and she shivered a moment, thinking of the dear people she would be leaving behind here. She leaned against the tree, sending out prayers. She prayed Fred's health would improve. She prayed Tilly would be able to cope with it, knowing the deep love they had for each other. She prayed Taryn would get over her leaving. When Miriam had kissed the precious child good-night and told her she was leaving, Taryn had clung to her, crying and begging her to stay.

Dear Lord, please take care of them all. Thank You

for letting me come back for a while, for being able to be a part of their family. I love them all so much.

And then she thought of Jake. She didn't know how she could leave him again.

But she knew she had no choice.

I love him, Lord. I don't think I ever stopped loving him. Please take care of him. Please—

She heard the sound of a truck engine, saw the lights sweep across the field as it turned into the driveway, then bob and weave as the vehicle came tearing down the lane, spewing gravel behind.

She straightened, then felt her mouth go dry as she recognized the truck that rocked to a halt, inches away from the back bumper of her car.

Her suitcase fell to the ground, her numb fingers unable to hold it, as Jake Steele flung the door of his truck open and strode toward her.

"Why are you going?" he demanded.

Miriam swallowed and took a step back. He was angry. She hadn't expected that.

She wanted to deflect his anger. "Did you find your mother?"

"No. And I don't want to talk about my mother. Right now, it's more important to me to find out why you keep saying you have to go without telling me exactly why. I know modeling isn't that important to you, Miriam. You said you came here to finish things off. Your farm isn't sold, and I know that you still love me. I would say there are a few unfinished things to go yet."

Miriam leaned back against the tree, watching him in the pale moonlight, unable to speak.

"Miriam…" He paused and took a step closer. "I asked you once before, and I'm going to ask you again. I love you dearly. I love you more than I've ever loved anyone. Will you marry me?"

His words laid aside all the defenses she thought she had built against him. Flimsy barriers, indeed. And for a bright moment she felt as if nothing was insurmountable.

"I told you I want to marry you," he continued, his deep voice softly caressing. "I want to take care of you. I want you to trust me. I want your problems to be my problems. I want you for better or worse, richer or poor—"

"You don't know what you're taking on," Miriam said with a shaky cry. Once again the burden of her debt pulled her down to earth, took away her hope.

"Then tell me. Tell me what I'm taking on."

Miriam looked at him, heard the pain in his voice. He loved her. She knew that as surely as she knew of God's love. As if from another part of her mind the words of the psalm Tilly read to her came into her thoughts. "You will restore my life again; from the depths of the earth, you will bring me up." Could these words be true for her? Could she and Jake find a way around this? Would his love withstand it? There was only one way to find out.

"I'm in debt for a hundred and twenty grand." The figure, spoken aloud, sounded even larger, even more insurmountable.

Jake's silence said more than any words he could have spoken. She wanted to curl up into a ball of misery; she wanted to let her sorrow overwhelm her. But she would have to wait until he was gone.

She pressed her fingers against her mouth as if to hold back her cries until then. Her eyes were firmly shut. She had watched him leave once, she couldn't do it again.

Then warm, hard hands gently pulled her fingers away. She felt his soft, inviting lips on hers. Slowly, gently, Jake pulled her into his arms, one hand curling around her neck, the other clutching her waist.

Miriam felt a melting begin deep within her, a softening. She slipped her arms around him, her eyes still shut tight, as if she were afraid to open them to reality.

Jake's mouth moved slowly, gently over hers, and then, as her arms tightened, with more urgency.

Miriam felt the warmth of his mouth, hard on hers, his arms holding her tightly against his chest. She kissed him back, unable to hold him close enough, unable to show him adequately what she was feeling.

He murmured her name against her mouth and kissed her over and over again, his hands caressing her back, her head, his fingers tangling in her hair.

Finally he drew away, but only to cradle her head against his, to hold her close to his pounding heart.

Miriam tried to absorb the onslaught of her own emotions as she leaned against his strength, her cheek pressed against his shirt, her arms holding him, his chin caressing her head again and again.

''Don't go, Miriam,'' he pleaded. ''Please don't

leave me again. I don't think I can go through this a second time." She felt his chest lift in a huge, shuddering sigh. "I don't care about the money, about your debt. We can figure this out. It's not too much to pay for having you with me. Nothing is."

Miriam closed her eyes, resting in this momentary haven, letting his words pull her along, beguile and captivate her. She had to trust him, had to believe him. Because if she didn't, what in life was there for her?

She lifted her face to look at him, and in the light of his truck's headlights she saw tears on his cheeks. With a trembling finger she touched them, awestruck at the sight, at the evidence of the depth of his feelings for her.

As she traced the path of his tears, she whispered his name, her own throat thickened with emotion. "I love you, too, Jake." She stopped, her voice breaking. Then the words came pouring out of her. "I don't think I ever stopped. I've never stopped thinking of you, wondering how you were, not daring to call because then I would hear your voice and start missing you all over again." She took a quavering breath. "It hurt so much to miss you. I didn't think I could go on. And now, to know that you still love me in spite of…in spite of everything…" She couldn't continue. Laying her head against his chest, she fought for control.

"Miriam, I have prayed to hear you say that." He laid his damp cheek on her head. "Say it again," he whispered.

"I love you." The words were muffled, but strong.

Then she looked up at him again, her hands cradling his beloved face. "I love you, Jake Steele. And I want to marry you more than anything."

He lifted his head and feathered a light kiss over her mouth, his gaze full of wonder, his fingers caressing her neck. "Oh, Miriam, I hardly dared hope. God has been so good."

Miriam reached up to touch his hair, her fingers reveling in its thickness. "You might not think so once you talk to your banker."

He shook his head. "I don't want to hear about that."

"But it's so much money," she couldn't help but say. "You couldn't afford to buy my land. How—?"

The rest of her words were cut off by his mouth covering hers. When he finally pulled away he touched her lips with his finger. "I said I don't want to hear about it."

She let her head drop against his chest as he lowered his hand. "I love you so much," she whispered. "I know we can get through this."

"Because we're doing it together, that makes it much easier."

As Miriam leaned against his chest, she let her prayer of thankfulness drift up to heaven. She had come here to rest, to recoup—and to leave.

But God had had other things in mind for her.

And she was grateful.

"Let's go home, Miriam," Jake murmured, giving her another tight hug. "There are a few people who want to know what's happening."

She caught him by the arm. "Jake," she said quietly. "I don't want to do the job, but it will pay me a lot of money. And if I don't do it, I stand to lose other jobs."

"So we'll buy you a plane ticket. That still gives you a couple of days here."

Miriam felt as if a huge weight had fallen off her shoulders. "It might work out."

Jake gave her a little shake. "You're not alone, Miriam. Not anymore."

He bent over to take her suitcase, and then, his arm around her, hers wrapped around him, as if they were afraid to let each other go, they walked to his truck. Jake tossed her suitcase in the back and helped her in, then pulled her against him as, one-handed, he spun the steering wheel around, and headed home.

Then he took off down the driveway, barely slowing for the turn off onto the road, and then taking off. He pulled to a halt at his own place, held her close a moment.

"I love you. I love you," he whispered, kissing her once again.

"I'm nervous, you know," she confessed.

"About what?"

"Taryn, Tilly. Will I be able to do it?"

"You know, Miriam, I think, deep down, you're not a model. I think you're a mother at heart."

His words comforted her, and together they walked up the sidewalk. Together they stepped into the house.

Taryn looked up from the kitchen table, blinked, then grinned as she saw Jake and Miriam.

"Daddy, Miriam," she yelled, running and throwing herself at both of them. Jake caught her, Miriam caught an arm, and the three of them held each other as Miriam's tears flowed freely.

"Let me guess—you talked her into staying," Simon drawled, turning around in his chair. He got up, shook Jake's hand and gave Miriam an awkward hug. Taryn got in the way, squealing with delight.

Tilly came into the kitchen to see what the commotion was about, and smiled broadly. "My goodness," she said, pressing a hand to her mouth. She, too, joined in the celebration.

They explained to Taryn what was to happen, and the child immediately began hugging and kissing Jake and Miriam indiscriminately.

Later, when Taryn was finally settled into bed, and Simon and Tilly had gone to bed, Miriam and Jake had some time to themselves again. They sat on the couch, Jake's arms firmly around Miriam as if he didn't dare let her go.

Miriam traced circles on the soft hair of his forearm, bemused at the difference ten years had made in this man she loved so dearly. "Jake," she asked quietly.

"Miriam," he replied, his voice teasing.

"I am serious." She hesitated, but she needed one more reassurance. "I need to know, Jake—are you sure you know what you're getting into?"

Jake sighed, his breath gentle across her head. "Miriam, I'm not worried. It's only money."

"But it's so much."

"It is. I won't deny it. But if you sold that land to

someone else I would have lost it anyway. I've been thinking I could sell one of the other quarters of land, by Rock Lake. Then I'd buy yours from you.'' He laid his cheek on her head. ''The rest of the debt we'll have to work into the farm debt.'' He hugged her again. ''I told you already, I'll do anything to have you stay with me.''

Miriam bit back her next protest, and relaxed against Jake, reveling in his strength, in the ability to lean on someone for the first time in years. It still felt strange—wrong almost—yet liberating to put all her fears and worries into someone else's hands.

Jake nuzzled her head. ''Have I told you I love you?''

''Not for about two minutes.'' Miriam turned her face up to him, and Jake kissed her.

''I used to dream of sitting with you on this couch,'' Jake said softly, tracing the line of her eyebrow, the curve of her cheek, the line of her lips.

''I did, too. I used to dream we could walk down Main Street holding hands, just like all the other lovers do.''

''Well, it's taken a few years, but we can.''

Then on that same couch, Miriam kissed her future husband.

And sent up a prayer of thanks. Their lives had taken some twists and turns to arrive at this destination, but they were finally here.

Together, at last.

Epilogue

"**N**ow stay close to me, it's really busy here," Jake said to Taryn as they made their way through the throng of people in the airport. She clung to his hand.

Jake had wanted to carry her, but according to her a big girl didn't need to be carried.

From speakers overhead a voice announced the arrival of yet another flight as Jake worked his way to the arrival gate.

People wearing trench coats and suits vied with individuals in blue jeans, sweatsuits and leather jackets for a spot close to the gate where the passengers from flight number 264 direct from New York were to arrive.

"Is she coming yet?" Taryn asked, clutching the bouquet of flowers Jake had picked up before coming here. "I don't want the flowers to die."

"They won't," Jake assured his daughter. "They'll still be fresh and pretty when you give them to her."

Taryn looked up at him, smiling widely. "When I get big I want to fly on a plane, just like Mims gets to."

"That would be fun, wouldn't it?"

Taryn nodded then buried her nose in the flowers, taking a deep sniff.

A burst of noise came from the arrival doors and Jake looked up, his expectations making his heart skip. She was coming. After a two-week absence, Miriam was coming home.

The doors swung open again and there, behind a group of laughing young kids, he saw her.

She wore a loose apricot-colored crop top over cargo pants. Casual clothing, yet Miriam managed to lend an aura of elegance and style to the simple lines.

Her hair shone under the bright lights, wisps of it accenting her face, her eyes, scanning the crowd as eagerly as Jake watched her.

She hadn't seen him yet, he realized as she paused, frowning lightly, clutching the large, oversize bag she always carried with her as hand luggage.

He noticed a few men glance her way then stop, their faces showing their obvious admiration. One man elbowed his neighbor who looked her way, then also stared.

For a moment Jake resented their gaping, but Miriam was unaware of the minor sensation she was causing.

She stood up on tiptoe, scanning the crowd, frowning.

Then, the frown melted, her eyes widened and she began to run.

"Jake," she called out, totally unselfconscious about her reaction.

Jake's heart quickened at the sight of her rushing toward him, her arms wide, laughing.

"You're here," she said.

He let go of Taryn's hand for an instant and caught her as Miriam flung her arms around him. He swung her up, holding her close, his head buried against her soft neck.

"Oh, Miriam," he murmured, "I missed you, I missed you."

They held each other a moment, yet unable to hold each other close enough, hard enough.

He pulled back and gently lowered her to the ground. They gazed lovingly at each other, then he lowered his head and with reverence kissed her mouth.

"How are you?" he asked, drawing slightly back, as he noted each dear feature, as if looking for any changes in her.

"Better. Now." She reached up and stroked his hair back from his face. "Much better." Then, she turned to Taryn.

"Hi, sweetheart." She dropped to one knee and hugged her tightly. "I missed you, little Pip."

"I missed you, too, Mims." Taryn held out the flowers. "We got these for you."

Miriam took the flowers, sniffed them appreciatively and grinned at Taryn. "They're beautiful. We'll have to put them in water when we get home, won't we?''

Taryn nodded, then took Miriam's hand. "Daddy can take your bag," she said imperiously.

"Yes, ma'am." Jake saluted, bent over and slung the bag over his shoulder. As he straightened he noticed a few puzzled glances from the men who had been ogling Miriam, as if they were wondering how some guy in blue jeans and a twill shirt managed to snag this exotic-looking woman.

"What's the matter, Jake?" Miriam asked, as she stood, holding Taryn's hand, her flowers clutched in the other.

"I'm still trying to get used to having all these guys staring at my wife."

Miriam frowned, then looked back over her shoulder in the direction Jake was glowering. "What guys?" she asked.

The men who had been looking, quickly averted their curious gaze.

"Oh, those guys," Miriam said, glancing back at Jake with a shrug. "It doesn't mean anything."

"Maybe not. But I don't like it."

Miriam leaned against him, smiling coyly up at him. "But I'm not looking, am I?"

"I hope not."

Miriam's expression grew serious. "Jake, I would love nothing more than to stay here every day. To be wearing dirty blue jeans and a shirt smeared with flour. You know that."

Jake grinned down at her, his heart overflowing with

love for the beautiful woman. "I know that. And only two more jobs and you'll be done."

Miriam sighed and nodded her head in affirmation. "Hallelujah. Goodbye to jet lag, to tight clothes, cranky photographers and temperamental clients."

"We did it, you know," he said as he slipped his arm around her. They began walking toward the exit. "It's just about done, that insurmountable debt you couldn't tell me about."

"Well, I'm really glad Simon was the one who bought the land. That way I can say I still own my old house," Miriam said, smiling lightly.

"Maybe someday we'll be able to buy it back, but for now I'm happy enough to rent it from him."

The automatic doors slid open at their approach, and Jake had to stop Taryn from wanting to go through them again.

"Miriam wants to go home," he said to her as they walked across the taxi lane toward the parking garage.

Taryn skipped beside them, still holding Miriam's hand. "I have a friend in grade one," she announced to Miriam. "She has a mommy and a daddy too." Taryn looked up at Miriam, a slight frown creasing her forehead. "But she doesn't call her mommy, Mims. You and Daddy said I didn't have to call you Mommy, but can I? Please?"

"Oh, sweetheart." Miriam stopped, and bending over, pulled Taryn into her arms. "Of course you can."

Jake watched the two of them, both beautiful, both

so very precious to him and felt a fullness wash over him at what Taryn had just asked.

Thank you, Lord, he prayed. *Thank you for my wife, my daughter. My family.*

Miriam stood and as she turned to Jake, he saw her wipe her eyes. She bit her lip and glanced up at him. ''Does it get any better than this?'' she asked, reaching out to him as well.

''I doubt it,'' he said, pulling her close. He caught Taryn in a hug, lifted her up and with one arm, held her as well.

He and Miriam exchanged another quick kiss and then, arm in arm, they walked down the ramp toward Jake's truck.

A father. A daughter. A mother.

*   *   *   *   *

Dear Reader,

When he was young, Jake Steele felt he had nothing to give Miriam Spencer because he was just a foster child. But because of the love of his foster parents, his life is different when Miriam comes back into it. I wanted to show, in this book, how vulnerable foster children can feel, even in a secure home. I also wanted to show that for some children, there is indeed a happy ending. I know, we have seen it in our extended family and in other foster families.

Foster parents give much to their kids, and in many long-term situations end up adopting them or making them a permanent part of their family in other ways. The foster child/parent bond can be as strong as the natural one.

I thank the Lord for the many people who open their homes to children who are not their own, and I pray they may receive the strength they need to do their work.

Carolyne Aarsen

Love Inspired

THE FAMILY MAN

BY IRENE HANNON

Davis Landing

Nothing is stronger than a family's love.

Hiring her old flame wasn't easy for magazine editor Amy Hamilton, but Bryan Healey was the best writer for the job. Yet working closely with the widowed single dad—and getting to know his adorable son—made Amy want this family man to be hers!

Steeple Hill®

www.SteepleHill.com

Available September 2006 wherever you buy books.

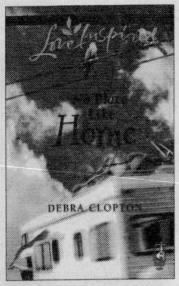

REQUEST YOUR FREE BOOKS!

2 FREE INSPIRATIONAL NOVELS
PLUS A
FREE
MYSTERY GIFT

Love Inspired®

YES! Please send me 2 FREE Love Inspired® novels and my FREE mystery gift. After receiving them, if I don't wish to receive any more books, I can return the shipping statement marked "cancel." If I don't cancel, I will receive 4 brand-new novels every month and be billed just $3.99 per book in the U.S., or $4.74 per book in Canada, plus 25¢ shipping and handling per book and applicable taxes, if any*. That's a savings of over 20% off the cover price! I understand that accepting the 2 free books and gift places me under no obligation to buy anything. I can always return a shipment and cancel at any time. Even if I never buy another book from Steeple Hill, the two free books and gift are mine to keep forever.

113 IDN D74R   313 IDN D743

Name	(PLEASE PRINT)	
Address		Apt.
City	State/Prov.	Zip/Postal Code

Signature (if under 18, a parent or guardian must sign)

Order online at www.LoveInspiredBooks.com

Or mail to Steeple Hill Reader Service™:

IN U.S.A.
3010 Walden Ave.
P.O. Box 1867
Buffalo, NY 14240-1867

IN CANADA
P.O. Box 609
Fort Erie, Ontario
L2A 5X3

Not valid to current Love Inspired subscribers.

Want to try two free books from another series?
Call 1-800-873-8635 or visit www.morefreebooks.com

* Terms and prices subject to change without notice. NY residents add applicable sales tax. Canadian residents will be charged applicable provincial taxes and GST. This offer is limited to one order per household. All orders subject to approval. Credit or debit balances in a customer's account(s) may be offset by any other outstanding balance owed by or to the customer.

LIREG05

CLASSICS

TITLES AVAILABLE NEXT MONTH

Don't miss these stories in September

FATHER MOST BLESSED
AND
A FATHER'S PLACE
by Marta Perry

Two single fathers each find
the woman of their dreams with a little help
from their children in two classic stories.

LOOKING FOR MIRACLES
AND
THE PRODIGAL'S RETURN
by Lynn Bulock

Love comes home in two beloved
Missouri-set romances.